OPERATION FORTITUDE

An absolutely gripping murder mystery full of twists

HILARY GREEN

Kim Maxwell Thrillers Book 2

JOFFE BOOKS

Joffe Books, London
www.joffebooks.com

First published in Great Britain in 2023

Cover art by Jarmila Takač

ISBN: 978-1-83526-052-4

AUTHOR'S NOTE

As with my other historical novels, while the main characters are fictional many of the subsidiary ones actually existed and many of the events depicted really took place. There is a saying that truth is often stranger than fiction, and in this case one of the most unlikely-seeming events is historical fact. I am referring to the involvement of King George VI in the plot to deceive Hitler about the location of the D-Day landings. British Intelligence went to great lengths to confuse the enemy about exactly where the landings were to take place. Regiments of tanks built of wood and canvas were created to deceive German aerial surveillance. Double agents fed back false information about troop movements. And one day two MI5 officials went to Buckingham Palace to see the King's secretary with a suggestion that he could help. The idea was for him to pay visits to troops in various parts of the country from which the invasion might be launched, apparently to wish them luck in the forthcoming battle. He even made the dangerous trip to the naval base at Scapa Flow, to suggest that the forthcoming invasion would be sea borne and probably directed at occupied Norway. The King took a willing role in the deception and he and the Queen were initiated into the secrets of the Special Operations Executive.

For this information I am indebted to Professor Richard Aldrich of the University of Warwick who very kindly gave me a copy of *Crown, Cloak, and Dagger*, the fascinating book he has written with Professor Rory Cormac detailing the involvement of the Royal family with the Intelligence Services from Queen Victoria onwards.

Other characters in my book who are based on people who really existed include 'M', the code name of Brigadier Colin Gubbins, the head of SOE; the notorious Klaus Barbie, head of Gestapo in Lyon; and Peter Ortiz and Henry Thackthwaite, the agents who were dropped into the Vercors to bolster the Resistance there. I have, of course, made my own interpretation of their personalities but hope I have done them justice.

CHAPTER 1

Vienne, Isère, South Eastern France. January 1944.

The man lay on his back, one leg twisted under him, arms outflung as if grasping for purchase and finding only thin air. The broken rungs of a ladder were scattered partly on top of him, partly on the ground around him.

The gendarme looked from the body to the turret of the small château.

'So what was he doing up there?'

'It seems the owners employed him to replace some tiles on the roof.' His informant wore the blue uniform of the *milice*, the paramilitary force of Frenchmen who supported the Nazi occupiers.

'Do we have a name for him?'

'According to his papers he is — was — Bernard Leblanc. He has a small builders' business in Vienne.'

'Was he on his own?'

'Apparently.'

'Working at that height without anyone to hold the ladder? Asking for trouble.'

'Not just that. It looks as if the ladder itself gave way. See, here? One of the rungs is broken.'

'Well, if he hadn't enough sense to keep his equipment in good order, he deserves everything that was coming to him. *Idiot*!'

* * *

In what had once been the salon of a manor house in Grendon Underwood, in the leafy Buckinghamshire countryside, a young woman settled herself at a desk in a small cubicle and clamped earphones on her head. She glanced at a clock on the wall, twiddled a knob on the radio set in front of her and was rewarded with a brief burst of Morse code. In response she transmitted an answering signal and the operator at the other end replied with a longer sequence of bleeps. The girl wrote quickly, transcribing the dots and dashes into five letter groups. Then she sent the code for 'Message received and understood', and signed off. The groups of letters did not form words. That was not part of her job. She tore off the sheet she had written on and gestured to summon a messenger, who carried the paper upstairs to the decoding room.

In a flat in Orchard Court, near London's Oxford Street — the HQ of the Special Operations Executive's F section — a tall man in the uniform of a colonel took up the receiver of a scrambler phone and listened with a growing expression of concern. When the call was finished he touched a button on his desk and said, 'Come in, Vera, please.'

An attractive, dark-haired woman in her mid-thirties responded to the request and took one look at her commander's face. 'What has happened?'

'Baker has been killed.' All SOE agents operating in France were known to their handlers by the name of a trade or profession.

'Oh no! An op that went wrong, or was he betrayed?'

'Neither, apparently. Accident, according to the message. He fell from a ladder.'

Vera frowned. 'I suppose these things happen, but somehow it doesn't sound like Baker. He has always been ultra safety conscious. Did the message come from his usual pianist?'

In SOE parlance, a radio operator was often referred to as a pianist.

'So the girl at Grendon said. She recognized his fist — or her fist in this case.'

'It's Pauline, isn't it, with that circuit? Did she give any details?'

'No, that's all. But it means Chandler circuit is without a leader. We need to get someone out there to clear up asap.'

Vera's frown deepened. 'Don't you think we need to find out exactly what happened? Was it part of a sabotage op or an intelligence-gathering operation? He must have had a reason for being up a ladder. If it was the latter, it may have alerted the Huns, in which case the whole circuit may be blown.'

Maurice Buckmaster shrugged impatiently. 'I suppose we could ask her for more detail, but we can't expect her to risk a long transmission. It makes it too easy for the German detector vans to pinpoint her location.'

'True.' Vera nodded. 'We really need to get someone on the spot.'

'I suppose you're right.' His face brightened. 'Here's an idea. That girl of yours — Maxwell. Is she anywhere in the vicinity?'

'Not too far away.'

'Get a message to her. She's got a good head for detective work. She proved that in the Lightning Bolt affair. Tell her to report to Hunter in Lyon. He's coordinating work in that area. He can point her in the right direction.'

'Very good, sir.'

* * *

Lyon. January 1944.

Kim Maxwell paused on the edge of the pavement and sup-pressed a thrill of recognition as she saw the place she had been ordered to report to. The windows of the building on the opposite side of the road proclaimed it to be the Bistro Le Renard Rouge. The Red Fox! Of course! And she had no doubt about the identity of the chef-patron. Every nerve in her body urged her to run across the street, throw open the door and walk in, but instead she strolled a little further down the road, her eyes taking in all the other people in the vicinity. It was this circumspection that had kept her alive and free for three months in enemy-occupied territory, and she was not about to abandon it now.

There was a parked car a few yards from the bistro, with a man and a woman in it. A little further on, a man was drinking beer and smoking a cigarette at a pavement café, though on this winter evening it seemed a trifle cool to sit outside. A woman pushing a pram passed her and walked on, and men carrying brief-cases headed in the opposite direction, on the way home from work. Some of them had come from the station, had been on the same train as her, but none of them had found some pretext to linger nearby while she was standing still. Kim went on down the street, took a left turn and stopped in a doorway that hid her from anyone following behind. No one passed her and when she peered out, there was no sign of anyone pausing to tie a shoelace or study an advertisement. She waited a little longer, then walked back towards the bistro. The man outside the café was just greeting a woman he had apparently been waiting for. He paid his bill and they walked off arm-in-arm. The couple in the car were now studying the menu in the window of the bistro and seemed to be having an argument. The man shrugged and turned away, and the woman followed. They got back into the car and drove away.

As sure, now, as she could be that she had not been followed and the bistro was not being watched, Kim walked up to the door and pretended to study the menu. In fact, she was looking beyond it to the interior and what she saw was not, at first sight, encouraging. The room was set out with tables covered in pristine white cloths and decked with candles and small vases of flowers. So far, so good and no more than she would have expected. It was the clientele that gave her pause. Almost all the tables were taken and more than half of them were occupied by German officers. But after the initial shock, Kim realized this was just what she should expect. The menu should have given her a clue, including as it did ingredients unobtainable for most people in that time of strict rationing. And then, there was the talent of the chef. If anyone, in this gastronomically critical city, could produce food to tickle the palates of the occupiers, it was the patron of the Red Fox.

She pushed open the door and was greeted by a blast of warm air scented with the smoke of Gauloises cigarettes and rich food. An attractive young woman in a dark dress and a white apron approached her.

'Does madame have a booking?'

'No, I'm sorry. I've only just arrived in Lyon. But I should very much like a table, if you can fit me in.'

'For yourself, or will someone be joining you?'

'Just me.'

'In that case, I am sure we can find you a place.'

She was led to a small table in a corner of the room, not far from the door into the kitchen. It was a position she would have rejected if this was a normal occasion, but as it happened, it suited her very well. She would be inconspicuous and could watch what was happening in the rest of the room as well as see who came in from the street. Her pulse was beating too fast for comfort, but she forced herself to behave normally. She ordered a good meal, more than willing to take advantage of what was on offer, and a half bottle of Côtes du Rhône Villages, and studied the customers. The German officers were clearly out for a good time. Wine flowed freely, followed by balloons of cognac, and the conversation was loud, almost raucous. By contrast, the few French customers were subdued, savouring their food as if it was forbidden fruit — which in fact it was — and unwilling to draw attention to themselves. She understood now what the couple in the car had been arguing about — the conflicting temptation

5

of the first decent meal they had had for months against the possibility of being labelled collaborators.

One of the Germans waved a waitress over and said something to her. She went back into the kitchen, and a moment later, a tall man with russet hair visible below his white chef's toque came out and approached their table. Kim shrank back in her corner and became absorbed in studying the menu, peeping over the top as the chef accepted the congratulations of his German customers. She watched him nodding and smiling as he basked in their approval, while her own stomach turned over with revulsion at the display. Was it possible that the man she knew so well had become a collaborator? The chance to do what he did best, and win such outspoken appreciation, must be a great temptation. He even appeared to have put on weight.

Kim lingered over her meal and ordered coffee, waiting for the other diners to finish. The civilians were the first to go, sidling past the Germans to reach the door without drawing their attention. At last, the Germans, too, had finished and paid their bills, adding, she guessed, generous tips for the waitress who had served them. The young woman who had greeted her on her entry came over with an apologetic smile.

'Forgive me, madame, but we shall be closing soon. It is almost time for the curfew.'

Kim smiled back. 'I understand, but before I leave, I should like to have a word with the patron. He and I are old friends.'

For a moment the professional facade slipped and Kim saw a look in the girl's eyes that asked, *What's behind this? Can I trust you?* Aloud, she said, 'Who shall I say is asking for him?'

'Tell him Madeleine is here.'

It was the code name she had been given and one she knew he would recognize.

'Very good, madame. A moment, please.'

The girl went out to the kitchen, and seconds later, the double door swung open and the chef appeared. Kim stood up and for a moment they stared at each other. Then he said, formally, 'Will madame please step into the kitchen?'

6

'With great pleasure,' she replied.

There were two other men in whites clearing up in there.

'Leave all that!' he commanded, throwing his toque aside. 'It's almost curfew. Get off home, both of you.'

They were quick to obey, stripping off their aprons and pulling on hats and coats. As soon as the back door had closed behind them he turned and swept her into his arms.

'*Mon dieu*! What a wonderful surprise!' He spoke into her hair, holding her close. Then he eased his grip and held her away from him, his expression sobering. 'What are you doing here?'

She looked beyond him to where the young woman was still waiting. He followed her eyes and smiled. 'This is Candice, my maître d'hotel or should I say maîtresse?' Turning to the girl he went on, 'Candice, Madeleine is an old friend.'

Kim extended her hand. '*Salut*, Candice.'

'*Bonsoir*, Madeleine,' the girl replied, but there was something in her eyes that was less than welcoming. Kim had seen her face as she withdrew from the embrace and it was enough to warn her to tread carefully.

'You should be on your way home, too, Candice,' he said. 'You don't want to be caught out after curfew.'

'And . . . and Madeleine?' she asked.

He smiled. 'She will stay here for the night.'

He untied his apron and set it aside, and Kim saw that the back of it was padded. Without it, his figure was as trim and athletic as always. Remembering her earlier disgust, she almost laughed at herself. How could she have forgotten what a consummate actor he was?

Candice collected her coat and hat, and bade them goodnight — reluctantly, Kim thought. As soon as she had left, he turned and put his arms around Kim again. 'Oh, *chéri*, it's so good to see you! I can't believe you're here.'

'Me, too,' she answered. 'When I got the order I had no idea it would bring me here.'

They kissed, a long, deep kiss that partly assuaged months of separation and anxiety. Then he said, 'Why are we standing in the kitchen? Come upstairs where we can be comfortable.'

He took her up to the living quarters above the restaurant. In the slightly shabby sitting room, furnished in typical provincial style in heavy oak and rather faded tapestry upholstery, he fetched a bottle from the dresser that stood against one wall.

'I think we need, and deserve, the best cognac.' He poured two generous measures. '*Santé*.' They clinked glasses. 'So,' he asked, 'what do you think of my little establishment?'

'It's perfect,' she said. 'As soon as I saw the name I knew it must be you.' She reached up and ran her fingers through his thick, tawny hair. 'Foxy doing what Foxy does best — and, of course, it's the perfect cover.'

Renaud Leroux, code name Roland, aka the Red Fox, and half a dozen other pseudonyms, laughed. 'It is, isn't it. Ironic that it should take SOE to set me up in the restaurant I always wanted.' He drew out a chair at a small, round table and sat opposite her.

'Now, I suppose we must talk seriously. You weren't sent here to sample my cooking.'

'Sadly not,' she agreed. 'Marvellous though it is, as always. I was told you would have a message for me — a job for me to do.'

He nodded. 'It seems the leader of a circuit based in Vienne, code name Baker, has met with an accident—'

'An accident? Really? Or is that a euphemism?'

'Apparently not. He fell off a ladder. The question is, what was he doing up the ladder. Was it part of an op? Was it really an accident? And who is taking charge of things at the moment?'

'How did Baker Street find out?' Kim asked. The headquarters of the organization was in Baker Street and this was a common shorthand.

'Message from his pianist,' Foxy replied.

'So the whole circuit isn't blown, if she is still operating.'

'Well, she was when the message was sent.'

'How long ago was this?'

'Three days.'

'And Buckmaster wants me to go and investigate,' Kim concluded.

'Yes, and do any clearing up that's necessary. He suggests you should assume control of the circuit until someone else can be dropped in, and that will give you cover for nosing about a bit.'

'OK. How do I make contact?'

'You should be at the Temple of Augustus and Livia in Vienne at 4 p.m. tomorrow. Carry a green umbrella, which I will give you. The recognition code will be "You seem to be prepared for bad weather" and the answer is "I've been caught out too often to take chances". I'll send a courier first thing in the morning to tell them to expect you. That is, assuming they are still picking up messages from the dead letter drop as arranged.'

'You are in touch with them, then?'

Foxy nodded. 'My role here is to act as a coordinator. There are several circuits operating along the Rhône Valley. They have been set up by a chap with the code name Roger. Amazing chap, prepared to go to any lengths, take any risk, but he can't keep in touch with all of them all the time. So the restaurant is somewhere people can come without arousing suspicion and leave messages. I have couriers who can travel round the area, and each circuit has a dead letter drop they are supposed to check every day. So far, it seems to be working.'

'Right. I can see this is the perfect set-up.'

He lifted his shoulders with a wry smile. 'It is, but sometimes I feel . . . it's too easy. Here I am, doing the job I love, while everyone else is taking the risks.'

'Don't kid yourself,' she told him. 'Your risk is as great as anyone's. It only takes one of your couriers to be caught and interrogated for the Gestapo to come knocking on your door.' As an afterthought she added, 'You can't enjoy pandering to the Nazis who come to eat here.'

'It makes me sick to my stomach,' he agreed, 'but it has its uses. When they are full of good food and fine wine they sometimes forget to be discreet. I've picked up a few useful bits of information.'

Kim paused, digesting the this. Then she said, 'Tell me about Candice. Does she know you are SOE?'

'Good lord, no! But I've let her guess that I have connections with the local Resistance. That's safe enough. She loathes the Nazis.'

'You do realize she's in love with you?'

'What gives you that idea?'

'The way she looked at me when you put your arms round me.'

He shrugged and coloured slightly. 'It's a crush, just a passing phase.'

'Don't brush it aside too readily. Remember, "hell hath no fury . . ."'

'You're right. We shouldn't be complacent. But if anyone's in danger, it's you, not me. So tell me what you've been doing. I thought your brief was to follow up on anyone who might have come under the influence of our old friend Dr Kline.'

'That's true.' Kim swallowed the last of her cognac and stretched her shoulders. 'Fortunately, Kline wasn't at the training school at Beaulieu very long before you, and I figured out that he was working for the Nazis. So there were a limited number of trainee agents who passed through there while he was operating. Of those, two who had apparently succumbed to his machinations and been turned, had already been "captured",' she made inverted commas with her fingers, 'and are presumably now reaping their reward in an SS holiday camp — unlike the rest of the poor bloody men and women who they betrayed. One had already been exfiltrated to the UK on medical grounds. That left three others. One was able to convince me that, like poor Lucien, he was able to resist Kline's attempt to hypnotize him, and I got the other two recalled for "debriefing". So as it happens, I was just

10

about to contact Vera Atkins and ask what she wanted me to do next when I got the message telling me to report to you.'

'I wonder what happened to Kline,' Foxy mused. 'He just disappeared when the balloon went up last time.'

'He cocked things up pretty badly,' Kim responded. 'I imagine he's hiding out somewhere in Spain, or South America, hoping Hitler's thugs don't find him.' She suppressed a yawn. 'Sorry. It's been a long day.'

He came round to stand behind her chair and lifted her to her feet. 'Come on. Time for bed.'

She nestled into his shoulder. 'I thought you'd never ask!'

CHAPTER 2

In a windowless office not far away a young woman stood to attention in front of a desk strewn with papers. The man sitting behind the desk was thick-set, heavy jowled, with eyes under bushy brows that held hers with a gaze she found impossible to break. His fingers tapped irritably on the desk.

'Your orders were to disrupt, to collect information, specifically names and descriptions. We wanted to flush out the whole viper's nest when the time came. Instead, you chose to act alone, against one individual, and attract unwanted attention in doing so.'

'But he was getting suspicious. I was afraid he was going to expose me.'

'Then you must have been careless. However it is, your usefulness here is finished.'

'But . . .'

He cut her words short with a raised finger. 'Fortunately for you, there is a way you can redeem yourself. You can be more use to us at home, with the connections you have.'

'At home? How am I supposed to achieve that?'

'That is up to you. Presumably someone will be sent to replace the man you killed. You must convince him that you can no longer remain in your current post.'

'And . . . and if I get back, how will I know what my orders are?'

'You will be contacted and given instructions. If you do your part efficiently, you may yet be involved in something far bigger than the mission you have just so spectacularly compromised. It will be your chance to redeem yourself, possibly to help change the course of history.' The dark eyes bored into hers. 'That is all. You may go.'

The woman clicked her heels and extended her arm in salute. '*Jawohl, herr doktor. Heil Hitler!*'

* * *

Kim collected two cases she had checked into the left luggage office and took the train to Vienne. It was not difficult to find the temple Foxy had mentioned, an impressive Roman structure of columns surrounding a raised platform, around which a busy square had developed as the modern town grew up. Kim could imagine, without difficulty, how it must have been before the war, with pavement cafés frequented by well-dressed men and women, market stalls loaded with produce and shop windows displaying fashionable clothes and desirable knick-knacks. Now the cafés were still there, but largely occupied by men in German uniform, and the market stalls had all but disappeared, their produce now subject to strict rationing or, more probably, sold on the black market. More jarring than anything, the temple itself was decked with a huge red banner displaying a black swastika in a white circle.

Kim stood in the shadow of one of the massive columns and leaned casually on the green umbrella Foxy had given her. It was not long before a young woman with blonde hair under a man's peaked cap approached her and spoke the pre-arranged code words. Kim responded as she had been instructed and the girl gave her a broad smile.

'Madeleine? My name is Sylvie. Welcome to Vienne.'

She was somewhere in her late twenties, as far as Kim could guess, stockily built with an open, slightly freckled face

13

and broad, capable hands. She was wearing trousers and the sort of blouson jacket worn by working men all over France.

'I was sorry to hear about the accident to our friend,' Kim said cautiously.

'To Bernard? Yes, it's shaken us all up rather.'

'Bernard? That was his name?'

'That's what his papers say. He was Bernard Leblanc.'

'So does that only leave two of you — you and your radio operator?'

'That's right. Her name is Pauline. I'll take you to meet her now.' She led Kim through narrow streets until they came to a row of tall, grey houses facing the river Rhône .

'This is where Pauline lodges. The owner is an elderly widow who can't manage stairs anymore, so she rents out the top floor, which is perfect for our purposes.'

A side door led straight onto a narrow staircase which bypassed the first two floors of the house and brought them to a door close under the roof. Sylvie tapped, a pattern of knocks that constituted a recognizable code, and the door opened.

The woman who stood there could hardly have been a greater contrast to Sylvie. Tall and willowy, with light blue eyes and a mass of chestnut brown hair that fell in waves to her shoulders. Glancing from her to Sylvie, Kim had a sudden mental image of a thoroughbred mare beside a sturdy pony, and it was reinforced by Pauline's reaction. She stepped backwards, her eyes widening in alarm, like a nervous horse.

'Who are you? What do you want?'

Sylvie moved forward. 'It's all right. Calm down. This is Madeleine. We had a signal telling us to expect her. Remember?'

Pauline seemed to recover herself. 'I'm sorry! Sorry! I didn't mean . . . It's just that I've been on tenterhooks ever since . . . Come in, do.'

The room was a garret, but it was comfortably furnished with a single bed and a large desk below a mansard window looking out towards the river. On the desk were a number of books and an open foolscap notebook.

'Please, come in and sit down. I'm sorry about my reception. My nerves are in tatters since Bernard died. Can I get you a drink? The coffee is undrinkable, but I have beer, or wine.'

'A beer would go down very well,' Kim said. 'Thank you.'

Pauline went into a small kitchen leading off the main room, and Kim wandered over to the desk. The books, she saw, were all the works of well-known French poets, and the notebook was covered in handwritten comments.

'That's Pauline's cover.' Sylvie had come to stand behind her. 'She's a student, preparing a thesis.'

'It gives me a reason for being closeted away here day after day,' Pauline said, coming back with three bottles of beer. 'And it means I can go on with work I started before the war. Not that I've managed to concentrate on anything lately.'

Kim looked at her. Her hand shook as she poured the beer. 'Were you close to Bernard?'

'Close? Not really. We only met occasionally. Usually, he sent me messages to transmit through Sylvie.'

'That's right,' Sylvie said. 'He was very security conscious. The less contact we had the better.'

'So how did that work with you?' Kim asked.

'Ah, well you see, I work for a local grocer. He's a sympathizer. I do his deliveries, by bicycle, so I get around quite a bit. I deliver Pauline's rations, and Bernard's, and the other people in the group. And if I've got something in my basket that's not strictly edible, who's to know?' She grinned cheerfully. 'And if I need to be out somewhere in the fields or the woods, I am a keen botanist on my days off.'

Once again Kim was struck by the difference between the two women.

'So, why has Bernard's death shaken you up so much?' she asked Pauline. 'After all, it was an accident, wasn't it?'

Pauline's eyes swivelled from Kim's face to Sylvie's. 'Well, it was, wasn't it? I mean . . . It's a shock, that's all.'

'I don't believe it was an accident,' Sylvie put in. 'I got to know Bernard quite well. He was meticulous about everything. He would have made sure that all his equipment was in good order and taken all the necessary precautions.'

'Tell me about him,' Kim said. 'What was his cover story?'

All SOE agents destined to be sent to France were given a new identity, complete with the necessary papers, and their 'legend', a back story giving their place of birth, their education, the names of their parents and siblings, wives or fiancées, and photographs of themselves — or someone very like them — at important events such as weddings or graduations. They were expected to learn and embroider this story so that they could give convincing answers if questioned by the authorities.

'He worked as a builder.' Sylvie told her. 'He told me his father was a builder and insisted he learned all the aspects of the business as he was growing up, so he was quite competent. He had a small yard out in the suburbs. He found it vacant when he arrived here and rented it. It meant he could travel around with ladders and sacks of cement and so on. Ideal for hiding weapons or *plastique*.'

'I can see that,' Kim agreed. 'So what was he doing up that ladder? Where was it?'

'A small château, out near Reventin-Vaugris. That's about 5 K from here to the south. He was up at the top of one of the turrets. I've no idea why. Maybe he was doing a genuine job. He did take on work from time to time, just to make his cover convincing — but who knows?'

'Who does the château belong to? Do we know?'

'A M. and Mme de la Fontaine,' Sylvie said. 'He likes to be known as M. le Baron, though titles like that have no meaning in France these days, of course.'

'How did you find out what had happened?' Kim asked.

'One of the local gendarmes is a friend. He loathes the Boches and passes us information when he can. He came to the shop where I work and told me.'

'Are the police satisfied that it was an accident, as far as you know?'

'It seems like it.' Sylvie shrugged slightly. 'They haven't been asking questions or conducting searches.'

'What has happened to the body?'

'It's in the morgue. We've been wondering what to do about it. I mean, we've no connection to him, as far as the police know. There won't be any living relatives they can contact. I suppose the authorities will arrange for him to be buried.'

Pauline, who had listened in silence, gave a sudden sob. 'It's awful! I can't bear to think of him being buried under a false name, without any friends present.'

Kim said, 'I'm afraid we can't be sentimental about it. At least he didn't die under torture, or in some godforsaken prison camp.'

Pauline sniffed and swallowed. 'Yes, I suppose that is some comfort.'

Kim thought. 'I still want to know why he was up that ladder. Was it possible that he was looking for a place to deploy an aerial. Maybe he thought it was time you found another place to transmit from, Pauline.'

The radio operator looked uncomfortable. 'Perhaps. He kept telling me I should find somewhere else.'

'How long have you been working from here?'

'Ever since I arrived. About three months.'

'Good heavens! It's a miracle one of the detector vans hasn't picked you up long ago. You must definitely find a new place.'

Again a look of panic flickered over Pauline's face. 'Oh no! I couldn't face it.'

'But you're not safe here,' Kim said. 'You must see that.'

'None of us are, are we? Not now that Bernard's dead. The whole circuit is falling apart. We can't go on operating without a leader.' Her tone was verging on hysteria.

'That's why I'm here,' Kim told her. 'I've been sent to take over until a permanent replacement can be dropped in.'

She regarded the other woman with curiosity. She must have gone through the exacting training given to all SOE operatives. She would have been assessed for her physical strength and her psychological stability, and she would never have been sent to France unless she satisfied her instructors on both counts. Yet now she seemed to be on the verge of falling apart. What was it about Bernard's death that had so unnerved her?

She recalled her attention to the immediate situation and turned to Sylvie. 'You mentioned other members of the circuit. Who did you mean?'

'There's a Resistance cell who have been working with us. The leader is called Luc Darnier.'

'What's he like?'

Sylvie frowned. 'It's complicated. He's completely dedicated, but he didn't always see eye to eye with Bernard. His group had been operating since the Nazis ousted the Vichy government and occupied southern France. I think perhaps he resented Bernard being dropped in to run the circuit.'

'Hmm. Interesting. Can you take me to meet him?'

Sylvie considered for a moment. 'Tomorrow would be better. I can deliver some groceries to him.'

'What does he do?'

'He's a pharmacist.'

'So I can just go to his shop and ask for some pills of some sort?'

'Yes, but there's a special way of doing it. I'll explain tomorrow. What is your cover?'

'I'll show you.' Kim fetched her larger suitcase and set it on the floor between them. Flipping the catches, she revealed a collection of women's underwear — vests and knickers and corsets, all in 'sensible' wool and cotton, and in a rather sickly shade of pink. Underneath were a pile of catalogues from a manufacturer in Toulouse. What she did not reveal was that under the catalogues the case had a false bottom, concealing a blonde wig and a pair of horn-rimmed spectacles, a pair of close-fitting black trousers, a black sweater and a pair of rubber-soled gym shoes, a large sum in French francs, a Webley Mark VI revolver and a double-edged Fairbairn-Sykes knife, named after the two men who had introduced it to SOE. Lethal weapons that she hoped she would never need to use. 'There!' she said. 'I'm a traveller in ladies' underwear — though heaven knows who actually wears this stuff.'

Sylvie chuckled. 'Well, good luck with selling that — but it's as good a cover as any, I suppose.'

'Tomorrow, then?' Kim asked. 'But first I need to check out this builder's yard. Have the owners repossessed it, do you know?'

'I don't think so,' Sylvie said. 'I've walked past it a couple of times and it's all locked up, just as it was when he left it.'

'Right. Can you show me where it is, this evening?'

'Yes. But now I'd better show you where you're staying. Bernard had a little house attached to the yard, but I don't think that would suit you. I've arranged for you to lodge with the grocer who employs me.'

'Does he know the risk involved?'

'Yes, he and his wife are supporters. They're prepared to take the risk.'

'Good.' Kim closed her case and stood up. 'Let's go, then.'

'So what is going to happen now?' Pauline asked nervously. 'Do you need me to send a message or anything?'

'Not yet,' Kim told her. 'I know where to find you if I do.'

'Take care! Make sure you're not followed.'

Kim looked at her. 'Trust me. I do know what I'm doing.'

Out in the street, she turned to Sylvie. 'Is Pauline always so twitchy?'

'No.' Sylvie frowned. 'I don't know what's got into her. She always seemed so cool, so efficient. But now . . .'

'Now she's gone to pieces.' Kim finished the sentence for her. 'And this is all to do with Bernard's death?'

'I suppose so. But then again, when we first heard about it, she took it quite calmly. It's only the last couple of days she's been like this.'

'Delayed shock, perhaps?' Kim suggested.

'I suppose so.'

Kim glanced behind her. It was the end of the working day and people were hurrying home, keen to get out of the chilly January wind. She could not see anyone among the crowd who seemed to be keeping pace with them, but checking for a tail was second nature. She drew her companion into a shop doorway. 'Let's wait here for a moment.'

Sylvie did not query the suggestion. These were familiar tactics to her, too. The crowd continued to surge past them and when Kim looked out, there was no sign of anyone hanging around. 'Tell me,' she said, 'how has the circuit been getting on — before Bernard's death?'

'Up and down, I suppose you could say. In the early days we had some pretty successful ops. Blew up the points on the main line between here and Lyon, scuttled a couple of coal barges on the river, ambushed a supply convoy. But then the Nazis started taking reprisals. After the ambush, they dragged out all the men in the nearest village, lined them up against a wall and shot them, in front of their wives and children. It was after that, that things got difficult between Bernard and Luc Darnier.'

'Understandably,' Kim said.

'But there's one odd thing, something that worried Bernard. Every time we arranged a drop of supplies, the Huns seemed to know in advance. The first time, one of our informants warned Bernard in time to send a message to tell HQ to call it off. Next time, the Huns were out in force, hiding in the forest all round the DZ. Someone spotted them and Bernard was able to use his S-Phone to contact the pilot and tell him to abort the mission. So the third time, he changed the time and place literally hours before it was due, but the Huns were there waiting for us anyway. There was a firefight and three of our men were killed. Luckily, the pilot must have seen what was going on and didn't drop his load.'

'But the Germans were warned, even when the arrangements were changed at the last minute?'

'Yes.'

'Well, whoever is doing it must have a very good line of communication with the enemy,' Kim said. 'Any ideas who it could be? Who knew what was going to happen?'

'Not many. Darnier had to be told, of course, because we needed his men to light the signal fires and collect the canisters when they were dropped. But he kept the time and place secret until the last moment — or so he said.'

'Could he be the source of the leak?'

'I suppose it's possible, but I find it hard to believe.'

'Well, there's a mole in the organization somewhere, that's obvious.'

'Do you think this has anything to do with Bernard's death?'

Kim lifted her shoulders. 'My gut instinct is that it may have, but I've nothing to back it up. I'll have to see what else I can unearth.' She shivered. 'Come on. There's no one following us. Let's get out of the weather.'

CHAPTER 3

M. and Mme Levigne, Sylvie's employers, gave Kim a warm welcome and showed her to a small but comfortably furnished bedroom. Over dinner she gave them the basic information they would need if anyone asked about her. Her documents gave her name as Madeleine Moreau and showed her to have been born and brought up in St Nazaire, on the west coast near Nantes. Her story was that her family had been killed in the British bombing of that city in November 1942 so she had moved inland and eventually found a job with the textile company in Toulouse. To explain her presence in their household, it was agreed she should say that she had been looking for a base from which to reach potential customers along the Rhône Valley, and they had been planning to let the spare room to bring in some extra cash. They were a pleasant couple, who had worked hard to build up a business, but they were also fiercely patriotic and loathed the Nazis who had occupied their country. Kim felt that she was as safe as it was possible to be under their roof.

After they had eaten, Sylvie returned and they told the Levignes that they were going out for a drink at a local bar. Instead, she led Kim through the darkening streets until they reached an area largely given over to small businesses and tradesmen of various sorts. She stopped outside a gate, through which they could see stacks of bricks and pieces of timber and the other impedimenta of the building trade. The gate was padlocked, but lock picking had been an essential part of their training for both of them, so it was less than a minute before Kim was able to swing it open.

'What are we looking for?' Sylvie asked.

'Anything incriminating,' Kim replied. 'Anything that might suggest Bernard Leblanc was not what he made himself out to be.'

She looked around the yard. It was almost dark and with blackout regulations in force, she dared not use her torch. 'If he's hidden anything out here amongst this lot, we've no chance of finding it. But it's more likely to be inside somewhere. Is that his office over there?'

The lock on the office door gave them a little more trouble but they were soon inside. There were blackouts on the windows so Kim risked turning on a lamp. 'I'll check the desk,' she said. 'You look through the filing cabinet.'

None of the drawers in the desk were locked and the papers they contained were exactly what might be expected for a business that had only been running a short time — receipts, bills, orders for materials, etc. Kim ran her hand under the desk, feeling for anything that might be taped there, but there was nothing. She pulled out the drawers and felt behind them for a hidden compartment but found none.

'Nothing here,' Sylvie said, closing the last drawer in the filing cabinet.

'No, I didn't expect there would be,' Kim said, 'but we had to be sure.'

'What about the safe?' her companion asked.

Kim shook her head. 'It's the first place the police, or the SD would check. It's not worth bothering to get it open. You said he had a house attached to the yard? Let's try there.'

They crossed the yard to a door in the opposite wall but here they found the lock had been changed for a new one which was harder to pick.

'He didn't want anyone getting in here,' Kim commented as she worked on it.

'So if there is anything . . .'

'It'll be in here.'

Eventually the lock yielded and they found themselves in a kitchen.

'Check the blackout,' Kim instructed.

'It's OK,' was the response.

The dim electric light over the table showed them an ancient gas stove, a sink and a range of cupboards. The room was clean, and the dust that had gathered in the last few days showed no sign of having been disturbed. Kim searched inside the stove and felt all round it for any loose panels but found nothing and the cupboards yielded nothing to Sylvie's investigation other than a few packets of dried goods and one or two tins. In a basket in a corner there were some potatoes and few wilted greens.

Sylvie suddenly stood still and swore softly.

'What is it?'

'It's nothing. Just . . . these are the groceries I delivered on my last visit. He'd hardly eaten any of them. It just made me realize — sorry! I'm just being a bit emotional.'

Kim went over to her and put an arm round her shoulders. 'It's OK. I understand. This is harder for you. You knew him.'

Sylvie sniffed back tears. 'I'm OK. Ignore me.'

Kim got down on her hands and knees and examined the floorboards, but there was no sign of a loose one. 'Let's try upstairs,' she said.

There was a small room at the angle of the stairs and, glancing in, she saw the usual foot block toilet with a wash basin and a small cupboard.

'You check in there,' she said. 'I'll start in the bedroom.'

There was only one bedroom, sparsely furnished with a single bed and a wardrobe which contained only the sort of clothes any working man might possess. She lifted the mattress, but found only cobwebs. There were no loose boards under the bed, either.

Sylvie came in. 'Nothing significant in the loo. I checked inside the cistern, just in case.'

Kim straightened up. 'Now where? He must have hidden stuff somewhere. Don't tell me it's out there in the yard among all that lumber.'

'Is there anything behind the wardrobe?' Sylvie wondered.

It was a struggle to shift the heavy piece of furniture, and at first it seemed their efforts had been wasted. Then Kim said, 'Just a minute. This looks deeper from outside than it does inside.' She tapped the back of the wardrobe and got a hollow sound in response. Feeling round, she located a small crack, just wide enough to insert her fingers. A pull, and part of the panel came away to reveal a space. Kim felt inside and retrieved a bag containing a revolver, like the one she carried in her own suitcase, a change of clothes, a toothbrush, two more sets of false-identity papers, and a considerable sum in French francs and American dollars. The revolver, she noticed, was loaded.

'Looks like he prepared a grab bag in case he had to make a run for it,' she commented. 'Well, this is what—'

They both froze at the clatter of a bucket being overturned in the yard below. For a few seconds they stared at each other, the same thought in both their minds. Then Kim made three silent strides to the door and switched out the light. They stood still in the darkness, straining their ears for any sound of movement. Kim's heart was thumping. Had the apparent acceptance by the authorities that Bernard's death was accidental been just a cover? Were they watching the yard to see who turned up to clear it? She should have been more careful, should have checked to make certain there was no one lurking in an alleyway or peering from a window opposite. Were they even now surrounded by the men of the SD? She felt in her coat pocket, then remembered that she was unarmed. To carry a revolver through the streets would have been too risky. She reached behind her for Bernard's bag and drew out his weapon, thankful for his forethought in keeping it loaded.

Standing where the door would hide her when it was opened, she slipped the safety catch off the revolver. It was futile to imagine that they could fight their way out if the building was really surrounded, but if there were only two or three of them . . . She might be able to create enough confusion to give Sylvie a chance to make a run for it. It was a faint chance, but she could think of nothing better.

The silence stretched out. Kim held her breath, waiting for the sound of footsteps on the stairs. She was aware that Sylvie had crept over to the window and lifted a corner of the blind, letting a gleam of moonlight into the room. Sylvie peered out, searching the cluttered yard for signs of movement. Then she gave a sudden, strangled laugh.

'*Merde*! It's a bloody fox!'

'What?'

'It was a fox prowling round. I've just seen it hop up on that pile of bricks and then over the wall. It was probably looking for rats or mice.'

Kim lowered the revolver. Her palms were damp and sweat prickled in her armpits. 'Bloody animal! I thought we were for it, for a minute.'

'Me, too,' Sylvie agreed.

'Come on.' Kim put the gun back in the bag and slug it over her shoulder. 'We've got what we came for. Let's get home.'

* * *

Next morning Sylvie arrived to collect the day's deliveries and Mme Levigne lent Kim her bicycle so she could go with her. They rattled through the narrow, cobbled streets until they reached a pharmacy in a prosperous residential area.

'I'll deliver these to the back door,' Sylvie said. 'You must go into the shop and ask to see the pharmacist about a personal matter you don't want to discuss in public. When you are taken into the private consulting room at the back you must tell him that you have trouble with an ingrowing toenail. He will know then that you are one of us.'

Kim followed her instructions and found herself facing a tall, lean man with an aquiline nose and narrow, dark eyes which had an upward tilt at the outer corners.

'Good morning, monsieur,' she began. 'My name is Madeleine Moreau. I believe we have interests in common.'

'You have been sent from London?' he asked.

'Yes.'

'May I ask why?'

'I'm instructed to take over Bernard's circuit until a more permanent replacement can be found.'

He regarded her sceptically. 'Is that so? Why would London send a young woman like you to run a circuit?'

Kim felt herself bristle. She was well accustomed to French misogyny, which was even worse than the British variety, but that did not make it easier to stomach. 'My superiors are sufficiently aware of my abilities to feel confident that I am up to the job.'

He shrugged. 'Well, then, I must assume that they are correct. What can I do for you?'

'Part of my brief is to find out exactly how Bernard died.'

His eyebrows rose. 'He fell from a ladder, from a considerable height.'

'Yes, we know that. The question is, why was he up the ladder in the first place?'

'Ah. You do not believe he was just replacing some broken tiles?'

'Do you?'

'No. He had a reason to be there.'

'Which was?'

'The building is a small château near the village of Reventin. Close by there is a small airfield. Not one used by the Armée de l'Air before the surrender, or by the Luftwaffe since the occupation. Before the war it was used by amateur fliers, people who could afford to keep a private plane. Since then . . .'

'Since then?'

'It has been very little used. But we have an informant, a young man who works as a mechanic there. He reported that from time to time some important people, high-ranking officers, use the airfield. We believe this must be for undercover operations of some sort. Bernard was keen to find out more. I believe his object in climbing that turret was to reconnoitre the situation.'

'With a view to what, exactly?'

Darnier's expression grew even more sardonic. 'Probably with a view to blowing something up. Our friend Bernard was very fond of making things go *bang*!' He illustrated the word with an expansive gesture.

Kim met his gaze. 'You didn't approve of that tactic?'

'Listen!' He lost the expression of detachment and spoke with manifest sincerity. 'Every time he blew something up, German reprisals became more violent. Last time we supported one of his ventures, the ambush of a German supply convoy, the entire male population of the village of Estrablin was put up against a wall and shot.'

'Yes, I heard about that,' Kim said. 'It was wicked.'

'Wicked? Yes! But we are dealing with men who will perform deeds even more wicked than that if they are provoked. How can I, in good conscience, support activities that are going to bring down such appalling revenge upon my own people?'

'So how do you see your role, as a member of the Resistance? What were you doing before Bernard arrived?'

'Propaganda. To keep up morale. To foster the spirit of resistance in non-violent ways by refusing to comply with regulations, minor acts of sabotage, that sort of thing. We have our own newspaper, *Vienne Libre*. It was enough to get us all arrested if we were caught, but not enough to provoke reprisals like that.'

Kim felt sympathy with his attitude, but it was not what she had been trained for. 'I understand what you are saying, but our mission, those of us who are sent from London, is to disrupt enemy movements and supply lines wherever possible. In doing so, we force the Nazis to deploy troops and equipment which they could otherwise send to the front line.'

'Listen,' Darnier said. 'Were you in France last summer?'
'Briefly.'

'You must have been aware of the atmosphere. We were certain that the Allies must invade at any moment. Once the Italians surrendered, we expected the invasion of southern France to follow very quickly. Here, in Lyon, we expected to be at the forefront of the liberation. We were prepared to go into action as soon as we got the word. But what happened? Nothing! No, not nothing. What happened was that the occupying Italian troops were withdrawn, or arrested, and the Germans took over, and they are much more heavy-handed than the Italians. Do you blame us for retrenching?'

'I can see that,' Kim conceded. 'But the invasion will come soon. It must come this summer.'

'Perhaps.' Darnier looked sceptical. 'When that happens, if it happens, the sort of tactics you people employ will come into their own. Then any disruption that prevents the movement of troops and equipment to the field of battle will he valuable. And the Germans may have too much to think about to spend time on reprisals.' He sat back. 'Until that time comes, there are other ways you could be useful.'

'Such as?'

'Does the name Klaus Barbie mean anything to you?'

'He's head of the Gestapo in Lyon. I've heard he has a very bad reputation.'

'He is a butcher!' Darnier spat the words. 'But do you know what his principal target is?'

'What?'

'Jews. Do they know in London what is happening to the Jews of Europe?'

'We've heard rumours of concentration camps, of Jews being rounded up in Poland. But is it happening here, in France?'

'Rumours!' He gave a brief humourless laugh. 'And yes, it is happening here in France. Jewish men, women and children are being rounded up and put into trains like cattle. Where they are sent, we do not know, but no one ever returns. And Barbie is tireless in locating them. People who have tried to hide them have been arrested and tortured to reveal their whereabouts.'

'How could I, how could we, help?' Kim asked.

'Tell your government what is happening. Somehow, some arrangement must be made to get these people out of the country, to a place of safety.'

Kim bit her lip. 'I can get a message back to my head-quarters, but it's hard to see what could be done. A mass exodus, such as you are describing, would be hard to organize in peacetime. In the present circumstances . . .'

Darnier sat back, suddenly deflated. 'Yes, of course. You are right. But tell your people. The world should know what these brutes are capable of.'

'I will do that,' Kim promised, 'but meanwhile . . .'

'To the business at hand. You ask me why Bernard was up that ladder, and I have told you what I suspect he was doing.'

'And you think his fall was an accident?'

Darnier lifted his shoulders. 'Of course. Why should you think otherwise?'

'I have no reason. I'm just trying to establish the facts.' Kim got to her feet. 'Thank you for your help. If you need to contact me, you can do so through Sylvie. But for the time being,' she paused and caught his eye, 'you can rest easy. I have no intention of making anything go bang.'

Cycling back to the Levignes' shop, she pondered on what she had learned. What could it be about that little-used airfield that had so intrigued Bernard? If it was being used for some covert activities, what might they be?

CHAPTER 4

At around the same time as Kim and Sylvie closed the gate of the yard behind them and set off through the dark streets of Vienne, in Lyon, Foxy Leroux said goodnight to his staff and bolted the door behind them. Candice had lingered, her eyes begging him to ask her to stay, but he ignored the appeal. He put out the lights and went up to his private rooms above the shop, but instead of preparing for bed he changed his clothes, putting on dark trousers and a black sweater.

Shortly after midnight he slipped silently out of a side door into an alleyway that led uphill away from the river. Keeping to the narrow, cobbled lanes he made his way southwards until he arrived outside a baker's shop close to the Place St Paul. The shutters were down, but when he tapped on the door it was opened at once.

'Come in. They are waiting for you.'

Inside the shop a little group of four huddled together, a man and a woman, both in their thirties he guessed, and two children, a girl of around ten and a boy, perhaps six years old. There was little in their dress to distinguish them from any other comfortably off bourgeois family in the city but one glance at their faces would immediately identify them as Jews, an impression confirmed by their haunted expressions.

For months now the Gestapo chief, Klaus Barbie, had made it his mission to root out all Jews in Lyon and deport them. Where they were sent no one knew, but nothing had ever been heard from those who were captured, and terrible rumours of concentration camps were passed from mouth to mouth.

'Come. It is time to move!' The speaker was the owner of the shop, a large, rubicund man whose normal cheerful manner was now displaced by anxiety. Foxy knew why. The family almost certainly lived on the other side of the river Saône, but to cross the Feuillée Bridge after curfew without being caught was impossible. There was nowhere to hide. So they came across in daylight, as if on a normal shopping errand, and someone had to conceal them until they could be moved on. The baker was one of those prepared to take the risk, but Foxy knew he would be glad to see them on their way.

He turned to the family and gave them a reassuring smile. 'You can call me Roland. Tell me your names. First names only will do.'

The man introduced himself as Leon, his wife was Sarah, his daughter Eva and his son Daniel.

'We can never thank you enough for helping us,' Daniel said, with a tremor in his voice.

'We must all do what we can,' Foxy said. He squatted down in front of the two children. 'Now, remember we must all be as quiet as mice. Imagine you are a mouse. You don't want the cat to catch you, do you?' They both shook their heads, looking at him with huge dark eyes full of doubt. 'The cat is asleep right now, so as long as we are quiet there is nothing to be afraid of.' He straightened up. 'Let's go. We've got a bit of a walk ahead of us.'

The couple took the children's hands, thanked the baker for his kindness and followed Foxy outside.

'Keep to the shadows,' he instructed. 'Don't worry. We shall soon be out of sight.'

He led them across the square and then to a door beneath a stone archway. At first sight it looked like the door of a house, but it gave to Foxy's pressure and revealed a dark space. He ushered the group through. Once they were all inside and the door was shut behind them he switched on a torch, showing a long passage with an arched roof, disappearing into the distance.

Leon whispered, 'This is a *traboule*, yes? I have heard of them but never seen one.'

'One of many,' Foxy confirmed. 'In this way we can cross the old city without risk of being seen.'

The *traboules* were a relic of the city's medieval past, when silk weaving had been its main industry. The weavers worked on the hill called the Croix Rouge on the other side of the river and they had created these passages running between and under buildings to allow them to carry their precious bales of silk to market without being exposed to the weather. Now they formed a network of secret passages — invaluable to the Resistance — of which the German occupiers were only just becoming aware.

Foxy led his charges through the labyrinth, twisting and turning but heading always south and upwards, away from the river. The light from his torch glowed gold on the sandstone blocks walling the passages. Some had elaborately carved arches supporting the roof, some opened out unexpectedly into little courtyards where they could look up and see the stars. These courtyards were surrounded by the walls of houses or apartment blocks, five or six storeys high, with lines of windows tightly shuttered to comply with the blackout regulations. Many had arched balconies decorated with carvings in the Renaissance style, where window boxes filled with flowers sent out a breath of perfume. In one courtyard, a circular tower housed a spiral staircase giving access to the upper floors. In others, doorways opened onto similar stairs. In another, a small fig tree grew in a pot and a little table and two chairs were set under it. From time to time the passage ended in a doorway leading out into a street, and Foxy waved the family to stay back until he was sure that it was deserted. The curfew kept law-abiding citizens indoors,

33

and within a few paces they were at another door, and into another passageway.

Eventually they reached the bottom of a long flight of steps, climbing out into the moonlight. Foxy paused and looked at his charges. They had maintained silence apart from that first query and even the children had not uttered a sound until just a few minutes earlier. Then he had heard Daniel whimper. He had ben immediately hushed by his parents but the meaning was not lost on Foxy. He knelt down by the little boy.

'You have been very brave so I think you deserve a ride. Climb on. I'll give you a piggyback up the stairs.'

The child hesitated until a nod from his father gave permission, then he wrapped his arms round Foxy's neck. Foxy stood up and looked round for the little girl.

'And you, *ma petite*? Can you manage this last climb?'

In the moonlight her small face was pale and shadowed with weariness, but there was no hesitation in the firm nod of her response.

With Foxy leading, Sarah holding her daughter by the hand and Leon at the rear they climbed upwards. A walled garden hemmed them in on one side and when they reached the top, Foxy set Daniel down and gestured to them to stay still. He went up the last few steps and peered cautiously round the edge of the wall. The stairs ended in a steeply sloping street, the Monte Saint-Barthelemy. It was a main road, and so, likely to be patrolled by the military. He waited until he was sure that there was no sound of approaching boots or vehicles, then he beckoned the family forward.

'Nearly there,' he encouraged them, leading them downhill. Above them, on the summit of the hill, the towers of the Basilica of Notre Dame de Fourvière stood out against the stars. A few hundred yards on, they came to a long wall on the opposite side of the road. A double flight of steps led up from the road to a door in the wall. Foxy climbed them and tapped softly on the door. It was opened by a woman wearing a simple dark blue dress with a veil over her hair. She stood back immediately and gestured to Foxy and his party to enter. Inside they found themselves in a small, beautifully decorated chapel with a domed roof. Leon and his family hesitated in the doorway, obviously uneasy about entering a place of Christian worship. The woman who had admitted them immediately reassured them.

'Come. I know you do not share our faith, but we are all children of God and must help each other however we can. You are welcome to rest here until you are ready for the next stage of your journey.'

She opened a side door into a small room where vestments hung on hooks in the wall.

'Sit, sit,' she said, indicating a bench. 'I will bring you some refreshment.'

She returned a few minutes later with wine and water for the adults and milk for the children, and a plate of biscuits.

Foxy looked at his watch. 'It is almost light. I will go and wait for our transport.'

'Where are we going?' Leon asked hesitantly.

'To Le Chambon-sur-Lignon,' he told him. 'It's a small village in the Haute-Loire, about a hundred kilometres from here. It's very remote, surrounded by forest, and the villagers have made a pact to give sanctuary to people of your race fleeing the Nazis. You will find many Jews there already and every one of the villagers has sworn never to reveal their presence. You will be safe there.'

'And they have all agreed to take such a terrible risk?'

'Yes. And as long as they keep their word, there is little chance of the Germans finding you. They have no reason to waste their time searching a small, insignificant place like Chambon.'

'It is a miracle!' Sarah looked at him with tears in her eyes. 'Such goodness to complete strangers!'

'How do we get there?' Leo asked.

'Transport has been arranged, but you may find the first part of the journey a little . . . unconventional.'

'What do you mean?'

35

Foxy grinned. 'You'll see. It should arrive any minute.'

Outside, he stood at the top of the steps, just inside the door, waiting and listening. In front of him, the city of Lyon was laid out at his feet and the sun was just rising over the hills to the east. He knew if he stepped out into the road and turned round, he would see the towers of the basilica above them just catching the first rays, but he resisted the temptation. He did not have to wait long before he heard the noise he was waiting for — the clip-clop of a horse's hooves and the rattle of milk churns. A farm cart came into sight, plodding steadily up the steep hill. When it reached him the farmer called to his horse, which stopped as if this was a regular routine, and he and a boy sitting beside him jumped down. The farmer looked up at Foxy and acknowledged him with a brief gesture. Then the two of them pulled back the tarpaulin that covered the cart and began to manhandle several churns of milk onto the pavement, where an equal number of empty churns awaited them.

Foxy went back into the chapel. 'It is time to move. Your carriage awaits!'

As they reached the door Leon suppressed a small gasp of dismay. 'This?'

'M. Pinchon will take you as far as his farm. Someone will be waiting there with some more comfortable form of transport for the rest of your journey. But for now . . . the Boches manning the roadblocks have seen this cart come by every morning. They know it's just the farmer bringing the morning milk. Why should they suddenly decide to search it?'

There was a low call from the farmer and in response, Foxy picked up little Daniel and carried him down the steps. 'Come along. Quickly now!' He lifted the boy into the cart and the other three scrambled in after him. There were some hay bales at the far end nearest the driver's position and they settled themselves on them. Foxy wished them *Bon chance!* and the farmer and his son piled the empty churns in front of them, pulling the tarpaulin over their heads.

The farmer and Foxy shook hands briefly, then he and the boy climbed back onto the driver's bench. He clicked to the horse and the cart with its hidden passengers clopped away into the distance.

Foxy lingered only long enough to thank the woman who had greeted them, and then he set off back the way he had come, keeping to the shelter of the *traboules* until he was back at the Place St Paul. The curfew had been lifted by then and the citizens of Lyon were going about their business. Men were heading for their offices or opening up shops, and women were joining the endless queues for whatever the ration allowed them, hoping that when they got to the head of the queue the commodity — whatever it was — had not run out. What the rations allowed was little enough, but even so, demand often exceeded supply.

There was a long queue outside the bakery and he could smell the fresh bread as he passed. Briefly, he imagined himself breaking a crusty baguette and spreading it with butter and he found himself salivating, but the image soon vanished. Bread these days was like eating sawdust, the limited supply of flour obliging the bakers to adulterate it with whatever substitutes came to hand.

He reached the bistro and let himself in. It was too early yet for any of the staff to arrive so he had the place to himself. He went up to his private apartment, made a cup of what passed for coffee and gnawed at a chunk of yesterday's bread. He washed and changed his clothes, then took a pencil and a sheet of paper and set about encoding a brief message. A glance at his watch told him he had little time to spare. In the bathroom he removed a panel behind the bidet and extricated a radio transmitter and receiver. With practised skill he unwound the aerial, threaded it across the room and out of the small window overlooking the alley. Then he put on his headphones, tuned the set to the correct frequency and sent out a recognition signal.

Back in Grendon Underwood a young woman in FANY uniform heard it over her headphones and smiled. Right on sked! She did not know who was sending the Morse code bleeping in her ears, but she recognized his 'fist' — his unique manner of using his Morse key — and he was always exactly on schedule with his transmissions. There was an exchange of code words, then Foxy sent his message which, when decoded by the girls 'upstairs', read simply: 'Four parcels successfully delivered.' The incoming message was equally incomprehensible until he had time to decode it. He signed off, returned the radio to its hiding place, and went downstairs to let his staff in and begin the day's food preparation. After a night without sleep he was less responsive than usual to the kitchen banter, but the men and woman who worked with him were accustomed to his occasionally taciturn manner and accepted it. After all, a chef who was a genius was entitled to be moody from time to time.

Once he was sure everything was in hand he went back upstairs and spent half an hour decoding the message. When he had finished, he went back to the kitchen and found the errand boy who was one of his most trusted couriers. 'Go to Jean Jacques and tell him that André has a horse suffering from colic that needs urgent attention.'

Jean Jacques was a vet who travelled from farm to farm to care for the animals, including the many horses which the farmers relied upon more heavily than ever in the dearth of petrol or diesel. For this reason, he had fitted out his truck with a *gazogene* burner, which produced gas from burning wood to fuel his engine. Vets were one of the small bands, which included doctors and priests, who were permitted to travel after curfew.

The dinner service was almost over when the vehicle chugged into the yard behind the bistro. Jean Jacques was invited into the kitchen for a beer and was still there chatting to the patron when the staff left for the night. As soon as they were out of the way, he led Foxy outside. In the back of the truck, underneath a mound of loose hay, were three large boxes. The two men carried them inside and Foxy prized open the lid of one. Inside were a dozen Lee-Enfield rifles.

The message Foxy had decoded earlier had told him there had been a parachute drop at a location used by one of the Resistance cells the SOE agent Roger had set up. Some of the weapons would have been retained by that cell. The rest were to be distributed to others, at Foxy's discretion. For the time being, they had to be hidden where other members of the kitchen staff would not come across them. He and Jean Jacques carried them down into the cellar and concealed them in a space behind the wine racks lining the walls.

Once the vet had gone, Foxy was at last able to climb the stairs to his own apartment and fall into bed.

CHAPTER 5

After her meeting with Darnier, Kim strapped her sample case to the carrier on her borrowed bicycle and pedalled out towards Reventin. There was little traffic here as the main road to the south ran away to her right, along the bank of the Rhône, so she was surprised to find a check-point in position a few miles from the village. It was manned by a couple of men of the *milice* — the Nazi-supporting militia who had usurped many of the functions of the gendarmerie. The man who stopped her was big, with shoulders like a bull and a gut that overlapped the waistband of his trousers. He was topped by a very small, round head with dark hair cut short and sleeked down to his skull so that it looked as if it had been painted on.

He made the usual demand to see her papers, and having scrutinized them, ordered her to open her case. She did so readily.

'You see, monsieur, this is my stock-in-trade. I am a traveller for the firm that produces these fine garments. I am hoping to find a customer somewhere in the next village.' Kim put on her most seductive smile. 'I am sure a gentleman of your fine figure must have a wife, or a girlfriend, who would appreciate a small gift. Would you like to select something from my samples?'

'Huh!' he snorted. 'If I wanted to give a woman lingerie, I'd find something a bit sexier than this.'

Kim sighed elaborately. 'Well, there you are. You see how hard I have to work to persuade people to buy. But times are hard and a girl has to do what she can to earn her daily bread. But perhaps I shall be lucky in Reventin. May I go now?'

'Yes, get on your way — and good luck selling that rubbish!'

Kim thanked him and mounted her bike. In the village she found a small haberdasher's shop and kept up the pretence of trying to persuade the owner to order from her catalogue. As she was about to leave, empty-handed, a light aircraft passed low overhead.

Kim gasped. '*Mon dieu*! I thought he was going to hit the roof of that house across the street. Is he going to crash?'

'Oh, don't worry,' the woman behind the counter said. 'It happens all the time. There's an airfield just the other side of those trees.'

It was not difficult to find the road that led to the airfield, but when she got there Kim understood why Bernard had been looking for a vantage point from which he could see what was happening. The whole area was surrounded by a high fence topped with barbed wire, and the gate was guarded by another man in the uniform of the *milice*. Such tight security was more than might be expected for an airfield used exclusively by amateur fliers — unless high-ranking German officers enjoyed going up for the occasional 'flip'. Kim cycled past, giving the guard a casual wave, and stopped once she was out of his sight. Behind the airfield the ground rose in a thickly wooded slope, and she could just make out the top of a turret protruding above the trees. It was the obvious observation point, if you could get up there.

She mounted her bike again and after ten minutes hard pedalling, found that the road bent at the top of the hill and passed the entrance to a building. In England, it might have been a manor house, but here in France, it had the architectural embellishments that earned it the title of a château.

There were no vehicles on the sweep of gravel leading to the main doors, and she could see no sign of anyone working in the gardens. She was tempted to investigate further but was unable to think of a reasonable excuse for her curiosity, should she be challenged. So, after watching for a few minutes, she cycled on, heading back to the city.

Next morning, she drew Sylvie out into the yard behind the shop and told her what she had learned from Darnier and from her expedition of the previous afternoon.

'So he was looking for an observation point,' Sylvie said. 'That makes sense, but we still don't know if the fall was an accident.'

'No, we don't, but I think it's a mistake to dismiss things as accidents too readily in our line of work. Can you think of anyone who might have had reason to want to get rid of Bernard? What about the villagers whose menfolk were shot? I know Darnier blames him for that, but somehow, I can't see him sneaking up and pulling the ladder out from under Bernard. Can you?'

Sylvie shook her head. 'I know they didn't see eye to eye about a lot of things, but I can't believe he'd commit murder in cold blood.'

'What about the people in that village? One of them might have wanted revenge.'

'It's possible, but I don't think any of them would know who he was. They would blame the Resistance but they wouldn't have any idea that there were British agents involved.'

'Unless someone leaked the fact to them. You said you thought there was a mole in the circuit somewhere.'

'That's true,' Sylvie agreed. 'I could go up there on a bird-watching trip on my next day off and see if I can pick up any local gossip.'

'Good idea,' Kim agreed, 'but be very careful. We don't know who we can trust now.'

Sylvie nodded. 'Don't worry. I'll just drop a few leading questions and see what it stirs up.' She started back into the house, then paused and turned back. 'I wonder what happened to his camera.'

'His camera?'

'Yes. When Bernard was carrying out a recce, he always took photographs. He said it was better than relying on memory. If he was going up to that turret to observe the layout of the airfield, he would have taken his camera with him.'

'My God!' Kim exclaimed. 'If the police picked it up they might have found God knows what incriminating stuff on it.'

'But if they had, it would have stirred up a real hornets' nest and the SD would have been brought in. Instead, it's all gone very quiet. It didn't look as though his yard had been searched, did it? It seems the police have just put it down as an accident and forgotten about it.'

'We didn't find a camera when we searched there ourselves,' Kim said. 'What kind was it?'

'An expensive one. What was it called? A Contax, that was it.'

'Did he develop the film himself? We didn't find any equipment or chemicals either.'

'Maybe he got Darnier to do it. The chemist's shop is where you go to get films developed usually.'

'Of course. So could Darnier have the camera?'

'I don't see how, if Bernard had it with him when he fell.'

'True,' Kim frowned. 'So what happened to it?'

'Maybe one of the gendarmes pocketed it as a bit of loot and just hasn't bothered to get the film developed.'

'That's a possibility, I suppose. I wonder if it might have fallen into some undergrowth. I think I need to go to the château and do some poking around.' An idea was crystallizing in her mind. 'Was it reported in the local paper?'

'There was a brief paragraph on an inside page. It won't have made much impression.'

'Never mind. It's not important.' Kim smiled at her. 'You'd better get on. M. Levigne will be wondering where you've got to.'

* * *

Next morning Kim made her way back to the pharmacy and asked, as before, for a private consultation with the owner. Darnier was not pleased to see her.

'You should not come here. Contact me through Sylvie if you need to.'

'There are a couple of things I need to ask you,' Kim said. 'If you can tell me what I need to know, I'll keep my distance from now on.'

'Very well. What is it?'

'You mentioned that your group produces a newspaper. How do you get it printed?'

'We have a sympathizer at ECAM — the Ecole Catholique des Arts et Metier. They moved here from Paris in 1940. They have their own printing press.'

'Would they do a small job for me? I want some business cards showing I am a journalist employed by one of the Lyon papers.'

Darnier looked puzzled, but he answered, 'I'm sure that could be arranged. Which paper?'

'What would you suggest?'

'*Le Progrès* is the one with the widest circulation.'

'Make it that one, then.' She handed him a slip of paper with the wording she required. 'How soon could you have them ready?'

'That depends on my contact, but it shouldn't be a long job. Now, you said there were two things . . . ?'

'Yes. I need to talk to your contact at the airfield. I want to get more detail about what he's seen going on.'

'Very well. I'm sure that can be arranged. I'll send you a message through Sylvie when I've had a chance to get in touch with him. Is that all?'

'Yes.' Kim stood up. 'Oh no. Just one thing more. Can you by any chance lend me a camera?'

'A camera?'

'If I'm going to pose as a reporter, I should probably have a camera. Nothing expensive, just something basic.'

'Well, yes. I think I can find you one.' He disappeared into a back room and came back with a Kodak Brownie camera. 'Will this do? It's got a film in it.'

'Oh, yes, that would be fine. Thank you.' Kim took the camera and added, as an apparent afterthought, 'Do you develop films here?'

'We have a darkroom, yes.'

'Did Bernard ever bring you films to develop?'

'Yes, he did, from time to time. I always did those myself, in case there was anything that might arouse suspicion.'

'When did you last develop a film for him?'

'Oh, several weeks ago. Why?'

'I just wondered if he had left his camera with you for any reason.'

'Left it with me? No. Why do you ask?'

'I haven't come across it, that's all. I expect it's in his house somewhere. Thank you, monsieur, that's all I need. I won't keep you any longer.'

He rose too, but then seemed to have second thoughts. 'There is just one thing that occurred to me after we spoke yesterday. You asked if I knew anyone who might wish to harm Bernard.'

'Yes! Have you thought of someone?'

'It is only a rumour, but there was gossip about an affair.'

'An affair?'

'Between Bernard and the wife of a *milicien*. But it seems unlikely to me. Why would he want to have anything to do with someone connected to the *milice*?'

'As a source of information, perhaps? What is the name of this *milicien*?'

'Georges Duboeuf. His wife, if I remember correctly, is Lili. They live out in the Les Charmilles area, I think.'

'Could you get me the address?'

'I'll ask around. But be careful. You don't want to mess with people like that.'

'Don't worry. I won't take any chances.'

45

Cycling back to her base at the Levignes' shop, Kim decided it was time she checked in with her superiors in London. There was little definite to report, but she should at least let them know that she was safe and still working on the mission she had been given. So when she got back, she sat down and carefully encoded a message, then she made her way back to the house from which Pauline operated.

To her dismay, when Pauline opened the door, she saw that both her hands were bandaged and she was supporting herself on a walking stick.

'*Mon dieu*! What has happened to you?'

Pauline looked shamefaced. 'It's so silly. I tripped on the stairs. I seem to have sprained both my wrists and twisted an ankle.'

'Have you seen a doctor?'

'Oh no! That would be too risky. He might ask questions I couldn't answer.'

'Not if your cover story is as watertight as it should be,' Kim said. 'Can I come in?'

'Yes, of course. I'm sorry, I'm not being very polite.'

Kim took a quick glance round the room. Everything was much as it had been on her first visit. There was no sign of a search, but something about Pauline's demeanour set off a warning signal in that part of her mind which acted on instinct honed by long experience.

'Let me have a look at your wrists,' she said, moving to the other woman.

'Oh, there's nothing to see,' Pauline protested. 'Really, it's not serious. Just a bit inconvenient. I can't use my hands very well.'

'So there's no question of you transmitting a message for me?'

'I'm afraid not. Sorry. I'm being a bit useless, aren't I?'

'It doesn't matter for now. Show me your set. I'll send it myself.'

Rather reluctantly, it seemed to Kim, Pauline showed her where the set was hidden above a loose ceiling panel and how to extend the aerial round the room and out of the window.

'Watch the street for any sign of a detector van,' she instructed, then settled herself in front of the set and sent out a signal. She had no regular 'sked' so she had to hope that one of the girls in Grendon would pick it up. The response came quite quickly. She identified herself and provided the requisite recognition code, then tapped out her message. The 'message received' code followed and she signed off and shut down. It had taken only minutes, but it was a relief to return the set to its hiding place without any warning from Pauline that a detector van was outside, or the dreaded sound of jackboots on the stairs.

'I'm so sorry you had to do that yourself,' Pauline said. 'I feel such a failure.'

There were tears in her eyes but Kim was unable to conjure up any sense of sympathy.

'Well, you are certainly not much use to us in your present state,' she agreed. 'Did you say you have been here for three months?'

'Yes.'

'Where were you before that?'

'This was my first deployment. I'd just completed my course at Beaulieu and they gave me leave to go home for Christmas. I was called back the day after Boxing Day and dropped the following night.'

'Home for Christmas?' Kim regarded her with a touch of envy. 'You were lucky!'

'I think Papa probably pulled some strings. There was a ball he had to attend. Mama died some years ago and he likes to have me with him on occasions like that.'

'Oh, really?' Kim murmured.

Heading back through the city streets she went over the conversation in her mind. *Papa . . . Mama . . . a ball he had to attend.* So that explained the 'thoroughbred racehorse' look. It was not a great surprise. She knew from experience that the men at the top of the SOE liked to recruit from the upper classes of society. It was an extension of the 'old boy' network in which they had grown up. Not that that, in itself, meant that they recruited the wrong girls. Kim had met a good few of them and found them as tough and as courageous as any agents she had come across. There was something to be said for the policy. Girls from that class were usually well-educated, spoke perfect French and were well-travelled and able to hold their own in any company. Most of them had independent means, which allowed them to indulge in dangerous sports like skiing and riding, to hounds. Her own background, as the daughter of a diplomat, was perhaps slightly less exalted but not so very different. But the mystery remained. What was it about Bernard's death that had so undone Pauline? This kind of weakness in a member of the circuit was a threat to them all. She found herself wondering if Pauline's injuries were genuine, or if they were self-inflicted. Either way, she was a liability. Arrangements must be made to send her back to England at the earliest opportunity.

Her first thought was to send a new message asking her superiors to arrange an exfiltration by air, but that meant relying on Darnier's group to suggest a suitable landing ground and prepare it. She remembered what Sylvie had told her about the Germans' apparent foreknowledge of parachute drops arranged by Bernard. Someone, somehow, was passing on the details and she could not risk a Lysander aircraft being shot down, or it and its pilot being captured when it landed. She had to find a secure way to make the arrangements and a location outside the area where Darnier and Bernard had operated. There was only one solution. She took the next train back to Lyon.

The Bistro Le Renard Rouge was busy, as usual, with parties of German officers occupying most of the tables. Kim was greeted, as before, by Candice but beneath the professional courtesy she sensed a brooding hostility. She ordered a meal and was enjoying a plate of *escargot a la bourguignonne* when Candice approached her table.

'Is everything satisfactory, madame?'

'Perfectly, thank you. My compliments to the chef.'

Candice lowered her voice. 'Monsieur asked me to tell you to wait until we close, then to allow fifteen minutes. After that, come to the kitchen door. It is at the side, down the little alley.'

'Thank you,' Kim replied. 'Please tell monsieur that I shall follow his instructions.'

She finished her meal in a leisurely manner, by which time most of the other diners had paid and left. She paid also, and walked out into the street. The problem now was to fill in the fifteen minutes without making it obvious that she was waiting for something. There were few people about now, and most were hurrying to get home before the start of the curfew. Anyone loitering would look suspicious. She walked briskly down the street, took a left turn, then a right, and found herself in a maze of narrow, cobbled streets. For a while she was worried that she might not find her way back, or might run into a German patrol who would want know why she was out after curfew, but her sense of direction held good and she finally found herself back on the right road. A glance at her watch told her almost twenty minutes had passed.

The door in the alley gave to her touch and she found Foxy alone in the kitchen. He held out his arms and hugged her close. 'Thank God! I was beginning to get worried.' Then he drew back and looked at her. 'Is something wrong?'

'Nothing immediate, but I need your help with something.'

His tone became businesslike. 'Right. Come upstairs and tell me about it.'

In his shabby sitting room she described Pauline's strange behaviour. 'To be honest, I'm not sure that those injuries are genuine. I wouldn't put it past her to fake them in her current state of mind. The girl's a mess and she could be a liability.'

'You're right. You need to get rid of her. Why don't you ask HQ to repatriate her?'

'I would, but there's a problem.' She told him what she had heard from Sylvie and his expression was grave.

'That's bad. You've got a traitor in the group somewhere.'

'I know, and I'll take steps to smoke him out, but right now I need you to contact London and arrange the exfiltration. Is there a landing ground we could use, preferably somewhere between here and Vienne?'

'I can think of a couple of possibilities. I'll have to contact the Resistance groups in the area and see what I can work out with them. It may take a day or two.'

'I understand that. I'll just have to keep an eye on Pauline and stop her from doing anything stupid.'

He frowned. 'You don't think, do you, that she could be the source of the leak?'

'It had crossed my mind,' Kim admitted. 'I shall certainly alert Baker Street to the possibility. It'll be up to them to interrogate her when she gets home.'

'Could she be another of Kline's converts?'

'I don't think so. She's been out here for three months and she told me she was deployed almost as soon as she passed out of Beaulieu. She just had time to spend Christmas with her family. The course at Beaulieu lasts about a month, which means she would have started there in mid-November. And we have good reason to know that Kline had skedaddled by November 9th. So he would never have had a chance to get at her.'

He sighed and reached for her hand. 'I wish we were working together. I worry about you, and I shall worry even more now I know you've got a traitor in the group.'

'I know.' She squeezed his fingers. 'But we're lucky to have this much contact. You know our lords and masters think having couples working together is bad for security. I'm only here now because Bernard was killed.'

'Are you any nearer solving that one?'

'I'm not sure. I think I know what he was doing up that ladder, but I don't know yet how that relates to his death. He wasn't popular with the head of the local resistance, but I don't see that as a basis for murder.' Speaking of Darnier reminded her of their first conversation. 'By the way, is it true that Jews are being rounded up and sent to concentration camps?'

He nodded soberly. 'Oh yes.'

'I suppose there's nothing we can do about it?'

'For the vast majority, no. But for individual cases . . .'

'What?'

'There are ways of getting a few away to a place of safety.'

She looked at him. 'You're involved, aren't you.'

'In a small way.'

'For God's sake, be careful, my darling. What we do is dangerous enough, without adding to it.'

He shrugged. 'I know, but it's not something I can turn my back on.' He stood up. 'Why are we wasting time talking when we could be in bed?'

She moved into his arms. 'Why, indeed?'

CHAPTER 6

Next day Sylvie brought a message from Darnier. 'The young man from the airfield will meet you tonight. Be in the Bar des Sportes at seven o'clock. Take the green umbrella. He will apologize that Jacques is unable to keep your date because his mother has been taken ill and has sent him to explain.'

At seven, Kim entered the bar. It was the sort of place frequented by young people, particularly young men. There was snooker table, table football and a juke-box. She had carefully kept her clothes unremarkable but had made-up her face and put on a colourful scarf, as if she was making the best of what was available under rationing to impress a boyfriend. The green umbrella was propped beside her chair. She had to wait about ten minutes until a man in his twenties, slightly built with a narrow olive-skinned face, came in and hesitated by the door, looking around nervously. Seeing the umbrella, he came over, and spoke the message she had been given, like an amateur actor speaking his lines.

She smiled up at him. 'Well, if Jacques can't make it, I guess I'll have to make do with you. Why don't you sit down. This could be your lucky night.'

She saw him blush and his expression was an endearing mixture of shyness and relief. He fetched a beer from the bar and took a seat opposite her, pushing a small package across the table.

'Jacques sent you a gift.'

'Oh, how sweet of him!'

She opened the wrapping. 'Chocolates! Wherever did he find them?' Inside the box there was a neat pile of business cards, identifying her as a reporter working for *Le Progrès*. 'Oh, that's lovely,' she cooed. 'Please thank Jacques for me.'

He blushed again and mumbled something. Undercover work did not come naturally to him.

'I'm Madeleine,' she said. 'What's your name?'

'Pierre,' he replied. 'Pierre Jervaux.'

'You work at the airfield out at Reventin, don't you?' She deliberately kept her tone light, as if she was just making conversation.

'Yes. Yes, I do.'

Four boys were playing the table football not far from where they sat and the noise they were making was more than enough to cover their conversation.

'You told M. Darnier that there have been some odd things happening there.'

'Yes, well, most of the planes are laid up for the duration — you know, not much chance of pleasure flights at the moment. But there are a couple that don't belong to any of the members of the aero club — bigger, able to fly longer distances. Every now and then we get instructions to prepare them for a flight, check them over, fuel them up. There's no problem getting the fuel. Then an army catering van drives in and food is delivered. Not the usual rations. Luxury stuff. Foie gras and champagne. That sort of thing.'

'And then?'

'Then some bigwigs arrive, high-ranking officers. They have a meal, a feast I'd call it, and then one of the officers and a pilot board the plane and they take off.'

'Do you have any idea where they are going?'

'No. They don't file any flight plans.'

'Is this at night?'

'Late evening. We have to light a flare path for them.'

'And when do they come back?'

'It varies. Sometimes after an hour. Sometimes longer.'

'And these planes, how far could they fly?'

'A long way, like I said.'

'As far as Berlin?'

'I should think so.'

'Or the Spanish border?'

'Easily.'

'What about across the Channel?'

'To England? Yes, I suppose so. But they'd get shot down, wouldn't they?'

'Not necessarily.'

Kim sat back. There was a lot to think about here. No wonder Bernard had been curious.

'Do you get any warning about when it's going to happen?'

'A bit. Sometimes the order comes through to get the planes ready the day before.'

'Do you live locally?'

'In Les Charmilles.'

'Do you know the grocer's shop belonging to M. Levigne in the middle of town?'

'Yes, I know it.'

'Next time you are told to get a plane ready, could you come there and ask Monsieur . . . ask him if he has any bananas.'

'He wouldn't have! I haven't seen a banana for months.'

'I know that. But he will understand that it is a message for me. I want to find out who flies in these planes.'

'You can't. You won't get near the airfield.'

'Never mind. Leave that to me. Just bring the message. Can you do that?'

She saw him straighten his shoulders. 'Yes. Yes, OK. I can do that.'

Something was nagging at the back of Kim's mind. *Les Charmilles. Where had she heard that before?* Then it came to her.

'You said you live in Les Charmilles?'

'Yes. Is that important?'

'I was just wondering, have you ever come across a *milicien* called Georges Duboeuf?'

'Duboeuf? Yes, everyone knows him. He's a pig!'

'In what way?'

'Likes to throw his weight about. No one was surprised when he decided to join the Milice.'

'What does he look like?'

'Funny-looking fellow. Heavily built but with a tiny head. Likes to swank around in his uniform, but we all think he looks stupid.' He stopped and looked at her. 'Why do you ask?'

'I think I may have come across him, manning a road-block near the airfield.'

He nodded. 'I'm not surprised. The security is really tight, even when we're not expecting anyone.'

Kim sat back and finished her drink. She had plenty to think about. She smiled at the young man on the other side of the table. 'Thank you for giving up your evening, Pierre. You've been a great help. I think I should be going now.'

He stood up. 'It was nothing, ma'amselle. I'm glad to be of service.'

She shook his hand. 'You won't forget — next time you expect something to happen?'

He grinned. 'Bananas!'

'Exactly!' She grinned back, then on an impulse, leaned forward and kissed him on the cheek. 'Goodnight.'

CHAPTER 7

The following morning Kim delved into the hidden compartment in the bottom of her suitcase and pulled out the blonde
wig, a smart navy skirt and a bright blue jacket. The transformation in her appearance was confirmed by Mme Levigne's
startled expression when she went down to the kitchen.

'Who? . . . What?' She gazed at Kim in confusion.

'It's all right, madame,' Kim reassured her. 'It's only me,
but I wanted to be sure no one would recognize me today.'

'Well, you can certainly be sure of that,' her hostess
responded. 'You gave me quite a shock.'

'I'm sorry,' Kim said. 'I'm afraid it's a necessary part of
what I do.'

'Don't worry about that. If it helps you to avoid the
Boches that's all that matters. I won't ask where you are going.
Just take care.'

'I will,' Kim promised.

There was a more direct route leading to the château that
did not involve passing through the little town of Reventin
so Kim took that, hoping to avoid roadblocks. She arrived
without passing one and rang the doorbell. A middle-aged
woman in an apron opened the door.

'Yes?'

Kim smiled. 'Madame le Baron?'

'Goodness, no! I'm the housekeeper.'

'Oh, forgive me. Is madame at home — or monsieur?'

'They're here, but they don't receive visitors — except for the doctor and the curé.'

'Oh, I see. Then perhaps I could address my questions to you — Madame . . . ?'

'Durand. What questions?'

Kim proffered her card. 'I'm a reporter with the *Le Progrès*. My editor read something about a tragic accident that happened here a few days ago and he has sent me to find out the details.'

She saw at once that she might have struck lucky with Mme Durand. Something in the woman's face told her that she relished the prospect of telling her story to a newspaper.

'*Le Progrès*? That's a Lyon paper, isn't it? What do Lyon folks care about what happens here?'

'Oh, there are always readers for a human-interest story — especially one with a tragic ending. Now,' Kim got out her notebook in a businesslike manner. 'Can you tell me in your own words what happened?'

'There's not much to say, really. The man was replacing some tiles on one of the turrets and he fell.'

'Can you show me where?'

The woman led her round the side of the building and pointed upwards. 'He was working on that turret, there.'

'So high up!' Kim made a point of taking a picture of the turret. 'How did he fall?'

'No one knows. He started one afternoon, just before I left. I don't live in. I came to work in the morning and there he was, flat on the grass.'

'So you found the body?'

'Yes.'

'And the poor man had been there all night?'

'Must have been.'

'But didn't the Baron or his wife know what had happened?'

'No. They're both stone deaf, you see, and they don't go out much. They're very elderly and rather frail.'

'My goodness. It must have been a shock for them.'

'I suppose.' The woman shrugged. 'They didn't really take it in, I don't think.'

'So who sent for the police?'

'I did.'

'And did they investigate?'

'Not what I'd call investigate. They seemed to think it was his own silly fault for being up there on his own, without anyone to hold the ladder.'

'That's a bit casual. But then, it was just an accident.'

'Was it?' Mme Durand looked at her meaningfully.

'You don't think it was?'

'I picked up the bits of the ladder after they'd gone. Thought it would make firewood, if nothing else. One of the rungs was broken and it didn't look to me as if it was rotten. It looked to me as if it had been cut.'

'Cut?' Kim's heart missed a beat. 'You mean someone deliberately sabotaged his ladder.'

'My husband was a carpenter. I know the difference between wood that's split and wood that's been cut with a saw.'

'Did you mention it to the police?'

'That lot? One of them was *milice*. I don't want to get involved with the likes of them.'

'No, I see.' Kim was thinking fast. 'I don't suppose you have still got the ladder?'

'Burnt it. Like I said, made good kindling.' She turned away to the front door. 'Look, you'd better not put that in your paper. I shouldn't have spoken. I don't want to cause any trouble.'

'No, no. Of course not,' Kim reassured her. 'I won't print that. Tell me one more thing. Did the baron or his wife call the builder in?'

'No, no. They wouldn't notice if the place was falling down about their ears. The chap just rang the doorbell one day and said he'd noticed some loose tiles on the turret and would they like him to put them right.'

'I see.' Kim looked up at the turret again. 'There must be quite a view from up there.'

'Oh yes. You can see for miles. Not that I've been up there lately. Too many stairs!'

'You don't think . . . I hardly like to ask . . . could I go up there and take a photo from the window. Just so readers can get an idea of how high up it is.'

The housekeeper paused, then shrugged her shoulders. 'I don't see why not.'

'Monsieur and Madame won't mind?'

'Oh, they won't notice. Like I said, they're stone deaf and they only use the ground floor now. They're in their drawing room on the far side of the house. Come on. We'll go in the back door.'

She led Kim through a kitchen and along a passageway to the foot of a spiral staircase. 'You go on up. Like I said, too many stairs for me.'

At the top of the stairs there was a small circular room right under the tiles, with a little window. Kim opened it and leaned out. As she expected, she had a perfect view of the airfield in the valley on the far side of the trees. She paused a few minutes, catching her breath and looking for any sign of movement around the hangars at the end of the runway. Then she closed the window but did not latch it and went back down to where Mme Durand was waiting for her. She offered to take her photo but the response was a hastily shaken head.

'I don't want any of this to come back to me. You keep my name out of the paper.'

'Of course,' Kim agreed soothingly. 'You've been such a help and I'm most grateful.' Then, as an afterthought, 'I'd like to send you a small gift, to say thank you. Are you here every day?'

'Every day except Wednesday. That's my day off. But there's no need, really.'

'Oh, I'd like to do it. Not everyone is as willing to help as you have been.' Kim put her notebook away and shouldered her camera. 'I must be on my way. Goodbye — and thank you again.'

She collected her bicycle and rode down the drive. As she reached the road, she saw something that sent a shock wave through her nerves. About to disappear round a bend in the road that led to Reventin was a figure in the dark blue uniform of the Milice. His cap obscured the shape of his head, but surely those bull-like shoulders could only belong to one man. Was it pure coincidence that Georges Duboeuf happened to be passing the château just as she was leaving, or was he following her? What was the connection between him and his wife and Bernard? Was she an informer for the Milice? Even if she was, how could she know about Kim's mission? Bernard had been dead before Kim arrived. These thoughts chased themselves round her brain as she cycled back to Vienne.

When she arrived at the Levignes' shop, she found Sylvie waiting for her.

'One of Hunter's couriers brought a message for you,' she said, handing Kim a sheet of paper.

It was a page torn from a railway timetable and at a casual glance would have told anyone reading it nothing more than the times of trains to and from Lyon to Paris. When Kim held it up against a window it became apparent that there were tiny pinpricks under some of the numbers. She took a pencil and carefully wrote those numbers on a page in her notebook. Still, they would have meant nothing to most people.

Sylvie was looking over her shoulder. 'Poem code?'
'Yes.'
'Fine, if you happen to have a copy of the poem.'
'Don't worry. I know it by heart.'

Some time ago, seeking a code that was foolproof but simple enough to be used by agents who had the courage and cunning to operate in enemy territory but who had little time or patience for encoding and decoding complex messages, Leo Marks, the head of coding for SOE, had come up with the idea that each man or woman should choose a poem that he or she knew by heart to be the basis of their personal code. Some of them had even then insisted that they were incapable of remembering poetry of any description and girls in the FANY encryption team had had to resort to making up verses personal to each of them — sometimes including lines that were scurrilous or bordering on the obscene. However, that had not been necessary when it came to choosing a poem for Foxy Leroux, and Kim knew very well what it was. La Fontaine's fable about the cunning fox and the crow.

She took a new page and wrote:

Maître Corbeau, sur un arbre perché,
Tenait en son bec un fromage.
Maître Renard, par l'odeur alléché,
Lui tint à peu près ce langage:
Eh ! bonjour, Monsieur du Corbeau.
Que vous êtes joli ! que vous me semblez beau!
Sans mentir, si votre ramage
Se rapporte à votre plumage,
Vous êtes le Phénix des hôtes de ces bois.

'Read out the numbers for me,' Kim instructed.
'1, 3, 1,' Sylvie obliged.
'Line 1, third word, first letter. S. What next?'
1, 3, 2.'
'Line one, third word, second letter. U. Go on.'
'1, 4, 2.'
'Line one, fourth word, second letter. N.'
'0, 1, 4, 2.'
'New word. Then the same. Another N.'
'1, 1, 6.'
'First line, first word, sixth letter. E.'
'9, 4, 6.'
Ninth line, fourth word, sixth letter. X.'

'2, 1, 1.'

'Second line, first word, first letter. T. Sunday next!'

By the same laborious process they translated the rest of the message.

'Sunday next, side door, bring P,' Kim read out.

'What does side door mean?' Sylvie asked. 'And there's no time given.'

Kim grinned. 'Don't worry. I know exactly what it means. It means he's arranged a flight to take Pauline home.'

'Today is Friday,' Sylvie said. 'So it's the day after tomorrow. I suppose we'd better warn Pauline.'

Kim frowned thoughtfully. 'I think we'll keep it to ourselves until the last minute.'

'Does that mean you think Pauline could be the source of the leaks?'

'I don't know. But the fewer people who know what we're planning the better.' She tore the page out of her notebook. They were sitting in the kitchen, where the cooking was done on a big wood-fired range that was never allowed to go out. Kim lifted the cover and dropped the page into the flames. 'Meanwhile,' she said, 'I should like to meet the rest of Darnier's group. Do you think you could arrange that with him?'

'Yes, of course,' Sylvie responded. 'I'm sure Luc can't have any objection. I'll ask him tomorrow when I take him his groceries.'

'And what about the people in that village where the men were shot in reprisal?'

'I get Saturday afternoon off. I was thinking of going birdwatching in that area.'

'Excellent,' Kim said.

On her return from her rounds the next day, Sylvie reported, 'Luc says they meet most Saturday nights in the bar of the Hotel du Temple. The owner is one of them, so it's secure and no one would question why a group of people meet in a bar. He says you are welcome to join them. Any time after eight o'clock.'

Kim spent the next day strolling around the city, trying to estimate the strength of the occupying forces in the area and making careful notes of the cap badges and other insignia worn by the German troops she saw in the streets and the cafés. Such information might not have any direct relevance to her current mission, but it was still useful intelligence to be passed on to her superiors.

She was in her room, brushing her hair ready to join the Levignes for dinner, when Sylvie rode into the yard. It had been a fine day, and with her sun-flushed face and tousled hair she looked a real country girl, perfectly at home in what Kim guessed was her natural milieu. She ran down to join her.

'Good day?'

Sylvie grinned. 'Yes, super. It's so lovely to be out in the open in this weather.' Then her smile faded. 'Sometimes, you know, you can almost forget for a few minutes that we're at war and imagine you're at home — or out here on holiday.'

She looked so disconsolate that Kim felt a sudden rush of sympathy. She put an arm round her shoulders. 'One day this will all be over, and we will be able to come here on holiday.'

'Will we? I wonder.'

'Yes! Of course we will. We have to hold on to that thought.' Kim noticed that she had a pair of binoculars hanging round her neck. 'Where did those come from? You didn't bring them out with you, did you?'

Sylvie's smile returned. 'Picked them up in a pawn shop just round the corner. I thought, if I'm going to pose as an ardent naturalist, it's the sort of thing I should have.'

'Well done, you!' Kim became serious. 'Did you manage to get any useful information at Estrablin?'

Sylvie grimaced. 'Not a lot. I pretended I'd only just heard about the massacre and wanted to find out if it was true. The villagers didn't want to talk about it. They were afraid if they did, the Germans might come back and punish them further. But there was one useful encounter. You know the Boches were supposed to have shot every man between the ages of fifteen and sixty? Well, I spotted a lad who was obviously over fifteen hanging about in the background. When I was about to leave and the women had all gone back inside, he came over and stopped me. It seems he was in the woods with his girlfriend when the Germans drove in, so he hid there and watched it all. You could see he was eaten up with guilt at being the only one left alive. He kept asking, 'What else could I have done?' and, of course, I told him there was nothing. The point is, he is consumed with anger, not so much at the Boches but at the Resistance. He blames them for setting the ambush and bringing that terrible retribution down on the village.'

'Understandably,' Kim commented.

'He kept saying that if he knew who was running the Resistance cell, he would kill him with his bare hands or denounce him to the Germans.'

'Did he seem to make any connection with Bernard?'

'No. He's looking for someone French. I don't think any of them have any idea that we are involved.'

'Hmm,' Kim mused. 'I wonder if Darnier has any idea how hated he and his team have become. I know he blames Bernard for the reprisals. He might go to great lengths to make sure there is no repeat of the ambush.'

'Even to the extent of killing Bernard? Surely not.'

'He may feel his own life has been put at risk. If anyone dropped a hint to that boy, or one of his family, that he was the leader of the group that set the ambush, he would either end up with a knife in his back or in a Gestapo cell.'

'I can't believe anyone would betray him to the enemy, however furious they were.'

'No? I've heard of plenty of instances where men and women have been prepared to denounce their neighbours in order to curry favour with the occupiers. In this case, they might think it was justified.'

'You really believe Luc Darnier would go that far?'

'He might not do it himself. There are probably men in his cell that wouldn't be so particular, if he gave the order.'

'I know he and Bernard didn't get on, but it's a long way from that to murder.'

Kim thought for a moment. 'Tell me about Bernard. Was there more to it than a disagreement about tactics?'

Sylvie hesitated for a moment. 'I hate to speak ill of the dead, but Bernard wasn't the most tactful person. I don't know anything about his background, of course. None of us are ever told the real identity of another agent, or what they did before they joined SOE, but my guess would be that he was an army officer. He liked to give orders and expected them to be obeyed without question. That didn't go down well with Luc.'

'How about the rest of the group?'

'It was OK as long as the operations were successful. Give him his due, Bernard was very good at planning and carrying them out. I think most of them felt that, at last, they were really hitting the Germans where it hurt. After the ambush they were all cock-a-hoop until the news came of the reprisals. Then things turned sour.'

'What was Bernard's attitude?'

'He thought it was, I think the word was regrettable, but this is war and sometimes innocent people get hurt. He'd been sent out here to do a job and he was going to get on with it.'

'So Luc Darnier had good reason to want him out of action,' Kim said. 'I wonder if there is anyone in the group who feels strongly enough to do the deed — or is sufficiently loyal to Darnier to do it on his orders.'

CHAPTER 8

Shortly after eight Kim entered the bar of the Hotel du Temple, which, in spite of its name, was one of the less prepossessing hostelries in the city. Rather shabby, situated down a side street and without any entertainment to attract soldiers on a night off, it offered as secure a meeting place as could be found.

A group of men and three women were seated around a long table on the far side of the room, Luc Darnier among them. Seeing Kim, he got up and came to meet her. He greeted her with a formal handshake and led her over to the table.

'*Mes amis*, let me introduce Madeleine who has been sent to us to replace poor Bernard.' He smiled. 'She assures me that she is not as fond of loud explosions as he was.' He went round the table giving her the names of the rest of the group. There was Jean Claud, a small man with glasses and receding hair, who told her he was a notary, the French equivalent of a solicitor. Next to him sat Charles, the youngest of the group. He had been a prisoner of war and had been returned home as part of a scheme to exchange prisoners for men to do forced labour in Germany. His hatred of the Nazis was unfeigned and had led him to seek out Darnier. Then there was Guillaume, a large man with hands like hams, who worked as a smith, and cited his patriotic duty as his reason for joining the Resistance. Jules and Marie were a married couple who owned a small holding on the edge of the city and whose son had been sent to Germany under the Service de Travail Obligatoire. Prudence and Louise were teachers who had both lost brothers in the fighting. That left Antoine and Olivier, both farmers who had been forced to hand over most of their herds to feed German families while their own people went hungry.

Introductions over, Charles leaned forward. 'When do we get back to hitting the Boches where it hurts most?'

Kim glanced at Darnier. 'I thought the general feeling was that it was better to keep a low profile to avoid any further reprisals.'

That let loose a barrage of argument. Some of the group backed Charles, but the majority took Darnier's line that the price of further action was too great. One of the most vociferous was Guillaume, who insisted that the final decision was up to Darnier, as their leader, and should be obeyed. It crossed Kim's mind, looking at him, that she could imagine him cutting through the rung of the ladder on Darnier's orders.

She interrupted the discussion to say, 'Tell me something. I know Bernard had a builder's yard as part of his cover. Do any of you have access to it?'

'I have a key,' Darnier said. 'It was where we stored the arms and ammunition.'

Kim's blood ran cold. How had she not thought of that? *Mon dieu*! Suppose the police decided to search it? Or a new man took over the business and found it?'

'Don't worry,' Darnier reassured her. 'As soon as we heard what had happened we went to the yard with Antoine's cattle truck and got it all out. It's hidden in one of his barns now.'

Kim breathed a sigh of relief. But she had the answer to her question. Darnier, or one of the others, could have got into the yard and tampered with Bernard's ladder.

She said, 'Before we can even begin to discuss what our future actions might be, we need to find out who killed Bernard.'

There was a gasp and they stared at her in incomprehension, except for Jules and Marie who exchanged a look which said that all their suspicions had been confirmed.

'But it was an accident, wasn't it?' Prudence said.

'I have reason to believe it was not,' Kim replied.

'And do you have any evidence to back that up?' asked Jean Claud, the notary.

'Nothing concrete, as yet,' she told him. 'What I am looking for is a motive. Who might want to kill Bernard?'

'I think the answer to that is obvious,' Jules said at once. 'Georges Duboeuf. Bernard was having an affair with his wife.'

'How can you be so sure of that?' Kim asked.

'Because I saw them meeting on several evenings. There's a path that runs along the border of my land down to a spot by the stream. It's very secluded — popular with courting couples. Two or three times I was working late just as it was beginning to get dark, and I saw Amelie — that's Duboeuf's wife — going down it. I recognized her because she and Marie were at school together. I wondered where she was going, the first time. Then a few minutes later, along comes Bernard. I waited, and after ten minutes or so, he comes back, and then she follows him.'

'Ten minutes?' Guillaume queried with a snort. 'That's a pretty speedy fuck!'

'No need for that sort of language!' Darnier reprimanded him. 'There are ladies present.'

'Sorry! Sorry.' Guillaume subsided. 'But really, that's not much proof they were having an affair.'

'Why else would they be meeting up secretly?' Jules demanded.

'Maybe they were just making an appointment to meet again,' his wife suggested. 'Perhaps she was letting him know when her husband would be out of the way.'

Kim had a surreal feeling that she was attending a meeting of the parish council, or whatever the French equivalent was, rather than a resistance group. 'The point is,' she put in, 'do we have any reason to think Duboeuf knew what was going on?'

'Not much gets past him,' Jules said. 'He's always nosing about, looking for trouble.'

'If that is right,' Darnier said, looking at Kim, 'it could be a motive for murder. But I doubt very much if it can ever be proved. The *milice* have more or less taken over the functions of the gendarmerie in this area, and they are not going to investigate one of their own.'

Walking home after the meeting broke up, Kim turned over in her mind what she had learned. If Jules was right, Duboeuf certainly had a motive, but he didn't look the type to go to the trouble of sawing through the rung of a ladder to get his revenge. A direct confrontation would be more in his line. On the other hand, Darnier had admitted he had access to the yard where Bernard kept his equipment. But was his fear of the revenge provoked by Bernard's methods sufficient motive to kill him? And in either case, what were the chances of finding definite proof?

Kim passed a restless night, but in the morning she had to put further consideration of what she had learned to the back of her mind. The priority now was to get Pauline to the rendezvous with the plane that would take her back to England. It was Sunday, so Sylvie was not due to deliver any orders. Instead, they had to go to church. They had both been taught that it was necessary to abide by the conventions of the society they were living in and regular attendance at church was part of that. Kim no longer had much faith in religion but her upbringing had been cosmopolitan and she was accustomed to different forms of worship, so it was not difficult to fit in with the congregation at Mass. When the service was over, she and Sylvie strolled together into the square surrounding the Roman temple.

Sitting over ersatz coffee at a pavement café, Kim said, 'Have you ever come across a character called Georges Duboeuf?'

Sylvie grinned. 'Georges Ducochon, that's what he should be called, with his fat belly and his little piggy eyes.

Yes, everyone knows him, swaggering around in his milicien uniform. Why do you ask?'

'His name came up last night. Some of Darnier's group think Bernard was having an affair with his wife.'

'Bernard?' Sylvie's eyes widened in surprise. 'I think that's very unlikely. He may have had his faults, but he was, above all, a professional. He would never have let himself get involved in something like that.'

'That's what I assumed,' Kim said, 'but there seems to be a certain amount of circumstantial evidence. I'll have to follow it up. But not today. I have to get Pauline to Lyon.'

'Do you want me to come?'

'No, there's no need. But I'll be gone overnight. We'll catch up again tomorrow.'

When Pauline opened the door of her flat, her wrists were still bandaged, but Kim was glad to see that she no longer needed her stick. The blue eyes widened in an expression of alarm.

'Oh, it's you. I wasn't expecting . . . Do you want to use the radio?'

'Not this time,' Kim told her. 'I've come to help you pack. You're going home.'

'Home? But when? How? There haven't been any messages from London since you were last here.'

'Don't worry about that,' Kim said. 'I have other means of communication. Now, what do you need to take with you?'

'But . . . but suppose I don't want to go back?'

'I'm afraid you don't have any choice. Orders are orders. Come on.'

It did not take long to gather together Pauline's few personal possessions and pack them into a rucksack.

'What about the radio?' she asked. 'That was dropped with me. I suppose it ought to go back with me.'

'No, don't worry about that,' Kim said. 'I'll clear all that away tomorrow.'

'I should tell my landlady.'

'Best not. I'll explain after you've gone.'

Pauline looked around her with a hunted expression. 'Where are we going? We've never set up a landing strip. None of the DZs are big enough for a plane to land — and there have been problems, you know, with security.'

'That's why we are not using the local people,' Kim told her. 'We're going to Lyon.'

Trains were infrequent on a Sunday so they had to take an earlier one than Kim would have liked, which left them with time to hang around in Lyon. They ate a meal in a small restaurant not far from the station and then, as curfew approached, Kim led Pauline through the old part of the city until they reached the Bistro Le Renard Rouge. As they approached, the main door opened and a group of German officers spilled out onto the street, talking and laughing loudly. Pauline gasped and Kim gripped her arm and walked her firmly down the other side of the street. One of them called after them, with an obscene invitation.

'Ignore them,' Kim ordered. 'Keep walking.'

Once round the corner she drew her companion into a doorway. 'Now we have to wait until the coast is clear.'

When her watch showed ten fifteen, they headed back to the restaurant in time to see the staff hurrying out of the alley at the side.

'In there?' Pauline asked. 'Are you sure?'

'Back entrance, this way,' Kim responded.

The back door was unlatched and the kitchen was empty apart from Foxy. He had changed into dark clothes and was wearing a coat with a hood pulled low over his forehead. Instead of embracing Kim, he greeted her with a nod.

'This is Pauline?'

'Yes.'

'Right. This way. The transport is a bit unconventional, but it will get us where we need to be.'

The gazogene truck was in the back yard and Foxy made rapid introductions.

'This is Jean Jacques. He's the local vet. Hop in the back.'

'I apologize for the smell,' the vet said. 'I've cleaned it out as far as possible but it was full of sheep until a couple of hours ago. There are some bales of hay to sit on and I've left a space behind them, here, see? If we happen to be stopped, get down in there and pull these blankets over your heads.'

'If all else fails, make a noise like a cow in calf,' Foxy suggested maliciously.

'What about you?' Kim asked.

Foxy was pulling on an overall. 'I'm the assistant vet.'

The truck swung out of the yard and both women found themselves coughing. The fumes from the gazogene burner were choking. Fortunately the sides of the truck were composed of open slats and by keeping their noses close to one of them, they were able to breathe. The truck ground along, climbing into the hills, and after an hour of being jolted around they were relieved when it came to a standstill. The rear doors were opened and Foxy called them out.

They were on a plateau several hundred feet above the city, looking out over the tops of the trees that clothed the hillside. Looking around her, Kim saw that rocks had been cleared to one side, leaving a stretch of short grass just long enough for a small plane to land. The pilot would need to be skilful — the runway ended in a sheer drop into a ravine.

A dozen or so men in dark clothes were busy putting the finishing touches to three piles of wood — the signal fires that would direct the plane in to land. One of them came over.

'This is André,' Foxy said. 'His *maquis* are pretty well in charge of this whole area.'

They all shook hands and André said, 'So, you are Madeleine. Roland has spoken of you.' Roland was the code name under which Foxy operated. 'I'm delighted to make your acquaintance. We have half an hour to wait. Shall we sit down?'

They seated themselves on some tree trunks that had been roughly carved to form benches and André produced a flask of eau de vie and passed it round. It was cold up at this altitude and Kim huddled into her coat, wishing Foxy would put his arm round her. But he kept his distance. She looked up at the sky. The moon was almost full and rags of cloud were being swept across it by the wind. It reminded her vividly of another night when she had waited and watched for a plane that was to take her and the young man she had rescued from the Nazi torturers back to safety. That hope had been extinguished in a hail of bullets. She could only hope that tonight would be different.

To distract her mind from such thoughts, Kim asked André about his organization. The *maquis* were groups of men, and a few women, who had taken to the hills and the wild places rather than submit to German domination. In some cases, all they wanted was to escape from the STO, or from retribution for some act that had brought them into conflict with the authorities, but very often they had then transformed themselves into very effective resistance fighters. Kim had experience of another such group in the Morvan hills and knew how much damage they could do to the occupying forces. From what André told her, his men had taken a slightly different approach. With the support of the local farmers and villagers they had more or less created an independent enclave, into which the German troops entered at their peril.

'We run our own hospital and more or less maintain law and order,' he told her. 'Most importantly, we prevent the produce from the farms being shipped out to Germany and make sure it's distributed fairly among the local communities.'

He was interrupted by a sudden crackle of static and Kim saw that he was holding an S-Phone, a device that would allow him to communicate with the pilot of an incoming plane once it came within range. André jumped up and signalled to the men waiting by the fires. Lighted torches were thrust into dry wood, and very quickly, flames shot skywards. Over the sighing of the wind Kim heard the drone of an aircraft engine. Pauline jumped to her feet.

'It's coming!'

'Yes.' Kim joined her. 'You'll be home for breakfast.'

André's radio crackled again and she heard him exchanging code words with the pilot. The Lysander, or 'Lizzie' as they were affectionately known, came into view over the crest of a nearby hill, flying low. Guided in by the fires and reassured by contact with André, the pilot came straight in to land. The wheels touched down, the plane bumped and swayed over the uneven ground, and for a breathtaking moment, it looked as if it might not be able to stop before it reached the precipice. Just in time, it came to a standstill and men hurried forward to take hold of its wings, helping it to turn so it could taxi back to the point where it had touched down. There, more men swung it round again ready for take-off.

Kim gripped Pauline's arm and hurried her across the grass. The door to the rear cockpit was opened and Kim had a brief glimpse of the pilot's face as he leaned round from his seat. She threw Pauline's rucksack into the cabin and pushed her up after it.

'Goodbye. Give my love to Blighty!'

The door was closed, she stood back and the engine revved. Watching it gather speed, Kim wondered if the runway was long enough to compensate for the extra weight of a passenger. The little plane hurtled towards the edge of the precipice, and around her she heard a low murmur of voices as men urged it upwards. At last the tail came up, and then what seemed like inches from the drop, the wheels came unstuck and the plane flew free. They watched it gain height and then circle back to pass over them, waggling its wings in farewell. The fuselage of Lysanders destined for operations like this was painted black underneath, to make it harder to spot them at night. For a moment it was a dark silhouette against the stars and then it was gone. The sound of the engine faded and Kim realized Foxy was standing beside her.

'Well, that was very neatly done,' he said, and put his arm round her.

She snuggled closer. 'That's better. I was beginning to think you'd forgotten who I was.'

'I don't trust that little baggage we've just sent off,' he said. 'The fewer stories she can tell about us the better.'

74

CHAPTER 9

When Kim walked into the grocer's shop next morning, M. Levigne greeted her with the words, 'Someone has left you a message. At least, I assume it's a message. A young man came into the shop and asked if I had any bananas. Of course, I told him I hadn't and he said it didn't matter. Just tell Madeleine I expect there will be some tomorrow. Does that make any sense to you?'

Kim replied with a smile. 'Yes, thank you. It does.'

Up in her room, as she unpacked her overnight bag, she thought through the implications of the message. Presumably Pierre meant that he had been ordered to prepare a plane for a flight tomorrow. Today was Monday, so he meant Tuesday. Damn! Why couldn't it have been a day later, when the housekeeper at the château had the day off? She wondered what time she finished. Pierre had said that the flights were always preceded by a farewell meal and took off in the evening, presumably so that they would have the cover of darkness by the time they reached their destination. So if Mme. Durand knocked off at around 5 p.m., that would still be long enough to break into the back door and get up to the turret while it was still light enough to see what was going on. She would just have to hope so.

By 5 p.m. next day, Kim was crouching in the under-growth at the edge of the forest opposite the château. It had rained earlier and the ground was damp, but in the last hour or two the sun had come out and the scent of new growth rose from the earth all around her. Under the shelter of the bushes nearby she found a clump of violets just starting to open. She thought how good it would be to go for a long hike through the woods, and remembered her conversation with Sylvie. One day, she promised herself, we'll come back and enjoy this beautiful country as it deserves.

Her reverie was interrupted by the imposing front door of the château opening. Mme Durand came out and care-fully closed the door behind her. Kim was surprised, hav-ing assumed that she would use the door leading into the kitchen. It was not important, however. The main thing was that the coast was clear and there was plenty of light left. The housekeeper disappeared round the side of the building and returned wheeling a bicycle. She mounted it and rode off towards the town. Kim waited a few minutes longer, in case she had forgotten something and came back. Then she crossed the road and skirted the edge of the grounds until she reached the back of the château.

For a moment she stood with her ear close to the kitchen door, listening. Madame had said the owners spent all their time in their apartments in the front of the building, but there was always the chance that one of them might decide to venture into the kitchen in search of a snack. When she was certain that all was quiet, she pulled out her lock pick and set to work. She had taken careful note of the lock when Mme Durand had let her in and knew it would give her no trouble. The lock clicked open and she turned the handle and pushed. The door remained firmly shut. It had been bolted from the inside.

Kim stepped back, swearing under her breath. Why had she not thought of that? That was why the housekeeper had left by the front door. Picking a lock was one thing, but there was no way of opening the bolts without doing serious damage to the door. She looked along the back of the building. There were windows she had noted before, probably giving onto the kitchen and various larders and utility rooms. They were all shuttered. She moved along, trying the shutters on each in turn, but they, too, were bolted from inside. Clearly, Mme Durand made a point of leaving everything secure.

Kim stood still, grinding her teeth in frustration. She must find out what was going on at the airfield, and the turret above her was the only way to do so. She considered ringing the doorbell and trying to persuade M. le Baron that she had some legitimate reason for needing to go up there, but she could think of no convincing excuse. She could tell them the true reason and appeal to their sense of patriotism, but that was too risky. They might well decide that the safest course of action was to call in the police — or the Milice. She gazed up at the turret above her head — and suddenly she knew how she was going to get there.

The turret was at the corner of the building and the window she had looked out of on her previous visit was at right angles to the wall she was facing. Just to her right, close to the corner, a drainpipe ran up to the gutter at the edge of the main roof. The turret stood above that, above the apex of the roof. Kim had spent her youth climbing mountains and her SOE training had seen her scaling sheer cliffs in Scotland. She had no doubt that she could shin up the drainpipe and then clamber up the tiled roof. The tricky part would be reaching round and up to the window she had so providentially left unlatched. It might be impossible, but it was the only option and it was worth a try.

As she had expected, the first part of the climb gave her no problems. Scaling the sloping roof was harder. The tiles were smooth and one or two of them were loose. She spreadeagled herself across them and inched her way upwards until she was astride the apex. She worked her way forward until she was right up against the wall of the turret and there, to her delight, she discovered that a shallow cornice ran around it at the level of the apex. She could find a foothold on that, but the question was whether she could reach high enough to grasp the sill of the window. Cautiously she stood up, steadying herself against the wall of the turret with her left hand. She reached out and rested her right foot on the cornice, then she stretched her right arm round the corner, feeling for the windowsill. For a moment she was unable to locate it, then reaching a little higher, her fingers met wood. She inched forward, reaching up, until she was able to get a firm grip. This was the dangerous bit. She edged round the corner, her feet on the cornice, her left hand feeling for the edge of the window. She found it and pushed it open. Even as she did so, the cornice began to crumble under her weight. Grabbing the windowsill with both hands, she struggled to pull herself up. It took all her strength, but at last her head and shoulders were inside the room and she was able to twist round, grip the top of the frame and pull the rest of her body through.

Panting, she crouched on the floor for a few moments until her pulse had steadied. Then she got up and looked out. Below her, the tops of the trees stretched away down the slope. Beyond them, the Rhône glittered in the late-afternoon sun. In the distance, rows of vines marched over the hills and valleys along the margins of the great river. And closer, just beyond the trees, was the airfield. Kim had borrowed Sylvie's binoculars, which she had slung over her back while she climbed. She pulled them round and focused them on the airfield.

There was much more activity then the first time she had looked. An army truck was parked near a long, low building that must serve as the club house when the airfield was used in peacetime by amateur fliers. Near it were two sleek saloon cars. The most surprising item stood on the tarmac, ready for take-off. It was a Lysander, just like the one that had taken Pauline away, complete with the RAF roundels painted on its fuselage. Kim concluded it must have been captured intact when a similar venture had been ambushed by the Germans. It would be, of course, the perfect vehicle for anyone wanting to make a clandestine landing in Britain. Kim's pulse began to quicken again. This could be vitally important information. Someone was being sent to spy, or perhaps carry out some act of sabotage. Now she need to see who, and get as good a description as possible.

She had to wait another half an hour, and the sun was almost down before the door of the building opened and three men came out. One was obviously, from his dress, the pilot, one was in the uniform of a Hauptsturmfuhrer in the Gestapo, but it was the third man who caused Kim to gasp in disbelief. Dressed in civilian clothes, short, and broad in the shoulders, with a head that looked too big for his body, even at this distance, the sight of him sent a shudder through her nerves.

The pilot climbed into the cockpit and the engines started. The officer and the civilian shook hands and the civilian got into the rear cockpit. Kim watched as the plane taxied out onto the runway and heard the distant roar as the engines revved up. Moments later it was airborne, climbing away into the last rays of the setting sun.

Kim sat back, her thoughts whirling. This information had to be sent to London as soon as possible. She thought of Pauline's radio set, but she did not trust its security. There was one person she could rely on to get the message out safely, and if she hurried, she could just make the last train to Lyon.

But first, she had to get down to ground level again.

Soft-footed, she padded down the long spiral staircase. Reaching the ground floor, she made her way to the kitchen. It was easy to draw back the bolts and she had left the lock undone from her earlier attempt. She slipped out and carefully relocked the door behind her. Mme Durand would be surprised to find the door unbolted, but Kim guessed she would simply conclude that it must have slipped her mind. She darted down the drive and across the road to where she had hidden her bicycle. She was already pedalling hard towards Vienne when, from the corner of her eye, she caught sight of a figure standing in the shade of an oak tree close to where she had been hiding. Only when she was well past did it register in her mind that it was Georges Duboeuf.

CHAPTER 10

Arriving at the Renard Rouge, Kim decided that she might as well enjoy her lover's cooking. Eating in the restaurant she would be less conspicuous than she would be hanging round the streets. She had not bargained for the reception she got from Candice when she asked for a table. The enmity in the girl's eyes was unmistakable and for a moment Kim thought she was going to refuse, but she apparently thought better of it and conducted her to the table by the kitchen door she had used before.

'Please tell M. le Patron that I will join him at the usual time,' Kim said, and Candice's haughty sniff had to be taken as assent.

The food was excellent, as always, but this time Kim found it impossible to relax and enjoy it. The loud conversation from the German officers who occupied most of the tables grated on her nerves and it seemed a long time before they finished their brandy and called for the bill. As the restaurant emptied, she paid and left, walking away with apparently purposeful strides until it was safe to double back. She waited until she saw the staff leaving, Candice among them, then she went to the side door and into the kitchen. Foxy was waiting for her with an anxious look on his face.

'What's happened? Is something wrong?'

'No, I've got news, that's all.'

He relaxed and laughed. 'So have I. Guess who was in here last night, enjoying my coq au vin and a bottle of Margeaux in the company of that butcher, Barbie? None other than our old friend Dr Kline.'

If he had expected her to be surprised, he was disappointed. Kim met his eyes and raised her eyebrows. 'And guess who I saw climbing into a Lysander with British markings four hours ago.'

It was his turn to gape in amazement. 'Not Kline?'

'None other.'

The stared at each other for a moment, the brief triumph of their mutual surprise forgotten.

'Kline on his way back to Britain?' Foxy said. 'That is very bad news indeed.'

'It is,' Kim agreed. 'And it's news we must get through to Baker Street at the earliest opportunity. When's your next scheduled transmission?'

'Not till early tomorrow, but I can try tonight and hope someone picks it up.'

'Well, we'd better get busy coding,' she said.

Up in Foxy's sitting room they sat down together with a copy of his poem and began the laborious process of encoding the message. It took them some time to agree on the exact wording. There was so much information to impart, but the message had to be kept short. In the end, the message read: *Attn M. Kline back in UK. Infiltrated by air 07/03.*

'M.' was the code name of Brigadier Colin Gubbins, the head of SOE operations and the man with whom both Kim and Foxy had worked on a previous assignment.

As soon as the message was ready, Foxy fetched his radio set from its hiding place and sent out his call sign, hoping one of the FANY girls at Grendon would pick it up. It was not long before he got a response and was able to send his message.

Once the radio set was back in its hiding place they were finally free to talk.

'Tell me how you managed to see him taking off,' Foxy said.

Kim described the events of her evening and he reached out and cupped her cheek in his hand.

'Dear God, girl! You could have been killed.'

'No chance,' she assured him. 'I've done worse climbs when I was at Arisaig. So have you.'

'I doubt it,' he responded. Then he said, 'This may mean a more dangerous situation back home than you realize. I overheard something Barbie was saying to Kline.'

'You were close enough to overhear them? Suppose he recognized you.'

'Unlikely,' he assured her. 'I never had much to do with him when I was at Beaulieu. We'd worked out his nasty little game and put a stop to it before I got to the point of being psychoanalysed by him. Anyway, what have we always said? People simply don't notice servants and domestic workers. The chances of Kline even looking at my face were remote, and why should he associate a slightly overweight French chef with a fit-as-a-butcher's-dog British trainee agent he might have passed in a corridor a year ago? No, I was safe enough.'

'So what did you overhear?'

'You won't have forgotten his penchant for cryptic code names. Operation Kugleblitz kept us guessing for weeks. Well, last night I heard him mention an Operation Enthaupten.'

'What on earth does that mean?'

'It translates as *beheading*.'

'Beheading? You don't think he's planning to have another go at assassinating Churchill, do you?'

'Well, he's the head of the government.'

'Dear God! I thought we'd scotched that plan.'

'So did I. But there's no more we can do about it from here. It's over to the chaps at Baker Street now.'

'I suppose so,' Kim said slowly. 'I have to admit, I'd like to be back there, working on it.'

'After what happened last year?'

'It couldn't be worse than what might happen to either of us out here, if we get caught,' she said soberly.

'Then we just have to make bloody sure we don't get caught.'

* * *

Getting off the train at Vienne next morning, Kim felt a stab of alarm. Georges Duboeuf was standing beside the ticket collector, checking the papers of each passenger. Her papers were in order, but this sort of check was not unusual and she had never seen Duboeuf carrying out this duty before. It bothered her that he seemed to keep turning up wherever she went.

When she reached him and offered her papers, he met her eyes with a grin. 'Ah ha! Been trying to offload that glamorous underwear on some other unsuspecting women?'

Kim lowered her gaze modestly. 'No, monsieur. I have a friend in Lyon.'

'Ah, of course.' He handed back her papers with a wink. 'I'm out of luck, then. A pretty girl like you. I might have known.'

As she walked away, Kim felt a sense of relief. Was it possible that Duboeuf's constant presence was due to nothing more sinister than a man's attraction to a pretty girl? Had he been watching her to see if she already had a boyfriend?

She left her case at the Levignes' and then headed for the house where Pauline had been staying. She was guiltily aware that she should have cleared the apartment earlier, but the urgency surrounding the preparations at the airfield had put it out of her mind. She had taken Pauline's key before she left, so she let herself into the flat. Once she had removed anything incriminating, she would visit the landlady, hand back the key, and explain that her tenant had been suddenly called away to attend a sick relative.

She began with the desk, checking for any paperwork that might look suspicious. There was the draft of the thesis

Pauline had been working on and several books of poetry, all in keeping with her cover story. Then Kim went through all the cupboards and the wardrobe. Apart from one or two items of clothing Pauline had, presumably bought while she was living in France, there was nothing.

So far, so good. Pauline had been meticulous about leaving nothing that might give a clue as to her real identity. That left just the radio set.

Kim knew it was hidden behind a loose ceiling panel, and it took only a moment to locate it and lift it down. The tricky bit would come later. She would not risk hiding it at the Levignes'. If the shop was ever searched, its presence would be enough to have them handed over to the Gestapo. A poor reward for their kindness in accommodating her. She decided instead to take it to Luc Darnier and let him find a suitable hiding place. That way, if the 'Grocer' circuit was ever reconstituted with a new leader and a new wireless operator, they wouldn't have to risk infiltrating with a radio set.

The dangerous part for her would be cycling through the streets with it. It was contained in an innocent-looking suitcase and the chances of any gendarme or *milicien* asking to search it were small. Just the same, she would be glad to get rid of it.

She was about to replace the ceiling panel when it occurred to her to check that there was nothing else hidden there. Reaching in, her hand encountered another object. What had Pauline thought was so precious, or so dangerous, that it needed to be hidden away? Kim drew it out. It was a camera, and across the front of it was the name Contax.

Kim sat down abruptly.

There was no doubt in her mind — this was Bernard's camera. If he had taken it with him when he went up his ladder, as Sylvie thought he certainly would have done, then Pauline must have been present when he fell. How else could she have come by it? And, more importantly, why had she hidden it? Why had she not mentioned that she had it? There could be only one reason.

Kim thought back to that image she had been given of a weak and nervous woman. Had it all been a carefully constructed illusion? Pauline had been through exactly the same training she had undergone herself. It had puzzled her how someone so easily frightened could have survived it. Had that all been an act?

Perhaps he had told her that he intended to climb up to the turret. A trained agent would have had no difficulty in breaking in to Bernard's yard. Kim and Sylvie had proved that easily enough. Once there, Pauline could have found his ladder and partially sawn through one of the rungs. Kim herself had been taught how to conceal the cut with a little sawdust and some glue. If she had intended to kill him, she would have followed him to see if her trap had worked. Perhaps even to finish him off, if the fall had not been enough. Then she would have seen the camera and realized it would provoke enquiries, so she had taken it and hidden it. But why had she killed him? Jealousy? Could she have been in love with him, and been pushed into a desperate revenge by the rumours of his affair with Amelie Duboeuf? It seemed far-fetched.

Kim caught her breath. Suddenly everything fell into place. The aborted supply drops! There was clearly a mole in the organization somewhere and who was better placed to know every detail of the arrangements than the radio operator who received the instructions? There was only one explanation — Pauline was a double agent, working for German intelli-gence. Immediately Kim's mind went back to her previous assignment. It was known that Kline, during his time at the SOE school at Beaulieu, had turned several people, most of them women. But Pauline's name had not been on the list she had been given of agents who had trained there while Kline was employed. Surely, she had passed through well before his day? Maybe it happened long before that. There were such things as 'sleepers' — apparently innocent charac-ters — ready to be activated when they were needed. Pauline, or whatever her real name was, might have been one of those.

Was it possible that she was jumping to conclusions? It seemed to Kim that this was the only explanation that fitted the facts.

With this conclusion came another, more urgent, thought. If she was right, she had just dispatched this viper into the heart of SOE. Where would she be now? She would have undergone a rigorous debriefing, but she had fooled Kim and could undoubtedly do the same to the handlers who were questioning her. So once they had garnered, as they thought, all the information she could give them, she would almost certainly be sent north, to that remote castle in the Highlands of Scotland that was known among SOE operatives as 'the cooler' — a place to which agents were sent when they were no longer operational but knew too much to be allowed to rejoin civilian society. Once there, Kim thought, there would be very little harm she could do, but would she stay there? It was clear now that the charade she had played out was designed to get her sent home, so there must be a reason. And now Kline was in England too. Kim felt a chill in her stomach at the thought that they might be operating together.

One thing was clear. M. must be informed, immediately. It would take too long to make her way back to Lyon and wait until the restaurant closed for Foxy to be able to use his radio set. But she had the means to hand, in the shape of the suitcase sitting on the desk in front of her. She had refused to use it while Pauline was there because some instinct told her that she was not to be trusted, but now she had gone, there was no reason not to employ it for this urgent communication.

Sitting down, she rapidly encoded a brief message. With practised hands she deployed the aerial and powered up the set. She did not have a regular 'sked', so she had to send her call sign several times before it was picked up. Having established contact and transmitted the necessary security code, she began to send her message. Probably because she had earphones clamped to her head, she did not hear the sound of boots on the stairs. It was only when the door was slammed open that she twisted in her chair and found herself facing two men in the uniform of the SS Feldgendarmerie, with pistols in their hands. And behind them was the rotund body and the tiny head of Georges Duboeuf.

CHAPTER 11

The restaurant was closed, but as on previous occasions, Foxy was not finished for the night. Once again, he changed his clothes and the slightly overweight chef was transformed into a lean, dark-clad secret agent. He made his way to the bakery on the Place St Paul. Waiting for him this time were an elderly couple accompanied by a young woman carrying a baby. After brief introductions, Foxy led them to the entrance of the *traboule*. As he closed the door, the woman pulled back with a gasp.

'Ah, no! I can't do it. I can't bear caves and confined spaces.'

Foxy switched on his torch. 'But this is not a cave, madame. See how beautiful the arched ceiling is? This is a place that men and women have used for generations and they sought to make it as lovely as the rest of their city. And soon we shall come to a courtyard where we can look up and see the stars.'

The elderly man touched the woman's arm. 'Come, Marta. You must be brave for the sake of the little one.'

Reluctantly, the woman allowed herself to be drawn further into the passage. Foxy regarded the sleeping child with some anxiety.

'He will not wake? It is imperative that we make no noise. People live in the apartments above us and they will not expect

88

to hear sounds of movement at this hour, after the curfew. Most of them would say nothing, but there are always one or two who are keen to curry favour with the enemy.'

'He's a very good baby,' she assured him. 'If he wakes, he will not cry.'

'Very well,' Foxy said. 'Follow me.'

He led the way through the warren of passages, pausing in the open courtyards to allow his charges to see the sky and take a breath of fresh air. In this way they came, without incident, to the foot of the long staircase leading up to the Monte Saint-Barthelemy. He was about to offer to carry the child when something made him stop and gesture to the others to stay back. At the top of the stairs he had seen a brief glow of light. As he watched, it came again. Someone was drawing on a cigarette.

At that moment the baby woke and let out a wail. Above him, Foxy heard a sharp exclamation and the stamp of feet as a sentry came to attention.

'Back!' he hissed, waving the other three back into the *traboule*. 'Follow me.' He led them at a run back the way they had come. Behind them, he could hear the clatter of boots coming quickly down the stairs. 'Faster!' he ordered, catching the elderly woman by the arm. The younger woman was clutching the baby to her, smothering its cries in her breast. They reached the first courtyard and he flung open the door leading to the spiral staircase. 'Up there! Get to the balcony and get down below the parapet. And for God's sake, keep quiet!' As they moved to obey him, he caught the man's arm. 'If I am not here when . . . when the coast is clear, go back, go up the stairs, turn left, go to the door at the top of the steps. Knock and you will be given shelter. Now, hide yourself!'

The fugitives scurried up the stairs and Foxy turned and ran on down the next *traboule*, making his footfalls as loud as his rubber-soled shoes would allow. He heard the pursuers thundering along behind him and knew that, so far, his ruse had worked. When, seconds later, an SS officer and three men ran into the next courtyard, they found Foxy leaning casually against the ornamental pot containing a small olive tree. As they skidded to a standstill, he spread his hands in a placatory gesture.

'OK, you caught me.'

The officer cast his eyes round the courtyard. 'Where are they?' His French was correct, though heavily accented.

'Where are who?' Foxy enquired innocently.

'They've gone ahead!' the officer exclaimed, reverting to German. 'You and you, get after them. They can't have got far.'

Two men dashed off along the next *traboule*. The officer returned his attention to Foxy. 'Don't think you can fool me. I know what you're up to.'

'I admit it,' Foxy said. 'But I'm surprised an officer in such an elite regiment is bothering himself with a bit of black-market smuggling.'

For an instant the German looked disconcerted. 'Black market?'

'I mean, I know it's illegal but I didn't think it would warrant the attention of an officer like yourself,' Foxy said.

'What are you talking about?'

Foxy unslung the pack he was carrying on his shoulder. 'OK if I open this?'

The officer levelled his pistol at him. 'Don't try anything.'

'Do I look that stupid?' Foxy undid the pack, careful to avoid any sudden movement, and slid out an oblong package wrapped in oilskin. 'This is what you're after, isn't it?' He unwrapped the package and disclosed a box containing ten packets of Lucky Strike cigarettes. 'These are good. Top quality Virginia tobacco.' He held out the box. 'I'm sure you know someone who would appreciate a packet of these. More than one packet, perhaps?'

For a brief moment he saw temptation flicker through the officer's eyes. 'Where did you get them?'

'An old chap I know owns a barge and plies between here and Besancon. Smugglers bring them over the border from Switzerland.'

'His name?'

Foxy shrugged. 'I couldn't tell you if I wanted to. All I know is the barge is called the *St. Christophe*.'

At that moment, one of the men the German had sent ahead came breathlessly out of the *traboule*.

'No sign of them, sir,' the man panted. 'They must have gone to ground somewhere.'

'Come on!' the officer said, turning back to Foxy. 'Stop trying to delay things. Where are the Jewish pigs you were escorting?'

'Jewish pigs?' Foxy said. 'I don't know what you're talking about.'

'You had people with you. I heard a child cry.'

Foxy lifted his eyes to the shuttered windows of the apartments above them. 'There are people living all round here. There must be dozens of children. It's not unusual for a baby to cry at night, I'm told.'

He saw that he had sown a seed of doubt in the officer's mind, but he was not so easily distracted. 'Papers!'

Foxy handed over his identity card.

'Leroux? The Bistro Le Renard Rouge? I've heard about it. They say you're a good cook.'

'I am. Perhaps you and a lady friend would like to sample my food. On the house, of course.'

Just for a moment he thought he might have won, but then the second man reappeared, shaking his head and shrugging in a gesture of defeat.

'Take him,' the officer ordered. 'You're coming with us, Leroux. Commandant Barbie wants a word with you.'

As he was frogmarched back the way he had come, Foxy spared a thought for the fugitives. If the old man had acted on his whispered instructions, he might yet have saved three more lives — four counting the baby.

* * *

Kim was sitting, hunched, on the narrow bed, her arms wrapped round her updrawn knees. They had taken her

91

watch, but she guessed it must be after midnight. At least this was an ordinary police cell, not a cellar, and the small, barred window high up in the wall was still visible, even at this time of night, so she was not in complete darkness. That, and the fact that she had not so far been interrogated, kept her worst nightmares at bay. But she knew the time would come and her whole attention was focused on one question. Would she be able, this time, to withstand whatever torture they chose to inflict? Could she, somehow, avoid naming Sylvie? And the Levignes? That kindly couple whose only crime was to give her hospitality. Could she keep them out of it? Then she remembered. Duboeuf had been tracking her. He would know about Sylvie and the Levignes. They were probably even now in detention, possibly in this same building.

She had expected to be questioned, probably brutally, as soon as she was brought here, but apart from a routine demand for her papers, the officer in charge had asked nothing. He had simply ordered his men to lock her in the cell.

She had heard Duboeuf protest, 'Aren't you going to interrogate her?' He had sounded disappointed, and she guessed he was looking forward to seeing her beaten.

When the officer replied curtly, 'Not yet,' Duboeuf had pressed further.

'Let me get at her! I'll soon have her singing like a canary.'

She shuddered. The Gestapo interrogators she had suffered under last time she was caught had been merciless but efficient. This man, if he had his way, would torture and humiliate her for the sheer pleasure of it.

The hours passed slowly. Eventually the little window above her grew brighter and she heard the distant sounds of the city coming to life. Traffic rumbled past, and the voices of men and women in the street outside floated up to her. Then she heard movement on the far side of the cell door. A hatch opened, a plate and a tin cup were thrust through it, and the hatch clanged shut again. Kim climbed stiffly off the bed to investigate and found a hunk of baguette and a cup of ersatz coffee. This was a surprise, too. It seemed she was being treated like any other prisoner held in police cells. The bread was even freshly baked.

After she had eaten and drunk the coffee, she was gripped by the need to empty her bladder. There was a bucket in the corner, which so far she had avoided using, but now it was becoming a necessity. She was about to give in when there was the grating noise of bolts being withdrawn and the door opened. One of the Feldgendarmes who had arrested her the previous day commanded 'Out!', illustrating the order with a jerk of his head.

In the outer office she was confronted by the officer who had been in charge when she was brought in. With a tremor in the pit of her stomach, she noticed Duboeuf lurking in a corner of the room.

'You are to be taken to Lyon,' the officer said. 'There is someone there who wishes to question you.' The spasm in Kim's gut intensified. This was her worst fear. She was going to be handed over to Klaus Barbie, and she was well aware of his reputation. Rumour had it that he had tortured to death Jean Moulins, the man sent by General de Gaulle to organize resistance to the occupiers. 'These men will drive you,' the officer went on. 'Take her away.'

One of the Feldgendarmes stepped forward and secured her hands behind her back with handcuffs, then prodded her towards the door. Outside, a staff car was waiting. She became aware that Duboeuf had followed them out.

'I'll drive,' he offered. 'I know the roads better than you do. If there are any hold-ups, I know ways around.'

One of her guards shrugged. 'OK. If that's what you want.' He gave Kim a shove. 'Get in.'

She scrambled into the back seat and one of the guards got in beside her. The other one sat beside Duboeuf in front. Duboeuf let in the clutch and the car pulled out into the morning traffic. They drove for some while along the main road towards Lyon and the two guards chatted in German, making lewd jokes about some French girls they had seduced on their last night off. Kim wondered if they thought she and

Duboeuf couldn't understand German, or if they just didn't care. The car took a turn to the right, onto a minor road, but the Germans did not appear to notice. A little further on, Duboeuf veered off again to the right and Kim saw that they were heading up into the hills.

What, she asked herself, *is the man playing at? Did he have some idea of taking them somewhere where he could have his way with her before handing her over to the authorities?* She wondered which was the worst prospect — enduring whatever sadistic pleasure he had in mind or being at the mercy of Barbie. She concluded that the first option would not necessarily preclude the second. Unless, and here she found a glimmer of hope, his plan involved doing away with the two guards. If she could offer some service to him that he would find irresistible, he might remove the handcuffs — and he was unaware of her training in unarmed combat.

At that point, one of the Feldgendarmes suddenly became aware of the change in their route.

'Hey! What the fuck are you playing at? Where are we going?'

'Short cut,' Duboeuf replied. 'I happen to know the Resistance are planning an ambush on the main road. Trust me!'

'Doesn't look like a short cut to me.'

'I know this country. You don't. Believe me, this is the best way to avoid trouble.'

The two Germans exchanged looks and one muttered in his own language, 'He's driving. Not much we can do about it.' A little further on, Duboeuf pulled off into a small clearing.

'Call of nature,' he explained, opening the door. As he did so, his eyes met Kim's and seemed to convey a message. She felt a sudden thrill of hope. Whatever game he was playing, it didn't fit with his earlier subservient attitude to the Nazis. Was it possible that she had misjudged this man?

Acting on instinct, she immediately demanded, 'I need to go, too.'

'You'll have to wait,' the one sitting next to her said.

94

'Oh yes? Do you want me to pee all over the seat? You'll have to sit in it for the rest of the journey if I do.'

He hesitated a moment, then said, 'All right. Get out. But stay where I can see you.'

'That's German courtesy for you,' she said mockingly. 'Will you get off on watching me?'

They were both out of the car by now. Duboeuf had walked away a short distance and was peeing with his back to them. The guard looked around. 'Over there, behind that bush. But stay where I can see your head.'

Kim's heart was beating fast. Had Duboeuf deliberately contrived an opportunity for her to escape? She indicated her bound hands. 'How am I supposed to manage like this?'

'Oh, let the woman have a bit of privacy,' his companion said. 'You can keep your gun on her. She can't get far.' With a grunt, the German produced the key and unlocked the cuffs.

'Go on, then. But remember, any funny business and you're a dead woman.'

Kim walked a few yards to where a couple of scrubby bushes gave some shelter, pulled down her knickers and squatted. It was a relief to be able to empty her bladder at last. As she stood up, she heard two shots close together. Spinning round, she found both Germans on the ground, both shot neatly through the head. Duboeuf was standing there, grinning, a smoking pistol in his hands.

Catching her eye, he called, 'Well, come on then! Don't stand around. Let's get out of here!'

CHAPTER 12

In a cellar below the Hotel Terminus in Lyon, Foxy faced Klaus Barbie across a table on which was set out an array of implements. Some of them he recognized, but there were others whose use he could only guess at. Since his arrest he had been forced to stand facing a wall with his arms above his head until his whole body was shaking with the strain. It was almost a relief to be bound, as he now was, to a chair.

Barbie considered him in silence for a few minutes, a look of anticipation on his face. He appeared to be giving himself time to savour the prospect. At length, he said, 'So, let us not waste time with futile denials. You will say that you are only a simple restauranteur and have done nothing worse than smuggle a few black-market cigarettes. But we both know that is not true. You are a smuggler, yes. But of Jewish pigs. Where were you taking them?'

Foxy had been in some tight corners but he had never suffered serious physical pain. He remembered that Kim had suffered, when she was captured by the Gestapo, long before he met her. She had been unwilling to give him the details, but he had wormed them out of her in the end. He had often asked himself whether he would be able to show the same courage. Now the moment had come to find out.

'I don't understand,' Foxy said. 'What Jews are you talking about?'

'The ones you were attempting to take out of the city, of course.'

'But I was alone when I was arrested. I know nothing of any Jews.'

'Come now! This is just a waste of time. We know quite well that you have been busy conducting these scum through the *traboules*. It is useless to deny it. Hasn't it occurred to you that you have been betrayed? The young woman concerned was most specific.'

The shock hit Foxy like a blow to the stomach. Betrayed? By a young woman? Could they have already arrested Kim and she had broken down so quickly? But another thought was forming through his confusion. He was being questioned about helping Jews to escape. Not about his work for the Resistance. Was it possible that whoever had betrayed him did not know about that? Or, a more terrible idea, that if Kim was in Gestapo hands, she had chosen to give them that part of the story in order to protect the rest of the circuit?

Barbie was watching him with a smile, enjoying the effect of his revelation. 'Oh yes. She was quite insistent. But you know the saying: "Hell hath no fury like a women scorned".'

A woman scorned? Not Kim. Candice. Candice knew nothing about his work for SOE. That was why he was not being asked about that. She must have guessed he was helping Jews to escape and seen that as a way to get her revenge. Relief vied with desperation as he tried to take in the new information. Perhaps Barbie had no suspicion as to his real purpose in France, but how long would it be before he let something slip under interrogation?

He forced himself to answer. 'I still don't know what you are talking about. I have no knowledge of any scheme to smuggle Jews through the *traboules*.'

Barbie gave a theatrical sigh. 'Ah, what a pity. So we must resort to more painful measures.' He stood up and came round the table to stand over Foxy. 'I wonder which part of your anatomy is most precious to you. Your eyesight, perhaps? Or your manhood? Perhaps we shall find out.' He turned away and picked up an instrument from the table. 'But we shall start with something less draconian.' He gestured to one of the guards standing behind Foxy. 'Remove his shoes.'

CHAPTER 13

Duboeuf was driving quickly along a track leading deeper into the mountains. For a few seconds after the shots that had killed her German captors, Kim had hesitated, unsure whether to turn and run and take her chances in the forest. Duboeuf had returned his gun to his pocket and raised his hands.

'*Mon dieu*! I've shot the Boches. What more do I have to do to prove which side I'm on? Come on! You're needed somewhere else.'

'I don't understand,' Kim said, as the car rattled and bounced over the rutted track. 'You're with the *Milice*. You work with the Boches.'

'Can you think of a better cover?' he asked. 'I cooperate with them over small things, so they trust me with bigger things.'

'So you're with the Resistance?'

'I'm not *with* anyone. I hate the Boches, but I work alone. I've no wish to be mixed up with that ineffectual bunch Darnier runs.'

'And Bernard?'

His tone softened. 'Bernard was my friend. He was a brave man, a man I was happy to work with.' He was silent for a moment. 'You thought I might have killed him, didn't you?'

'It crossed my mind.' Kim was frantically recalibrating her ideas. 'So, his meetings with your wife were just a cover up?'

'Exactly. We let people think they were having an affair, but really, she was just passing on information I thought might be useful.'

'But are you in contact with London? Does anyone there know about you?'

'No. I told you, I work alone. Bernard tried to recruit me, but I refused. I didn't mind cooperating with him, but I value my independence.'

'So how was it I kept bumping into you at every turn?'

'I've been keeping an eye on you since you arrived.' He cast a brief glance at her. 'When Bernard was killed, I guessed someone would be sent to clear up after him.' He raised an eyebrow. 'I wasn't expecting a girl, but when you started hanging round the airfield I knew it must be you.'

'But you betrayed me to the Feldgendarmes.'

'No!' For a second he took his eyes of the track to look at her. 'No. I didn't. They must have been waiting for you to start transmitting. I'd followed you to the house and then I saw the detector van in the side street. I knew what was going to happen so I joined them and pretended I had always suspected you and wanted to see you arrested. They're so used to me hanging around they didn't question it. But I don't understand how they were there so quickly.'

'I think I do,' Kim said. 'And I'm pretty sure I know who killed Bernard.'

'Who?' he asked sharply.

'The girl who lived in that house. She called herself Pauline.'

'But she worked with Bernard. She was one of yours.'

'That's what I believed. Now I think she was a double agent. I think Bernard had begun to suspect and that's why she engineered his death.'

'*Salope!*' Duboeuf almost choked on the swear word. 'The bitch! Where is she now?'

'Back in London. I sent her home.'

'Do they know she's been working for the Nazis?'

'No. I had only just worked it out and I was about to send a message to warn the people I work for when you burst in with the Gestapo. My guess is, they had detected her transmissions weeks ago but they had been warned off as long as she was working for them. But as soon as it became known that she was no longer in France, they were free to move in.'

The car lurched around a hairpin bend and Kim realized that they were now deep in the mountains above Lyon. 'Where are we going?' she asked.

'I told you, you're needed. Your friend from the Renard Rouge has got himself arrested. We're going to join a group run by a guy called André. He seems to think he knows a way to get him out.'

For a moment Kim thought her heart had stopped beating. Foxy, in the hands of the Gestapo? The idea was unbearable.

'Roland?' she croaked, from a throat suddenly dry. 'When?'

'Is that his name? He was picked up yesterday.'

'And this man André? Who is he?'

'Runs an outfit like the one Darnier is in charge of, but a damn sight more effective. You'll meet him in a minute. We're almost there.'

* * *

The village where André and his *maquisards* had made their base was really no more than a collection of isolated farmsteads. Kim looked around, trying to pick up landmarks from her previous visit, but that had been at night and she soon recognized that the area he had chosen as a landing ground must be higher up, well away from the village. They were stopped on the road some distance away by three armed men, but it was obvious that they knew Duboeuf.

'Mademoiselle Madeleine is a friend,' he told them. 'André has asked me to bring her.'

They were waved through and as they drove on, he tilted his head towards Kim. 'I suppose that's not your real name?'

'It's what it says on my ID card,' Kim replied, and he accepted it with a grunt.

André was waiting for them in the kitchen of one of the larger houses. He shook hands with Duboeuf. 'Bravo, Georges! You found her. Thank you.' Then he took both Kim's hands. '*Ma chère*, Madeleine! I am so sorry that we meet again in these circumstances.'

Kim was struggling to contain the sense of panic and despair that had gripped her since Duboeuf's revelation, and his kindness almost undid her. 'What happened?' she asked, forcing the words through a throat that ached with unshed tears.

'According to my informant, he was arrested while trying to smuggle a Jewish family to safety through the *traboules*. You knew he was involved in that business?'

'Yes, he told me. I told him he shouldn't take the extra risk, but he felt he couldn't ignore what was going on. Where is he?'

'In the Hotel Terminus. That's where Barbie has set up his HQ.'

'So it's the Jewish involvement. Nothing to do with his work for SOE?'

'We think not. But the longer he's in Barbie's hands, the greater the likelihood that Barbie will make the connection. He will be delving into every corner of his life. Roland is a brave man, but even brave men break eventually.'

Kim swallowed. She knew better than most how hard it was to withstand torture and the thought of her beloved Foxy being subjected to some of the things she had suffered made her want to fall on the ground and howl. Only one thought kept her going.

'Georges said you have some idea about getting him out,' she said.

'Yes. It's a long shot — a pretty desperate one to be honest — and it will require you to put yourself at great risk too. But if you can pull it off, it might work.'

Somewhere, from a part of her mind she kept shuttered most of the time, a vision of a dark cellar and a door that could not be opened forced itself into her consciousness. With a supreme effort of will she suppressed it.

'Tell me what you want me to do.'

* * *

Foxy was no longer bound to a chair. Naked now, he was suspended by his wrists from a bar set into the ceiling, his feet — swollen and inflamed from the extraction of his toe nails — barely touching the ground. He could feel blood trickling down his arms from where the fetters that held him had cut into the flesh. He had lost all sense of time. He'd had neither food nor drink since his arrest. His tongue was swollen with thirst.

The door of the cellar opened and Barbie came in, followed by two of his henchmen. He walked over to where Foxy hung and looked him up and down.

'So, now. Tell me where you were taking those Jewish pigs.'

Foxy could only manage an inarticulate croak.

'Give him water,' Barbie ordered.

A man came forward with a bucket and tipped the contents over Foxy's head. He stuck out his tongue in a desperate attempt to get some of it into his mouth.

'Now, speak!' Barbie ordered.

In the long hours before it became impossible to hold any idea in his mind except his pain, Foxy had had time to think. He realized that Barbie had no idea of his real purpose, the real reason he had been sent to France. He had accepted his cover story as the chef-patron of the Renard Rouge and was only concerned with his efforts to save some of the Jews who lived in the city. He knew that if he was to have any hope of survival, he must keep his inquisitor's mind fixed on that. It was tempting, sorely tempting, to offer up some information, to betray the kind sisters of the Perpetual Rosary who sheltered the families he brought to them. But he knew that one betrayal must lead to another, and eventually to the location of the village where the Jews were being given sanctuary. The only way was to maintain the story he had started with.

'I've told you. I know nothing about any Jews,' Foxy mumbled.

Barbie sighed. 'I was afraid it would come to this.' He held out a hand to one of his men. 'Give me the knife.' A long, narrow-bladed knife was placed in his palm. He stepped closer to Foxy. 'So, what shall it be? Your eyes, or your balls?'

* * *

The next morning a young woman was admitted into the room Barbie had commandeered as his office in the Hotel Terminus. Her fair hair was drawn back from a face bare of make-up and eyes that were reddened from weeping. A simple smock partly concealed her swollen belly.

Barbie looked up from the papers on his desk. 'Well, speak up!' he demanded. 'I've agreed to give you five minutes. Don't waste my time.'

The woman approached, her shoulders bowed and hands clasped in a gesture of appeal.

'Monsieur, you have the father of my child in your custody.'

'What of it? He is here because he has refused to follow the laws of the Reich. He deserves all he gets. It is useless to petition me on his behalf.'

'Monsieur, it is not for him that I have come to beg, but for my unborn child.'

Barbie turned his head away with a shrug. 'What have I to do with that? You should have chosen a better man as a husband.'

'But that is why I have come.' Tears were on the woman's cheeks. 'We were betrothed, but not yet married. Unless you help me, my child will be born without the blessing of the church.'

'So? You should have thought of the possible consequences before you allowed yourself to be seduced. I ask again, what has this to do with me?'

'I have come to beg you to allow us to be married. That way, our child will not be born out of wedlock and when . . . if . . . when my man is released, we shall be able to live as a family, according to the law. You are a man who believes in the rule of law, monsieur. I believe your people, the Nazis, set great store by the sacredness of the family. Will you allow us that small consolation?'

For the first time Barbie looked directly into the woman's face. 'And if I were minded to agree, how is this to be accomplished?'

She answered eagerly. 'I have spoken to Father Michel at St Bartholomew's Church. It is only a few streets away from here. If you name a time, your men could bring my fiancé there. It would take only a few minutes, and he could be guarded all the time and returned here afterwards.'

Barbie looked at her for a long moment. 'And what could you offer me in return?'

Slowly, the woman sank to her knees, her bowed head hiding the loathing in her eyes. 'I will do whatever it pleases you to ask.'

The German's hand was at the fly of his trousers. 'Then I think we may be able to come to an agreement.'

CHAPTER 14

The congregation in St Bartholomew's Church was almost lost in the echoing space of the nave and the high-vaulted roof. A much larger gathering would have seemed sparse in that place, but as it was, there were only a handful present for this hastily arranged ceremony. The bride wore a simple blue dress that hung loosely over her swollen belly, which was partly concealed by a bouquet of pink roses. Next to her stood an older man, who may have been her father, and behind her were two young women, bridesmaids presumably, who also carried bouquets. In the front pews half a dozen young men and two women constituted the witnesses. Their expressions were composed, as befitted the occasion, but a close observation would have revealed the tension in the set of their shoulders and their rapid glances around the church. Any regular worshipper at that church could have told you that the priest who waited in his vestments at the altar was not Father Michel but a much younger man. A curate, perhaps?

For several long minutes the assembled company waited. There was no choir, nor organ music to cover the silence. Then the doors at the back of the church clanged open and a small procession entered. Two uniformed Gestapo officers, followed by a man whose hands were shackled behind him, and then two more Gestapo. At the sight of them, the bride and her companions let out cries of dismay, which were hastily suppressed. Half the man's face was concealed beneath a bloodstained bandage, and he shuffled awkwardly in shoes that seemed too big for him. The guards marched him to stand beside his bride at the altar, where one of them undid the shackles. For a moment, bride and groom gazed wordlessly into each other's faces. Then the priest spoke the first words of the service.

It was a truncated version of the marriage mass and the young priest seemed in a hurry to get through it. Bride and groom made the necessary responses, the witnesses stood and knelt as the liturgy required, but their words were mumbled, their movements automatic and their attention was focused not on the figures at the altar but on the four guards.

When the moment for the Eucharist arrived, the priest seemed more nervous than ever. He fumbled with the paten, nearly causing the communion wafers to fall, and then he dropped the chalice. He dived down behind the altar to retrieve it. When he stood up again, he was holding, not a chalice, but an MP 40 submachine gun.

The bride dragged her new husband to the floor. Over their heads, four short bursts from the machine gun brought the four Gestapo men crashing to the floor in a pool of blood. The bride scrambled to her feet, as two of the witnesses ran forward to lift the groom bodily and carry him towards the vestry at the back of the church. The bride and her two attendants dropped their bouquets, revealing pistols hidden beneath, and followed, their rear guarded by the rest of the wedding party. In the vestry, the real Father Michel, bound and gagged at his own request, nodded encouragingly. The bride paused long enough to drop a kiss on his cheek and murmur, 'Thank you, Father'. Then the whole party left by a side door.

In a small side road at the back of the church waited two cars and the *gazogene*-operated van belonging to the local vet. Already, the groom had been loaded into the van, and concealed behind some bales of straw, the young bull, which until now had been the only occupant, bellowed his objection to the disturbance. The bride, moving with surprising agility for one in her condition, climbed in beside the driver, and the van pulled away. Some of the witnesses jumped into the two cars and followed. The rest simply melted away into the passing crowds going about their usual business in the city.

Almost an hour later, the vet's van came to a standstill in the yard of the farm where André had set up his headquarters. The bride jumped down and ran to open the rear doors.

'Wait! Wait!' Jean Jacques, the vet, hurried to join her. 'Let me get Hermann out first.'

Hermann the bull was coaxed out and led away. Kim, minus her padding and her blonde wig, scrambled into the van, almost afraid of what she was going to find. As she did so, the bales of straw were dislodged and Foxy struggled into a sitting position. He twisted his head from side to side, taking in his surroundings with his good eye, and focused on Kim.

'Well,' he remarked, 'that wasn't quite what I imagined for our wedding — but sod this for a honeymoon!' And he passed out.

Kim threw herself across the bales to grab him in her arms, simultaneously laughing and weeping. 'Oh, my love! My dear love! What have they done to you?'

André's hand gripped her arm. 'Come along, *chérie*, let's get him into the house. It will be more comfortable.'

Foxy was carried into the farmhouse and laid on the big bed in the room upstairs that must have once accommodated the farmer and his wife. The room was scented by the bunches of dried lavender that hung from the low beams, and the open dormer windows let in the bleating of sheep and the noise of chickens scratching in the yard below. At the same time, a pony and trap drove into the yard and a silver-haired man carrying a black bag got out. In the bedroom, Kim was kneeling by the bed. Foxy opened his unbandaged eye.

'Kim? It is you, isn't it?'

'Yes, my love. It's me.'

'That's good. Back there, I wasn't sure who I was marrying.'

She touched the bandage. 'What has he done to you?'

'Oh, he gave me a choice. It was this or my balls. You know what they say — an eye for an eye . . .'

He drifted into unconsciousness again. André came into the room and stooped over Kim.

'*Chérie*, this is Doctor Dufrais. He has looked after me and my men ever since we came here. You can trust him completely. Let him see what needs to be done for our friend here.'

Kim rose unsteadily and the doctor leaned over the bed. 'So, what have we here? What acts of bestial cruelty has that monster perpetrated now?' He started to remove the bandage from Foxy's head, then paused and looked at André. 'Perhaps the young lady should wait outside?'

Kim began to protest, but André took her by the arm and urged her towards the door. 'Let's allow the good doctor to get on with his work, shall we?'

To Kim, the next minutes seemed endless. At last the doctor came out, his face set.

'How is he?' Kim begged.

'He has been cruelly treated, but he will recover. He is strong, and he will need all his strength.'

'And his eye?' Kim forced the words out.

'Gone, I am afraid. There is nothing I can do to remedy that. But the wound is clean and it will heal in time.'

Kim thought for a moment she was going to be sick. The room spun around her. André took her arm. 'Come downstairs. You need a brandy. I've got a bottle stashed away for moments like this.'

Kim shook her head. 'No. I want to be with him.'

'He is sleeping now,' the doctor said. 'I gave him a strong sedative. He will sleep for several hours. When he wakes, he will be in great pain. Give him two of these every four hours.' He handed Kim a bottle of pills. 'I wish I could give you morphine, but alas, that has been unobtainable for months. These will help.'

André took the doctor downstairs and Kim went back to where Foxy lay. She touched his face but there was no response. Remembering his strange, shuffling gait when he was brought into the church, she carefully lifted the blankets and saw that his feet had been freshly bandaged. She did not need to ask why.

For the next four or five hours she held his hand and refused to move, despite the entreaties of André and the two young women who had acted as her bridesmaids. One of them, Jeanne, was married to one of the *maquisards*. The other, Prudence, had joined them after her mother and father had been shot for harbouring a downed American airman. Both loathed the Nazis and were prepared to do anything in their power to thwart them and, despite the risk involved, they had not hesitated to play their parts in the wedding charade. They came to sit with Kim when they could, in between feeding the livestock and cooking for the men. They brought her soup, which she barely touched, and ersatz coffee which she sipped and then allowed to go cold. All she could think of was how she might break the bad news to Foxy when he woke — and how he might react.

At last Foxy gave a deep sigh and opened his good eye. Kim leaned over him.

'It's all right, my darling. You're quite safe.'

He scanned the surroundings, his eye swivelling from side to side.

'Where am I?'

'In André's village. Don't worry. He's doubled the patrols and everyone is on his guard. If the SS have followed us, they won't get through.'

He focused on her face. 'Did I imagine it, or did we get married?'

'We went through a form of the service.'

'Not the real thing?'

'No. Jules, who performed the ceremony, is not in Holy Orders. He was studying for the priesthood but gave it up when the war started.'

'So, not binding then?'

110

Kim experienced a twinge of dismay. 'No.'

He sighed. 'Oh well, better luck next time, eh?'

She kissed him on the lips. 'We don't need words in church to keep us together.'

He was quiet for a moment. Then he said, 'The eye? I suppose there's no hope?'

She shook her head, unable for a moment to frame the words. 'No, the doctor says there's nothing to be done. I'm so sorry, darling.'

He managed a smile. 'Don't worry. I'll wear a black eye patch and look piratical, and women will be captivated by my air of mystery.'

She felt laughter rising in her throat. 'I'll get you a parrot to sit on your shoulder.'

He laughed in response, a faint, dry sound but a laugh nonetheless. 'Just make sure it can say "pieces of eight"!'

It was a poor attempt at an imitation but enough to send Kim into a spasm of helpless giggles. This was the irrepressible Foxy she knew and loved. She buried her face in his shoulder and sobbed with laughter.

When she had regained control, she asked, 'Are you in pain?'

'My bloody feet are killing me, but you know how that feels.'

She nodded. That was something that still gave her nightmares, but she reminded herself that however great her suffering at the hands of the Gestapo, she had escaped without lasting injury.

'The doctor left some pills.' She poured water from a jug Prudence had set to hand and lifted his head so he could swallow the tablets. As she laid him back on the pillow, she said, 'Rest now. We can talk again later.'

The local farmers owed a debt of gratitude to André for preserving their herds from the German requisitions and, as a result, he and his men were well supplied with fresh food. Foxy was fed eggs beaten up in milk, beef broth and home-baked bread. Within two days he was able to get up and hobble downstairs to join the rest of the group. Looking around her properly for the first time, Kim was surprised to see Georges Duboeuf, minus his Milice uniform.

'I didn't thank you properly for getting me out of the Gestapo's hands,' she said.

'No problem,' he replied. 'You had a lot on your mind at that point.'

'Just a minute!' Foxy interjected. 'What's all this? Out of the Gestapo's hands?'

Kim explained to him how she had been arrested and how Duboeuf had contrived her release.

'Dear God!' he exclaimed. 'If I'd known what was going on while I was shut up in the Hotel Terminus, I think I'd have gone mad.'

'Just as well you didn't, then,' she responded. 'But Georges, I didn't expect to find you still here.'

He shrugged his shoulders. 'I could hardly go back and take up my duties with the Milice after I shot those two goons. André has kindly allowed me to join his outfit.'

Kim turned to André. 'You two knew each other already?'

'Yes. A couple of months back, Georges heard a rumour that the SS had infiltrated an informer into the group. He warned me and I was able to identify the man and . . . deal with him.'

Kim turned back to Duboeuf. 'Can you give me any news of Sylvie, and the Levignes?'

'As soon as I could I told Sylvie you had been arrested. It gave her time to go to ground. I'm not sure where, but she said she had a safe place. The Levignes? Not so good, I'm afraid. The Gestapo raided their shop and took them both away.'

Kim bowed her head. 'Those poor people! Their only crime was to give me their hospitality.'

'How much do they know about you?' Foxy asked.

'Very little. Just the name on my identity card and the story that I'm a travelling saleswoman who needed a place to stay for a week or two. Of course, they guessed that was just a cover, but that's all they could tell the Gestapo.'

'Well,' André said heavily, 'we must hope for their sakes that the Boches believe that.'

Foxy had insisted on getting up, but it was obvious that he was still in considerable pain. Apart from the damaged eye socket and his feet, his wrists were swollen and cut from where the handcuffs had dug into them while he was hung from them, and the muscles and tendons in his shoulders had been strained almost to breaking point. There were bruises all over his body where one of the guards had kicked him and he suspected he had a broken rib, maybe two.

'He should be back in England, getting proper treatment,' André said.

'I know,' Kim replied. 'But how can we organize an exfiltration flight without radio contact?'

'Don't worry about me,' Foxy said. 'I'll be fine here, as long as André can put up with me.'

'You're welcome to stay,' the Frenchman assured him, 'but I'm not sure I can guarantee to keep you out of Barbie's hands. He won't rest until he's got you back and, although I trust all my people implicitly, there is always the chance that one of the locals might let something slip.'

'That makes it even more urgent to fix a flight,' Kim said. 'I suppose there's no chance of getting your radio set out of the Renard Rouge?'

'Hopeless,' Foxy said. 'Barbie will have men watching the place day and night. But what about your radio operator in Vienne? Surely that's the answer.'

Kim clapped her hand to her mouth. 'Oh God! With everything that's happened it went out of my mind. Pauline is the traitor. She's a double agent and I'm pretty sure she killed Bernard.'

'Good God! Are you sure? How do you know?' Foxy leaned forward intently.

As briefly as possible Kim explained about the discovery of Bernard's camera hidden in Pauline's apartment and the conclusions she had drawn. 'We knew there must be a mole in the circuit, and who better placed to pass on information to the Huns? And the only way she could have come by Bernard's camera is if she was there when he fell off that ladder.'

'Perhaps he lent it to her?' André suggested.

'If that was the case, she would have handed it over in case it had useful information on it, not hidden it away with her radio set,' Kim said. 'I thought from the start there was something odd about her. She seemed determined to convince me that she was on the verge of a nervous break-down, but I felt all along she was putting it on.'

'And we've just shipped her back to England!' Foxy exclaimed. 'Have you warned Baker Street?'

'No.' Kim shook her head despairingly. 'That's how the SS caught me. I was using her set to warn them, but I hadn't managed to send the message before the Huns marched in and arrested me.'

'That makes getting access to a radio set our top priority,' Foxy said. 'God knows what mischief she could be making back in England.'

'I take it you don't have any means of communicating with London?' Kim asked André.

He shook his head. 'I relied on Roland. So did all the groups in the area.'

Foxy nodded. 'That was my chief function, coordination and communication.'

'And as far as I know, there is no one from SOE anywhere near Vienne,' Kim said. 'The only contacts I have are north of here. I think I might have to go to Paris.'

'Too risky.' André shook his head. 'Don't forget you are also a wanted fugitive. Barbie will have been told about your escape. He may not connect you with the pregnant, blonde woman who conned him into that fake marriage ceremony, but the SS in Vienne have the papers with your false identity and a description of you.'

Kim ran her hand through her hair. 'Of course they do. My God, what a mess!'

'Yes.' Foxy was slumped in his chair. Suddenly, he jerked upright. 'Wait a minute! What am I thinking about! I know the solution.'

'You know?' André queried.

Kim leaned forward. 'Go on.'

'André, how far is it to Vercors?'

'Vercors? About 150 kilometres, depending on the route you take.'

'What is Vecors?' Kim asked.

'It's a mountainous plateau in the foothills of the Alps,' André told her. 'Very rugged. Practically inaccessible.'

'That's the whole point,' Foxy said. 'I've just remembered a message that came through to me a day, no two days before I was picked up. You remember, *chérie*, I told you about the guy with the code name Roger, who had set up resistance circuits all along the Rhône Valley?'

'The one you were acting as coordinator for?'

'Yes, that's him. Very impressive character. He's been back in the UK being debriefed, but I got word through one of the couriers that he's back in France and in the Vercors. The message was that a large number of *resistants* are congregating there with the intention of establishing a semi-independent enclave. The plan is to make it a centre of resistance activity sufficient to tie down a large number of German units, in the event of an Allied landing in the south of France.'

'Is such a landing imminent?' André asked eagerly.

'That I can't tell you,' Foxy said. 'But the point I'm making is that Roger will have radio contact with London. If we can get there, we can at least get a message through about Pauline and possibly arrange an exfiltration flight.'

'That's brilliant!' Kim said. 'How do we get to this place?'

'That won't be easy.' André shook his head dubiously. 'There's no direct train service, and anyway, we couldn't risk using public transport. Barbie's men will be watching all routes out of the area. That means private car, or something similar, and I know we don't have gas for a trip that long.'

'You're forgetting that I have contacts with other groups like yours that Roger set up all along the valley,' Foxy said. 'If we can get in touch with one or two, they might be able to organize some form of transport from one group to the next.'

'That sounds feasible,' André agreed.

'So, how do we go about making contact?' Kim asked.

Foxy rubbed his chin. 'A day or two ago that wouldn't have been a problem, as the couriers always came to the restaurant. They will know to steer clear of that from now on and I've no way of getting in touch with them.'

'Do you know the location of the nearest group to here?' André asked.

'It must be Patrice's lot. They are based in the village of St Jean de Bournay.'

André calculated quickly. 'That's about thirty kilometres away. We should be able to get you that far.'

'Well, it's a start,' Kim said. 'Hopefully they will be able to pass us on to the next group.'

'We still need to fix you up with a new identity and some kind of disguise,' Foxy said.

They were in the big kitchen of the farmhouse which was the hub of André's organization. Two of his most trusted lieutenants were eating a late lunch at the long table. They had not been part of the conversation but there had been no attempt to keep the discussion secret. Now one of them, a man in his middle years who rarely spoke but who had the reputation of being one of the bravest among them, got up and came over.

'Forgive me for interrupting, but I think I may have a solution.'

'Go on, Laurent,' André said.

'My daughter was much the same age and build as Madeleine here. I still have her papers. With a few . . . adjustments to her appearance, I think Madeleine might pass as her.'

André stood up and put his hand on Laurent's shoulder. '*Mon cher*, that is a most generous offer.' He turned to Kim. 'Laurent's daughter, Amelie, was shot when she tried to prevent the Boches from taking away the family's only milk cow. She knew her little brother and sister needed the milk. That's why Laurent came to join us.'

'That is a terrible story,' Kim said. 'I'm so sorry. What has happened to the little ones now?'

116

'They live here, in the village,' Laurent said gravely. 'André took us all in and we are safe here. That is why I am happy to do anything I can to help. I'll fetch the papers.'

He was back in a few minutes, holding out a wallet which contained all the papers every citizen of occupied France was obliged to carry. The identity card showed a grainy picture of a young woman and gave her description. *Age: 25. Height: 1 m 60. Hair: Brun. Eyes: Noisette.*

'I'm about the right height,' Kim said. 'I suppose you could call my hair brown, though it's darker than that. I'm not sure what "noisette" means.'

'Hazel,' André said. 'I reckon you could say that about your eyes, too.'

'It's a really good fit,' Kim said. 'Thank you, Laurent. But are you sure you want to part with these?'

Laurent shrugged. 'I don't need them to remember her. If they can be useful, you're welcome to them.'

'It won't stand up to close examination,' Kim said. 'I'll have to memorize the other details and make up a back story to go with it. But it should get me through a casual check at a roadblock.'

'Then we can go,' Foxy said, 'if you can find us some transport.'

'I'll get a message to Jean Jacques,' André said. 'His gazogene truck is our best chance and he can hide you in the trailer.'

'Not with that bloody bull again, please!' Foxy begged, but he looked more cheerful than Kim had seen him since his rescue.

CHAPTER 15

Jean Jacques arrived at André's HQ the following day. When Kim explained to him what they were hoping to do he ran a hand through his thinning hair with a frown.

'You don't think it's feasible?' she asked anxiously.

'It's feasible, all right,' he replied. 'I'm just wondering what story I can tell the Boches if I get stopped at a roadblock. Why am I going to St Jean de Bournay? There must be vets closer they could send for if some of their animals need attention.'

'I see your point,' Kim murmured. 'But you are the only person we can think of who has the means to get Roland there. He's not fit enough to walk.'

'Who is your contact there?' Jean Jacques asked Foxy.

'He's a farmer. I only know him as Patrice, but the farm is called Ferme des Peupliers.'

'Well, that's a good start,' the vet said. 'It's mostly sheep and pigs in that area. OK. I have an idea. A farmer friend of mine has a prize hog that he wants to sell. I could say your friend Patrice is buying it.'

'Oh no!' Foxy groaned. 'First a bull. Now a prize hog!'

Jean Jacques laughed. 'Don't complain. How do you think we got through that roadblock when I brought you up here? You can thank Hermann for that.'

'Hermann?'

'Most of these young conscripts are city boys who've hardly even seen a cow. They were not going to climb into the trailer to search if it meant getting past a rather irritable bull. And I suspect most of them would feel the same about a large porker.'

Foxy sighed resignedly, but he was grinning at the same time. 'Oh, very well.'

Jean Jacques returned next day with the pig in the trailer. Foxy was ensconced behind it, on a bed of hay and concealed by bales of straw, while Kim, wearing farm-worker's dungarees and with her hair tied up in a scarf, sat beside the vet. Their route took them along minor roads winding through the wooded hills and valleys of the department of Isère. They were stopped twice at roadblocks manned by members of the Milice but they only glanced casually at their papers and peered briefly into the trailer before waving them on. By midday they were on the outskirts of St Jean de Bournay. A girl on a bicycle with loaves of bread in her basket knew the farm and gave them directions, and a short while later Jean Jacques drew to a standstill in the farmyard. A woman stopped in the act of tipping a bucket of leftovers into a pig pen and came over.

Kim jumped down and greeted her. '*Bonjour, madame.* We are looking for Patrice.' She realized that this was not the farmer's real name, but the use of the code name would alert anyone in the know that she was working with the Resistance.

The woman looked her up and down suspiciously. 'Patrice? Who wants him?'

'I was told to tell him the runt of the litter is called Cyrano.' It was the password used by the couriers working for Foxy.

The woman continued to stare at Kim for a few seconds longer. Then she said, 'He's inside. It's the midi. He is resting.'

Kim was familiar with the sacred French midi, the lunch break that lasted a couple of hours.

'I'm sorry to disturb him,' she said, 'but it is important.'

The woman, whom she took to be Patrice's wife, disappeared into the house and a few minutes later a lean, wiry man with a mop of unkempt dark hair came out to join them.

'You're not the usual girl. What's happened?'

'There has been a . . . a problem,' Kim told him. 'We have an injured man in the trailer. He needs a bed for the night and some form of transport tomorrow. We are heading south.'

'What's happened to Roland? He arranges all that sort of thing.'

'It is Roland who needs your help.'

'Roland? *Mon dieu*! What happened?'

'I'll explain later. Please, can we bring him in?'

She could see that Patrice was unhappy about this turn of events, but he said, 'Very well. Where is he?'

Jean Jacques had opened the back of the trailer and Patrice was confronted by the sight of a large hog.

'What's this?' he demanded. 'Is this some sort of joke? You tell me there is an injured man and you show me a pig?'

'The pig is yours, if you want him,' Jean Jacques said. 'The patient is back there.'

The pig was removed and shut up in the barn, and Jean Jacques and Kim set about removing the bales of hay. Foxy hauled himself into a sitting position. His face was flushed and beaded with sweat.

'Dear God! I thought I was going to suffocate,' he said, coughing. 'The fumes from that gazogene boiler nearly killed me.'

Jean Jacques clapped a hand to his brow. 'I should have thought of that. You were much closer to it than we were.'

'Come on,' Kim said. 'Let's get you out of there.'

Between them, she and Jean Jacques helped Foxy out. Patrice stared at him.

'This is Roland?'

'Yes.'

'He can't stay here! The Boches are looking everywhere for him. There are posters up all round the village describing a man with only one eye and red hair. You'll have to find somewhere else.'

'There is nowhere else,' Kim said desperately. 'Please, it's only for one night. He's been tortured. You can't turn us away.'

As Patrice hesitated, Foxy raised his head and looked at him. 'I was always told that Patrice was a brave man who would do anything to spite the invaders.'

It was enough. Patrice lifted his shoulders and said, 'OK. Bring him in. Marie, fetch some cider.'

Supported on one side by Jean Jacques and on the other by Patrice, Foxy hobbled towards the farmhouse. As they reached the door, they heard the sound of a bicycle bell behind them and a postman rode into the yard. Patrice looked round and swore.

'*Merde*! Get inside, quickly!'

In the stone-flagged kitchen they lowered Foxy onto a wooden settle. His breathing was ragged and Kim was worried. The woman Patrice had addressed as Marie came over with a mug. Her earlier suspicion seemed to have given way to concern.

'Here, drink some of this. It's good cider.' She glanced up at Kim. 'Poor fellow! He's in a bad way.'

Foxy drank thirstily and seemed to revive. 'It is good! *Merci, madame.*'

Marie looked at Kim and Jean Jacques. 'Sit down, please. Have some cider. You must be tired.'

Patrice came in carrying some letters and closed the door behind him. 'He would arrive just at that moment! That Pepin can never resist sticking his nose into other people's business.'

'Do you think he saw us?' Kim asked.

'Only your backs, but of course he wanted to know who you were. I told him you'd brought a pig I bought at the market. But I don't trust him. The Boches are offering a good reward for information and Pepin is always short of money.'

'Then the sooner we are on our way the better,' Foxy said. 'Can you find us some form of transport?'

'Where to?' Patrice asked.

'My next contact is in St-Siméon-de-Bressieux. It's about another twenty-five to thirty kilometres.'

Patrice nodded thoughtfully. 'That shouldn't be too difficult, but the problem is getting hold of fuel.' He looked at Foxy. 'And you're in no condition to walk far.'

'I'm afraid not.'

'OK. Let me think about it. The main consideration is to keep you away from any main roads. Meanwhile, you need to rest and eat. Marie, is there any of that soup you made for our lunch left?'

'Plenty' the woman replied. 'And there's bread and cheese to go with it.'

Jean Jacques got up. 'I should be heading back.'

'But you must eat first!' Marie exclaimed. 'Please, sit down again. It will only take a few minutes to warm the soup.'

'What about the hog?' Patrice asked.

'As I said, he's yours if you want him.'

'How much?'

'Consider it a gift in return for your hospitality to my friends. The owner will understand.'

As soon as they had finished eating, Jean Jacques insisted that he must be on his way. He kissed Kim on both cheeks.

'*Merde alors*! I won't say good luck.'

'Thank you for everything,' Kim answered warmly.

Foxy hauled himself to his feet and embraced him. 'I owe you a lot, *mon ami*. And I forgive you for the bull — and the pig!'

'Take care of yourselves,' the vet said. 'And when all this is over . . .'

'When all this is over we shall come back and celebrate properly,' Kim promised.

While they were eating, Patrice had been outside watching the lane leading to the farm. As soon as Jean Jacques had left, he said, 'I'm worried that that idiot Pepin may be blabbing as we speak. I think you would be safer in the loft over the barn, if you don't mind.'

Neither Kim nor Foxy had any objection and they were soon ensconced in the loft, with blankets over a bed of hay and a jug of cider to tide them over. In truth, Kim was glad to have a few quiet hours. Foxy needed the rest and after the tensions of the drive, she was happy to relax beside him. The day was overcast and chilly and it was pleasantly warm in the barn.

They were both jerked out of a doze as the shadows were lengthening in the yard below them. They had been aware of the farmyard noises of pigs grunting and chickens clucking, and the clank of buckets as Patrice and Marie came and went across the afternoon, but suddenly there were new voices calling to each other and the whirr of bicycle wheels crossing the yard. There were spaces for ventilation in the eaves where the roof met the sides of the barn and Kim wormed her way across to one so she could look down. With a chill in her stomach she recognized Pepin the postman accompanied by three men in the uniform of the Milice. She turned to warn Foxy but he was already sliding across to join her.

In silence, the two fugitives watched as the *miliciens* hammered on the door. Patrice opened it, glowering in simulated irritation.

'What the hell do you want, disturbing honest folks while they are enjoying an aperitif after a hard day's work?'

The next part of the exchange was inaudible, but they saw one of the *miliciens* indicate Pepin.

Patrice responded with a sudden gust of laughter. 'You're taking this idiot seriously? You must be mad. But come on. If you really think I've got something to hide, you'd better come in and have a look round.'

'He's a cool customer!' Foxy whispered.

All three disappeared into the house, followed by Pepin. It was dark enough for lanterns to be lit and they watched the lights move from room to room in the house as the *miliciens* searched. Before long the only light came from the windows of the kitchen and Kim heard the faint clink of glasses.

'He's got them on the cider,' Foxy murmured. 'Good man! It's strong stuff.'

Half an hour passed and the sounds of laughter floated up to them. Then the door opened and the four men reappeared, followed by Patrice with a lantern in his hand. He gestured to them to follow him, which they did, somewhat unsteadily, and he led them to one of the pens that lined the yard.

'He's showing them the pig!' Kim hissed delightedly.

The men peered into the sty then stepped back, and there was more laughter and a lot of back slapping before the visitors got back on the bicycles and wobbled off down the lane.

'Oh, well done! Well done!' Foxy exclaimed.

Soon after that, Patrice came into the barn and called up to them. 'I reckon you can come down now. They swallowed my story about buying the pig. I don't think they'll be back. Marie's cooking dinner.'

The farmhouse kitchen was redolent with the smell of frying bacon and andouillette sausage, both rare treats under rationing, and very soon Kim and Foxy were sitting with a steaming plate in front of them.

As they ate Patrice said, 'I think I may have found a way for you to get to St Simeon. Can you ride a horse?'

'I can,' Kim said. 'I'm not sure about Foxy?'

He grinned. 'I lived in the States for years, remember. I'm no horseman, but I reckon I can sit on anything other than a bucking bronco.'

'That's good,' Patrice said. 'One of my group is a forester. He keeps horses for getting about and for dragging out timber, and he knows the countryside like the back of his hand. I had a word with him this afternoon and he will lend you horses and come with you as guide. Then he can take the beasts back with him. Will that do?'

Kim looked at Foxy. 'Are you up to a long day in the saddle?'

'I guess I'll have to be,' he said. 'It's got to be an improvement on being stuck behind that gazogene burner.'

'So we're agreed?' Patrice asked.

'Agreed,' said Kim and Foxy in unison.

'Good, you need to be ready for an early start tomorrow.'

* * *

Patrice's friend Mattieu arrived while they were still at breakfast, bringing with him three Percherons, France's most popular work horses. Solidly muscled, standing at around sixteen hands, they were ideal for pulling heavy logs, but not the perfect choice for riding. Kim's head hardly came up to their shoulders. She knew, however, that horses like this were placid natured. They would pose no problem for an inexperienced rider, which she suspected was the case with Foxy, in spite of his bravado.

In any other circumstances Kim would have thoroughly enjoyed the day. It had rained overnight but as they set off the sky cleared and there was a real promise of spring in the air. They rode along woodland tracks and the narrow lanes that threaded their way between fields where new lambs bleated and gambolled, avoiding roads and skirting round small villages. Occasionally they were able to see down to the road that ran along the bottom of a valley and twice they saw convoys of troop carriers heading in the same direction as themselves. If they were also heading for the Vercors, Kim reflected, it did not bode well for the resistance fighters gathering there.

Her more immediate worry, however, was Foxy's condition. It had been hard enough to get him mounted in the first place. His feet were still much too sore and swollen for him stand on his own, but with the combined muscle power of Patrice and Mattieu, they had succeeded in boosting him into the saddle. Once there, he seemed fairly comfortable, but as the day wore on, Foxy's tightly clamped jaw as he suppressed his groans tore at her heart. Remembering the bruises on his chest and abdomen and the possibility of a cracked rib, she could imagine that every step would be agony. Mattieu had proved to be of a taciturn character, and as the hours passed, Foxy gave up the effort of conversation, so they rode mostly in silence. That in itself did not bother her — she was happy to listen to the birdsong and the bleating of the lambs. She just wished Foxy could enjoy the ride.

Marie had given them bread and cheese and a flagon of cider for their midday meal, but Kim soon realized that if they dismounted, Foxy would never be able to get back in the saddle, so they snacked as they rode.

It was mid-afternoon when they saw the ruined castle that marked the little town of St-Siméon-de-Bressieux. Foxy's contact there was none other than the mayor, and couriers were instructed to go straight to the town hall. To ride up to it on their big horses, however, was hardly the way to keep a low profile, so Kim left the two men with the horses in the shelter of a patch of woodland just before they reached the first houses, and went on foot.

CHAPTER 16

St-Siméon-de-Bressieux was a prosperous town of hon-ey-coloured buildings. As Kim approached the town, the citizens were just returning to work after the midday break. Shops were opening up and housewives were heading for the covered market with their shopping baskets. Kim mingled with the crowd, trying to look as if she belonged there. The mairie was a surprisingly imposing building for a town of this size, and Kim felt a tightening of her gut as she approached. Like all municipal buildings it was draped, by order, with flags bearing the Nazi swastika. That did not, of course, indicate the sentiments of the people inside, but nevertheless, it felt unpleasantly like walking into the lion's den. It did not help that a board outside displayed a large 'WANTED' notice, with a description of Foxy. Barbie was casting his net wide.

It occurred to her as she made her way to the town hall that she was not very suitably dressed to be calling on the mayor. She was still wearing the overalls that Jean Jacques had lent her and the headscarf that partly hid her hair. She had been glad of them on the ride — being in a skirt would have been extremely uncomfortable. She consoled herself with the thought that, these days, with so many of the men either dead or prisoners of war, and the younger ones shipped off to Germany as part of the Service de Travail Obligatoire, a great many women were having to take on the work the men would have done, and dress accordingly.

A bored-looking woman behind a desk in the foyer asked her business, but her expression changed when Kim gave the reply Foxy had taught her. 'I have a message for M. le Maire from his Aunt Claudine.' She was immediately led up the stairs to the mayor's office, a large room furnished in heavy oak with windows looking out onto the town square. The mayor, a small man with greying hair and spectacles — an unlikely looking rebel — rose at once and shook Kim's hand.

'*Bonjour, madame*! What brings you to St-Siméon?'

'Your aunt sends her compliments and asked me to tell you that little Georges has taken his first steps.'

'Ah, I am delighted to hear that. So tell me, in what way can I be of service?'

'I have an injured friend who need a night's lodging and help with his onward journey.'

'And where is this friend?'

'He is waiting for me at the edge of town. It is important that he is not recognized.'

The look in the eyes behind the glasses sharpened. 'Indeed. Do you have transport?'

'We are on horseback at the moment, but the horses have to go back where they came from. My friend cannot ride much further.'

The mayor nodded briskly. 'I know exactly the right place for you. Mme de Vaux will be happy to put you up for the night at the château.'

He lifted a telephone on his desk and dialled a number. When the call was answered, he said, 'Mme la Comtesse, I have a visitor with me. She has come with a message from my Aunt Claudine. She has a friend with her and they need somewhere to stay for the night. I thought you might have a room for them.'

Kim did not hear the answer, but the mayor put the phone down with a smile and turned to her. 'So, that is all arranged. Madame will be glad to accommodate you and your friend. I will find someone to show you the way.'

After a second brief conversation on the phone he led Kim downstairs to a back entrance where they found a boy of about twelve waiting with a bicycle.

'Pierre,' the mayor said, 'this lady's friends are waiting for her. She will show you where. I want you to take them to the château.'

'Very well, Papa,' the boy responded.

The mayor looked at Kim. 'You need have no anxiety. Pierre understands the need for discretion. Now, I wish you good luck and a pleasant evening.'

He shook her hand again and turned back into the building. For a moment Kim hesitated. It all seemed too easy, as if it had been well rehearsed. Was she being led into a trap? But what choice did she have? Foxy had had no suspicions about the members of this circuit. She had to trust his judgement.

'Madame?' The boy was waiting for her. He was tousle-headed, just at the gawky stage where his arms and legs seemed too long for his body, but his expression reassured her. He knew he had been given a serious responsibility and was determined to live up to it.

She smiled at him. 'It's this way.'

'So,' she asked as they walked, 'do you often help out your father like this?'

He looked sideways at her and she could see he was weighing up how much it was safe to say. In the end he gave a small shrug. 'I do errands for him, when he asks me to.'

She was tempted to push her enquiries further but she understood that he had been warned not to give any details of their operations to any stranger, even one who seemed to be on the same side. It would not be fair to press him. So she asked innocuous questions about his family and his favourite subjects at school, but even here his replies were guarded. He had been well-trained, and that increased her confidence.

They found Mattieu dismounted and holding the reins of two horses while they grazed at the side of the track, but Foxy was still in the saddle, his head drooping with weariness.

'Pierre is going to show us where we can stay the night,' she told him, taking the reins and clambering into the saddle.

The boy had been studying Foxy's face and Kim realized with a shock that he must recognize him from the description on the poster. But he said only, 'Your friend looks tired, madame.'

'Yes, he is,' Kim agreed.

He gave her a reassuring smile. 'It is only five minutes to the château.'

The Château Bonnard was typical of its kind — a pretty miniature replica of the grand buildings that lined the Loire, with a steep-pitched roof and pointed turrets. As they rode up to the entrance, the front door opened and an elderly, grey-haired manservant came down the steps.

'Madame La Comtesse is waiting for you. Please dismount. Your horses will be taken care of.'

Kim slid to the ground and handed her reins to Mattieu. She went round to Foxy and saw him brace himself as he swung his leg over the horse's back and lowered himself to the ground. For a moment he clung onto the stirrup, then he straightened up, but as his feet took his weight, he staggered and would have fallen without Kim's grasp on his arm. The butler saw what was happening and came quickly forward to support him on the other side.

'*Doucement, monsieur, doucement*! Gently, gently! Come, this way.'

As they helped Foxy up the steps to the front door, the butler said over his shoulder, 'Pierre, show the other gentleman the way round to the stables.'

In the main hall, a tall, elegantly dressed woman, her white hair dressed in a chignon, waited to receive them. Seeing Foxy, she came forward quickly. '*Ah mon dieu! Le pauvre*! Come, come. You can rest yourself here.'

She led them into a beautifully furnished salon and instructed them to lower Foxy onto a chaise-longue. Kim was suddenly aware that both she and he were covered in dust and horsehair.

'Madame, your lovely furniture! We're too dirty . . .'

'Rubbish!' the old lady replied. 'Now, sit here and have something to drink. Then Gaspard will show you where you can refresh yourselves after your journey.' She turned her attention to Foxy. 'Is there anything we can do for you? Shall I call our doctor? He is one you can trust, I promise you.'

Foxy shook his head and summoned a smile. 'No, no, madame. I shall be fine after a rest and a wash. Please, do not concern yourself.'

Their hostess's obvious concern allayed any remaining doubts in Kim's mind and she realized they had been very lucky. After a glass of *pastis* they were taken upstairs — Foxy leaning heavily on Gaspard's arm — to a spacious bedroom and a bathroom where the bath was already filled with scented water. Kim bathed quickly, while Gaspard helped Foxy to undress. As the extent of his injuries was revealed she heard the butler click his tongue in shock, but he refrained from asking questions, and very soon Foxy was lowering himself into the warm bath with a sigh of relief. Kim had carried a satchel with a change of underwear and a toothbrush for each of them, given by members of André's team, as they had arrived with only the clothes they stood up in. She was worried that neither of them had anything else to wear other than their travel-stained clothes, but to her relief, she found a beautiful negligee laid out on the bed for her and a silk dressing gown for Foxy.

'Madame suggests that you come to dinner *en déshabillé*,' Gaspard said. 'Meanwhile, Lucille, her maid, will clean your clothes.'

'What has happened to Matthieu, who came with us?' Kim asked.

'He is in the kitchen, with cook,' was the reply. 'He was invited to join madame and yourselves for dinner, but he preferred to remain there. He is staying in the room that belonged to the head groom before the war.'

Dinner, though the menu was limited by the rigours of rationing, was served with the same elegance as if it were a pre-war dinner party. It was clear that the number of staff was greatly reduced and confined to Gaspard, Lucille, a cook and a maid of all work, but the countess was determined that standards must be maintained. As they talked, they became aware of just how much she and her family had suffered. Her elder son was a prisoner of war, held somewhere in Germany, and the younger had been killed during the battle to stem the German advance at Sedan. Her daughter-in-law had volunteered to work as a nurse at a hospital treating injured servicemen, leaving her seventeen-year-old son with his grandmother.

'And where is your grandson now?' Kim asked.

The countess raised her eyebrows. 'I thought perhaps you would be able to guess. He has gone to join the *maquis* in the Vercors.'

'The Vercors!' Kim and Foxy exclaimed with one breath.

'But of course!' was the response. 'Once the STO was announced, he realized that it would be only a matter of months before he turned eighteen and found himself being shipped off to work in Germany. The only alternative was to go to the *maquis*. But I assume that is where you are heading, also?'

'That is the plan,' Foxy agreed. 'Getting there is not so easy under the circumstances.'

The countess nodded. 'I understand. I will not ask why there are wanted notices all over the town for a man fitting your description. Nor will I enquire how you came by your injuries. It is better not to know too much.' She set down her wine glass and stood up. 'So how do you intend to go on from here?'

'At the moment, I don't know the answer to that,' Foxy told her. 'Up to now I have been able to make use of a network of contacts I have built up over the last year, but this is the furthest south my network reaches. From here on, we shall have to trust to luck.'

'We are hoping you may be able to suggest some way forward,' Kim added.

The countess nodded again. 'I shall give it some thought. Meanwhile, I suggest you both get as much rest as you can. I'm sure you are in need of it.'

No one had queried Kim's relationship to Foxy. She was not wearing a wedding ring, but it was assumed that they would sleep together. It was a luxury neither of them had experienced for some time — sleeping in a large, comfortable bed with clean sheets — but Foxy's injuries meant that intimacy had to be confined to a cuddle. Nevertheless, Kim slept well and woke refreshed as the first gleams of sunlight filtered through the curtains. She lay for a while, basking in the pleasure of her surroundings. It felt for a moment like the first day of a holiday, but reality soon reasserted itself. They must move on as quickly as possible. She nudged Foxy, who came to with a groan, but when he tried to rise, he slumped back onto the pillows.

'Give me a moment. I've stiffened up after yesterday's ride. My bloody back is giving me hell, and my legs are not much better.'

Kim massaged his muscles as well as she could but any pressure on his ribs elicited a sharp yelp of pain, and when she examined his feet it was clear that they had swollen up again. He was in no condition to travel. Leaving him to rest, she went downstairs and was directed by Gaspard to the morning room where the countess was eating breakfast. When Kim explained her concerns, her hostess's response was immediate.

'I shall send for Dr Magritte. I can assure you that he is to be trusted. He has cared for members of our group when they have been wounded. He will be able to help.'

The doctor arrived surprisingly promptly. After examining Foxy, he joined Kim and the countess, grave-faced.

'I have not asked your friend for details of what happened to him, but whoever was responsible should answer before God for his brutality. However, what matters now is your current situation. What he needs is rest. I have given him some more painkillers. He must not undertake another journey like the one you did yesterday.'

'I know you are right, doctor,' Kim said, 'but we need to move on.'

'You can stay here as long as you need to,' the countess said.

'It is noble and generous of you to say that,' Kim responded, 'but it would not be fair to you. There must be people who saw me in town yesterday, and it is possible we were followed here. It only needs one person to yield to the temptation of the reward to bring the Milice, or the SD, here to search. Besides that, there are many reasons why we need to complete our journey — reasons beyond our own security.'

'Hmm. In that case,' the doctor said, 'we must find some way for our friend up there to travel without undue exertion. The principal difficulty, as I see it, is the need to hide his face. Other injuries can be disguised to some extent, but the damage to his eye is impossible to conceal.' He picked up his black medical bag. 'I have an idea — not one that will be very appealing — but under the circumstances . . . I need to talk to a colleague. I shall return later with his answer.'

With that, he took his departure, leaving Kim and the countess to speculate about what the idea could possibly be.

Foxy spent most of the day sleeping. The countess attempted to entertain Kim by showing her round the château, but she was too much on edge to respond as she felt she should. The threat she had spoken of to her hostess was very real and she found herself constantly listening for the sound of vehicles approaching. When she heard it, late in the afternoon, her heart began to thump. Very few people had the petrol to run cars these days. It could be the gendarmes, or the Milice, or possibly a German staff car. If Foxy had been recognized as they passed through, it was quite likely that someone would have betrayed him for the reward. She got up, intending to run upstairs to Foxy, searching her memory for possible hiding places. But it was too late. The vehicle stopped outside and the butler was already opening the front door. It was a measure of the tension Kim was under, that for a moment, she failed to recognize the doctor who had examined Foxy earlier.

Over a glass of *pastis* in the drawing room, he explained his idea.

'I warn you that this will not seem a very attractive proposition, but it is the only way I can think of to convey our friend to where you need to go without his face being visible. I have spoken to my colleague, the undertaker. He is prepared to bring the hearse here, with a coffin. We would, of course, make air holes to allow Monsieur Roland to breathe and we could put in cushions and blankets to make it more comfortable. I will prepare a death certificate, giving the cause of death as typhus, which should deter any official from making a close inspection. We will give him an address in Pont-en-Royans, which is the entrance to the Vercors, and say he is being taken home to be buried. You, of course, will be the grieving widow. You will need to invent a reason for his being here in the first place.' He paused for breath and looked at Kim. 'All these are details. The question is, do you think our friend could bring himself to be closed up in a coffin for the duration of the journey?'

Kim shook her head. 'It's not for me to say. That has to be up to him.'

They went up to the bedroom where they found Foxy awake and sitting up. The doctor explained his idea again and asked, 'So, what do you think? Is it possible?'

'How long is the journey?' Foxy asked.

'An hour, perhaps a little longer. The hearse will have to travel at a suitable pace.'

Foxy looked at Kim, but she tried to keep her expression neutral. She knew she could not have contemplated the idea. It would bring back too many traumatic memories. But she knew, too, that it was probably the best, possibly the only way of getting him to safety. She saw the same thought taking root in his mind. He returned his gaze to the doctor.

'Then the answer is yes. I think it's a brilliant idea. Thank you, doctor.'

'What happens when we get to Pont-en-Royans?' Kim asked.

'The coffin will be taken to a chapel of rest. It belongs to an undertaker who is a colleague. There, M. Roland will be released and the empty coffin, suitably weighted I assume, will be buried.'

Another problem occurred to Kim. 'What about papers? The ID cards we have at the moment will not fit with that story.'

'That is not a problem,' the doctor said. 'If you remember, the mayor is one of us. He will be able to supply everything you need. Give me twenty-four hours to arrange everything. You will need new names for a start. Any ideas?'

Foxy thought briefly. 'Fabrice. Fabrice Marchand.'

'And I'm his wife Amelie,' Kim said. She decided to keep the name she had been given by Laurent in memory of his daughter.

'Very good,' the doctor said. 'You will have papers in those names by tomorrow.'

The next day they said goodbye to Mattieu, who shrugged off their thanks with a brusque '*Il n'y a pas de quoi*' and set off for home leading the two spare horses. The rest of the day was spent creating a 'legend' that would back up the new identities being created for them.

* * *

'How does it happen that you are here in France?' Kim asked. 'Fabrice Marchand would have been called up and probably either killed or taken prisoner.'

'OK. Taken prisoner and then exchanged as part of the deal with the Boches over STO. That happened. And I came here to join my wife.'

'And what am I doing here?' Kim asked.

'You are employed by me as a secretary/companion,' the countess suggested. 'And when your husband came back from the POW camp, I offered him a job in the kitchen.'

'But he caught typhus and died,' Kim said. 'The really difficult thing is why on earth are we taking your body to the Vercors.'

'Oh, that's easy. I grew up there and my dying wish was to be buried beside my parents in the churchyard at Pont-en-Royans. So my very generous employer,' with a nod to the countess, 'has agreed to arrange the transport.'

Kim stretched her arms. 'Well, it won't stand up to any in-depth interrogation, but it should be enough to satisfy a routine enquiry. We can embroider a few extra details between now and tomorrow.'

* * *

The next morning a hearse drew up outside the château and a coffin was carried in and set down in the hallway. Kim was ready, wearing a black coat, which the countess had found in her daughter-in-law's wardrobe, over a dark dress belonging to Lucille, and a small hat with a veil — the perfect image of a grieving widow.

The undertaker greeted her with a solemn, '*Bonjour, madame.* My condolences on your loss,' and the four pallbearers bowed their heads in greeting. It was clear that they all intended to play their parts to perfection.

Foxy, dressed in a suit that had belonged to the countess's son and hastily altered by Lucille, had recovered enough to hobble downstairs and was looking down at the coffin.

'It's been lined with something soft,' said Kim, who had examined it carefully, 'and there's a cushion for your head.'

'What about air holes?' he asked.

'Here.' Kim pointed to some ornamental scroll work, which cleverly concealed a number of tiny holes. Unless you were looking for them, they would be impossible to detect.

He raised his head and looked at her with a wry smile. 'Married a couple of weeks ago and buried today. We didn't have long to enjoy wedded bliss, did we?'

She leaned up and kissed him. 'Like you said, better luck next time.'

'I'll drink to that,' he said, and climbed into the coffin.

Kim handed him two bottles, one full of water, one empty for emergencies. Then the undertaker's men put on the lid. As she watched them securing it, Kim almost cried out. It was too close to the nightmare that still haunted her dreams and she knew she could never have endured such incarceration. She still had nightmares in which she was locked in that tiny, lightless cell with no idea whether she would ever get out. Her heart swelled with pride at Foxy's calm acceptance.

The men lifted the coffin and carried it out to the hearse. The countess embraced Kim and wished her good luck.

'We can never thank you enough,' Kim said tearfully.

'Live, and fight to drive these monsters back where they came from,' was the reply. 'That's all the thanks I need.'

CHAPTER 17

The hearse was stopped twice at roadblocks, but after a cursory glance at their papers they were waved through. Soon after passing the second one, Marceaux, the undertaker, gestured ahead.

'There! Behold the Vercors!'

Kim caught her breath. Ahead of them, rising out of the cultivated fields and vineyards, was a solid wall of granite, perhaps a thousand feet high. From this distance it appeared unbroken, an impregnable fortress.

'And people live up there? How do they get there?'

'There are gateways, valleys that run through the cliffs. Pont-en-Royans is at the start of one of them.'

Pont-en-Royans was the most stunning village Kim had ever seen. At the mouth of a narrow valley carved out by a swiftly flowing river, the houses clung to the steep sides of the cliff, one above another, as if suspended in mid-air. Painted in shades of pink and cream, their terracotta, tiled roofs were backed by a band of thick forest, above which the bare granite cliffs reached skyward.

The hearse threaded its way through the narrow streets until they reached the church at the highest point. Here, the coffin containing Foxy was lifted out and carried into a small side chapel, where they were greeted by the curé.

Marceaux smiled reassuringly at Kim. 'Have no fear, madame. We are in good company.' He turned to the priest. 'Father, we have brought you a guest to be sheltered, not a corpse to be buried.'

The priest did not seem unduly surprised. 'Then you are welcome, madame. And our mysterious guest. Perhaps we should release him?'

The bearers set the coffin down on a trestle and Marceaux produced a screwdriver and unscrewed the lid. When it was lifted away Kim caught her breath. Foxy lay exactly as he had lain before the coffin was closed, his hands folded on his chest and his one visible eye shut. For a terrible moment she thought he was dead, suffocated, in spite of all their precautions. She leaned over him and whispered, 'Foxy? It's all right, *chéri*. We're safe.' The one eye opened and focused on her face, then he smiled and stretched.

'Married, buried and resurrected — and it's not even the third day. Help me out. I think I've seized up completely.' Sitting up, he caught sight of the curé. 'Sorry, Father. I didn't mean to blaspheme.'

The priest stepped forward with a smile. 'I think, under the circumstances, He will forgive you. Here, take my hand.'

Between them they helped Foxy out of the coffin and he stretched and eased his stiffened limbs.

'What now, Father?' Kim asked.

'I'm sure you could both do with some refreshment. Our mayor, Louis Brun, also owns a restaurant. I'll take you there now.' He looked at Marceaux. 'We can arrange the burial later on.'

Minutes later they were being welcomed by a short, plump man into a small restaurant which was perched a little below the church. Kim introduced them both as Madeleine and Roland. It seemed that everyone in the village, from the mayor and the curé down, was a supporter of the Resistance and found nothing unusual in the arrival of two more refugees.

'Mind you,' Brun said with a wink, 'they normally arrive on the funicular from Grenoble, not in a hearse.'

'Where do they go then?' Foxy asked.

'There is a farmhouse — Ambel. It's pretty remote. We have set up a centre there for them, but now there are so many that there are other camps all over the Vercors. Mostly they are young men, *refractaires*, escaping the STO. That obviously does not apply to you. May I ask why you have come?'

Kim and Foxy exchanged glances — how much should they reveal, even in this apparently safe space?

'We are British agents,' Kim said. There was no point in concealing their true identities, she decided. Not if they were going to finish their assignment. 'Escaping from the Gestapo. Roland was caught in Lyon. You can see what they did to him.'

'At the hands of Klaus Barbie, I presume. The Butcher of Lyon,' Brun said grimly. 'You are not the first to come here to escape from him.'

'We urgently need to communicate with London,' Kim said. 'Is there someone with a radio set?'

Brun nodded. 'You need to talk to Eugene Chavant — he is the commander. But first you must meet our American and British guests. They have a radio operator with them.'

'American and British?' Foxy queried.

'They were dropped by parachute a couple of months ago — an American and an Englishman. I will speak to them on the telephone and tell them you are here.' He went into the rear of the shop and they heard him speaking on the phone.

'How does he know their nationalities?' Foxy asked. 'They should be undercover, with assumed names.'

Kim shrugged. 'Curiouser and curiouser. I suppose they must be genuine. We'll have to wait and see before we make a judgement.'

Brun came back smiling. 'One of them will come to pick you up very soon. Meanwhile, let me get you something to eat and drink.'

While Brun busied himself making omelettes, Foxy followed him into the kitchen and introduced himself as a fellow chef. Kim heard them exchanging jokes about the experience of running a restaurant and was glad to hear Foxy laughing.

They had just finished eating when there came the sound of a car drawing up outside. Going to the door, they were confronted by the sight of a large, bright-yellow limousine. Extricating himself from it was an immensely tall red-headed man in the uniform of the American Marines. He strode up to Foxy with his hand outstretched.

'Hi! I'm Peter Ortiz. Welcome to the Vercors. Hey! Looks like you've been picking a fight with the wrong guy.'

'You could put it like that,' Foxy agreed. 'I'm Roland.'

'And this young lady?' Ortiz turned to Kim.

There was something slightly condescending in his tone that put Kim's back up. You can call me Madeleine,' she responded coolly.

Ortiz looked from one to the other, eyebrows raised. 'OK,' he said slowly. 'You're French, right?'

'We're both British,' Kim said. 'We work for SOE. If you radio Baker Street, they will confirm our identities.'

'Hey,' he exclaimed. 'Don't get me wrong, I'm not doubting your story. But we weren't told to expect anyone to join us.'

'We haven't come to join you,' Kim told him. 'It's a long story but you can see Roland has been tortured and we need to get him back to the UK. Also, we have vital information for our bosses in Baker Street. So if you can give us access to a radio, we can try to arrange to be exfiltrated.'

Ortiz's manner changed. 'OK. Let's get you up to HQ. You need to meet Henry and Eugene and we'll introduce you to our radio operator. Jump in.'

Kim and Foxy exchanged a few brief words of thanks with Brun and climbed into the back of the limousine. Ortiz leaned round from the driver's seat and proffered a flask.

'Take a pull. It's good bourbon. And here,' waving a pack of American cigarettes, 'do either of you smoke?' When they both said no, he reached into the glove compartment and pulled out another package. 'Well, maybe you'd prefer some of this.

'Chocolate!' Kim exclaimed. 'I haven't seen a big bar like this since before the war.'

'Well, help yourselves,' the American said. 'Plenty more where that came from.'

The car ground upwards along a narrow, winding track through the forest, while Kim gorged herself on the chocolate and Foxy made the most of the contents of the hip flask.

'Where are we going?' Kim asked.

'Little place called St-Martin-en-Vercors. Chavant has set up his HQ there.'

'And Chavant is . . . ?' Foxy enquired.

'He's the head of the Combat Committee. Remarkable guy. Served in World War l, decorated several times. Mechanic by trade, and used to run a café in Grenoble. He was one the men who first came up with the idea of making Vercors a fortress for the *maquis*. He's got a real tight organization going here. He's got *Post* and *Telegraph* people working with us, the local gendarmes are on side, every point of access to the plateau is covered by sentinels linked by phone, or when that's not possible, by courier. There's a system of motorcycle couriers standing by. He's even got the director of the local hydroelectric plant on our side.'

The trees they were driving through changed from oaks and chestnuts to firs as they climbed higher and eventually came out onto a plateau above the tree-line. If Kim had seen signs of spring in the countryside below, there were none here, and snow still lay thick on the ground. St Martin was a tiny village set in a little valley. Ortiz drew up outside what was probably a farmhouse in more peaceful times, and shepherded them inside. In a long, low-ceilinged room, with bunches of herbs and strings of onions hanging from the beams, they were greeted by a middle-aged man in civilian clothes and a slightly younger, athletically built man in the uniform of a captain in the Royal Army Service Corps. The civilian was introduced as Eugene Chavant and the soldier as

Henry Thackthwaite. Having delivered them, Ortiz excused himself on the grounds that he had other duties to attend to.

When they were settled at the long kitchen table with glasses of rough red wine in front of them, Thackthwaite said, 'Right. Who are you and which outfit do you work for?'

Kim glanced at Foxy and he nodded. There was really no point in hiding their identities any longer. 'I'm Lt. Katharine Isobel Maxwell and this is Sergeant Renaud Leroux. We belong to F Section, under Maurice Buckmaster. If you can contact HQ, someone there will vouch for us. Our code names are Madeleine and Roland.'

'So what are you doing in France, and how come you are here?' the captain asked.

'I'm not at liberty to go into details,' Kim said. 'The basic fact is that we were both working as agents in the Lyon and Vienne area and we were both blown. I was lucky and escaped but . . .' She hesitated. The nickname Foxy seemed too informal for the occasion . . . 'Roland was handed over to Klaus Barbie, with the results you can see — or guess at. He needs to be airlifted home and I have vital information that must go directly to M.'

Thackthwaite asked a few more questions, then said, 'OK. I'll get our pianist to send an enquiry on his next sked. That will be this evening, and with any luck we should get a response by tomorrow morning. Until then, please consider yourselves our guests.' He turned to Foxy. 'Is there anything we can do for you? We have a doctor here, and a small hospital.'

Foxy shook his head. 'Thanks, but I had the dressing changed yesterday and it'll be fine till tomorrow. Now, do you mind if we ask a few questions?'

'Fire away.'

'You and your colleague here are both in uniform. You're not undercover. What's the idea behind that?'

Thackthwaite grinned. 'We are the first Allied liaison officers to appear in France since 1940. Our purpose is to show that the Allies are committed to supporting the

Resistance and to coordinate the *maquis* into a force that can hold down significant German forces in the event of an Allied invasion on the south coast.'

'Is that what is being proposed?' Kim asked.

'I'm not in a position to know for certain, but we are told that it is being considered as a real possibility.'

'And if it happens, will you be able to hold out here?' Foxy asked.

'If we get the heavy weapons I am asking for,' the captain said. 'There have been several arms drops in the last few months and we are well supplied in some ways, but we need mortars and heavy machine guns if we are to hold the access roads.'

Chavant spoke for the first time. 'This area is perfectly suited to a large drop of troops by parachute. With reinforcements like that, we could cut communications between the main German army and those defending the south. The Vercors could become a command centre for General de Gaulle.'

'Wow! That's ambitious!' Kim said.

'It's what we are working for,' Thackthwaite replied. 'What the top brass make of it, we have no way of knowing.'

'Meanwhile, we carry out a great deal of sabotage,' Chavant put in. 'Last month we sabotaged the transformers at the St Bel works in Grenoble and stole 2,700 kilos of explosives, and a week later we blew up twelve locomotives.'

'That's impressive!' Kim said.

'And what is the Huns reaction to all that?' Foxy asked. 'I can't believe they just let you sit up here and carry on like that without reprisals. Is this place really impregnable?'

'Far from it,' Thackthwaite said with a sigh. 'Since the Italians surrendered and the Huns moved into Grenoble things have changed considerably. The Eyeties never bothered us much but the Germans are a different matter. There was a terrible massacre of resistants in the city last November. They've made several incursions in recent months. Last January they forced their way up from St Eulalie onto the plateau and burned the village of Les Barraques, and a few days later they came up through the Gorges du Nan. The *maquis* strategy when under attack is to melt away into the forest, but that leaves the poor bloody civilians to take the rap. Six of them were burned alive in one building. The Huns are deploying their Alpine troops. High cliffs and deep snow are no deterrent to them.'

'So what's the answer?' Foxy enquired.

'Unless we get the weapons I keep asking for, and the reinforcements, we can't hold this place. It won't be a fortress — it will be a trap. My advice is that we should concentrate on mobile, guerrilla tactics. Unfortunately, the *maquis* are not the only elements to consider. There is also a large military contingent, troops who came up here when the Huns moved into Grenoble. The commander is Narcisse Geyer and he regards the *maquis* as an undisciplined rabble. His idea is that we should all sit here quietly, without provoking the Germans, until there is an Allied landing. Then join up with them.'

'The man is a coward!' Chavant said bitterly. 'He and his men would rather not fight at all if they can avoid it.'

Thackthwaite swallowed the last of his wine and looked at his watch. 'It's getting late and I guess you to could do with turning in. Eugene, where can they sleep?'

'There is enough room,' the Frenchman said, 'but I have to ask a delicate question . . .'

He looked enquiringly at Kim. For a moment she was at a loss to understand. Then she laughed. 'Thank you, monsieur. One room is all we require.'

'*Eh bien*,' he said with a smile. 'Follow me.'

* * *

Waking next morning, Kim felt for Foxy's hand. 'How are you, my love?'

He stretched gingerly and smiled. 'Improving. I had a good long rest lying in that coffin. Some of the aches and pains are easing.'

'That's good,' she said, but she could tell from his movements that he was making light of his injuries.

Down in the kitchen Thackthwaite greeted them with a smile. 'Good news. Baker Street confirms your identities but they want to know what the dickens you are both doing here.'

Kim asked, 'If I encode a message, and give you the necessary security checks, could your radio operator send it for me?'

'Yes, no problem. Let me have it as soon as it's ready.'

There was fresh bread for breakfast and real milk for the ersatz coffee. 'It may not look like it now,' Chavant told them, 'but in the summer this place is idyllic. There is good pasture for the cattle, and land for growing wheat and corn.'

As soon as she had eaten Kim settled down with a borrowed pad and pencil to encode her message. It was not an easy task. She knew she must keep it short. Even here, a radio operator could not risk a long transmission that would allow the enemy to pinpoint his position. Also, she was afraid of saying too much until she had definite proof. In the end she wrote: *Pauline not to be trusted. Roland injured. Urgent exfiltration requested.*

Ortiz reappeared just as she was finishing. 'Look, I've got a feeling we got off on the wrong foot yesterday, but when two strangers turn up out of the blue and want access to our radio set . . . well, it's no wonder I was a bit suspicious. Right? Now I've heard your story from Henry, all I can say is I take my hat off to you. It takes real guts to do what you do. Can we start again?'

Kim smiled. 'Of course. I don't blame you for wanting to check us out. But we weren't expecting an American officer in full uniform, either.'

'OK' he grinned back. Guess you two might like the guided tour. Care for a drive?'

Having handed her message to Thackthwaite, Kim pulled on a borrowed coat and joined Foxy in the yellow limousine.

'Can I ask you something?' Foxy said.

'Sure. Fire away.'

'How did you acquire this magnificent vehicle?'

Ortiz laughed. 'We were dropped outside a little village called Eymeux. It's about sixteen kilometres from

Pont-en-Royans. Our local guide turned up in this. He'd "liberated" it from the home of a known Nazi sympathizer.'

'And you have enough petrol — sorry, gas — to run it?' Kim queried. 'I thought it was almost unobtainable.'

'Oh, no problem there,' Ortiz said. 'These *maquisard* guys had done a good bit of liberating stuff on their own account. They've managed to seize more than one petrol tanker from depots in Grenoble.'

'That's amazing!' Kim said.

'What these guys are capable of never ceases to surprise me,' Ortiz agreed.

Over the course of the next few hours he gave them a comprehensive tour of the plateau. Although at first sight, under the covering of snow, it seemed desolate and uninhabited, there were little villages hidden away in small valleys where the local people had obviously led peaceful and prosperous lives until war disrupted them.

The narrow road climbed and twisted, clinging to the sides of deep canyons that bisected the plateau. Kim wondered who had made it.

'It's the logging company,' Ortiz told her. 'They own a large part of the forest around here.'

The biggest surprise came when they drove through a tunnel that connected the northern side of the plateau with the southern side. The difference in the vegetation and even the style of the houses was like moving from rural France to a Mediterranean island. Conifers were replaced by cypresses, and where the snow had melted, the hillsides were covered in the sort of scrub you might find in Provence.

During the course of the drive, Ortiz introduced them to several *maquis* camps, spread around the area.

'How many *maquis* are there up here?' Foxy asked.

'Several thousand.'

'It must be a nightmare keeping them all supplied,' Kim suggested.

'It's not easy,' the American agreed. 'Your people have dropped a lot of cash, but it's never enough. But these guys have learned to live off the land. Chavant got a local poacher to teach them how to snare rabbits and hares. And a while back, a group raided an army warehouse in Grenoble and took away hundreds of pairs of boots. In summer they hire themselves out to local farmers to help with hay making and ploughing. They get by.'

'And will there be enough of them to hold the plateau against the Boches if there is an Allied landing?'

'Only if there is a drop of a large number of airborne troops,' Ortiz said grimly.

As they drove into the village they passed a man in the uniform of a French officer, riding a magnificent bay stallion. He acknowledged them with a brief nod and rode on.

'Who was that?' Kim asked.

'That,' Ortiz answered with a wry smile, 'was Narcisse Geyer of the 11th Cuirassiers.'

'Haughty-looking bugger,' Foxy commented.

'Got it in one!' Ortiz replied.

'Edward mentioned him last night,' Kim recalled. 'I gather there is no love lost between him and Chavant.'

'None at all,' Ortiz agreed.

Back at the farmhouse in St Martin, Thackthwaite greeted them with a smile. 'We've had a response from London. They will arrange an exfiltration flight for you during the next moon period.'

'Which is when?' Kim asked. 'Must be a week or so.'

'Any time around 10 March,' he replied. 'We are expecting a big drop of arms and supplies at that time.'

'So it could be a soon as five days.' A huge sense of relief swept over her. She had been praying for this for days now but it had always seemed a distant prospect. Now at last she had a definite date to look forward to.

CHAPTER 18

With time to fill, Kim made a point of getting to know the *maquisardes*. There were women as well as men, who acted as couriers and also as spies who could go down to the towns around the plateau and return with vital information about German troop movements.

One of Chavant's most trusted couriers — Genevieve — was based in the town of Villard de Lens.

'You should come to Villard,' she said. 'Give yourselves a day out. Before the war it was a very popular ski resort, and the Hotel Splendide is the best on the plateau. It still manages to hang on to a hint of its former glory. You can get quite a decent meal there.'

'How would we get there?' Kim asked. 'I can't expect Peter Ortiz to drive us around all the time.'

'On the bus,' was the unexpected reply. 'There's a bus goes every morning from St Martin to Grenoble.'

'Even now?' Kim asked.

'Why not? For the local people life has to carry on as close to normal as possible. Some of them work in Grenoble. Will you come?'

'I'll have to talk to my . . . my partner,' Kim said. 'But it would make a change from hanging around here.'

Foxy's attitude was the same. 'Let's go. I'm tired of sitting around waiting for something to happen.'

So early the next morning they boarded the bus along with a crowd of local people — men in working clothes, women carrying baskets, some with small children on their laps. It had snowed again and the sides of the narrow road were banked up with drifts. The route took them down through what they had learned to call the Gorges de la Bourne, one of the many canyons carved out millennia ago by a river, and the road turned and twisted, clinging to its sides. For short time Kim forgot the war and marvelled at the spectacular scenery.

'Do you ski?' she asked Foxy, amazed that she had never thought to put the question before.

'I used to, back in the States,' he replied. 'Don't know if I'll ever be able to try it again.'

She squeezed his hand. 'Of course you will. If Nelson could command a ship in battle with one eye, I'm sure he could have skied if given the opportunity.'

He returned the squeeze. 'Don't know how he'd have managed with only one arm, though. At least I've still got two.'

'One day, we'll come back here and ski,' she said. 'I bet there are some terrific runs.'

As if to jolt them back into the present, the bus rounded a bend and skidded to a stop. Peering ahead, Kim saw with a shock that they were nose to nose with the first vehicle in a column of German personnel carriers.

'Dear God!' she murmured. 'But there haven't been any warning.'

'Sit tight,' Foxy said. 'Remember, we're just innocent civilians going to visit a friend.'

'But they need to know, back at St Martin,' she whispered.

'No way we can do anything about that right now,' he returned.

An officer had jumped out of the leading vehicle and was waving his arms at the bus driver. 'Move! Get out of the way!'

'Easier said than done,' Foxy muttered.

The driver reversed and backed the bus into the bank of snow at the side of the road. The wheels spun on the icy surface and it was clear that it was impossible to move further.

'Out! Out!' the officer shouted. 'Everyone off the bus.'

Unwillingly, the passengers descended, pulling their coats closer around them and delving into pockets and bags for gloves and scarves. The German was giving orders to some of the men in the first truck and they climbed out, bringing spades and shovels.

'You men,' the German gestured at the passengers. 'Clear the road. Get digging.'

One of the soldiers thrust a spade into Foxy's hands. Kim was about to protest but he gave her a warning look and she was suddenly gripped by a cold fear. Was it possible that Barbie's search for his escaped prisoner had been pursued even to here? She remembered the posters, the sketch of a man with one eye covered. If this German officer looked closely at Foxy, would he recognize him as a wanted man? Foxy had turned his back and was digging along with half a dozen other men, clearing the snow along the edge of the road. It must have been costing him, still recovering from his injuries, but he kept his head down and dug with the rest of them.

Eventually they had widened the road sufficiently to allow the convoy to pass, and the spades were handed back. But they were not out of danger yet.

'Papers!' the officer demanded.

Kim still had the false papers the mayor of St-Siméon had given her, and Foxy had his. She frantically ran over in her head the story they had prepared about his release from prison camp and her job as secretary to the countess. It had been a sketchy tale when they concocted it and now she had half-forgotten it. She prayed that neither of them would be required to elaborate on it.

It was only the men who had to show their papers. Kim held her breath as the officer took Foxy's and scrutinized them, looking from the photograph to his face and back again. After a long moment he returned them and moved on to the next man. For a moment, she caught Foxy's eye and they exchanged a look of mutual relief. After that, all the men had to turn out their pockets and submit to being searched, but it was only cursory. A check to see if they were carrying weapons, Kim surmised. At last they were ordered back onto the bus. Kim slipped her hand into Foxy's.

'Are you all right?'

'I'll live,' he returned, but his breathing was uneven and she could feel an electric tremor running from his hand to hers.

'*Courage, mon brave!*' she whispered.

'Main thing is,' he whispered back, 'all this delay has given them a chance to prepare back at St Martin.'

'If they even know what's coming,' she murmured. 'We have to find a way to warn them.'

'I don't see what we can do till we get to Villard,' he said.

'It's another half hour to Villard,' Kim said. 'By that time the Huns will be in St Martin. We must get off at the first opportunity and hope to find someone with a telephone.'

They left the bus at the end of the gorge, where the road turned north for Villard. There was a small café there but the owner shook his head regretfully when asked if he had a telephone. They were standing in the doorway, trying to think of some way to warn their friends, when a small car came at a reckless speed down the road from the direction of Villard. Kim jumped out, waving her arms to stop it and it drew up with a squeal of brakes.

'Madeleine! What are you doing here? I thought you were on your way to Villard.' The driver, to Kim's amazement, was Genevieve. 'Did you meet a German convoy on the road? I've been told one passed through Villard at the crack of dawn, before anyone was awake.'

'They are on their way up to St Martin right now,' Kim said urgently. 'We have to warn them!'

'It's no good,' Genevieve said. 'There's no chance we could get there before them.'

Foxy leaned into the car. 'Perhaps there is, if you know a way round to bypass them. We were on the bus and met them head on. It took a good twenty minutes to dig away enough snow so they could get past. And in these conditions, they can't move very fast. Is there no other way?'

'Jump in!' Genevieve said. 'There's a logging track that goes over the hill and meets the main road nearer to the turn off for St Julien. If we can get across, we might still beat them.'

The narrow track climbed steeply towards the ridge that separated the two valleys. The encircling trees had provided some shelter from the recent snowfall, so it was passable — just — but they were glad that the car was fitted with snow chains. At each hairpin bend Kim stared ahead, hoping to catch a glimpse of the valley, but it was not until they crested the ridge that they were able to see down to the road leading to St Martin.

'There!' Foxy exclaimed. 'They are just coming out at the head of the gorge. If we can get down there quickly, we might beat them.'

Genevieve took the track down at hair-raising speed, the car skidding and sliding until Kim felt certain it must overturn. They reached the road barely fifty yards ahead of the leading vehicle in the convoy, and Genevieve swung the car onto the road.

'We've done it!' Foxy whooped.

But even as he spoke, they heard the crack of rifle fire and the car shuddered and swerved. Peering back, Kim saw the officer in the leading jeep on his feet, aiming his rifle at them. There was another crack. They all heard the sound as one of the tyres blew out and the car skidded off the road, ploughing into a snowdrift. Foxy managed to force a door open and the three of them scrambled out and took shelter behind it. Kim automatically felt for her pistol, but of course none of them was armed. It was suicidal to carry a weapon where there was a chance of being searched. They couldn't run through the deep snow, and trying to escape by the road would make them easy targets. She ground her teeth and wondered if her false identity would stand up to the interrogation she knew must follow.

Genevieve peeped over the door and gasped. 'They're turning off! They aren't heading for St Martin.'

Kim got cautiously to her knees and peered back along the road. It was true, the leading vehicle had turned down a side road and the convoy was following.

'Where does that go?' Foxy asked.

'To St Julien — but I can't think why they would be going there,' was the reply.

Kim got somewhat shakily to her feet. 'Well, they aren't aiming for St Martin, which is a comfort, but we need to get there as soon as we can. They may be coming back.'

Foxy was inspecting the car. 'Do you have a spare wheel?'

'Yes, of course.'

'Well, if we can push the car out of this snowdrift and get the wheel on, we might yet make St Martin in time.'

It took all their combined strength to get the car back on the road. Kim was acutely aware of the pain Foxy must be in, but he never faltered or complained. Genevieve produced the spare wheel and ten minutes later they were on their way. As they screeched to a stop outside the farmhouse, Edward Thackthwaite came to the door.

'*Mon dieu*! What has happened to you?' he asked, looking at the bullet holes in the car.

'We met . . .' Kim began, but she was interrupted by the sound of sustained gunfire and the explosions of grenades from somewhere down in the valley.

'What . . . ?' Thackthwaite began.

'There's a German convoy at St Julien,' Kim told him. 'We met them on the way. We were trying to get here to warn you. Genevieve was fantastic, she got us over the ridge, but they shot us up and blew the tyre out.'

'What is down there?' Foxy asked.

'La Matrassiere. It's the HQ of the military wing. Geyer is down there.'

'Can we do anything to help?'

'How many of them are there?' Thackthwaite asked.

'I counted ten trucks,' Kim said. 'All packed with men.'

Thackthwaite shook his head. 'We can't get a big enough force together in time to face up to that sort of strength. But that's not the way we operate anyway. Geyer's men will have simply headed into the forest. The Boches may catch up with some of them but they will never find them all. Going by previous incursions like this, they won't stay long. They will take any equipment that's been left behind, set fire to the buildings and then they'll bugger off back to Grenoble. But we must be prepared in case they decide to come on here.'

Chavant had joined them. 'What I want to know is how in the name of God were they able to drive up from Grenoble and through Villard without anyone hearing them.'

'They came before dawn,' Genevieve said. 'Everyone was asleep. I woke up just in time to see the last truck disappearing but all I could do was follow them. The road is too narrow to overtake.'

'But what about the sentries?' Chavant demanded. 'Someone must have been asleep on the job.' He turned to Genevieve. 'We have to thank you for your wonderful effort.'

'*Pas de quoi*,' the young woman murmured.

There was something in her voice that made Kim look at her sharply and she caught her breath as she saw that the sleeve of Genevieve's coat was soaked with blood.

'*Mon dieu*! You're wounded. Why didn't you say anything?'

'It's nothing. Just a graze,' Genevieve said, but her voice betrayed her.

'Take her to the hospital,' Thackthwaite ordered. 'I must help Eugene with the preparations.'

Kim obeyed. The *maquis* had set up a well-equipped hospital, run by a local doctor who was a supporter. His examination showed that a bullet had ripped through her heavy coat and opened a gash in her upper arm that required stitches. Leaving her in his care, Kim went to find Foxy and see what help was needed in preparing the defence. A group of men had already been sent half a mile down the road, to where a sharp bend provided some cover. They were armed with grenades to slow the convoy down and to provide an early warning of its approach. Another, larger group was heading on foot across the hills to set up an ambush on the road up to Villard. The remaining men were hurrying around the camp, collecting vital equipment and supplies.

'There's no intention of making a stand,' Thackthwaite said. 'As soon as we hear the grenades going off, everyone will head for the woods. The Boches may set fire to the farmhouse but at least they won't get any of the weapons or signalling equipment.'

There followed a tense hour or two, until a spy sent to watch the road further down came back to report that the convoy was heading back for the gorge.

'Well, they will get a nasty shock on the way home,' Chavant said with relish.

The camp was beginning to return to normal when Narcisse Geyer rode in and dismounted at the door of the farmhouse. He looked exhausted, no longer the haughty officer they had seen before.

'What happened?' Chavant asked. 'We heard gunfire.'

'We were attacked,' was the terse reply.

'What was the result?'

Geyer sat down and took a mouthful of the brandy Thackthwaite set in front of him.

'They came across the fields from St Julien, on skis. We were in the process of setting up a new HQ at the farm belonging to the Peyronnet family in La Matrassiere. There were two officers and three men there. They didn't stand a chance. Then they set fire to the farm.' Geyer's hand shook as he took another gulp of brandy. 'After that they came on to my HQ at Les Combes. We'd heard the shooting so we had a few minutes warning. Most of us were able to reach the forest, carrying everything we could grab hold of, but one of my men is missing. The Boches set fire to Les Combes and then headed back the way they had come. But not before they took two of our radio sets, one in contact with Algiers and one with London, plus the codes.'

'Well, they won't get back unscathed,' Chavant said. 'We've set an ambush on the Villard road.'

It was almost dark when the men of the ambush detail returned.

'Did you get them?' Chavant asked.

The leader shook his head gloomily. 'We never saw them. When we realized they weren't going to show up, we went down the way they should have come. We met a shepherd out looking for a lost sheep and he told us he'd seen them. Instead of taking the road to Villard, they turned left at the Pont de la Goule Noire and went down to Pont-en-Royans.'

Chavant gave vent to a few choice expletives. Then he patted the man on the arm. 'Not your fault, *mon brave*. The bastards are just too cunning. We must learn from this so they won't get away with it again.'

The mood at dinner that night was sombre.

Spirits were raised next day by a message from London. There was to be a drop of supplies on the night of the full moon, 10 March, two days away.

'Was there any mention of an exfiltration flight as well,' Kim asked eagerly.

'I'm afraid not,' Thackthwaite said. 'But you had better be ready to leave, just in case.'

The drop zone was a couple of kilometres west of the village. Kim and Foxy went along with the rest, in the hope that the message had merely neglected to mention that there would be a Lysander landing to take them back home. Kim was more anxious than ever to get back to England. The longer they had to wait, the more time Pauline — or whatever her real name was — would have to act on her orders, whatever they might be. And more immediate than that, Kim was worried about Foxy. The exertions of a few days ago had opened up some of his wounds and she knew he was in constant pain.

It was a freezing night. In the moonlight the snow-covered peaks glimmered with breathtaking beauty, but Kim was in no mood to appreciate them. She had waited so many times on different fields in other parts of France, listening out for the sound of an approaching aircraft, but the wait never got easier. The sound, when it came, was louder and deeper than she expected. Signal lights flashed from ground to air and back again, then the fires were lit and five Stirling bombers flew overhead.

Parachutes blossomed like exotic flowers and men ran in all directions to catch hold of them and detach their precious cargo. The sound of the bombers had faded into the distance but still she stood, straining her ears in the hope of hearing the familiar note of an approaching Lysander. The silence remained unbroken except for the muffled voices of men as they loaded the containers onto handcarts to bring them back to the village.

The haul was stowed away in a deep cave where an enemy incursion was unlikely to find them. Chavant and his officers were delighted. It was the biggest drop of weapons they had ever received. But Thackthwaite was unsatisfied. There had been none of the heavy weapons he felt were essential for the defence of the plateau.

Kim and Foxy tried to hide their own disappointment. The 'moon period' lasted only a few days. Soon there wouldn't be enough light for aircraft to find their target.

Two days passed, then Thackthwaite came quickly into the farmhouse kitchen where they were having breakfast.

'Good news! There is going to be second drop and this time we've been told you two should stand by to be airlifted out.'

Kim caught her breath. 'When?'

'Tomorrow — 16 March.'

By morning Kim and Foxy had said goodbye to the friends they had made and packed their few possessions ready to leave, but during the day there was a heavy fall of snow and the frost deepened, making all movement around the plateau difficult. Nevertheless, the fires were set that evening and the *maquis* gathered in readiness. Kim and Foxy said

159

goodbye to Eugene Chavant and Peter Ortiz and went with Thackthwaite to join the reception party.

Kim looked at the sky. The clouds had cleared and the moonlight almost eclipsed the stars. In many ways it was a perfect night for flying, but there was no telling how deep the snow was on what would be the landing strip. It was one thing for a bomber to overfly the target and drop parachutes, something quite different for a light aircraft to land and take off. Chavant had sent men to clear the snow as far as possible and there was now a narrow strip of flat ground, banked all round by large drifts. The surface that remained, however, was more like an ice rink than a landing ground. Kim was very much afraid that the pilot of the Lizzie would decide that it was too dangerous to attempt a landing.

At the appointed hour, the drone of the Stirlings approached and soon the parachutes were falling thickly all round. Kim counted sixteen of them. As the sound of the bombers faded, a terrible silence ensued. Even the voices of the men collecting the containers seemed to be muffled by the snow. Kim was about to turn away when Foxy said, 'Listen!' Faint at first, then growing louder, they heard the unmistakable note of a Lysander's engine.

Thackthwaite produced a high-powered torch and began to flash a Morse code recognition signal. The plane came into sight, flying so low it seemed almost to skim the tops of the surrounding hills, and an answering light winked from the cockpit. Kim held her breath. Would the pilot risk landing in those conditions?

The plane overflew, then pulled up and banked away.

'He's not even going to try it?' Kim could not keep the tears out of her voice.

'Wait,' said Foxy.

The engine note changed as the plane turned again and came in for a second run. The wheels touched down on the icy ground and the plane skittered sideways, then corrected itself and ran on to the far end of the cleared strip. Men were ready there to help it turn. It taxied slowly back to where they waited and turned again, engine running. Kim and Foxy were already almost beside it.

The cockpit cover slid back and a young face framed by a flying helmet looked out at them.

'Not sure if this thing will get off the ground with the extra weight of two of you, but hop in and we'll give it a go.'

Kim looked at Foxy. He was already shaking hands with Thackthwaite, but he turned at the steps leading to the rear cockpit.

'Come on! What are you waiting for?'

'No,' she said, stepping back, 'you go! I'll catch the next one,' as if Lysanders were a regular bus service.

He reached for her. 'Either we both go, or neither of us. It's not negotiable.'

'Get on with it!' the pilot shouted. 'Before the Huns track us and shoot us down.'

Kim turned to Thackthwaite and reached up to kiss his cheek. '*Merci, mon brave — et merde alors!*'

'*A toi aussi!*' he replied. 'And for God's sake, tell them in London we can't hold this place without reinforcements.'

Foxy was already in the cockpit. Kim squeezed in beside him and closed the cockpit cover. It was a squeeze in a space intended for one man, but they managed to fit themselves in and close the cover. Men were hanging onto the wings, waiting for the signal. The engine revved and the plane trembled like a greyhound on a leash. Then the men jumped aside and the little plane shot forward, gathering speed. It was impossible to see ahead from her seat, but Kim could picture the plane hurtling down the landing strip, heading for the banked-up snow at the far end.

Would the wheels unstick before they crashed into it? There was a lurch and the angle changed as the nose lifted, the engine straining at full throttle. There was a jolt as the wheels brushed the top of the snowbank, then suddenly they were free and clear, rising into the moonlit sky.

Kim huddled closer to Foxy. 'We're going home, my love.'

He hugged her. 'I do believe we really are.'

CHAPTER 19

The plane had to land once to refuel on the way home, so by the time they approached Tempsford airfield the sun was up. Looking down as they came into land, Kim was struck, as she so often was when she returned to England, by how verdant the countryside looked. After the snow and ice of the Vercors it was a comforting sight.

Slightly less comforting, as she and Foxy extricated themselves from the cramped cockpit, was the sight of an ambulance drawn up beside the official car that waited for them. Of course, she remembered, she had said in her signal that Foxy was wounded. She should be glad that he would soon be getting the care he needed, but she had not anticipated being separated from him so quickly, before they had time to make their reports to their senior officers.

'I don't need a bloody ambulance,' Foxy spat when he saw it. 'I'm not a bloody invalid!'

The ambulance was crewed by two women in FANY uniform, while a third waited by the door to the car.

'Sorry, sir,' the first of the three said in response to Foxy's outburst. 'We've got orders to take you to Millbank, to the Queen Alexandra. I expect it's just for a check-up.'

Kim touched Foxy's arm. 'Go with them, *chéri*. You know it's the sensible thing. I'll come and visit as soon as I can.'

Still protesting, but less volubly, Foxy was led away and Kim turned to the FANY driver by the car. 'Are you here for me?'

'Yes, ma'am.'

Ignoring the open rear door, Kim slipped into the front passenger seat. 'OK. Where are we going?'

'I've been given an address in London, ma'am. Kensington.'

'Oh, right.' Kim sat back as the car swung out of the gates. She had half expected to be taken to one of the safe houses the organization kept in and around London, but the Kensington address she was delivered to was an even more tightly guarded secret. It was a place known only to M., the head of SOE, and was the place where she and Foxy had stayed during the previous operation they had conducted under M.'s direction. This was a relief. It meant that her message had got to him and he had seen the seriousness of the situation. So, she would not have to explain everything to Maurice Buckmaster, the head of F section, before being passed on to M.

The hall porter at the block of flats was expecting her and handed her a key to the front door. She let herself in with a pang of nostalgia. This was the place where she and Foxy had first made love, and where, between them, they had brought about a successful conclusion to what had been called Operation Lightning Bolt. Now, it seemed, they were to be embroiled in another dangerous scheme devised, she suspected, by the same man who had been her nemesis last time — the man she had last seen boarding a plane at a secret airfield.

On the table in the hallway she found a note in M.'s handwriting. *Make yourself at home. I shall be with you at 1800 hours.*

In the kitchen there was a fresh loaf and a small pack of real butter, and the fridge was stocked with milk, eggs and cheese — the equivalent of a week's ration. It was a long time since her last, hurried meal at St Martin. She ate a boiled egg with the bread and butter and then made her way into the bedroom. The memory of her first night with Foxy was so strong it brought tears to her eyes, but she had not slept for over twenty-four hours, and as soon as she slipped under the covers, she fell asleep.

She woke abruptly with a twinge of panic. M. was coming at six o'clock. What time was it? To her relief her watch showed her it was not quite five.

She had a bath and wondered what to wear. She didn't want to dress in the clothes she had worn on the journey again: a pair of slacks and a sweater loaned to her by one of the *maquis* women, grubby and sweat-stained from constant wear. She opened the wardrobe. To her amazement, inside was the dress she had been wearing the last time she stayed in the flat. She had left it in favour of the French-made garments she was given before her last mission. There was even some of her underwear in a drawer.

Clean and dressed, she felt ready for her forthcoming meeting with M. It wasn't quite six, so she made herself a cup of tea and a piece of toast and took them into the living room.

Whoever had been tasked with stocking the fridge for her arrival had also thought to leave a selection of newspapers with the previous day's date. Kim picked one up and leafed through it. The headlines were mainly concerned with the battle raging around Monte Casino. Normally she would have read avidly, but today she found it impossible to concentrate.

She turned the pages and found herself looking at a photograph on one of the 'society' pages. The caption read, *The Hon. Davina Westerham greets guests at the ball given by her father, Lord Westerham, to celebrate her engagement to Squadron Leader Paul Darnley*.

But it was the face of the attractive young woman in the foreground that sent a shock wave through her.

She was still staring at it when she heard the sound of a key in the lock. She jumped to her feet as a dapper figure in the uniform of a brigadier in the 24th Guards Brigade entered the room.

'Well, Kim. Here we are again.' The voice with its Scottish lilt was warm, but the piercing eyes under the heavy brows searched her face as he held out his hand.

Kim suppressed the instinctive reflex to come to attention in the presence of a superior officer and shook the hand.

'Sir . . .'

He overrode her eagerness. 'How are you? I've just had a report from the surgeon at the Queen Alexandra. When he told me what our poor friend Foxy had suffered, it made my blood boil. But you are uninjured, yes?'

'I'm fine, sir, thank you, but . . .'

'Let's sit down, shall we? I believe there is still a bottle of Black Label in that cupboard. Can you find a couple of glasses?'

'Sir, I've got to ask you.' Kim ignored the request and picked up the paper. 'What is this woman doing in London? Why is she not in the cooler, up in the Highlands?'

He studied the picture for a moment. 'Ah, yes. Davina . . .'

'That's *her*. That is Pauline! I sent you a warning.'

'Yes. I remember.'

'So why is she on the loose, free to host balls and God knows what?' In her anxiety Kim forgot the deference due to his rank.

He handed the paper back to her and said mildly, 'Why don't you find those glasses and I'll explain.'

When they were both seated with a measure of whisky, he said, 'There's a very good reason that young woman is "on the loose" as you put it: she's no longer a member of the service. She was demobbed on health grounds soon after she came back to England.'

'On health grounds?'

'She was seen by a psychiatrist who diagnosed a complete nervous breakdown.'

'Nervous breakdown!' Kim snorted.

'I assumed you were aware of her mental state. That was why you had asked for her urgent exfiltration, isn't it?'

'It's all a charade. She's extremely dangerous. I warned you in my message.'

'You said "not to be trusted". I thought that was because of her fragile condition.'

'She's not "fragile",' Kim said, 'she's just a damn good actress. She's a double agent, and I'm pretty sure she killed Bernard.'

'Good God!' M. rarely looked disconcerted, but he did now. 'Tell me the whole thing.'

Kim poured out the story of how she came to suspect Pauline. 'It was when I found she was hiding Bernard's camera, that I knew for certain,' she finished. 'How else could she have got hold of it?'

M. listened with a frown. 'You've convinced me. But the evidence is circumstantial. I would need better proof before I could take any action.'

'But people have been interned on weaker grounds for suspicion, surely?' Kim said.

'Maybe. But this young woman has friends in high places. Her father was a close confidant of the ex-king and still has connections at court. Pressure was brought to bear on me to allow the psychiatric assessment at all. Now that she is no longer a serving officer, I no longer have any authority over her.'

'But . . .' Kim began, and was interrupted by the sound of the front door opening. There was a murmur of voices, and then the sitting room door opened and in walked Foxy. He was still wearing the camouflage jacket and trousers loaned to him by one of Chavant's men, but his missing eye was now covered by a neat black patch.

M. jumped to his feet. 'Good God, man! Why are you not in the hospital?'

Foxy tried to look apologetic. 'Sorry, sir, but there really wasn't any point in me occupying a bed that might be needed for someone really sick. They've patched me up, if you'll forgive the pun,' he indicated his eye, 'and there's really nothing they can do about broken ribs, except recommend rest. I thought you might have sent Kim here, so I took a chance. Luckily the hall porter recognized me from last year and brought me up.'

Kim was hovering. She wanted to run and put her arms round him but the presence of M. inhibited her.

After a brief pause, M. said, 'Well, you are here now, so you had better sit down. Kim, can you fetch another glass?'

When he was seated with a glass in his hand, Foxy looked at Kim. 'Have you told him about Kline?'

'Kline?' M. said. 'I was coming to that. I got your message. What makes you think he's back in England?'

Kim briefed him about her investigations into the private airfield and how she had seen Kline board a flight.

'But there's more,' she added. 'Foxy, tell M. what you overheard.'

'He came to the restaurant with that swine, Barbie. From what I could hear, they were planning some big operation.'

'And that was before Kim saw him take off in a plane with fake RAF markings?'

'The night before.'

'And did this big operation have a name?'

'Operation Enthaupten.'

'Enthaupten? Beheading?'

'Yes.'

M. was silent for a moment. 'That is very worrying indeed.'

'Do you think they are planning to have another attempt on the Prime Minister?' Kim asked.

'I certainly suspect that they are hoping to do something to destabilize the country, and I guess they are getting increasingly desperate. They must be aware that it is only a matter of months, perhaps weeks, before the Allies open a Second Front with a landing in occupied Europe. They will need to act fast.'

'Is there going to be a landing soon?' Kim asked.

M. raised an eyebrow. 'I'm not privy to that sort of knowledge, and even if I was, I couldn't tell you. But it must come soon. Everyone knows that.'

'I'm convinced Pauline is in some way involved in whatever is being planned,' Kim said.

'Oh yes. Pauline? What's happened to her?' Foxy asked.

Kim showed him the picture in the paper and M. explained again how she had gained her freedom.

'I was convinced at the time that she really was in a bad state and that the pressure put on me was simply by people worried about her welfare,' he said. 'It's obvious now that we need to keep a very close eye on her.' He refilled their glasses. 'But right now I want to hear your reports. How did you end up in Barbie's clutches, Foxy. And how did you get free again?'

Foxy began to recount the circumstances of his arrest.

'What did you think you were doing, smuggling Jews out of the city?' M. interrupted. 'That was never part of your brief.'

'I know that,' Foxy said, 'but you need to understand — our government needs to understand — that Jews are being arrested all over France, not just in Lyon. They are put on trains and no one knows where they are sent, but they never come back.'

'I've heard the rumours,' M. said heavily, 'but that is not something we should be getting involved with. It is for others much higher up the chain of authority to deal with.'

'With respect, sir,' Foxy persisted, 'I believe we should. These people need our help.'

'And the best way to help them is to drive the Nazis out of their country,' M said. 'Which is what you are supposed to be helping to do. Let's get back to the issue at hand. You were caught. Then what?'

Foxy glossed over the details of his treatment at Barbie's hands, only emphasising that it seemed the Nazi had no idea that he was with SOE.

'So how did you get away?' M. asked.

'That's where Kim comes in,' Foxy replied.

Kim then related the story of her own arrest, her release and the fake wedding which had set Foxy free. As M. listened, the corners of his lips twitched, then spread into a broad grin.

'Well, that's about the cheekiest and riskiest plan I've ever heard of, but it worked. Congratulations. Now, there's just one more point to clear up. You were picked up from the Vercors plateau. How did you manage to end up there?'

They explained between them what had led them to travel to the Vercors and when they had finished, Kim added, 'That reminds me, sir. Thackthwaite asked me to give you a message. He says that in the event of an Allied landing in the south of France, there would be no way they could hold the plateau without significant reinforcements and heavy weapons.'

M. frowned. 'I made it clear to De Gaulle and his lot when this whole project was mooted that I cannot guarantee any such things. I was given to understand that the Vercors was impregnable, and what he calls his Secret Army could not only hold out but provide considerable assistance in cutting German lines of communication.'

Foxy and Kim exchanged glances. 'It's not impregnable,' Foxy said heavily. 'We've seen that. Without reinforcements, it's not a fortress, it's a trap.'

'Well, that is not part of your remit,' M. said firmly. 'So I don't expect either of you to involve yourselves. We've got serious matters of our own to concentrate on.' He looked at his watch. 'Have either of you eaten?'

They both shook their heads. 'Not since lunch,' Kim said.

'Right. I don't want you out in the streets. Ring this number. It's the chef at the Kensington Palace Hotel. Tell him to send up the best dinner he can conjure up and that the order comes from the brigadier. We have an arrangement, so he won't question it.'

He got up. 'I want you both to rest up here until further orders. I'll get someone to bring you fresh supplies and I'll come round at about six o'clock tomorrow. We'll talk further then.'

He left and at last Kim felt free to put her arms round Foxy. 'You! You're incorrigible! You should have stayed in the hospital.'

'But aren't you glad I didn't?' he asked, and kissed her.

Half an hour later they sat down to the best meal they had eaten for months and then they went to bed. Foxy's broken ribs made sex difficult, but they found ways round the problem and fell asleep in each other's arms.

* * *

When M. arrived the following evening, they saw from his expression that he had something very serious on his mind. Instead of settling in an armchair with his habitual glass of whisky, he moved to the table.

'Sit down, both of you. We need to talk.'

They sat as commanded and he looked from one to the other. 'You have both signed the Official Secrets Act and I know you understand the need to abide by it. But what I am about to reveal to you requires your utmost discretion. You have both proved yourselves reliable and resourceful. You will need those attributes if we are going to foil what I believe is the most damaging plot our enemies have yet devised.'

Kim caught Foxy's eye and saw that he was experiencing the same combination of excitement tinged with fear as she was feeling.

'Go on, sir,' Foxy said.

'Last night, after I left you, a terrible possibility struck me. I was at first unable to work out what part Pauline, or Davina to give her her proper name, could possibly play in any plot to destabilize the country. Then it struck me. She has got herself engaged to Squadron Leader Darnley. You might have noticed that he does not appear in the photograph beside her. The reason for that is that he suffered terrible burns to his face when his Spitfire was shot down in '43. Dr McIndoe has done wonders for these boys with his plastic surgery, but Darnley is still terribly disfigured and burns to his hands make it impossible for him to fly again. I found myself wondering why a girl like Davina would be prepared to marry a man in that condition. Don't get me wrong, I know there are women who are sufficiently selfless and compassionate to do that, but Davina doesn't strike me as that type.'

'Nor me!' Kim murmured.

'Then another consideration struck me,' M. went on. 'Darnley is as well connected as his fiancée. His father was an equerry to the late King George V. So when he was told he would be restricted to ground duties only, because of his hands, someone must have pulled a few strings and got Darnley appointed as an aide-de-camp to the present king.'

'Oh God!' Kim broke in, in spite of herself. 'So she, Pauline or Davina, now has access to the royal court.'

'Precisely.'

'*Enthaupten*!' Foxy breathed. 'Beheading. Not the P.M. The King!'

'That is exactly my thought,' M. confirmed. 'In addition, we have the fact that her father was an intimate of the current Duke of Windsor.'

'Are you saying it's the same plot as last time,' Kim said. 'They still want to put Edward back on the throne.'

'That is the only conclusion that makes sense,' M. agreed.

'I can't believe it!' she said. 'Are these people completely obsessed?'

'So it would seem,' M responded. 'But there is an added complication that only a very few people will be aware of. His Majesty is currently working for us.'

'For SOE?' Kim said incredulously.

M. permitted himself a small smile. 'Perhaps I should say *with* us. The King has been aware of our operations for some months. He spent four days at Massingham, our HQ in Algeria. Since then he and the Queen have visited Tempsford and also Gaynes Hall — both locations you two will be familiar with. I'm told that they were shown some of our useful gadgets. You know the sort of thing. Exploding wine bottles or rocks, etc. I'm told Her Majesty was particularly amused by the exploding horse dung.'

Kim and Foxy exchanged looks, in equal measure amused and incredulous.

'More to the present point,' M. continued, 'and this is where your vow of secrecy becomes paramount, you will be aware, like everyone else, that we, together with our American allies, are planning to open a Second Front by landing troops in occupied Europe. As I told you, I am not privy to the exact date, but that is not important. The critical point is not when but where. At what point on the coast will the landing take place? Around Calais or further south? Perhaps a thrust from North Africa towards the Riviera, or even north into occupied Norway. It is vital that the enemy are kept guessing about that so that they cannot mass their troops to repel the invasion.'

Foxy nodded. 'I can see that.'

'A great deal of time and ingenuity has gone into deceiving them about the location,' M went on. 'As a part of that, a week or so ago, two gentlemen from MI5 spoke with Mr Lascelles, the King's private secretary, and put it to him that His Majesty could play a big part in this deception.

'The plan is that he should visit his troops in various different parts of the country, but all at locations from which it is possible that the assault could be launched, depending on the target. For example, he has recently inspected troops in the south-east, the obvious area for them to be concentrated if the invasion was planned to take place in the Calais region.'

Kim caught Foxy's eye and he nodded to show he was as impressed as she was by the planned deception.

'We know that the Germans have their spies here, but what the Huns don't realize is that we have turned many of them, and they now work for us. They will report the King's visit to their controllers, who will pass it on to the High Command, who will draw the obvious conclusion. But then, if His Majesty makes an inspection elsewhere, the Hun may decide that the real invasion will come from there, aimed at a different part of the coast. We are calling it Operation Fortitude.'

'It's brilliant!' Kim said.

'But doesn't this make him more vulnerable, if he's travelling around the country?' Foxy suggested.

'That is exactly my point,' M. agreed. 'It means that our job is even more vital.'

'Where does Pauline/Davina come into this?' Kim wondered.

'The King's movements are, of course, kept a closely guarded secret,' M. said. 'Only at the last minute are the press informed, so that the visit can be reported for the benefit of our German spies. But Squadron Leader Darnley is bound to know in advance, and perhaps he has been persuaded that his obligation to be discreet does not extend to his fiancée. At the very least he will probably tell her he is going to be away for a few days.'

'She isn't working alone, of course.' Kim said. 'Have you had any luck tracking down Kline?'

M. shook his head. 'Not so far. The trouble is, by the time you were able to get a message to me, he had already been in the country for some days.'

Kim sighed and shook her head. 'If only I'd been able to get that signal off before the Boches grabbed me.'

'Not your fault,' M. said. 'We must be thankful that you were able to send it at all. However,' his face brightened, 'we have one asset of whom you are not aware, and which you will find surprising.'

'Go on?' Foxy prompted.

'You will not have forgotten Justin Verney?'

'The man who owned the house in Flood Walk where I was kept prisoner,' Kim said. 'You can't be using him, surely?'

'I had an idea when we picked him up trying to leave the country that he might come in useful,' M. said. 'It struck me from the start that he did not belong with the likes of Lyndham and Hastings.'

'That's true,' Kim agreed. 'I'm pretty sure he was the one who threw me a blanket when I was locked in that cellar. He probably saved my life. But why was he working with them?'

173

'It seems that he has certain sexual proclivities that could get him sent to jail if the authorities were informed,' M. said. 'It makes him very vulnerable to blackmail — or in the present case, to a suggestion that from now on he works for us. To do him justice, I think he came to hate everything that Lyndham and Hastings stood for, but he didn't know how to get out of their clutches.'

'In what way is he now an asset, under the present circumstances?' Kim asked.

'You would not have guessed from your previous encounter with him, but he is a professional photographer, and he specializes in portraits of people in what we call high society — noble ladies and gentlemen, debutantes, the rich and well connected. He is a bit of a darling of theirs, gets invited to all the best parties. You get the picture?'

'I'm beginning to,' Kim said.

'There is another aspect to him,' M. went on. 'He has some useful connections with the royal household. You probably aren't aware of this, but men of his persuasion are valued as royal servants. Presumably because they are unlikely to have wives or families, they are seen as particularly loyal and devoted.'

'And no threat to royal princesses,' Foxy remarked dryly.

'There is that, too,' M. agreed. 'Anyway, whatever the reason, Verney has two ways of obtaining useful information. He can pick up any titbits of gossip about, for instance, the Hon. Davina, where she goes, who she is seen with. He can also keep an ear to the ground for any hints of disloyalty to the current king. There are still a lot of people in court circles who think Edward was unfairly hounded from the throne.'

'What about us?' Kim asked. 'What do you want us to do?'

'Your role is slightly limited by the fact that Davina knows you, so we can't put you in any position where you might come face to face. But you, Foxy. You never met her?'

'Yes, briefly. I organized the flight that brought her home.'

'Ah,' M. looked disappointed. 'It that case my idea will not work.'

174

'I'm pretty certain she wouldn't recognize me,' Foxy said. 'You remember, Kim? I was wearing a coat with the hood pulled well down. And it was dark. Anyway, I look rather different now.'

'Well, if you think it's worth a gamble,' M. said, 'I think it might be time for Rufus Foxton to make a reappearance. Verney will recognize you, of course, from the meetings you attended at his house, but you were not there for the final acts, and we can invent a back story for you to explain your temporary disappearance.'

'This might help,' Foxy said, touching his eye patch.

'Yes, I'm sure that can be incorporated. Foxton will be the wealthy, sophisticated young American you presented yourself as last year. Go to a few parties. I'm told Davina has a busy social life. Make friends with her and when you feel safe enough you can mention your links with the German American Bund, hint at your disquiet about the way the war is going . . . well, I don't need to tell you. You did it all off your own bat last year. Your objective is to find out who her friends are and ingratiate yourself with them.'

'Sir,' Kim put in, 'Foxy's only just discharged himself from hospital. Don't you think it's a bit too soon—'

'Forget it!' Foxy interrupted her. 'I'm not being asked to engage in a fist fight or abseil down a mountain. I'm fit enough to lounge around with a cocktail in my hand.'

'It may not stop at that,' Kim objected.

'Kim has a point,' M. said. 'Perhaps I am asking you to go back to work too soon.'

'Believe me,' Foxy said, 'I'll recover quicker if I've got something to occupy my mind — and I'm no good at doing jigsaws.'

'Well, take it easy. Don't put yourself in any situation that might turn dangerous,' M. said.

'Just tell me where the best parties are,' Foxy responded. 'But I'll need to go back to my little bolthole in Clapham to collect my Rufus Foxton wardrobe.'

'You'll need money, too,' M. said. 'I imagine you are both owed a good deal in back pay. I'll make sure yours is paid into your Foxton account, if that's OK with you.'

'Fine,' Foxy agreed.

'What about me?' Kim asked. She was beginning to worry that there was no role for her. 'What can I do?'

'Your job is to seek out the times and places where the King is likely to be most vulnerable. I think we can assume that he is safe enough as long as he remains inside Buckingham Palace. I will keep you informed about his movements when I know them myself, which may not be until a day or two before. Think as you would in France if you were targeting a German general. Where are the weak spots and how might they be exploited?'

'I understand what you are saying,' Kim said, 'but there will be other forces involved in protecting him. I don't want to tread on anybody's toes.'

'I don't want to involve the police or the regular army. To do so would involve too many explanations, bearing in mind that as far as the Army High Command is concerned, SOE does not exist. I'm going to give you a small team to work with, but I want to keep it "in house" as far as possible. I shall ask the CO at Beaulieu to find four of his best trainees to work on a special assignment under your command. How does that sound?'

'I can see what you are asking me to do,' Kim said. 'I just wish there were more concrete details. But I suppose that will come when we know His Majesty's next move.'

'I'm afraid that's the way of it at present,' M. agreed. 'I'll give you more information as soon as I know it. Meanwhile, you need a base to work from. I don't want this flat to become known to too many people. I'll find you a safe house where you and your team can get to know each other. And you, Foxy, in your Rupert Foxton persona, had better check into a suite in one of the better hotels. I'll cover your expenses.'

Foxy nodded.

M went on. 'One further thing. We need to be able to keep in touch. The headquarters in Baker Street was set up under the name of the Inter Services Research Bureau specifically so that men and women in a variety of uniforms could be seen coming and going without arousing comment, so if we need to meet face to face, we can do it in my office there.'

Foxy started to say something and stopped.

'Yes?' M. asked.

'Rupert Foxton won't be in uniform.'

'Good point. I presume you still have the uniform you were issued with when you joined up?'

'If I can still get into it,' Foxy said with a grin.

'Well, you may need to have something done about that. Rupert Foxton will need to be able to transmogrify into Sergeant Leroux when we need to meet. But I suggest we keep such meetings to a minimum to avoid alerting the opposition. I suggest, Foxy, that you make a habit of having lunch or afternoon tea at the Savoy. Hand your coat to the cloakroom girl and if you need to contact me, leave a coded message in a brown envelope in the pocket. If I need to get in touch with you, you will find a similar envelope in the pocket when you collect your coat. Understood?'

'Yes, perfectly.'

'Now you, Kim. I'm afraid the Savoy is going to be a bit out of character for you. But there is a news vendor who has a pitch in Trafalgar Square, on the corner of the National Gallery. An envelope left with him will find its way to me and likewise he will pass on any communication I have for you. Is that all clear?'

'You spoke of a coded message,' she said. 'Are we using a poem code? If so, what poem shall it be?'

'Do you have a preference?'

'Foxy and I use the La Fontaine Fable about the fox and the crow. Do you know it? *Maitre Corbeau sur une arbre perché* . . .'

'I vaguely remember it from my long, distant school days,' M. agreed. 'But I can look it up. We'll use that if it's what you are used to.'

'Suppose something happens that means we need to speak to you urgently,' Foxy said.

'Then you have my personal phone number. Only use that in an emergency.' M. stood up. 'That's as far as we can go for the moment. I'll get back to you as soon as I've got things moving.'

When M. had left, Kim looked ruefully at Foxy. 'We're going to have to work, and live, separately.'

He sighed and put his arms round her. 'So it seems. Let's make the most of today.'

CHAPTER 20

The following evening a tall, russet-haired gentleman in immaculate evening dress, wearing a black eye patch, entered the underground ballroom of the Dorchester Hotel. After two bombs had fallen on the Café de Paris, killing the band and most of the dancers, most hotels in London had turned their underground storage spaces into restaurants and ballrooms to escape the bombs during the Blitz. It was the only way to provide London society with the entertainment everyone craved.

The newcomer ordered a dry martini at the bar and surveyed the dancers gyrating to the music of Lew Stone and his orchestra. A little further along the bar a man in the uniform of an RAF officer glanced round and caught his eye.

'Good evening.'

'Good evening,' the newcomer responded.

'Haven't seen you around here before.'

'No, it's my first time. I only arrived in London a couple of days ago.' The accent was pure east-coast American.

'Oh, right. You're from the States, right? What brings you to London?'

'Oh,' he waved his glass vaguely, 'business, business.'

The RAF man studied him for a moment. 'You're not in the Services. I mean, not in uniform, so I assume . . .'

He indicated the eye patch. 'Precluded by injury, I'm afraid.'

'Of course, of course.' The RAF man looked embarrassed. 'Sorry. Didn't mean to intrude.'

'That's quite all right.' The stranger put down his glass and extended his hand. 'Rufus Foxton.'

His hand was taken. 'Dick Johnson. Most people call me Johnny.'

'Pleased to meet you, Johnny.'

The conversation continued while Foxy surveyed the dance floor. After a while he said, 'You know, I'd really like to make the acquaintance of some of these lovely ladies. You couldn't introduce me, could you?'

Minutes later he was seated at a table in the company of the RAF man, two of his fellow pilots and their girlfriends. He asked each girl in turn to dance, and they each returned to the table flushed with the pleasure of having been in the arms of superb dancer. He bought a round of drinks and chatted easily, all the time scanning the dance floor. But so far he had drawn a blank.

He was considering making his excuses and moving on to one of the other hotels when a new party entered the ballroom — two men, in uniforms that identified them as members of one of the Guards regiments, and three young women. Foxy suppressed a grin of satisfaction. 'Jackpot.'

The Hon. Davina Westerham crossed the room, laughing at something one of the men had said. 'Three women and only two men,' Foxy mused internally. 'Ideal!' Of course, he thought, her fiancé, being so badly disfigured, would probably not wish to attend a very public gathering like this. Which left the Hon. Davina without a partner, and opened an opportunity for an attractive man with the requisite *chutzpa*, the Yiddish word that summed up the quality of nerve, or audacity.

His opportunity came a few minutes later when the band leader announced a gentleman's excuse me. Davina took to the floor with one of the guardsmen but within a few bars, another man tapped her partner on the shoulder with a murmured 'excuse me' to take his place. Foxy led one of the RAF men's girlfriends onto the floor and very soon he felt the expected tap and yielded her up. He wove his way through the dancers until he reached Davina, tapped her partner on the shoulder and stepped into his place.

'Good evening, ma'am.'

'Good evening.' He was aware that she was studying his face, trying to place him.

The dance was a foxtrot and she yielded to his lead as smoothly as if they had danced together many times before. Within a minute, he felt a hand on his shoulder. Without missing a step, he glanced round. 'Forget it, buddy. I've been wanting to dance with this lovely lady all evening. I'm not giving her up now.'

'Oh, I say . . .' the disappointed partner began, but Foxy whirled her away out of his reach.

She was looking at him with a slightly mischievous smile. 'That was naughty.'

He smiled back. 'I'm afraid I don't always abide by the rules.'

'Well, thank you, anyway,' she said, looking over his shoulder. 'That chap is a terrible dancer. He'd have trodden all over my feet.'

'A lady like you should never have to put up with a man like that,' he replied. 'Let me buy you a drink.'

He manoeuvred them to a table and ordered champagne, and as they raised their glasses, he said, 'By the way, my name's Rufus. Rufus Foxton.'

'I'm Davina Westerham.'

'An unusual name for an unusually beautiful lady.'

'You're a flatterer.'

'Not so. That is nothing but the unvarnished truth.'

He was able to say that quite sincerely. She was indeed very beautiful. Her chestnut hair fell to her shoulders in glossy waves and the delicacy of her pale skin was thrown into sharp contrast by cherry-red lipstick. He gave himself a mental warning. It would be easy to forget that this lovely girl was a double agent.

'So,' she said, 'what part of the States are you from?'

'Boston, Massachusetts,' he told her.

'And you are over here doing what? You're not a GI.'

'No, ma'am. I escaped the draft because of this,' indicating his eye patch.

'So what brings you to London?'

'I'm here on behalf of a client who is a collector of art, paintings in particular.'

'Isn't that rather a strange thing to be doing in the middle of a war?'

'Not at all. My client is worried that wonderful works of art may be damaged, or stolen, in this futile conflict.'

'You regard the war as futile?'

'Yes, I do. America and Britain and Germany should be brothers-in-arms, not enemies.'

She studied him for a moment. 'You want to be careful who you say that sort of thing to. It might get you into big trouble.'

He shrugged. 'I don't see why. What's the point of killing one another when there's peace to be had for the asking?' Having sown the seed, he changed the subject. 'Let's not talk about war. Drink up and let's have another dance.'

They danced together for the rest of the evening and he had to admit to himself that he enjoyed it. As the leader of the band announced the last waltz, he said, 'Look, I've really enjoyed myself tonight. Could we make this a regular date?'

She raised her eyebrows. 'Has it escaped you that I'm engaged?'

'I saw the ring. But where's the man it belongs to?'

'He doesn't like dancing.'

'Well, then. Perhaps I could be your regular dance partner. How about that?'

She drew back and looked him over. 'Look, I'm not making any promises, but I come here most evenings and if you're here as well . . .'

He smiled and nodded. 'Fair enough. I'll be here. Can I see you home?'

For a moment she appeared to consider the idea then she shook her head. 'I think I should go back with the people I came with. I've already neglected them rather rudely. Thank you for a pleasant evening. Goodnight.'

He bowed slightly. 'Goodnight, ma'am.'

CHAPTER 21

Kim had been invited to go down to Beaulieu to interview potential candidates for her 'special training exercise'. She had been happy to catch up with some old friends, though her memories of her time there were somewhat mixed. She interviewed a number of trainees put forward by their tutors and had finally chosen four — one girl and three men. All of them, in keeping with the regime designed to prepare them to work undercover in France, had been given French names and for the duration of their training spoke only French. None of them ever used their real names and their identities were known only to those who had recruited them. Kim explained to them that for the purpose of this exercise they would have to revert to English, and she suggested that they might use any nickname they had acquired when they joined up, or at school.

The girl was a subaltern in the Women's Motor Transport Company, a branch of the ATS which was made up largely of FANYs who had agreed to be absorbed into the regular army. She was very small, no more than 5' 2", with a mop of unruly dark curls and intense blue eyes. Since her childhood, she had been known as Mouse. She would be the driver for the team.

The first man Kim selected might have been a model for the ideal 'clean-cut' Englishman, with a square chin, blond hair and blue eyes. Ironically, he was Welsh. His surname was Lamb, so inevitably he was called Larry, after the well-known Children's Hour character. He held a degree in engineering and was a second lieutenant in the Royal Army Engineering Corps. He was presented to her as a student who had shown particular talent in the use of explosives.

Number two was Mac, a large, taciturn Scot, a lieutenant in the Gordon Highlanders, whose particular expertise was unarmed combat. He was the muscle in the team.

The third was in some ways the odd one out. He had been recruited into SOE directly from civvy street, having avoided the universal call-up because of a history of childhood asthma. He had been a professor of modern languages at Queen Mary College, part of the University of London. He had grown up in France, and had been searching for an organization that would allow him to contribute to the war effort. His expertise was in tactical planning. He was, unsurprisingly, known as Prof.

The safe house M. had found for Kim was a tall, rather shabby Victorian house in the middle of a terrace on a road leading off Balham High Street. It belonged to an elderly couple who had moved out of London to escape the bombing and were happy to rent it to the War Office as a place where service men and women on leave could stay while they sampled the delights of the metropolis. At least, that is what they were told. The Blitz had displaced so many people that the population was in constant flux, but even in peacetime, Balham was the sort of place where people got on with their lives without being questioned by nosy neighbours.

Once Kim had settled her team there, she gave them the rest of the day off, to amuse themselves as they pleased, giving credence to the fiction that they were there on leave. She, meanwhile, paid a visit to the news vendor in Trafalgar Square. There was a message for her, calling her to a meeting with M., so she headed at once for the Inter Services Research Bureau in Baker Street.

Since she was no longer undercover, Kim was back in uniform, so she blended seamlessly with the men and women from various services going in and out of the building. Waiting outside M.'s office was a man in the uniform of a sergeant in the Sussex Yeomanry. He was reading some notices on a board and had his back to her. She moved towards him. 'Foxy?' He turned round. Suddenly, she was catapulted back a year, to her first meeting with her students as a tutor at Beaulieu. '*Mon dieu*, Roland!'

He laughed. 'Takes you back, don't it?' His accent had automatically changed to fit the costume, back to the cockney twang he had grown up with.

She stared at him. There was no black eye patch. But your eye . . .' she stammered.

'Good, isn't it? They gave it me before I left the hospital. I didn't fancy it at the time. I think the eye patch is more glamorous. But now it comes in useful.'

It took her a moment to understand. While one eye was glinting with amusement, the other looked back at her, expressionlessly. It was a good imitation, but it was glass.

She caught her breath. 'My God! For a moment there I thought I was going mad. You might have warned me.'

'I only thought of it when I was getting into this outfit.' He came closer and took her hand. 'Sorry if I gave you a shock.'

The door opened and M. appeared. 'Come in, both of you.'

It was obvious from his expression that he had something important to say.

'I've just received information from MI5 that the King intends to make a journey to Lincolnshire and Yorkshire to inspect airborne troops, leading, we hope, to the impression for our German spies, that the invasion may come from the air rather than by sea. On this occasion, the family will also be involved. The Queen and Princess Elizabeth are travelling with His Majesty.'

''Struth!' Foxy interjected. 'The perfect opportunity to bump them all off.'

'Exactly,' M. said grimly.

'How are they travelling?' Kim asked.

'By rail, in the royal train. So, if your intention was to "bump them off", how would you go about it?'

'I'd mine the track.'

'That is what I would expect,' M. agreed, 'but where? The first stop is RAF Waddington, so they will leave the train in Lincoln and a car and a police escort will be waiting for them. The distance from London St Pancras is roughly 120 miles. After that, the royal party will go on to visit other units in Yorkshire. That leaves several hundred miles of railway track to inspect. An impossible task.'

'Could we get the army involved?' Foxy suggested.

'It would require hundreds of troops, troops which are already heavily engaged in preparations for what we are calling D-Day. I can't imagine what the reaction of the High Command would be to such a request, on the basis of the very sketchy information we have. Let's face it, it's mainly guesswork.'

'There's another point,' Kim said. 'If we are right, and that is what Kline and Davina and their helpers, whoever they are, are planning, where are they going to get the necessary explosives?'

'How did we get them, when we were in France?' Foxy said. 'They were dropped to us by the RAF.'

'I suppose the Luftwaffe might risk a similar drop,' M. said, 'but our air defences are so tight now I doubt they would get through. They'd be picked up on radar the moment they crossed the coast.'

'Maybe they already have them. It's possible Kline brought them in with him.'

'One thing puzzles me,' M. said. 'If their ultimate objective is to place ex-King Edward on the throne so he can sign a peace treaty with Hitler, they have to convince the general public that Germany is our friend. It's going to be hard to do that if they can be shown to be responsible for the death of our current royal family. King George and Queen Elizabeth have made themselves very popular by enduring the Blitz alongside the rest of London instead of retreating to the safety of Windsor or Balmoral. Edward would never be accepted if he was suspected of being complicit.'

'No,' Kim agreed. 'It would have to look like an accident.'

'Or the action of some other enemy of the state,' Foxy suggested. 'What is the IRA getting up to these days?'

'You make a very good point there,' M. said. 'We have intelligence that there have been extensive contacts between German agents and members of the IRA. I have no doubt that they would be happy to cooperate in the scheme.'

'And they would be the fall guys. The assassination could be blamed on them, leaving the Huns with clean hands.'

'That is all very well in theory,' M. said, 'but it doesn't help us with the immediate problem.'

'Could it be suggested that His Majesty cancels the trip north?' Kim asked.

'Not on the flimsy grounds we could offer,' M. said. 'We desperately need better intelligence. Foxy, how are things progressing with your attempts to get close to Davina?'

'Quite well,' Foxy told them. 'She comes to the Dorchester most evenings and treats me as her regular dance partner. Last night she invited me to a party at her father's London house, so I seem to be making progress. But so far, I haven't seen anything that connects her to Kline, or to any kind of plot. But of course I don't know what she does during the day. I can't follow her around without arousing suspicion.'

'I could set my team to follow her and report where she goes and who she sees,' Kim offered.

'Are they good enough to do that without alerting her?' M. asked.

'They should be. They were all passed as ready to be dropped into France. If they can operate there under the noses of the Huns, they ought to be able to manage it in London.'

'And I will keep my eyes open at this party for any useful connections,' Foxy said.

'Do it,' M. said. 'At the moment she is our only connection to whatever is going on. We must just hope, somehow, she will give us a way into the puzzle.' He stood up. 'Very well. Report back to me at the same time tomorrow. Time is short. We need a breakthrough.'

* * *

When Kim assembled her team the next morning, she had made a decision. It would be unfair to involve them on the basis that this was only an exercise. On the other hand, she was aware that the full importance of what they were being asked to do must remain secret.

'I have to tell you,' she began, 'that you have been brought together on the basis of a lie. This is not just an exercise to test your readiness for deployment in France. It is a project that could have enormous significance for the safety of this country. We believe we have a double agent who is a young woman from an aristocratic family and well placed in what we like to call "society". We have reason to believe that she is at the heart of a very dangerous plot. I can't tell you any more than that, but it is crucial that we have as much information as possible about her. So I am tasking you with the job of following her.'

She saw them exchange glances, a glimmer of excitement in each look.

'You will work in pairs, Mouse with Larry, and Mac with the Prof, and I want a twenty-four-hour watch on her. I want to know where she goes and who she sees, and who comes to the address I shall give you. Many of the people she is with will be exactly what you might expect from a young woman in her situation — friends of her own age, officers on leave, family members. Incidentally, you may see her with a tall man with a black patch over one eye. He's one of ours. What we are looking for is anything out of character, any associates who do not fit in her social circle. If you see anyone like that, one of you should attempt to follow him or her and find out where they live, or are lodging, so we can keep an eye on them, too.'

She opened her shoulder bag and took out a folder containing the newspaper cutting and a copy of the photograph

Davina had been given for her fake French-identity card. 'This is the young woman you will be following. Her name is Davina Westerham and her father is Lord Westerham. Her mother is dead and her only brother is a POW. She is engaged to an RAF officer who is currently serving as an aide-de-camp to the King. The Westerhams have a big house in Mayfair and a country estate in Kent. Be warned, she has had the same training as you, so she will be alive to the possibility of being followed. Do not, under any circumstances, approach her. Your job is to watch and record, that's all.'

'We'll need to be in civvies, then, presumably,' Prof said, 'if you want us to blend into the background.'

'Yes, of course,' Kim agreed.

'I've got one set of civvies with me,' Mouse put in, 'but we might need to change our appearance, like we've been taught at Beaulieu, if we are following someone.'

'I've thought of that,' Kim told her. She took out her wallet. 'I'm giving each of you five quid. There are plenty of second-hand clothes shops round here. See what you can buy that will allow you to make a quick change.'

* * *

Leaving them to their shopping, Kim went to check out the surroundings of Lord Westerham's London home.

Wester House was a mansion situated on Mount Street in Mayfair. Unlike many of its neighbours, it had escaped damage in the Blitz but to Kim's delight, the building opposite, which had been converted into luxury flats, had not been so fortunate. Many of the windows had been blown out and were boarded up, but it seemed some of the flats were still occupied.

She had dressed in civvies and come prepared with a brief case and a buff folder full of papers. In a cubicle off the main foyer she found the hall porter, apparently absorbed in *The Racing Times*.

'Good morning. I'm from the Ministry of Housing. We are carrying out a survey of available accommodation to house refugees or people who have been bombed out. I can see there has been some bomb damage, but are any of the flats still habitable?'

The porter was a small man who had managed to stay surprisingly plump in spite of rationing He put down his paper reluctantly and heaved himself to his feet. 'The back of the building's still more or less intact, ma'am, and some of the owners are still in residence. But Jerry's made a right old mess of the flats at the front — windows blown out, floorboards gone.' He rubbed his nose. 'I reckon it wouldn't take too much to make them so people could live there, if they weren't too choosy, but I don't know what the other residents would say if they had to share the place with a bunch of refugees.'

'The residents will have to accept whatever the ministry decides,' Kim told him with some asperity. 'Can you show me, please?'

With bad grace he led her to the stairs. 'Lift's out of commission, so this is the only way up — aside from the fire escape.'

By the time they reached the first floor he was wheezing. 'It's me chest,' he gasped. 'Me asthma. That's why I'm not in the forces.'

After inspecting the flats with rooms facing out to the street and apparently taking careful notes, Kim informed the man that she would be returning later with workmen to start repairing the damage.

Later that day she returned with the Prof, who carried a clipboard and a measuring tape, followed by Mouse carrying a briefcase, and Mac and Larry dressed as workmen.

'We shall make a start on one of the first-floor flats at the front,' Kim said. 'Number 3. Can I have the keys please?'

Flat number 3 had windows that faced directly onto the facade of Wester House.

'This will be our forward base,' she told them. 'We'll remove just enough of the boards over the windows to give us a view of comings and goings opposite. You'd better make a bit of noise from time to time, as if you're actually doing some work. I'll get some home comforts organized for you. Two of you will be here, ready to follow our quarry. The other two will be back in Balham with me. So if you need back up, you can telephone. There's a pay phone in the front hall. One pair can do the daytime shift, eight a.m. to four p.m., the other pair the evening, four p.m. till midnight. Two will also stay overnight, taking it in turns to sleep and you will swap duties the next night. I don't think you'll get any trouble from the porter. He told me he goes off duty at six. But you had better leave by the main entrance around 5.30 and then come back in up the fire escape. Understood?'

'What about the other residents?' Prof asked.

'It won't matter if they see you during the day. You have a good reason for being here. But you will have to be very careful not to make any noise at night. Any further questions?'

None were forthcoming. Kim looked at her watch. 'It's just after three. Who wants to take the first shift?'

'We will,' Larry said, adding with a grin at Mac and the Prof, 'That means you two are on the night shift.'

Kim returned to Baker Street and looked up an old friend in the stores department. A couple of hours later a van driven by Mac drew up outside the block of flats, and he and Prof carried in a stepladder, some planks of wood and some crates with tools sticking out of the top. Underneath the tools were sleeping bags, a paraffin stove, a kettle and some provisions.

Kim, meanwhile, reported as ordered to M's office.

Foxy was there before her. 'You remember I told you I'd been invited to accompany Davina to a party last night? Guess who was there taking photographs.'

'Our friend Justin Verney?' Kim asked.

M. nodded in confirmation. 'He came to see me first thing this morning. I think we may have a chink of light.'

'How so?' Kim asked.

'After he had taken the formal pictures, he made a point of snapping as many of the guests as possible. These are the results.'

M. spread half a dozen photographs out on the desk. 'These men are all known to us as having previously expressed support for Moseley and his fascists. Several of them also belong to the English Array. You will remember some of the men we had dealings with last year were members.'

Foxy studied the pictures. 'I remember that chap. He was friendly with Hastings and that crowd.'

'But Hastings and the others were arrested after they held me prisoner and I escaped,' Kim said. 'I thought we'd rooted out the dangerous ones.'

'So did I,' M said grimly. 'But it seems not. The English Array has gone underground, but several of the men in these pictures are known to be members. As such, they are ardent royalists who believe the country needs a king who will be an absolute ruler with what amounts to a feudal system under him. They are misogynistic, anti-Semitic and against any form of democracy. And they do not regard our current monarch as a suitable ruler. They will be well aware that their friends have been interned under defence regulation 18B, but it seems that has not put them off. To find them all gathered together at a time like this is alarming, to say the least.'

'It fits in with my experience of last night,' Foxy said. 'I was probed as to my allegiances and my attitude to the war. I made a point of bringing up my association with the German American Bund and protests against the war in the States. I think I convinced them.'

'That's good,' M. said. 'We may be able to use your connections. But going back to last night, Verney made another useful discovery. He noticed that a small group of the men in these pictures had taken themselves away from the general gathering and met in the library. He hung about outside, trying to eavesdrop, but the door was too thick and the voices too quiet. He was about to give up when his host came down the hall and he needed a reason to be where he was. So he lifted his camera and, in his words, blundered into the library. All conversation stopped and someone demanded to know what the hell he thought he was doing. He said something about not wanting to miss taking a picture of any of the guests, apologized for intruding and backed out. The point of all this is, as he walked in and before his presence was realized, he heard one sentence — or a part of one: "It all depends on the Irishman".'

Foxy let out a low whistle. 'The Irish connection. So I was right.'

'It would seem so,' M. agreed. 'It would certainly explain where they are getting their bomb-making experience from. It gives us something to work on, but time is desperately short. We have five days before the royal party sets out on its journey.' He turned to Kim. 'Has your team come up with anything?'

Kim shook her head. 'We were only able to set up the watch this afternoon. I haven't even had a report from them yet.'

'And your association with Davina?' M. looked at Foxy. 'Any suggestion of an Irish connection?'

Foxy also shook his head. 'None so far.'

M. sighed. 'Well, I will institute investigations into any possible Irish suspects, but it all takes time. We must just pray that one of us gets a breakthrough before it's too late. If the worst comes to the worst, I shall have to tell MI5 of our suspicions and see if they can persuade the palace to change their plans.'

CHAPTER 22

The following evening Kim was waiting for Larry and Mouse to return to the Balham house at the end of their spell of duty. She heard the front door slam and feet thudded up the uncarpeted stairs.

'Evening, ma'am,' Larry greeted her, and she saw at once from his face that something unusual had happened.

'Well? What have you got to report? Have you seen the lady?'

'Oh yes,' Mouse said breathlessly. 'She went out this morning and we followed . . .'

'We lost sight of her for a couple of hours, Larry interrupted, 'because she went somewhere we couldn't follow her.'

'Where?' Kim asked.

'You'll never guess,' Mouse put in, wide-eyed. 'Buckingham Palace.'

'Not through the main gates,' Larry said. 'She went into a side entrance. We hung around outside and she came out a couple of hours later, but there's no way of knowing what she did or who she saw inside.'

'Of course not,' Kim said. 'It's not so surprising. Remember I told you she's engaged to one of the King's aide-de-camps? Presumably, she was visiting him.'

'I'd forgotten that,' Mouse's face fell.

'A long visit though, during what are presumably working hours for him,' Larry said. 'Or doesn't that apply in those circles?'

'I've no idea,' Kim admitted, 'but two hours in the middle of the day is taking a bit of a liberty, I should say.'

She made a note to pass on to M. in her next report.

* * *

The breakthrough M. had wished for came two days later. It started with a phone call from Mouse.

'I'm frightfully sorry but I've had to drop back. I think our target has spotted me. We followed her to Harrods and she went into Ladies' Fashion. Larry waited outside and I went in alone. A man hanging around there would look suspicious. She took a dress from the rack and went into a changing cubicle, but when she came out, she hadn't been trying on the dress. She'd been changing her own clothes. She went in wearing a smart suit and a hat, and came out in a shabby overcoat with a scarf over her head. Well, it's just the sort of thing we've been taught to do at Beaulieu if we think we are being followed, so she must have spotted me, don't you think?'

'Possibly,' Kim agreed. 'She might have some other reason, but you are probably right to drop back. Where's Larry?'

'I managed to get out before she did and I tipped Larry off about the change of clothes. She came out a minute later and caught a 390 bus, heading north. Larry just had time to jump on after her. So I don't know where they are now. Sorry. I think I've made a mess of it.'

'No, you haven't. You've done the right thing. Go back to the observation base and wait there to see if she comes back. I'll follow this up.'

Kim rang one of the secretaries at the Baker Street HQ. 'Can you tell me where the 390 bus route goes?'

'Hang on a minute. I'll look it up.' There was a pause and the sound of pages being turned. 'It runs from Knightsbridge to King's Cross.'

'King's Cross!' Kim felt a jolt of dismay. 'OK. Thanks.'
She rang off, biting her lip.

Was Davina planning to take the train and follow the same route that the royal party would take next day? If so, was she planning to set the explosive charges herself, somewhere along the line? It couldn't be done in broad daylight. What were her plans?

An hour passed and the phone rang again.

'It's me, Larry.'

'Thank heavens! Where are you?'

'I'm in a phone box on the corner of Acton Street and Gray's Inn Road.'

'And where is your target?'

'I'm not sure. I had to make a quick decision. She went into a pub called O'Neil's and met up with a man who was obviously waiting for her. Middle-aged, sandy hair, respectably dressed but a bit shabby. Could be a travelling salesman or something like that. They talked for about ten minutes. I tried to listen in, but I couldn't get close enough to hear what they were saying — only the odd word or two. But I think the man had an Irish accent.'

'Irish?' Kim broke in. 'Are you sure?'

'Not completely. I just had that impression. Anyway, when the meeting broke up, I had to decide whether to follow the lady or the bloke. You said to try to establish the identity of anyone she met so I decided to follow him. He's staying in a small hotel on Acton Street.'

'Is he still there?'

'Yes. I checked the area. There's no route out the back and he hasn't reappeared, so he must be.'

'Is there anywhere you can shelter so you can keep watch without arousing suspicion?'

'There's a little newsagent's place a bit further along on the other side. I'll go in there and spin them a line about being a private detective.'

'Great! Stay there. If he moves, follow him. I'm sending Prof to take over.'

Prof had been passing the time before the next shift by trying to interest Mac in a game of chess. He looked up when Kim called his name. 'Where do you want me to go?'

Kim rapidly brought him up to date with what Larry had told her. 'This man could give us a vital clue. It's essential that you keep an eye on him, wherever he goes next. Do you need a London map?'

He shook his head. 'I was a student here. I know the King's Cross area quite well.'

'Right. Do you have money? Take this. You may need to pay for a taxi, or a train fare. Send Larry back, in case the target has spotted him. Mac, I want you to go to the observation base and take over from Mouse.'

The rest of the day passed in nail-biting inactivity. Kim felt sure they had located the Irishman referred to in the conversation Justin Verney had overheard the night before. She wished she had gone herself to follow him, but knew her role was to act as coordinator for any future action.

Mouse returned to report that Davina had come home, looking as smart as when she had set out, so Kim was comforted by the knowledge that at least Mac would keep her under observation. Shortly after that, the phone rang again.

'Skip?' It was Prof's voice. 'I've got a problem. I've been up and down Acton Street and all round the side streets, but there's no sign of Larry.'

'You're sure you're in the right place? Did you find the hotel?'

'Yes, there's only one in this street.'

'What about the newsagent's shop?'

'It's closed.'

'Is there anywhere else he could be hiding himself?'

'No, unless he's inside the hotel.'

Kim thought fast. There were two possibilities. One, the Irishman had spotted Larry and had deliberately led him away, possibly looking for a quiet spot where he could silence him. Or he had set out for a new destination and Larry had followed. On balance, the second option seemed more likely.

If it had come to a fight, Larry was perfectly capable of looking after himself.

'OK, Prof. You'd better come back. There's nothing we can do until Larry makes contact.'

As evening drew in, she and Mouse cooked sausage and mash for the three of them and it was almost time for Prof to relieve Mac when the phone rang again.

'It's me, Larry. I'm at King's Cross station. I'm afraid I've lost my target.'

Kim's heart sank. 'Where did you lose him?'

'Somewhere between London and Lincoln.'

'You've been to Lincoln? No, wait. Come back here and we can talk properly. I don't want to do this over the phone.'

Larry arrived twenty minutes later. He looked tired and worried.

'I'm sorry. I've let you down.'

'Just tell me exactly what happened.'

'OK. He came out of the hotel not long after I called you and went to St Pancras station. I got in the ticket queue behind him and heard him ask for a return ticket to Lincoln, so I bought one too. I didn't dare sit in the same carriage, in case he had noticed me, but I got in one just behind. It was a slow train, stopping at every station, and every time I watched out of the window in case he got off. I'd more or less decided he really was going all the way to Lincoln when we stopped at place called North Hykeham. I watched as usual and then, just as the train was pulling out, he jumped off. By the time I got the door open, we were gathering speed and past the platform. I suppose I should have jumped and risked it, but I reckoned I wouldn't be able to do much with a broken leg so I stayed put.'

'Quite right, too,' Kim said.

'The train didn't stop again until we got to Lincoln, so I caught the next one back and got out at North Hykeham. It's a pretty small place and I had a good wander round but I couldn't see any sign of our man. God knows where he went, but that's it, I'm afraid. Sorry.'

'Don't be.' Kim was already on her feet. 'You may just have given us the clue we need. Stay here and get yourself something to eat. Prof, I want you to go to our forward observation point and bring Mac back here. All of you, get some rest while you can. We shall be on the move at first light. I'm going back to HQ to collect some gear.'

A call to the private number M. had given her for emergencies brought him to the office just as she arrived. After briefing him, she collected a requisition document for a vehicle and a number of items of equipment. She also collected four Welrod pistols, plus ammunition, to add to the one she was already carrying. At the last moment, she also picked up a grab-bag she kept stored in a locker.

When she joined up at the start of the war, she had been renting a furnished flat. Her diplomat father had spent most of his life abroad and he and her mother were currently in Geneva, so there was no family home where she could leave things. She had sold or given away most of her possessions and stored the rest in a suitcase in a secure storage locker, but she had kept a few items in case they ever came in useful, and they were in the bag.

It was almost dawn when she returned to the safe house and found her team ready and waiting. As they drove north with Mouse at the wheel of the jeep, she briefed them.

'I've told you part of what this is all about. Now I'm going to give you the full picture. You've all signed the Official Secrets Act, so I don't need to remind you that this goes no further than between us. We believe that there is a plot to assassinate the King and replace him with the Duke of Windsor.'

There was a gasp of incredulity from the back of the vehicle.

Kim went on, 'Today, His Majesty is travelling north on the royal train to inspect airborne forces preparing for the invasion of France. The Queen and Princess Elizabeth will be with him. It is a perfect opportunity for the plotters to eliminate almost the whole family. We think the people behind this have allied themselves with the IRA — hence the interest in this mysterious Irishman. We are assuming that there will be an attempt to blow up the train but we didn't know where, until you gave us the clue, Larry. If the Irishman is planning to mine the tracks, the chances are he has done so somewhere within a short distance of North Hykeham.'

'I wondered what the dickens made him get off there,' Larry said. 'It looks like the back of beyond.'

Kim spread a map on her knee. 'There are a lot of abandoned sand quarries that have filled up with water in that area, so I am assuming the railway line runs on an embankment. Does that accord with what you saw, Larry?'

'Yes, I remember looking down and seeing a lot of little lakes, or ponds.'

'Right. If I wanted to derail a train, that is where I would do it, so that it would roll down the embankment, causing maximum damage, and because of the terrain it would take longer for the emergency services to reach it.' She ran her hand through her hair. 'It's guesswork, of course, but that's all we have to go on.'

'What time is the King due?' Prof asked.

'He's scheduled to arrive in Lincoln at 11.55. That doesn't give us much time. The important question is, how is the Irishman going to detonate his mine? He can't use a pressure switch, like the ones I know you're familiar with, because the first train to pass over would set it off. Time pencils are not accurate enough. He needs to be sure it goes up exactly as the royal train passes. So he needs to have line of sight and be close enough to detonate it. We need to look for wires stretching from the mine to where he has hidden himself. With me so far?'

'Yes, Skip,' four voices murmured in unison.

'Mac, I want you to scout the terrain to the west of the line. Prof, search the area to the east. He may have created some kind of hideout, or he may be hiding in plain sight, pretending to be an innocent bystander. Look for someone angling in one of the ponds, or birdwatching. If you see someone suspicious, challenge him and if you're in any doubt, take him down. I'm going to issue you all with a gun. We want him alive, if possible, but the vital thing is to stop him detonating his mine.'

'Suppose we come across someone who really is just fishing or watching birds?' Prof asked.

'Assume the worst, but don't shoot unless you see him go for a detonator.'

'What do you want me to do?' Larry asked.

'You're the one with most experience of explosives. I want you to search the line south of the station. You've done the bomb-disposal course, so you know what to do if you find something. I'll cover the line north of the station. We'll go as far as we can within the time, but my guess is that he won't have bothered to trek that far from the station. Mouse, you will stay with the vehicle and be ready to bring it to wherever it may be needed. Those rucksacks contain walkie-talkies. We'll each have one and Mouse will be our communications hub. If anyone finds anything, call her up and she can pass the word to me. My call sign will be Alpha. Larry, yours is Beta, Prof, you're Gamma, and Mac, you're Delta. Mouse is Epsilon. Any questions?'

'It occurs to me,' Prof said, 'that if our man is watching the line, he's going to see us. It won't be difficult to guess what we're doing.'

'That thought had struck me, too,' Kim agreed. 'But what can he do? Even if he is equipped with a sniper rifle, a shot will give away his position. He can't hope to take all of us out before we get to him. And there's no point in him detonating his mine prematurely. All he can do is hunker down and hope we don't find it in time.'

They parked the jeep on a side road running along slightly higher ground east of the line, at an intersection with the road leading from the village to the station. There they shouldered the heavy rucksacks. As they fanned out, she checked her watch.

'It's 10.40. I reckon the train will pass here at about eleven forty-five. Let's get to it.'

Avoiding the station itself, where questions would have been asked, Kim ducked through a wire fence and climbed the embankment to the line. Turning north, she began to walk along the track, searching for a lump of plastic explosive stuck under one of the rails and the tell-tale wires leading from it. After covering some five hundred yards, she had found nothing. She called Mouse.

'Alpha to Epsilon, are you receiving me? Over.'

Mouse's voice came back with a crackle of static. 'Epsilon to Alpha, receiving you loud and clear. Over.'

'Anything to report? Over.'

'Nothing so far. Over.'

'OK. Over and out.'

Kim looked ahead. A short distance away, a bridge carried a road across the track. She looked at her watch. Just after eleven. She began to worry. What if her deductions had been wrong? What if the mine, if it existed, was laid somewhere else, or if it was here and somehow she had missed it? She shook herself and forced her mind to focus.

She walked on, under the bridge, studying the ground. It was when she straightened up to ease her back that she saw it.

Not on the line.

Up close to the point where a central column supported the bridge. A dark lump and close to it, something else — a box about the size of a shoe box.

She walked back and studied the bridge. It was a modern concrete construction. In order to carry the road up from the low ground to clear the railway, it was long, sloping up to a flat surface and then down. If that charge was blown as the train passed underneath it would bring several tons of concrete down on it.

She moved back and studied the interior of the bridge. The concrete pillars gave no toe holds for even the most experienced climber. No, there was only one way to reach that bomb.

She called up Mouse. 'Bring the jeep to the bridge that crosses the line half a mile north of the station. Park it in the middle.'

By the time Kim had scrambled up to the level of the road, the jeep was approaching. She waved it into position and opened the back to extract her grab bag. In it was her climbing equipment from the days, long ago now, when she used to climb mountains with the man she expected to marry. Since then, she had had plenty of experience while at the SOE training school at Arisaig, and she had kept her equipment handy just in case it was needed. She blessed the guardian angel who had prompted her to grab that bag from her locker.

Rapidly, she uncoiled the rope and handed one end to Mouse. 'Make that fast to the tow bar.'

Mouse, well-trained, asked no questions but did as she was told. Meanwhile, Kim struggled into the harness and clipped onto the rope.

'The explosive is under the bridge. I'm going to abseil down so I can reach it.' She hung a set of cams onto her belt, together with wire cutters, and threw the end of the rope over the parapet. As she did so, she stubbed her toe on a padlocked metal box stencilled with the words, *PROPERTY OF LNER. DANGER. DO NOT TOUCH.*

She looked down at it for a moment, mildly puzzled about what it was doing there, but time was short and she could not allow herself to be distracted. She put one foot on the box, used it to lift herself over the parapet and lowered herself gently until she was hanging below the road bed and could see the underside of the structure.

After the bright daylight it took a few minutes for her eyes to adjust. The bridge was reinforced with metal girders. She tried to remember exactly where she had seen the explosive but it was very different from this angle than from looking up from ground level. Eventually she spotted it, attached to the rusted metal, just at the junction with the supporting pillar. Kim glanced up and saw Mouse's face peering down at her. She gave her a thumbs up and then reached out and grabbed hold of one of the girders and pulled herself forward so that she was under the bridge.

She made a temporary anchor with the rope and braced herself against the girder with her knee. Then she felt around the lump of explosive with one hand and found what she was looking for. A detonator was impaled in it. She followed the wires with her fingers as far as she could reach. They led up and through a narrow crack in the structure to the road above.

That LNER box! It must contain some device that could be remotely activated. If only she had investigated the box, she might have been able to disable it without the need to hang in mid-air on a rope.

She glanced at her watch. 11.37. It was too late to climb back up and find some way to undo the padlock. The royal train could pass here in less than ten minutes. She would have to find a way to disable the bomb from here. She wedged a cam into a small gap between the girder and the road bed and clipped her rope into it. Now she was stable enough to use both hands. It was just a matter of cutting the wires. She pulled the wire cutters from her belt and then hesitated.

If the device was booby trapped, cutting the wire could send her and the bridge up in smoke. She could see no sign that it was, and after all, the man who had set it had no reason to imagine that anyone would find it. She drew a deep breath and cut the wire. Nothing happened. She exhaled and chuckled to herself. Success!

In that instant, she felt the rope go slack. Instinctively, she grabbed hold of the cam with one hand and the edge of the girder with the other. The rope fell down past her and pooled beside the track. The only thing now that prevented her from joining it was the cam and her precarious grip on the girder. At that moment she heard the sound of the approaching train. The noise of the engine echoed round her as it came under the bridge.

A cloud of steam enveloped her and as it did so, the cam came loose from the crack under the girder and she fell.

CHAPTER 23

Larry watched the royal train pass him and disappear along the track. Then he shrugged the rucksack containing the walkie-talkie off his back and called Mouse. There was no response. He set off along the track towards the station. Part way along, Prof climbed up the embankment to join him.

'Looks like Skip guessed wrong. The train's gone through and I haven't heard an explosion. Unless she found the bomb in time. I've been trying to call Mouse but there's no answer.'

'Me, too,' Larry agreed. 'We'd better go back to the jeep and find out what's going on.'

As they reached the station, they were joined by Mac.

'Wild goose chase,' he grunted. 'I've not seen anyone suspicious and there's been no explosion. And these bloody sets are useless. I can't get any response.'

They climbed up to the junction where the jeep had been parked, then stood looking around.

'Where the dickens are they?' Prof asked.

'There's the jeep!' Larry exclaimed. 'Look, on that bridge.'

The jeep, when they reached it, was empty.

'Where the hell . . . ?' Larry began.

'Oh, no! No, no, no!' Prof had moved round to the far side of the vehicle. Mouse was lying between it and the parapet, face down, arms and legs spread out like a dropped toy. He knelt down and put his hand on her neck, feeling for a pulse.

'Anything?' Larry asked.

Prof shook his head. 'I think her neck's broken. She must have been looking over the parapet and some swine crept up behind her.'

'Where's the boss?' Mac asked. 'That's what I want to know.'

Prof had found the grab bag. 'There's climbing equipment in here. But no rope. You don't think . . . ?'

Larry looked down. 'You think she abseiled down for some reason and then someone cut the rope?'

'Aye,' Mac said, 'and here's the evidence.' He showed them where part of the rope was still fixed to the tow bar. It had clearly been cut.

They all gazed down at the railway line again.

'There's the rest of the rope.' Larry pointed down. 'At the side of the track.'

'We'd better get down there.' Prof said. 'There could be another train along at any moment.'

They reached the track in grim silence, each preparing himself for the sight of a mangled body, but there was nothing. The line was clear all the way under the bridge and beyond.

Larry craned his head to look up. 'That's what she was after! Look there.'

'You reckon that lump up there is *plastique*?' Prof asked.

'I'd put money on it. And Skip must have disabled it, or the man we've been looking for failed to detonate it. He must have spotted what was going on and done for poor Mouse then cut the rope. But then what?'

'Do you think he might have taken Skip?'

'Taken her body, you mean?' Mac said.

'She might have survived the fall,' Prof said. 'But not without injury.'

'Should we start a search?' Larry asked.

'What's the point?' Mac said. 'He must have transport. He could be anywhere by now.'

'We ought to retrieve that *plastique*, if that's what it is,' Prof said. 'It may provide some clues about its origin, maybe even fingerprints.'

'Easier said than done,' Mac grunted.

'If Skip could abseil down to it, so can I,' Larry said. 'We were all trained to do it up at Arisaig.'

They retrieved the rope and clambered back to the bridge. A hunt through the grab bag produced the rest of the equipment needed and with the rope fastened again to the tow bar, Larry lowered himself over the parapet.

'I'll keep watch,' Mac said. 'Whoever it was did for that poor lassie is probably far away by now, but we can't be too careful.'

A few breathless minutes passed while they all strained their ears for the sound of another approaching train, then Larry called up, 'Lower me another rope. I'll tie this stuff to it and you can haul it up.'

Once the package containing the explosive was safely on the bridge, Larry dropped to ground level and then clambered back up the embankment to join the other two men, coiling the rope as he went.

Prof was examining the explosive. 'It's *plastique* all right and here's the detonator but where did these wires go? How was he going to set it off?'

'Look here!' Mac had upended the metal box labelled with the initials of the rail company to expose wires that emerged from the base. 'The mechanism, whatever it is, must be in here. Let's see if we can get it open.'

'No, wait!' Prof said sharply. 'It says "danger".'

'Och, that's just to stop nosey parkers from meddling with it.'

'No, Prof's right,' Larry put in. 'It may just be to put people off, but it could be genuine. It may be booby trapped.'

'So, what do we do?'

'Shove it in the back of the jeep with the *plastique*. We'll take it back to HQ,' Prof said. 'This is way above our pay grade. We have to alert the top brass.'

They did as he suggested, lifted Mouse's body carefully into the jeep and set off back to London.

CHAPTER 24

Kim came round to find a coal-grimed face looking down at her.

'By 'eck, lass. I thought tha'd had it when you dropped out of the sky, like that. Whatever was tha doing up on that bridge?' Kim struggled to sit up, but a hand on her shoulder pressed her back. 'Lie quiet now. The ambulance will be here shortly.'

'Where am I?' she asked through lips that felt like rubber.

'Lincoln station, lass. You dropped onto the tender but we couldn't stop. Had to let you lie there on the coal till we got here. We had some very important passengers, tha see.'

'The King!' Kim said. 'Is the King safe?'

'Safe as houses, lass. Gone on his way with Her Majesty and the princess.'

Kim sank back. In the split second of her fall she had known she was going to die. Now the realization was slowly dawning on her that she was still alive. Gingerly, she tried moving her legs. It hurt, but the muscles responded. She clenched and unclenched her fingers. Her arms seemed to be intact as well. Her whole body ached as if she had been beaten, but miraculously, the damage seemed to be superficial.

'I thought I was going under the train,' she mumbled.

'You nearly did,' was the answer. 'I thought I was seeing things when you dropped onto the tender. Was you trying to end yourself?'

'No! No. I can't explain. Sorry.'

There was movement round her and the man stood up. Voices asked questions and were answered, then an ambulance man stooped over her.

'Can you hear me? We're going to get you to hospital. You'll be fine. Just take it easy.'

'No!' She tried again to sit up. 'I have to get back. People will be looking for me.'

'You can contact them later. You're in no state to go anywhere now. Just try to relax.'

Kim made a final effort and succeeded in propping herself up on her elbow. 'No, you don't understand . . .' Then she slumped back, unconscious.

* * *

Kim woke from a drug-dazed slumber to find M. sitting at her bedside.

'Sir?' She struggled up in the bed.

'Be easy, lass.' The Scot's burr was a little more pronounced than usual. 'From what I hear, you're lucky to be alive. But when you feel up to it, I'd like you tell me what happened.'

'Where am I?' She looked around the unfamiliar room.

'I had you transferred from the hospital in Lincoln to the Queen Alexandra. You don't remember?'

She sorted through a tangle of memories, trying to pick out reality from dream. 'Oh yes, the ambulance. That was . . . yesterday?'

'Last night. I thought it would be best. We can talk here without anyone asking questions. How are you feeling?'

'I . . . don't know. Sleepy.'

'They gave you a dose of morphine to help you through the journey. Your head will clear in a bit. Here, have some water.'

He poured water into a glass on the bedside table and slipped a hand under her head to help her drink. She swallowed and sank back onto the pillow.

'So it was yesterday that it, that I . . . Oh God! Mouse! What happened to Mouse?'

His tone was sombre. 'I'm sorry. Sub-lieutenant Collier is dead.'

'Dead? Oh no!' Her head was clearing and memory was coming back. 'Who? Was it the Irishman?'

'There's no way of knowing at the moment. All I can tell you is that her neck was broken, probably by someone trained in unarmed combat. But before we go into that any further, I want you tell me your side of the story.'

Kim closed her eyes for a moment, trying to disperse the last shadows of sleep. Then she began, at first hesitantly but with increasing fluency, to relate the events that had led up to her fall.

'I thought I'd had it,' she concluded. 'One second earlier and I'd have been under the train, not on top of it.'

'Thank God you were able to hang on for that split second,' M. said.

'The box!' Kim suddenly remembered. 'There was a metal box on the bridge. I'm sure it contained the detonator mechanism, if only I'd stopped to look. Someone needs to retrieve it and check it.'

'Don't worry. Your three men worked that out for themselves and had the sense to bring the box and the *plastique* back to London with them. Of course, they didn't know who to contact, so they reported back to the CO at Beaulieu and he sent them on to me. They were convinced that you must be dead and they were immensely relieved to learn that you had survived. I've sent the box to Cecil Clarke at Station 17. He'll be happy to have a new toy to play with.'

'What's happening now?' Kim asked. 'Are you looking for the Irishman?'

'I've had to bring MI5 and the police up to speed on what we are involved in. There is a countrywide search in progress and the ports with ferries to Ireland are being watched. I got an artist to work with your chap, Larry, and between them they managed to produce a reasonable picture of the man we are looking for. But it's little enough to go on if he has the sense to keep his head down and not try to leave the country, so I don't hold out much hope of catching him.'

'I've been thinking,' Kim said, 'he couldn't have got that explosive in place without help. He didn't have that box on the train with him. Larry would have noticed it. I imagine it's pretty heavy, so someone must have brought it to the bridge for him, in a vehicle of some sort. And unless he's an expert mountaineer, I doubt if he could have lowered himself down to fix the explosive unaided.'

'I agree,' M. said. 'He must have had an accomplice and I suspect it was the same person who killed poor Lieutenant Collier. The man himself must have been concealed somewhere within sight of the bridge and he wouldn't have wanted to leave the spot with the train due so soon.'

Kim met his eyes. 'An accomplice with unarmed combat training. Pauline? Have you arrested her?'

'Davina Westerham seems to have vanished off the face of the earth.'

'Vanished? How is that possible?'

'I've had your team keeping watch on the London house and I've sent some others to watch the country mansion in Kent. There's been no sign of her. Our friend Foxy has been doing his best to locate her. He tried calling at the London house but couldn't get past the butler — you can imagine how it went: "Sorry, sir, Miss Davina is not at home. No, sir, I'm afraid I can't tell you when she is likely to return," etc. Incidentally, I got Justin Verney to follow up on your report about her visits to the palace. It seems her fiancé has an aunt who is one of the Queen's ladies-in-waiting. I gather that "waiting" is a large part of what they do and to that end they have a sitting room of their own. Apparently, Davina has been making a habit of dropping in for a coffee and a gossip.'

'So that's where she is getting her intelligence,' Kim said.

'And possibly testing attitudes to a potential change of regime,' M. agreed.

'But as soon as she realized the plot to bring down the bridge hadn't worked, she disappeared?'

'Seems like that.'

Kim bit her lip in frustration. 'If only I hadn't pulled my team off watch, we'd know. But I needed them to search the railway line. She must have left just after I called my chaps off and driven north to meet up with the Irishman.'

'You can't blame yourself,' M. said. 'You acted with commendable speed, and without your courageous action we might . . .' He paused, 'I don't like to think about the situation we might be in now.'

They were both silent for a moment and then Kim felt able to bring up a thought that had been at the back of her mind since she woke. 'Is Foxy OK?'

'He's fine. Just very cross with me for forbidding him to visit you. I pointed out that we ourselves may be under surveillance and there's no reason for Rupert Foxton to be visiting this hospital.'

She smiled. 'Yes, you're right, of course. Are you expecting to see him soon?'

'Not unless he has something to report.'

'Do you think they will give up now?' Kim asked.

M. shook his head. 'I think they are too desperate for that. They know they only have a limited time to act. Once the Second Front is opened and our troops are back on French soil, it will be too late to talk about a treaty with Hitler.'

'And His Majesty? Will he be making any more trips?'

'We shall only know that a few days before it happens. But I suspect there will be others.'

'Then . . .' Kim pulled herself upright.

M. stretched a hand, palm outwards, towards her. 'No. There is nothing for you to do now except rest and get well. You will stay here until the doctors are ready to discharge you. And that's an order.'

She shook her head stubbornly. 'I don't even know what's wrong with me. I don't think I've broken anything.'

'On the contrary. You have torn a ligament in your ankle, you have two cracked ribs and severe bruising to your back — and you were suffering from concussion.' He stood up and looked down at her with a smile. 'Be thankful. It could have been so much worse.'

After M. left, Kim sank back onto her pillows and admitted to herself that she was in no fit state to go anywhere. A nurse came in with some pills for her to swallow and then returned with a cup of tea and some toast spread with honey. 'A special treat,' she was told. 'Tomorrow it'll be back to margarine.'

Kim was just beginning to drift off to sleep again when the door opened to admit a khaki-clad figure and Foxy bent to kiss her.

'What are you doing here?' she asked. 'I thought it was off-limits to you.'

'Off-limits to Rupert Foxton,' he agreed, 'but there's no reason for Sergeant Leroux not to call in for a check-up. After all, I was a patient here not so long ago.'

She stretched her arms round his neck and winced as he lifted her from the pillows. 'Oh, it's good to see you,' she whispered.

He cradled her closely and murmured into her hair, 'My darling, I came so close to losing you! What were you doing, climbing down from that bridge?'

'Doing my job,' she responded. 'Just like you would have done.'

He drew his head back and looked into her eyes. 'You're right, of course. If only this bloody war was over! I sometimes wonder if we have any chance of surviving until peace.'

'We've managed it so far,' she pointed out. 'Let's hope our luck holds.'

He kissed her and laid her back on the pillow.

'What about you? How are things going at your end?'

His face brightened. 'I think I may be on the right track. I've been invited to spend the weekend at the Westerhams' place down in Kent.'

'Really? Do you think Davina will be there?'

'I'd be surprised, but I might get some clue about where she's hiding out.'

'Why do you think you've been invited?'

'I've been pushing the idea that I might be sympathetic to their cause and I have friends in the States who could be influential in preparing public opinion there. I'm hoping that this might be the occasion for them to open up about what they are planning.'

She frowned up at him. 'You're sure they don't suspect you? Getting you down there, away from London, could give them a chance to . . . well, you know what I'm saying.'

'I know,' he agreed, 'but I haven't had any hint that they are on to me.'

'You must be on your guard. I don't like the thought of you putting yourself in their grasp without any back-up.'

He squeezed her hand. 'Don't worry. I can take care of myself. You know that.'

She was tempted to remind him that he had already had his head in the lion's mouth once and that she was in no position to rescue him a second time, but all she said was, 'Promise me that you'll tell M. where you are going and try to arrange some kind of emergency signal.'

'I'll make sure he knows what's going on,' he promised.

A nurse put her hand round the door. 'I think you should leave now, sergeant. The patient needs to rest.'

'I'm going,' he said, and bent to kiss her. 'Don't worry about me. Just concentrate on getting well.'

'I shall worry. You know that. Just make sure you come back to tell me what you've found out — if anything.'

'I'll be in touch,' he promised, 'but it may not be for a few days.'

When he had gone, Kim closed her eyes. His words echoed in her mind. *I sometime wonder if we have any chance of surviving until peace.*

* * *

Falcon's Nest was a gracious manor house set in woodland on a ridge of the Kentish Weald, close to the village of Hawkhurst. As he stepped out of the hired Bentley, Foxy wondered if the name was a deliberate homage to the Eagle's Nest, Hitler's command centre in the Bavarian Alps, or a happy coincidence. Perhaps it was just a reference to the name of the village. He put the thought out of his mind and approached the front door. It was opened before he rang by Rogers, the butler he was accustomed to seeing at Lord Westerham's London residence.

'Mr Foxton. Welcome to the Falcon's Nest. Let Jenkins here take your case. He'll be looking after you during your stay. His lordship is expecting you. He is in the library. This way, if you please, sir.'

Foxy, wearing an immaculately cut suit of dark-grey worsted over a cream silk shirt and a Yale bulldog tie, handed his case to the young manservant and followed the butler through the hallway, with its elegantly curving staircase, to a room at the back of the house. Three walls were lined with bookshelves containing books that Foxy suspected were bought by the yard for their bindings rather than their content. The long windows on the fourth wall looked out over an immaculate lawn lined with rose beds just beginning to put out new growth after their winter pruning.

Lord Westerham rose from a leather armchair to greet him. 'Rupert! I'm so glad you could join us.'

Foxy looked round the room. There were four other men there, all of whom he had been introduced to at a party, by Davina, and all of whose faces he remembered from the photographs Justin Verney had taken. All identified by M. as known fascist sympathizers.

'You know Reggie Lancing, I think,' his host resumed. 'And Pip Broklehurst. Have you met Bonzo Delauny and James Frost?'

Foxy shook hands all round and Frost said, 'Call me Jack, guys. Everyone does.'

Foxy recognized the ambience, the nicknames, the cosy club of old friends who had probably all gone to the same public school. It was something far from his own experience, but he had come across it often, before, when he had been pursuing his erstwhile career as a con man dealing in forgotten Old Masters. He knew how to blend in.

Rogers served pre-luncheon drinks and they chatted inconsequentially about the weather, golf, the absence of first-class cricket due to the war, the prospects of various horses in the flat-racing season about to begin at Newmarket. It was striking that there was very little discussion of the progress of the war, the topic at the top of most people's minds. There were questions to Foxy about how sport in America was being affected by the war. Fortunately, he had expected that and had made a point of studying reports in *The New York Times*.

Bearing in mind that he was supposed to have been 'home' during the months when he was actually in France, he had also made a point of becoming acquainted with an undersecretary at the US embassy to pick up as much information and gossip as possible.

At a lull in the conversation, Lancing — or Reggie as he insisted Foxy should call him — said, 'I hope you don't mind me asking, but what happened to your eye?'

Foxy touched the black patch and smiled. 'A duelling accident. I was keen to emulate the tradition of the Junkers, for whom a facial scar was a matter of pride. Unfortunately, my opponent was less skilled than I thought, and instead of giving me the scar I was hoping for I got this. But I wear it as a badge of honour nonetheless.'

The men's faces turned towards him almost as one. Foxy could almost feel the subtle change that had taken place in the atmosphere.

'You feel a kinship with the Junkers, do you?' Westerham asked at last.

'I would be honoured to claim that. My family originated in Bavaria and I have reason to believe that we came from Junker stock. One day, I hope to be able to trace my ancestry and prove it. Meanwhile,' he lifted his shoulders and touched the eye patch again, 'this will have to do.'

There was a brief pause, then Westerham said, 'It does you credit.' There was a murmur of approbation from the rest.

Luncheon was announced and as they made their way to the dining room, he took the opportunity to ask, 'Will Miss Davina be joining us?'

Westerham smiled at him indulgently. 'I'm sorry if you are disappointed, Rupert. Davina is in Scotland. We have a little place on the river Spey, and she's gone up there for the salmon fishing.'

'Really?' His face expressed innocent surprise. 'I had no idea she was a keen sportswoman. She never mentioned fishing to me.'

'Well, I think it's the peace a quiet she goes for. Sometimes, you know, she finds the London scene a bit too frenetic and she just needs to get away for a bit.'

They entered the dining room, and for a second, Foxy froze. Rising to greet them was a man whose face he had last seen at one of the tables in his restaurant in Lyon, dining with Klaus Barbie. He experienced an instant of panic, then reassured himself that in his present guise, he was unrecognizable as the plump and smiling chef-patron of the Bistrot Le Renard Rouge.

Westerham said, 'Ah, doctor! I'm glad you decided to join us. May I introduce our new friend Mr Rupert Foxton? Rupert, this is Doctor Winkler. He is staying with us for the time being.'

Leopold Kline extended his hand. 'Delighted to meet you, Mr Foxton.'

'Likewise,' Foxy said, forcing himself to shake the offered hand.

'Doctor Winkler is an old family friend,' Westerham said. 'Sadly, he no longer feels welcome in his own country, so he has taken refuge with us.'

'He is fortunate to have such generous friends,' Foxy murmured, his mind racing. The implication of what had been said suggested that Kline was posing, as he had done before, as a Jew, hounded out of his home country by the

Nazis. But how did that square with the fascist proclivities of Westerham and his friends? Then it occurred to him that it provided the perfect double-blind to avert suspicion. He wondered how much his host knew about the man behind the pseudonym.

Over lunch the conversation was as anodyne as before and Foxy began to relax. When the meal was over Lancing announced that he was going to take a stroll round the grounds to settle his stomach and 'Jack' Frost agreed to accompany him. The other two guests opted for a game of billiards, so Foxy found himself alone in the library with his host and Kline, a situation he felt certain had been planned beforehand.

'May I ask,' he said, 'how you two came to meet?'

'We owe a big debt of gratitude to Doctor Winkler,' Westerham said. 'You may find this hard to believe, seeing her as she is now, but there was a time when my daughter was extremely fragile.'

'In her health, you mean?' Foxy queried.

'In her mind.' It was Kline who answered. 'She suffered from incipient schizophrenia.'

'It first manifested itself in her early teens,' Westerham said. 'By the time she was eighteen the symptoms were so severe that we sought treatment for her at a clinic run by Doctor Winkler. She was under his care for almost two years.'

'I had no idea,' Foxy murmured. 'She told me that she spent two years at a finishing school abroad, but I thought that was in Switzerland.'

'That was what we told people,' her father said. 'After all, nobody wants to burdened with the stigma of . . . what shall I call it? . . . mental instability.'

'Of course, of course.' Foxy was busy processing what he had just heard. Presumably, the SOE recruiters had accepted the story about the finishing school. Knowing that she had spent that time under the influence of Leopold Kline explained a lot. They had realized it couldn't have been at Beaulieu. It had happened much earlier than that.

'And she is completely cured?' he asked.

'Completely,' Kline answered. 'But let us not spend too much time talking about her. I am curious to know more about you. Where in America were you born?'

Alarm bells were ringing in Foxy's mind. It had been a long lunch, accompanied by some excellent wine. The room was warm, his armchair very comfortable. Everything was combined to induce a feeling of relaxation. Westerham had wandered away to a table almost out of sight and was leafing through a book lying there. Foxy remembered how Kline had hypnotized trainee agents at Beaulieu, under the guise of assessing their psychological suitability, and had turned some of them into double agents. He suspected something similar was planned for him. He had never been hypnotized and told himself that he was probably one of those who would not succumb, but he could not be certain of that.

The questions were simple at first and Foxy had a well-rehearsed background story, much of which was based on fact, so he answered with confidence. However, in spite of himself, he found his eyelids drooping. He knew he must not succumb. It was vital to keep control of his consciousness. As the questions became more probing, he had to improvize but he managed to maintain a consistent narrative. He admired the Germans and deplored the war. He had many friends in America who felt as he did. Eventually he heard Kline say, 'When I tell you to wake up, you will remember nothing of this conversation. Wake up!'

Foxy blinked and wriggled his shoulders, trying to give the impression that he was coming out of a deep sleep. 'Goodness. I do believe I dropped off for a few minutes there. Do forgive me!'

'Nothing to forgive.' Westerham was sitting opposite him now. 'I blame the wine and a good lunch.'

Kline had disappeared.

Tea was served, and the other men rejoined them.

'Right,' Westerham said. 'Shall we get down to business? Rupert, you may have guessed that I did not invite you down here purely for the pleasure of your company. My friends and I have a scheme in hand in which we would appreciate your help.'

'Anything I can do, sure,' Foxy responded.

'We have certain aspirations for the future of our country. There are things happening here which we deplore and wish to change, and we have had the impression for some days that you share our views. We are now convinced of that fact.'

'Views such as?' Foxy assumed an expression of guarded curiosity, but beneath his outward calm his pulse had quickened.

'That this war has been and always was totally unnecessary,' Lancing said, fixing his gaze on Foxy.

'You got it. I agree wholeheartedly there,' Foxy said.

'We believe that rather than fighting Germany we should embrace them as brothers, which is why we were all impressed with your attitude towards the Junker tradition,' Westerham continued. 'We believe that there is peace to be had for the asking, but there are people who stand in the way.'

'People?' Foxy asked. 'Not sure I get your drift.'

'The establishment, so called.' This was Frost. His voice expressed vehement distaste. 'The jumped-up bourgeois, the low-bred rabble who have taken it upon themselves to run the country.'

Foxy feigned puzzlement. 'You mean your country's parliament?'

'That's the tail that wags the dog,' Lancing put in. 'That's the trouble with so-called democracy. Giving power to people not bred to wield it properly. But the real problem is higher up.'

'Are you talking about the Prime Minister?'

'He's part of it.'

'I thought he was an aristo,' Foxy said. 'Isn't his grandfather a duke?'

'He's a traitor to his class,' Westerham said. 'But the problem goes higher than that.'

'Higher?' Foxy queried, apparently nonplussed. 'You can't get any higher, unless you mean the King?'

'The usurper!' Lancing spat the word. 'If the true king had never been driven out of the country, we would not be at war now.'

Foxy looked round the group. 'You guys, really believe that?

'We know not,' Westerham emphasized. 'If Edward had remained king, he would have made a treaty with Hitler, and our two countries would have taken their rightful place in the world. Germany would rule Europe and we would be left to control our great Empire unimpeded.'

'OK,' Foxy said slowly. 'So, what is the answer?'

'A change of ruler,' Westerham said.

Foxy sat back and allowed himself a sceptical laugh. 'Hey, that's quite a challenge. How do you reckon to do that?'

'That is for us to work out. George is a sick man, it's common knowledge. He smokes too much. In time, cigarettes will kill him. And then what follows? England ruled by a girl not yet out of her teens? What red-blooded man will kneel and pay homage to that? We need a regime change, and we need it soon before . . . well, before things have gone beyond our reach to repair.'

Foxy took his time before replying. 'So, what do you want from me?'

'We need you to return to America and prepare public opinion for what is going to happen here. Am I right in thinking that the majority of Americans want nothing to do with this war?'

'Well, sure, at one time. But that was before Pearl Harbour,' Foxy said.

'But if the war in Europe was over, America could concentrate on defeating Japan,' Lancing said.

'That is certainly an attractive proposition,' Foxy agreed. 'If it means we don't have to risk the lives of our boys in a war that has nothing to do with us, I'm with you all the way.'

'That is the prospect we want you to promote among your friends in the German American Bund,' Westerham said. 'It is important that influential men understand the necessity of what we are planning to do and can bring the President round to our point of view. Will you do it?'

Foxy allowed a moment to pass, as if considering the request. Then he nodded decisively. 'I'll do whatever it takes, but it would help if I knew a bit more about what exactly you are proposing.'

'I think it is enough for you to know that we intend to bring about a change of ruler,' Westerham responded. 'The precise details are up to us.'

'Can you at least give me some idea of when this is going to happen? I have business affairs to settle before I can go back to the States again.'

Westerham exchanged glances with the others. 'I can't give you a precise date, but you can be assured it will happen within a month. So the sooner you can settle your affairs and get home the better.'

'OK, I can work with that.' He stood up. 'You can rely on me, gentlemen.'

There were handshakes all round and then Westerham looked at his watch. 'We've done a good afternoon's work. Now I think it's time to dress for dinner.'

CHAPTER 25

As soon as he returned from Kent, Foxy left an envelope in his coat pocket at the Savoy requesting an urgent meeting. Next day, he presented himself at the Inter Services Research Bureau where M. was waiting for him in his office along with Kim, her left ankle encased in a heavy bandage. She struggled to her feet as he entered. Foxy saluted his commander and turned to seize her hands.

'It's great to see you, but should you be out of hospital?'

'A question I myself have been asking, but to very little effect,' M. said dryly.

'I'm fine,' she insisted. 'I can't come to any harm sitting in a chair in this office, can I?'

'Provided that is all you do,' M. responded. 'I wish I could be sure it will be. But we are wasting time. Sit down, both of you. I want to hear Foxy's report. Was it a worthwhile weekend?'

'I think I can say it was,' Foxy said. 'I can now bear witness in court that Westerham and his cronies are plotting to change the ruler.'

'Was Davina there? Kim asked.

'No. According to her father she is in Scotland. He claims to have a place of some sort on the river Spey and she's gone there for the salmon fishing.'

Kim gave a dismissive snort. 'Davina? Salmon fishing? Watch out for flying pigs!'

'I thought I might go up there and check out the story,' Foxy said.

'No. I want you here keeping an eye on Westerham,' M. responded.

'I'll go,' Kim said.

'You will not!' Both men spoke simultaneously.

'That woman killed Mouse.' Kim's voice was taut with anger. 'I want to see her hanged.'

'She will face justice, never fear,' M. said. 'But right now we have a more immediate threat to deal with. I suggest we send your three men up there. They dealt well with the situation after they thought you had gone under that train and I believe they can be trusted to make enquiries without raising suspicion. Let's get back to the matter in hand. Who was there with Westerham?'

Foxy named the four men and went on, 'But more importantly, guess who else was there, posing as a Jewish refugee?'

'Not Kline?' Kim exclaimed.

'The man himself. He's calling himself Dr Winkler now. And listen, when Davina was supposedly at her finishing school in Switzerland, she was actually at a clinic run by Kline, being treated for incipient schizophrenia.'

'By God! That explains everything,' M. exclaimed. 'He will have hypnotized her there.'

'But this was before the war,' Kim objected. 'He couldn't have been planning to turn her into a double agent then.'

'It could have been '37 or '38. He would have seen war was inevitable, though,' M. said. 'Foreign powers are known to plant "sleepers" in enemy country, ready to be activated when required. I assume that as soon as Davina arrived in France, he made contact somehow and activated her.'

'But how could he have known that she would be picked out by our people for agent training,' Kim asked.

'I wonder if her father was in on it from the start,' Foxy suggested. 'He might have put her name forward in the right quarters.'

'That seems more than likely,' M. agreed.

Kim looked at Foxy. 'Are you quite sure he didn't recognize you?'

Foxy lifted his shoulders. 'I think I can be pretty sure of that from what followed. He tried the same trick on me.'

'He hypnotized you?' M. said sharply.

'He thinks he did. But I saw what was coming and played along.'

'What was he after?'

'I think it was mainly to make sure I was who I said I was. There were a lot of questions about my former life in America. Fortunately, the reality is pretty close to the story I've been telling, so I was able to give convincing answers. And there was a lot of probing about my attitudes to the war and to the fascist ideology. I fancy if I had been really under the influence, he might have got some very different answers and blown my cover completely. But as it is, he must have been convinced because it was after that Westerham really opened up.'

'And said what?'

'It was pretty well what we expected. They want Edward back as king and a peace treaty with Hitler.'

'And did they say how this was to be accomplished?'

'Not in detail. I tried to push them on that but they clammed up. There was some talk about the present king's health, his smoking and so on.'

'Could they be looking for some way of getting rid of him and making it look like natural causes?' Kim wondered.

'I don't know,' Foxy said. 'All I could get out of them is that it has to happen within a month.'

'We already knew that.' M. took out his pipe and began filling it. 'To have any chance of success they have to do it before the invasion. So we are no further forward on that front. What is supposed to be your part in all this?'

'I am to go back to the States and work on public opinion, preparing them to accept the change of ruler and the end of the war in Europe. I told them I couldn't leave immediately, but I don't know how long I can put them off without arousing suspicions.'

M. held a match to his pipe and did not speak until it was drawing properly. Then he said, 'So we know who, but we don't know how. We must pray for a clue of some kind before it's too late.'

'Is the King planning any more jaunts, do we know?' Kim asked.

'Not yet,' M. said.

'I suppose with Davina out of the way, they've lost their source of information on that front,' Foxy pointed out.

'True,' M. agreed. 'It's likely they will have less advance warning. But we are not much better off than they are. I am only told a few days in advance. But this idea of death by natural causes worries me. I find it hard to imagine how it might be accomplished. I think I will alert Justin Verney to that idea and see if his contacts in the palace can be any help.' He stood up. 'Meanwhile, Foxy, you had better make yourself look busy, as if you are winding up your business dealings. But don't lose sight of Westerham and the rest. You mix in their social circle, don't you?'

'As far as possible,' Foxy agreed.

'Keep that up. There must be others involved. Try to identify them. Above all, see if you can pick up any hint that something is about to happen. Kim . . .' he looked at her with an expression that combined concern and exasperation, 'I've got a germ of an idea that might be useful, but meanwhile, I'm sending you to our rehabilitation centre outside Leatherhead. Don't argue! I need you fit as soon as possible, so concentrate on getting that ankle fixed. Understood?'

Kim sighed. 'Understood, sir.'

CHAPTER 26

Flat on his belly, Larry wriggled forward through tufts of heather and fronds of dead bracken until he reached a vantage point that allowed him to look down at the fast-flowing river below him. A little to his left stood a house on a slight rise, facing out towards the river. The word 'house' seemed inadequate. Glenfarr House, Lord Westerham's 'little place in Scotland', was a miniature baronial castle. Its mellow sandstone walls rose to a battlemented gable, and in the centre a round tower was crowned by a pointed roof.

Two days earlier he and the other two remaining members of the team had received written instructions from Kim to take themselves up to Speyside.

'We think,' she wrote, 'Davina may be hiding out at Lord Westerham's hunting lodge. I know you are as keen as I am to get hold of the woman who killed Mouse, but for now you are just to watch her. On no account must you let her suspect your presence. You will get further instructions in due course. If she leaves there, follow her and report back on this phone number.'

They had been furnished with a jeep and provided with suitable clothing and other necessary equipment. After several days living in Balham, painfully aware of the absence of Mouse, and watching the Westerham's house without results, it was a relief to be on the move.

Posing as three comrades-in-arms enjoying a well-earned spell of leave, they had found accommodation in a small hotel. It had not been difficult to find out where Lord Westerham's property was situated, but none of the locals they chatted to seemed to be aware that one of the family was in residence.

There was a grunt and Mac wriggled into position beside him. 'There. Did I not tell you we'd have a good view from here?'

'You did, and you were right,' Larry agreed. The Scotsman had grown up stalking deer on the estate where his father was a gamekeeper, and Larry and Prof had been grateful for his expertise.

Larry put his field glasses to his eyes. 'Not much sign of movement down there.'

'True enough,' Mac agreed, 'but if she's in there she must come out sooner or later and we're bound to see her. We must just be patient. Just be grateful it's no raining.' He squirmed over onto his back and peered behind them to the edge of the forest that clothed the upper slopes of the glen. 'We need to make ourselves a wee hidey-hole back there. You keep watch and I'll see what I can contrive.'

An hour later, during which time Larry had had more than enough of the tranquil beauty of the scene, Mac came crawling back. 'I've made us a bit of a shelter there under the trees and I reckon we can see just as well from there. Come and look.'

Mac had built a rough tent of fallen pine branches thatched with bracken. The ground was covered in a thick carpet of fallen pine needles which made a surprisingly soft floor. It was dry and cosy, and from any further than a few yards it would have been almost invisible.

'Brilliant!' Larry declared.

'Aye, well. It'll serve to keep the wind and rain out if the weather changes,' the Scotsman agreed.

'One of us should go back and relieve Prof,' Larry said. 'He'll be wondering what we're up to.'

'You go,' Mac said. 'I'll keep watch.'

Prof was sitting in the jeep, which was parked a short way off the road in a woodland ride.

'Mac's set up a forward observation point at the edge of the trees,' Larry told him. 'Come on, I'll show you.'

By evening they had agreed a system of watches between them. One would always be in the hide, keeping watch for any sign of movement in the grounds of the house. One would remain in the jeep, in case their quarry left in a vehicle. They still had the walkie-talkies, so the watcher in the hide could alert the one in the car to follow. The third would either be sleeping or bringing provisions for the two on duty. It meant long stints on watch but they had all been conditioned to hardship.

'We'll have to check out of the hotel,' Prof said. 'We can't be coming and going at all hours without arousing suspicion. We'd better tell them we've decided to move on.'

'Bugger!' Larry muttered. 'I was enjoying sleeping in a proper bed — and I was getting friendly with that little dark-haired barmaid.'

'Aye, we noticed. Well, from now on you'll just have to make do with our company and a sleeping bag in the back of the jeep,' Mac told him.

On the second day, Prof was rewarded by a sighting of a slender figure wearing slacks and a headscarf strolling along the riverbank. But from the safety of the hide it was impossible to be sure if it was Davina.

'We need to get a close look, just once, to be sure it is her,' he said when he reported the news to the others.

'But how?' Larry asked.

'Look,' said Mac, 'we've got the gear. Next time we see her outside, one of us should pose as a hiker and ask for directions.'

Next morning, Mac radioed Larry in the car and he pulled on his walking boots and made his way down to the riverbank. His request for directions was met with a sharp response to the effect that he was trespassing on private land

and must clear off immediately. But when he rejoined the others, he was able to say, 'It's her all right.'

A telephone call to M.'s office confirmed that 'the filly is safely in the stable'.

* * *

Foxy, obeying instructions, had continued to develop his social life. With almost every man under forty having been called up, there was a dearth of suitable dancing partners and he was much in demand during his visits to the underground ballroom of the Dorchester Hotel. The atmosphere was becoming increasingly frenetic. The laughter was louder, the drink flowed more freely and the dancing grew wilder. Everyone knew, or thought they knew, that a major new offensive was about to begin. The men who were there were almost all in uniform and on embarkation leave, knowing they could be called back to their units at any moment. The fact that many of the them were American contributed much to the loss of normal British restraint.

It was not only on the dance floor where single men were at a premium. Foxy was invited to luncheon parties, asked to make up a four for bridge and as the weather grew warmer, to play tennis. In these settings he showed the same expertise as he did in the ballroom. He had been well-trained in his former life as the chef/confidante and occasional lover to a wealthy lady in New York and had fostered his skills in his later career as a dealer in Old Masters. In all these activities, he saw little of Lord Westerham, who seemed to have retreated to his country house, but Lancing and Frost were often included in the gatherings and treated him affably, though without any sense that they shared a particular bond. Foxy, in turn, watched who they spoke to and eavesdropped wherever possible, but to his increasing frustration he picked up no hint of what, if anything, was being planned.

Then one day, collecting his coat in the Savoy cloakroom, he found a note in the pocket. *Conway's having a party at Claridge's tomorrow night. Get yourself invited.* That was no problem. He already had an invitation. The party was for the twenty-first birthday of the eldest son, a lieutenant in the Guards. The boy's actual birthday was not until the following month, but the celebration had been brought forward on the grounds that when the day came, he might be 'otherwise engaged'. Nobody voiced the thought that if the expected landings on the French coast took place, he might never reach that milestone.

Foxy circulated among the guests, wondering why this particular event was so important. Before long he saw Justin Verney busy with his camera. They exchanged glances and when he had finished with his current subjects, Verney came over.

'Good evening. I don't think we've met. My name is Verney. I am a photographer. My card.' He handed a slip of pasteboard to Foxy. 'Would you be interested in getting a studio portrait? I can be available tomorrow, at about 10 a.m., if you are.'

Foxy looked at the card and then back at Verney. 'Thanks. I guess my folks would like that.'

Verney gave him a brief, tight smile. 'Oh good! See you tomorrow then.'

He moved on, leaving Foxy speculating about the possible reasons for this assignation. He had no further contact with Verney, but as the party drew to a close and he collected his coat, he felt an unexpected object in one of the pockets. He restrained the impulse to pull it out until he was in the taxi heading back to his hotel. It was a crumpled packet of Benson and Hedges cigarettes. Scrawled across it in red ink were the words *DO NOT SMOKE!*

Back in his room Foxy wrapped the packet in a clean handkerchief and put it in the safe. There was obviously something very wrong with these cigarettes, which could only have been planted by Justin Verney, but he was at a loss to understand why he had gone to such lengths to hand them over without being observed. Presumably, all would be made clear when they met the next morning.

Just before ten Foxy arrived at the photographer's studio, just off Albemarle Street. To his surprise, the door was locked. He waited a few minutes, assuming that after a late night Verney had overslept and would arrive shortly.

By 10.20, Verney had still not made an appearance. Foxy wondered if it was possible that he was already inside. Maybe there was a side door and he had just forgotten to unlock the main one. He made his way down a narrow alley at the side of the building. There was a door here, presumably leading into the rear of the studio. Peering through the grimy glass he saw that it opened onto a small kitchen. He tried the handle and to his surprise the door opened. He stepped inside.

'Verney? Hello? It's Rupert Foxton.'

There was no reply.

Foxy moved through the kitchen to a door on the far side and found himself in the studio. There were the usual screens and pedestals and drapes to provide background for his photographs and several spotlights and camera stands, but no sign of the photographer. Looking round, he saw another door. Of course, that must lead to a dark room. Verney must have lost track of time developing his film from last night.

Foxy tapped, and called Verney's name, not wanting to open the door and ruin whatever Verney was working on. There was no reply. He tapped again, louder.

'Verney?' Foxy demanded, shaking the handle. It turned under his hand. He cracked the door open and immediately stepped back, his hand going to his nose. Something in there reeked. He braced himself and went in. The room was in complete darkness. He fumbled down the wall and found a light switch. A dim red light flooded the room.

At the far end of the room, Verney hung from a hook in the ceiling which held one end of the line he used to dry his prints. A thin cord was tight round his neck. It was clear from the state of his trousers and the pool on the floor that in extremis he had lost control of his bowels. Foxy gritted his teeth and went closer. Verney was dead. There was no question of that. A foot or two away there was an overturned stool and, on a shelf nearby, lay a sheet of paper. Foxy produced the small torch which he habitually carried with help him and read: *I can't live with the shame any longer.* It was signed Justin Verney.

Careful not to touch anything, Foxy retreated. He wiped the light switch and the door handle with his pocket handkerchief, and did the same with the handles of the other doors he had opened. Then he closed the side door behind him and made his way back to the main road.

Like most of London, Albemarle Street had not escaped the destruction wrought by the Blitz and although the bombing seemed to have stopped, there was still rubble on the pavements, and potholes that made it necessary to walk with care. He picked his way down to Piccadilly, turned right and headed for the Ritz Hotel. From the foyer there he made a phone call to the emergency number M. had given him. After that he took the underground to Clapham and let himself into the little flat he kept as a pied-à-terre, where he changed into his army uniform. Half an hour later he was in M.'s office. The journey had given him time to recover from the shock but he still felt as if he could do with a stiff drink.

'Verney is dead,' he told him.

'Dead? How? When?'

'Hanged, in his studio. Sometime last night.'

'Suicide?'

'It's been made to look like it, but I've got good reason to think otherwise.'

'How's that?'

As concisely as possible Foxy related the events of the previous evening and produced the packet of cigarettes. 'I'm pretty sure it must have been Verney who left them in my pocket.'

M. lifted them to his nose. 'I'll have to send these to the lab to be analysed, but my guess is that they have been laced with some kind of drug. Where did Verney get them from?'

'I've no idea. I imagine he was going to tell me this morning.'

'And someone took good care to make sure that he couldn't,' M. said grimly. 'But a very alarming thought has come to me. It's possible that he got them from one of his contacts among the palace footmen. I happen to know that Benson and Hedges are the King's favourite brand.'

'Good God!' Foxy exclaimed. 'So that's what they meant by "natural causes". Would smoking those kill him, do you think?'

'I couldn't say without knowing exactly what is in them. But he is a very heavy smoker so I can't imagine it would be good for his health, whatever it is.'

'So, what happens now?' Foxy asked.

'This is MI5's department,' M. said. 'I'll get onto them to deal with Verney. It will probably be best if we let it be known that the suicide idea has been accepted, so there will be no police investigation. Let the perpetrators think they've got away with it.'

'I wonder why he slipped them into my pocket instead of waiting to give them to me this morning,' Foxy mused.

'Probably because he suspected that someone was on to him and he wanted to make sure we got the message.'

'That suggests that whoever it was, was there at the party last night.'

'Any obvious candidates?'

'Some of the usual suspects were there, including Lancing and Frost, but I didn't notice them taking particular interest in Verney. It might be someone we don't know about yet. Tell you what, though, Verney was taking photographs of the guests. If we can get hold of them, they might provide a clue.'

'Were there any prints hanging up to dry in the dark room?'

'I didn't notice any, but I confess I didn't stay to look around. The film might still be in his camera.'

'I'll ask MI5 to retrieve any they find and let me have them,' M. said. 'But much more urgently, we need to find out if any of these cigarettes have been substituted for the genuine article in the palace. They will have to send someone in to discreetly empty all cigarette boxes and replace them with new cigarettes.'

'That'll give them a headache, under current rationing conditions,' Foxy murmured with a brief grin.

'That's their problem. I'm sure they have ways and means,' M. said wryly. He gave Foxy a sharp look. 'I presume you didn't leave any traces of your visit.'

'No. I was careful not to.'

'That's good.' M. sat back and eased his shoulders. 'OK. Leave all this to me. I'll put the wheels in motion. Come here tomorrow, same time, and I'll update you on the situation.'

When Foxy returned next morning M. was looking a little more relaxed.

'MI5 have got everything in hand. Verney's death will be officially recorded as suicide. There was a note, apparently.'

'Yes, I saw it. But has anyone checked the handwriting?'

'I imagine not. It happens to be convenient from our point of view.'

'Did they recover any photographs?'

'Sadly not. The camera had been opened and the film exposed. Whoever was responsible obviously saw the possible danger.'

'Damn!' Foxy muttered. 'Have you heard back from the lab?'

'Yes. The tobacco in the cigarettes was mixed with cannabis and heroin. They say smoking them would initially bring on a sense of euphoria but too many could be fatal. Fortunately, it seems Verney enabled us to nip the problem in the bud. The man MI5 put in collected all the cigarettes that had been put out in the royal apartments and it seems they are all the genuine article.'

'So Verney's informant had slipped him some of the doctored fags before the plan had been put into action?'

'It seems so. MI5 are now, on some pretext, conducting searches of the rooms of all the palace servants and any possible hiding places where a supply of the doctored cigarettes might be stashed away — though heaven knows what the chances are of finding anything in that great warren of a place. Meanwhile, some senior members of staff, whom MI5 assure me are above suspicion, have been alerted to check every time the boxes are refilled. I don't see what more we can do at the moment.'

'I feel bad about Verney,' Foxy said after a moment. 'He started off on the wrong side, but he was doing his best to rectify that. I'd like to see his killer brought to justice.'

'So you will, in the fullness of time. As will the men behind him. But we have to play our cards carefully until we have positive proof of what they are planning and have them all in our net.'

'Speaking of the people behind the plot,' Foxy said, 'have you heard anything about Davina?'

'Kim's team have confirmed that she is at her father's house on Speyside. They have seen her out walking but so far, she seems to be keeping a very low profile.'

'At least we know where to get hold of her when the time comes — and she can't do much harm stuck away up there.'

'Let us hope it stays that way,' M. said.

CHAPTER 27

For almost two weeks the three men had maintained their watch on the house and its occupants, and the discomfort and tedium were beginning to tell.

'How long are we supposed to keep this up?' Larry demanded. 'I can't see that we are doing anything useful.'

'We keep it up until we're told otherwise,' Mac said dourly. 'Ours not to reason why.'

There was very little to break the monotony. They were familiar now with the staff of the household. They had watched the gardeners at work in the grounds, and from time to time a maid came out to hang up washing or a chauffeur appeared to wash one of the cars. There was a hen house in a small yard to one side and every morning a small girl, who looked to be no more than twelve or thirteen, came out to feed the chickens and collect the eggs. A baker's van called every other day and another van with the insignia of a local grocer came once a week. And at some point, on most days, they saw the slender figure of their quarry strolling along the riverbank. She was always dressed the same way, with a dark-red jacket over a plaid skirt. All this was carefully logged by the three watchers but it seemed to have little to do with the question uppermost in all their minds. Was this the woman who had killed Mouse? If so, what were they waiting for? If not, why were they not tracking down the real murderer?

One morning Mac had just taken over the watch from Larry, who had been on night duty and was busy heating water over a little primus stove to boil an egg for his breakfast. Prof was in the driving seat of the jeep, yawning and trying unsuccessfully to finish the crossword in the newspaper he had bought from the local village shop the day before. Suddenly his radio crackled into life.

'Obs position to base. Are you receiving me? Over.'

Prof grabbed the microphone. 'Base to obs. Receiving you loud and clear. Over.'

'Target is on the move in dark-green Riley, chauffeur-driven. Over.'

'On it!' Prof responded. 'Which direction?' He leaned out of the car. 'Larry! In! Quickly!'

Larry was already shutting off the primus. He jumped in as Prof began to reverse the jeep out of the little clearing where they had set up camp.

'South!' Mac's voice came over the radio. 'She's heading south.'

'On my way!' Prof responded.

He bumped down the rough track and then turned right onto the main road. It was never a busy thoroughfare, the only traffic being a couple of delivery vans and a farm cart. Prof could see a few hundred yards ahead of him a dark-green saloon.

'There she is!' he exclaimed triumphantly.

'Looks like she's heading into Broomhill,' Larry said.

'And what's in Broomhill?' Prof rejoined. 'A railway station.'

'And that line goes to Aviemore, where she can pick up a connection to Edinburgh and possibly the overnight express to London.'

Prof glanced sideways at his companion. 'If she is heading for the train, you'd better go with her. Have you got money on you?'

'Enough for a ticket to London? Just about. If I go, how will we keep in touch?'

'Damn! That's a good question.' Prof thought for a moment. 'I know. Do you still have the number for the hotel where we stayed when we first came up?'

'Yes, I'm sure I have.'

'Ring there and leave a message. I'll call in regularly to pick it up.'

'OK. That should work. 'Course, we may be jumping the gun. Perhaps she's just going shopping.'

They had come to a small village which seemed to owe its reason for existence to the railway that ran through it.

'Looks like we were right,' Prof said. 'She's heading for the station.'

As they drove into the station yard, they heard the sound of an approaching train. The green car had stopped and the familiar figure in the red jacket jumped out and hurried onto the platform.

'Quick!' Prof said. 'Or you'll miss it.'

Larry scrambled out of the car and ran into the station. The train was already moving and a porter shouted indignantly, but Larry ignored him. He launched himself and managed to grab the handle of a door. He wrenched it open and half fell into the carriage.

Prof watched the departing train and then drove slowly back to the camp. He made his way through the trees to the hide where Mac was crouching.

'She's got on the train. Larry's gone with her. Is there any point in us continuing to watch the house?'

Mac glanced up at him and then settled back into his position. 'She may be back in an hour or two. We don't know where she's headed.'

'True.' Prof sighed. 'Oh well, I'll take over. You get back to the jeep.'

Later that afternoon, Prof drove to the hotel. The manageress was behind the reception desk.

'I'm sorry to bother you,' Prof began. 'You remember my two friends who stayed here with me? Well, I've somehow managed to lose touch with one of them and I am wondering if by any chance he's rung here and left a message for me.'

The woman gave him a shrewd look, as if she guessed this was a fabrication. 'Aye, he has. But I don't know what you'll make of it. He says to tell you "It's not her" and he's on his way back.'

'Not her!' It took a moment for this to sink in. Prof improvised rapidly. 'Oh well. That makes sense. You see, the reason we all decided to come here on leave is that Larry — my friend, that is — met a girl in London and he fell for her hook, line and sinker. But before they could exchange addresses, they got caught up in an air raid and he lost touch with her. All he knows is that she lives somewhere in this area and she was on her way home. So he was desperate to come here and see if he could track her down. We'd almost given up, but this morning he saw a girl getting on the train at Broomhill and he felt sure it was her, so he jumped on the train too. But it seems he was mistaken.'

He stopped, almost breathless, and met the woman's eyes. Whether she believed his story or not was hard to tell, but her look suggested she was unimpressed.

'Aye, well. That's a wild goose chase and no mistake. Was there something else?'

Prof was about to leave when an idea came to him. After two weeks camping out, he was dirty and in need of a shave. 'I don't suppose I could rent a room for an hour, to have a bath and freshen up, could I?'

She pursed her lips. 'You can rent a room for the night. Whether you sleep there or not, is up to you.'

'Agreed.' He produced the money and was shown to a room.

'The bathroom is along the passage — but you'll remember that from your last visit.'

An hour later, bathed and shaved, Prof headed back to the camp. He felt guilty about affording himself the luxury, and to ease his conscience he bought fish and chips from a local shop and carried them back to Mac in the hide. They were still eating them when there was a rustle in the bushes and Larry joined them. He was sweating and weary.

'What a bloody waste of time! Did you get my message?'

'Yes,' Prof told him. 'When did you realize it wasn't Davina?'

'When we got to Aviemore. I managed to catch up with her in the queue at the ticket barrier. She'd taken off the headscarf and close up she looked nothing like Davina. Dark hair, older — probably one of the staff at the house at a guess.'

'Bloody hell!' Prof said. 'A decoy. And we fell for it.'

'She must have guessed we were watching,' Larry went on. 'Or why go to those lengths?'

'Possibly just a routine precaution?' Prof suggested.

'Question is,' Mac said, 'is the real one still here? Why set up the decoy if she's planning to stay put.'

'We need to get a close look,' Prof said. 'No good just assuming the red jacket and the scarf are enough. Perhaps I'd better smarten myself up and go and call at the front door. I can pretend to be an old friend from London, come to look her up.'

Mac shook his head. 'You'll get no straight answers that way. The staff will lie through their teeth if that's what they've been told to do. I've got a better idea.'

'Go on.'

'The wee lassie who looks after the chooks. They may not have thought to warn her to keep her mouth shut. We've a better chance of getting the truth from her.'

'How do you propose to do that?'

Mac laid a finger along the side of his nose. 'You leave that to me.'

As it began to get light next morning, Mac slipped out of the hide and began to make his way down the hill, using dips in the ground and clumps of gorse as cover. By the time the sun was up he was in position behind the hen house. As always, it was not long before the young girl came into the yard and went to let the hens out. As they left the hut with a flutter and a cackle, Mac stepped out from behind the hut. The girl jumped back with a gasp but Mac laid a finger to his lips and winked at her.

'Whisht, lass. I'm no going to harm you. I just want to ask a wee favour.'

'What?' Her eyes went from him to the house. 'What do you want?'

Mac produced an envelope. 'Could you give this to Miss Davina for me?'

'Why?'

He moved a little closer, lowering his voice to a conspiratorial murmur. 'It's like this, you see. Me and her met down in London and we're — well, I'm in love with her. But her daddy doesn't approve and he won't let us see each other. That's why he sent her to live up here. If I post this letter, they won't give it to her. The poor lass is like a prisoner here. But I saw you feeding the chooks, and I thought if anyone can slip a letter into her hand it would be you. Will you do it for me?'

The girl's eyes had widened and her face told him she was caught up in the romance of his story, but now she shook her head regretfully. 'But the mistress is no here.'

'Not here?'

'No. She went away yesterday.'

'Did she! Do you know when she'll be back?'

The girl shook her head.

Mac sighed sadly. 'Aye, well. I've missed my chance then. I'd best be on my way. But hark, you'll no let on to them inside that I was here? It would only make trouble for your mistress if they knew.'

'I won't say anything,' she promised.

'Good girl!' He put his hand in his pocket and produced a shilling. 'That's to say thank you for keeping our secret.'

Her hand closed over the coin. 'Thank you, sir. You can trust me. I'll not say a word.'

Back at the hide Larry was waiting.

'She's gone, if the little lass is to be believed — and I've no reason to think otherwise.'

'How the dickens did she manage it? You were watching the house, weren't you?'

'I was, and I never took my eyes off it. Prof took over later, but I think we can trust him to stay alert. So how . . .' he snapped his fingers. 'The baker's van! The baker called just after you and Prof had gone. She must have bribed him, or persuaded him, to give her a lift.'

'Where does he come from?' Larry asked. 'Have you any idea?'

'Aye. Grantown-on-Spey. It's on the side of the van.'

'Then I think one of us should go and speak to him.'

'You go. I'll keep watch here in case the lass was wrong and madam is still inside.'

Prof had been on night duty and was not best pleased to be woken when Larry started the van. He was still grumpy by the time they reached Grantown.

'How the devil are we going to justify asking questions about who he chooses to give a lift to?' he demanded. 'He'd be perfectly within his rights to tell us to get lost.'

'We'll just have to bluff it out,' Larry answered. 'You can do it. You've got the right accent and you look more presentable.'

It was not difficult to track down the baker and they caught the van driver just as he was about to set out on his rounds.

'Just hang on a minute,' Prof said, in his best official manner. 'We are here on government business and we need to ask you a few questions.'

The man looked alarmed. 'What about? I haven't done anything.'

'We are not accusing you,' Prof said. 'But this is a matter of national security. Did you pick up a passenger when you called at Lord Westerham's place yesterday?'

'There's no law against giving someone a lift,' the man said sullenly.

'No. But there is a law against obstructing members of the security service in the pursuit of their enquiries,' Prof replied.

245

The driver looked from him to Larry and decided it would be safer to comply. 'OK. I did. What about it?'

'Who was it?'

'One of the staff, works in the kitchen she said. She didn't give me her name. Just asked for a lift into Grantown to visit her old mother who lives out Cromdale way. She can get a bus from here to Cromdale. I dropped her off at the bus station.'

'What did she look like?'

'Pretty girl. Reddish sort of hair.'

Prof and Larry exchanged glances. 'Right. Thank you,' said Prof. 'That's all we need to know.'

The man's expression changed. Now he saw himself as playing a part in some dramatic plot. 'Spy, was she? Working for the Nazis?'

'No, no,' Prof waved the idea aside. 'Nothing like that. Thank you for your help. We'll let you get on with your round now.'

Larry waited until the man returned, disappointed, to his van, then said, 'I think the moment has come to use that emergency number we were given to contact HQ, don't you?'

CHAPTER 28

Kim was leafing languidly through a copy of the *Daily Mail*. She had complied with everything required of her by the staff at the rehabilitation centre and as a result she felt almost back to full fitness. Now she was bored and frustrated.

The papers were full of reports about the desperate battle being fought around Monte Casino in Italy, but her attention was suddenly caught by another headline. *THE KING TAKES LEAVE OF HIS FLEET*. Under the headline she read, *The King has taken his leave of his captains in the Home Fleet, and has bidden them, their ships' companies and their ships God Speed before battle*. There was further reference to the ships venturing into *cold and lonely waters*.

It was obviously another ploy in the game of deception designed to confuse the enemy. When the German double agents reported this visit back to their handlers it would present them with the possibility that, rather than an invasion across the Channel, what was being prepared was a naval expedition against occupied Norway. Whether Hitler's High Command were entirely convinced or not, they wouldn't dare withdraw troops from there to reinforce the defences along the Channel coast. They might even feel it necessary to send extra forces north.

That's all very well, Kim thought, *but how safe had the King been in those distant waters?* She knew that the Home Fleet was based in Scapa Flow, in the Orkney Islands, an area where German submarines might be lurking. But there was danger closer at hand, as she and a handful of others well knew. Her frustration at being sidelined grew. *What precautions are being taken against that?*

Her brooding was interrupted by a nurse. 'Matron wants to see you.'

In her office Matron looked Kim up and down. 'I've had a message from your CO. He wants to know if you are ready to be discharged. What do you think?'

'Yes!' Kim said firmly. 'I'm more than ready.'

'Well, I'm prepared to agree, as long as you don't put too much stress on that ankle. You will need to keep it bandaged to give it extra support, but as long as you aren't expected to walk long distances you should be fine. I've said as much to your CO and he's sending a car for you.'

In his office in Baker Street M. greeted Kim with a smile. 'It's good to have you back. How are you feeling?'

'Much better now I'm away from the hospital, thank you, sir,' Kim told him.

His expression grew serious. 'Good. Sit down. There have been developments.'

'The King went to Scapa Flow,' Kim said. 'I read it in the paper. Were we . . . were you informed in advance?'

'Yes, I was, but he was in the charge of either the RAF or the Navy at all times. There really was no way for us to be involved. So,' he smiled briefly, 'you didn't miss out on anything. But now we have something more important to consider. Your three chaps have managed to lose Davina.'

'Lose her? How?' Kim demanded. 'I thought they were better than that.'

'To do them justice, I don't think they can be blamed. She pulled a classic decoy operation, sending a double to get on the train heading south and then smuggling herself out in the baker's van disguised as a servant. With only three of them, it would have been difficult to cover all eventualities.'

'Where are they now?' Kim asked.

'On their way back to London. I've given them forty-eight hours leave, then they'll back in the house in Balham. After being on watch twenty-four hours a day for two weeks I thought they deserved it.'

'I suppose so,' Kim agreed unwillingly. 'But I'm sorry they let you down.'

'They are all very contrite,' he said. 'I think we can leave it at that. The question now is, where has Davina gone?'

'Not home, presumably.'

'No. Foxy has called at the house in London and at the Westerham's country home, and found no sign of her.'

There was a tap on the door. M. looked up. 'Ah, speak of the devil, I fancy. Come in.'

Foxy entered the room and Kim jumped up to greet him. He had been forbidden to visit her at the rehabilitation hospital and she had longed for the feeling of his arms around her. They had had so little time together since they returned from France. He saluted M. and reached out to take her hand.

'All right,' M. said. 'I'll give the two of you time to catch up later, but right now we need to get down to business. I need to bring you both up to date. First of all, I take it, Foxy, you've had no sighting of Davina?'

'No. I've hung out in all her old haunts and asked all her friends, but they still think she's up in Scotland.'

'Well, I can't see what else we can do until she decides to show her hand,' M. said. 'But there is progress in another direction. Kim, you don't know about this: Justin Verney is dead. Murdered, we think. Foxy, you'd better fill in the details.'

Foxy complied, recounting as briefly as possible his last encounter with Verney, the cigarettes left in his pocket and the discovery of his body.

'So who killed him?' Kim asked. 'It can't have been Davina's handiwork this time. She was still under observation in Scotland then, right?'

'Correct,' M. agreed. 'But we now have further information that I haven't shared with either of you yet. I was forced to hand over this part of the investigation to MI5 since we have no standing in this affair. It's really not SOE business and it's only by accident that we are involved. They have done a good job so far. They arranged for the rooms of all the palace servants to be searched and they found a stash of the drugged cigarettes under the bed of one of the footmen. He was arrested, of course, and has been cooperating to the best of his ability. It's exactly as I expected. He is, like Verney, a homosexual.'

He paused and sighed.

'I sometimes think we have made our lives, and the lives of those of us who care for the security of the state, far more difficult than they need be by making homosexual relations illegal. Whatever our personal feelings are about the act, to threaten otherwise law-abiding citizens with prison just makes them obvious targets for blackmail. That is what happened to this man. He was picked up by a stranger in the pub and invited to an address in Pimlico, where he was encouraged to take part in various sexual activities. Unbeknown to him there were hidden cameras, and a few days later he was confronted by the photographic evidence and threatened with exposure to the police. His only way to avoid that, he was told, was to take these cigarettes, and when the opportunity presented itself, to substitute them for the genuine articles in the cigarette boxes in the royal apartments. He had taken them and stored them under his bed but refrained from putting them out in the hope of finding a way out of the problem.'

'So was it him who alerted Verney?' Foxy asked.

'Yes. He had met Verney before and knew they had — well, tastes in common — so he confided in him and gave him a pack of the doctored cigarettes. Verney promised to pass them on to the relevant authorities, without revealing where he got them.'

'So Verney contacted you and asked to arrange a meeting,' Foxy said, 'and you told him to look out for me at that party. At which point, he planned to hand them over, but someone, somehow, found out and decided to silence him. Presumably whoever it is didn't know he had already passed the packet to me.'

'But who is this other man?' Kim asked.

'There is the rub,' M. admitted. 'He gave the footman an assumed name and so far, we have not been able to trace him. The flat in Pimlico is rented to a businessman who has been in South Africa for the last six months, so someone must have burgled their way in and set up this . . . this orgy or whatever you like to call it. We have a description but nothing more. Five are pursuing their investigations but they haven't come up with anyone yet.'

'I feel certain he was there at that party,' Foxy said. 'I definitely had the impression that something scared Verney off after he had spoken to me. That's why he shoved the fag packet into my coat pocket instead of waiting.'

'I've suggested to Five that that might be the case,' M. said. 'I understand they are working through the list of guests. Of course, even if the blackmailer was there, he may not have committed the murder. It wouldn't have been too difficult, with the right connections, to find someone to do the dirty work for them.'

'So where does all this leave us?' Kim asked.

'I think there's nothing more we can do in that direction at the moment,' M. replied. 'Besides which, another challenge has come up which is much more within our remit. Next Wednesday, His Majesty is going to Exbury House, a location which will be familiar to both of you from its proximity to Beaulieu. Now, as you probably know, it has been requisitioned by the Royal Navy as a base for training landing crews and has been renamed HMS *Mastodon*. After inspecting the ratings there, the royal party will board the royal yacht barge and cruise down the Beaulieu river to the Solent. There, the King will inspect the British Naval Assault Force which is being assembled ready for D-Day. Now, my worry is that this may well be the last opportunity Westerham and his gang have to carry out their plot before the invasion of France begins. They may resort to desperate measures. For that reason, I feel it is imperative that we have somebody actually onboard that barge.'

'Is it crewed by naval personnel or civilians?' Kim asked.

M. grinned. 'It is crewed by members of the Women's Royal Naval Service,'

'Oh, I see! So, can I become a temporary Wren?'

'Exactly what I was thinking,' M. said. 'The question is, can we get you trained up sufficiently in the time available so you can pass muster as the genuine article? How are you with boats?'

'I've had very little experience. I've never sailed or rowed. Frankly, I don't know one end of a boat from the other.'

'Hmm,' M. frowned. 'Well, hopefully we can arrange things so you are not actually needed to perform any vital actions, but the Navy are not going to be happy if spoil the smart, efficient image of the crew. I shall have to talk to someone sufficiently senior to fix things and then arrange for you to have three or four days' intensive training. Do you think you can cope with what's required?'

Kim grimaced. 'I can't say I like the prospect, but of course, I'll do my best.'

'Good.' M. smiled at her. 'I have every confidence in you.'

'What about me?' Foxy asked. 'Can't I pose as some kind of flunky?'

'I don't think there will be much need for flunkies,' M. said. 'All the required services will be provided by the Navy. Besides, I need you elsewhere. This game is coming to its end. Whatever happens, or doesn't happen, next Wednesday — and I very much hope there is no further attempt on the King's life — we need to reel in the various actors and get them behind bars. I am only holding back now because I am hoping the MI5 investigation bears fruit and I don't want to alert the rest of the conspirators until we can get them all in the bag. But I don't want to wake up one morning and find that Westerham has got wind of what is happening and disappeared. It's bad enough having lost track of his daughter. I won't lose him. So I want you to go down to his place in Kent — make whatever excuse you can come up with — and stick by him until after the King's visit to the south coast. After that we'll have to see exactly where we are, but it may be time to involve the police and have him taken into custody.

'There's Kline, or Winkler as he's calling himself, too,' Foxy reminded him. 'We don't want him slipping through the net again.'

'All the more reason for you to be there to keep an eye on him,' M. said. He reached for his pipe and began filling it. 'Right. We have five days to prepare. It will take me a day or two to arrange things with the Navy, Kim. I suggest you go and have a chat with your three men in Balham. Keep them on their toes in case we need them. After that, I think you both deserve a spot of leave. It won't be more than forty-eight hours, maybe less, but you can have the use of the flat in Kensington for that long. That way, I'll know where to find you when I need you.' He stood up. 'Off you go. I'll be in touch in due course.'

They rose to their feet and saluted, saying a simultaneous, 'Thank you, sir.' Outside the room, Foxy took Kim in his arms and swung her round. 'Forty-eight hours! Let's not waste a moment of it.'

Much as she wanted to go straight to the flat, Kim needed to check on her team in Balham first. She had not seen them since her fall and she felt she owed them at least an hour or two of her time.

'If M.'s given them leave, they probably won't be at home anyway,' Foxy pointed out hopefully.

As it happened, they found all three men sitting in the large, rather bare room on the first floor that served as a sitting room. Prof and Larry were playing chess and Mac was writing a letter. Kim let herself in and the three of them jumped up in surprise as she entered.

'Skip! It's so good to see you,' Prof exclaimed.
'Sure is!' Larry echoed.

Mac simply stood looking at her with a wide grin on his face.

'We thought,' Larry began, 'we were convinced you must have . . .' He broke off.

'Gone under that train,' Kim finished for him. 'It was a close thing, but I was lucky.'

Their eyes had gone to the khaki-clad figure who had followed her in. She drew him forward. 'Gentlemen, this is Renaud Leroux.'

'Afternoon, gents.' As always, when in uniform, his accent reverted to the cockney he had grown up with.

She saw them take in the sergeant's stripes on his sleeve and the thought was as clear as if it had been written across their foreheads: *Non-commissioned rank, i.e., not an officer, so not one of us.* That kind of service snobbery made her angry, especially when directed at Foxy.

'You might recognize him better in civvies, with a patch over one eye.'

Foxy took his cue smoothly. 'Rupert Foxton, at your service gentlemen.' The accent was now unmistakably American.

She saw them register the transformation and reassess him.

Prof regarded him with interest. 'So, what do we call you? Leroux or Foxton?'

He grinned. 'My friends call me Foxy.'

'And the black patch? Was that part of the disguise?'

Foxy turned his head and indicated the glass eye. 'A necessary one — courtesy of Herr Klaus Barbie.'

Larry started. 'Barbie? The man they call the Butcher of Lyon? We were warned about him. You served in France?'

'Foxy ran a very successful circuit from Lyon until someone betrayed him to the Gestapo,' Kim said.

It was Mac who stepped forward. 'Man, I'd like to shake your hand. It's a privilege to know you.'

After that they all shook hands and Kim said, 'Right, now the introductions are over, what does a girl have to do to get a cup of tea round here?'

When they were all settled with mugs of tea, she said, 'I'm sorry it's been so long. But I gather you've been kept occupied.'

They all looked downcast. 'We let you down,' Larry said. 'We're all sorry.'

'Tell me what happened.'

When they had finished, Foxy said, 'Well, it strikes me there's very little else you could have done, under the circumstances.'

'I agree,' Kim said. 'You've nothing to blame yourselves for.'

A sense of tension went out of the atmosphere.

Prof brought up the subject in the back of all their minds. 'What about poor Mouse? We aren't any nearer to catching her killer.'

'Not yet,' Kim said, 'but everything suggests it was the woman you've been watching. Davina had the same training as all of us, so she's quite capable of it.'

'And we let her slip through our fingers!' Mac said bitterly.

'Don't worry,' Kim told him. 'We'll find her eventually and when we do, she will pay the full price.'

'So what do you want us to do now?' Prof asked.

'Nothing immediately. It's a waiting game at the moment, but we anticipate developments in the near future. Just hold yourselves in readiness.'

Soon after this, she and Foxy took their leave and headed in joyful anticipation to the flat which M. kept as a safe house for agents.

* * *

They had only two nights together. On the morning of the second day Kim was instructed to report to the Royal Naval College to begin her training as a Wren. Foxy was ordered to find some excuse for going down to Lord Westerham's house in Kent. As they both prepared to leave, he took her in his arms.

'If M. is right and our enemies are getting desperate, you could be going into danger. Promise me you won't take any unnecessary risks.'

She looked up at him. 'You know that we shall both do whatever the situation seems to require. That's how we operate. But if M. is right and we are coming to the end of this particular game, maybe, if our luck holds, we might get a bit of a breather before we go onto the next thing.'

He sighed. 'I suppose that's the best we can hope for. Goodbye, my darling.'

'No!' she said. 'Never say goodbye. It's just *au revoir*.'

'You're right. *Au revoir, mon amour.*'

CHAPTER 29

In the impressive surroundings of the Royal Naval College on the banks of the Thames at Greenwich, Kim was interviewed by a somewhat bemused superintendent.

'I'm told you have no naval experience whatsoever, but for reasons I am not allowed to know, you have to be trained to look sufficiently competent to be part of the crew of the royal barge. Have you any idea how fierce the competition is for a posting like that?'

'I can imagine it must be, ma'am,' Kim agreed. 'I wish I could explain what this is all about, but I am restrained by the Official Secrets Act. All I can say is I will do my utmost not to let you, or the crew, down.'

'Hmm.' The superintendent looked if not reassured, at least resigned. 'Well, we must do what we can in the short time available. As a FANY I suppose you have at least some notion of military discipline and behaviour.'

Kim did not dispute that, but she was acutely aware that the training she had received was a far cry from what the superintendent imagined.

She was handed over to a senior Wren who gave her a crash course in protocol: how to recognize insignia of rank; how to salute, who to salute and when; correct forms of procedure in a variety of circumstances. She was also introduced to 'Jackspeak' — naval slang — without an understanding of which, it was made clear to her, she would be 'all at sea'.

She exchanged her FANY uniform for a navy jacket with brass buttons and a navy skirt, with the chic hat which, she had heard, was the main reason for many women choosing to volunteer for the Wrens rather than the ATS. The uniform had been designed, she was proudly told by the quartermaster in charge, by Edward Molyneux, the well-known couturier. As she looked at herself in the mirror, Kim had to admit that it was very smart. She was relieved to find that it also came with navy trousers for wearing on board.

In the afternoon, she was told to join some new recruits for drill. This was a new experience, whatever the commandant had thought, but she was naturally active and her SOE training had given her good coordination, so under normal circumstances this would not have been a problem. However, it was the last thing her damaged ankle needed and by the end she was limping and in considerable pain.

Evening was taken up with a lecture on the type of boat she would be expected to work on. The royal barge, she learned, was not the kind of ceremonial vessel luxuriously decorated and equipped with a throne that she had imagined. It was, in fact, a fast motor launch of the type used to transfer personnel from ship to shore or vice versa. By bedtime she was at least able to recognize the correct names for different parts of the boat and what their functions were.

Next morning, bearing a petty officer's insignia on her uniform, she was driven down to Hampshire, to the beautiful mansion of Exbury, now renamed HMS *Mastodon* — though why the Navy insisted on referring to all its shore stations as if they were ships was still a mystery to her. On her arrival she was directed to the office of the commanding officer, Captain Swinley. He looked her up and down as if the sight of her offended him, then he barked, 'I don't know who you are or why you're here, but while you are here you are under my command and will obey my orders. Is that clear?'

'Perfectly, sir,' Kim replied levelly.

'Right!' He almost seemed to be disappointed, as if he had expected her to disagree. 'I'm told you are to join the crew of the royal barge when the King comes here tomorrow. Understand this: if I have any reason to suspect that your behaviour will not be in keeping with the standards I expect, you will be stood down. I will not have you letting down the rest of the crew and giving His Majesty the impression that we are less than perfectly capable in the discharge of our duties. The regular crew understand that just because you are women that is no excuse for lax standards.'

Kim kept her face and voice neutral. 'I understand, sir. I shall do my best to fit in.'

'Very well. I'll get someone to introduce you to the people you will be working with.'

'Forgive me, sir,' Kim said. 'Do they know I am coming?'

'Yes, they have been warned. Don't expect a warm welcome.'

He called an orderly, who led her out of the house and down to the river, where a boat was moored alongside a jetty. Five women with overalls over their uniforms were busy polishing already shining brass and gleaming woodwork. At the orderly's call one of them, bearing the insignia of a Chief Wren, came down the gangplank to meet them.

'You're our mysterious supernumerary, I take it.'

Kim found herself grinning. 'Well, I've been called a few things in my time, but that's a first.'

The other woman's face relaxed. 'So what do we call you?'

'Maxwell — or Max, if you like,' she said, reverting to the name her FANY colleagues had always used.

'OK. I'm Jean Jackson, but I answer to Jacky.' She held out her hand. 'Welcome aboard.'

With considerable relief, Kim shook the offered hand.

'Come and meet the rest of the crew.'

All work had stopped by now and the other four girls gathered round. Kim was introduced and was aware that she was an object of much curiosity, but no apparent hostility.

259

'I'm told that we're not allowed to ask why you are here,' Jacky said. 'But I guess it must be something to do with the King's visit tomorrow.'

'It is connected,' Kim agreed, 'but I'm afraid I can't say more.'

They did not try to push her, or offer guesses about her purpose, for which she was grateful. Instead, Jacky said, 'I think we'd better go out for a little cruise so we can see where you fit in.'

It was a beautiful day and Kim decided that in normal circumstances there would be nothing pleasanter than cruising down such a beautiful river, but any pleasure she might have taken in it was soon banished by her own sense of incompetence. Her companions were a perfectly integrated team, working together as smoothly as a well-oiled piece of machinery and she was just in the way. By the time they returned, Jacky had given up the idea of giving her any responsibility.

'Look. When the King arrives, we shall all line up to be inspected. Then, once he's onboard and we're ready to cast off, the best place for you to be is on the top of the aft cabin. You'll be out of the way there. If anyone asks, you're there as a lookout. OK?'

'OK,' Kim agreed.

As they walked back up to the house, she said, 'How do you get on with Captain Swinley? I got the impression he doesn't like having a crew of women.'

'Oh, him!' Jacky said. 'He is the ultimate misogynist. He can't bear the idea of women in the Navy. You just have to put up with his jibes and let it all wash over you.'

The extent of the captain's misogyny was revealed the following morning. The establishment included male ratings, who were there being trained to crew the landing craft that would deliver troops to the beaches of France when the invasion started. The Wrens, apart from the women Kim had already met, were mostly there as a support, handling secretarial and domestic duties or working in signals. As HMS

Mastodon prepared to receive her commander-in-chief, orders were issued. The male ratings were to parade on the main lawn to be inspected. The women were banished to the top floor.

'It's not fair!' The exclamation was on everyone's lips.

For Kim, the restriction was more than an inconvenience. The whole object of sending her here was so she could be on watch at all times for any sign of someone with malign intentions. The King, she had been told, would certainly want to tour the gardens before he set off on his voyage. They had been laid out by Baron Rothschild when he owned the house and were famous for the collection of rhododendrons and azaleas, which were in full bloom. They presented a perfect opportunity for any would-be assassin. It was imperative that she was somewhere in the neighbourhood at all times.

Kim contemplated facing the captain and insisting that the order did not apply to her, but remembering his attitude when she arrived, she did not hold out much hope of achieving her ends that way.

'Isn't there any way we can creep down to the garden?' she asked Jacky.

'There's the fire escape,' someone suggested.

'Swinley will be livid if he spots us,' someone else said.

'He'll be too busy bowing and scraping,' Jacky pronounced. 'I'm game, if anyone else is.'

'I'm with you,' Kim said.

As the royal party drew up outside the front door, half a dozen Wrens opened the door leading to the fire escape and tiptoed down to the garden. The men were already drawn up in lines on the lawn, but the officers were being presented to the king on the terrace and were facing away from them. On the far side of the lawn there was a shrubbery and the Wrens made a beeline for that, rapidly hiding themselves among the bushes. If any of the men saw them, there was nothing they could do about it without breaking ranks.

While her companions peered round the bushes to watch the King as he moved along the lines, Kim's attention was elsewhere, searching the surroundings for any movement. She was painfully aware that a sniper could be concealed anywhere in the dense undergrowth, but the inspection came to an end without incident. The ratings were dismissed and there was some conversation between Captain Swinley and the King, at the conclusion of which the captain stepped back and the King moved off, alone, along the path that led to the rhododendron plantation. It seemed, Kim thought with a half-smile, that he found the captain's company inconducive to the pleasures of nature. She flitted silently through the bushes, always alert to any sign that she and the King were not alone. He strolled slowly, his hands clasped behind his back, stopping occasionally to inhale the perfume of a flower, and it occurred to Kim that such moments of private contemplation must be very rare for him and thus very valuable.

After fifteen uneventful minutes, the King returned to the house And Kim ran to join the crew of the barge. She found them already lined up along the jetty, polished buttons and boots shining in the sun.

'Good of you to join us,' Jacky muttered, but without malice.

Kim took her place at the end of the line and a minute or two later the royal party appeared. Jacky gave a command and they all came to attention and saluted. The King passed along the line, murmuring a few words to each of them.

'Good to see all you ladies so eager to serve,' he said to Kim. Captain Swinley was close behind and she suppressed a grin at the expression on his face.

The King boarded and took his place in the cockpit along with a couple of officers, and the crew moved to their allotted stations. Ropes were cast off and the barge moved out into the centre of the river. From her position on the roof of the aft cabin Kim had a good view of the rest of the boat. The cockpit, where the King was standing, was in the middle — *midships*, she mentally corrected herself. Three Wrens were in the forward cockpit, Jacky at the wheel. The other two were stationed on the gunwales on either side of the King's position. The engine was immediately under where Kim was sitting and she could feel its steady thrumming through her body. It was accessed through a hatch in another small cockpit in the stern.

As before, in other circumstances the situation would have been idyllic, but there was a constant reminder of the reason for the King's presence. Landing craft were moored all along the banks of the river, their captains and crews standing to attention, and as they passed each one the King returned the salutes. Kim was astounded by the number. It was the first time she had seen concrete proof of the magnitude of what was being prepared. It made her realize that this trip was not a ruse to confuse the enemy. These preparations were for the real thing, and it could not be long before the whole plan went into action.

It would have been easy to forget her purpose as she took in what she was seeing and she had to remind herself to keep a watch out for any unauthorized person on the riverbanks, or any activity in the river itself, but she saw nothing to arouse her suspicions. They came to the estuary and the barge moved out into the waters of the Solent, the smooth glide replaced by pitch and roll as they encountered the waves.

The hatch behind her opened and a Wren popped her head out, took a quick look around and disappeared again. Kim glanced back at her and then away again. Suddenly, all her senses were on full alert. She looked forward. All five members of the crew were still at their stations, and there should only be five. She thought back to that brief appearance, the angle of the head, a scarcely glimpsed profile. Then she knew.

Kim slipped back along the cabin roof and lowered herself into the cockpit. Carefully, she opened the hatch. The engine compartment was small, the engine itself taking up most of it, but bending to adjust something at the base of it was a slender figure. The opening of the hatch sent a shaft of sunlight into the compartment, warning the woman that she was being observed. The woman turned round. Kim's first thought was *Pauline!* Then she corrected herself. *Davina.*

'What do you want?' she asked sharply.

'I want to know what you are doing, for a start,' Kim replied.

Davina shaded her eyes against the light. 'You! It had to be you, sticking your nose in!'

'What have you done?' Kim asked tensely.

Davina stepped aside to display the device she had attached to the base of the engine housing. 'I've set the timer for four minutes. If you get out of the way, that just about gives us both time to slip over the side and swim far enough away to escape injury.'

'Oh no!' Kim said. 'I'm not moving, so you had better deactivate that thing before it blows us both to smithereens.'

'Can't be done,' Davina said.

The blood was pounding in Kim's ears but her mind was icily cool. 'Get out of my way. I'll do it if you can't.'

'Don't be a fool! Do you want to die? Jump while there's still time.'

'No. Either you stop that thing or we both go up. Your choice.'

Kim looked at her. The carefully designed impression of fragility had gone. She had shed the uniform jacket and hat and without them it was obvious that she was in peak condition, as fit and tautly muscled as Kim — or as Kim had been until the fall from the bridge. If it came to a fight, they had both had the same training in unarmed combat, but Kim knew she was at a disadvantage. But what choice did she have?

Davina moved forward as if she was going to try to push past, but as she reached Kim, her left foot shot out and she kicked her hard on the shin. It was a blow that would have had Kim crumpling up in agony but for the heavy bandage she had wound round her lower leg to support her ankle. Kim was momentarily knocked off balance, but she recovered in time to see Davina's clenched hands raised above her head, ready to bring them down in a killing blow to the back of her neck.

Kim lunged upwards. Her fist passed between the upraised arms and caught her assailant under the chin. Davina's head shot up and she staggered back until the engine casing blocked her way. Kim threw herself forward and brought her knee up to strike Davina in the abdomen, but the cramped space meant that the blow was less effective than she intended. It was Davina's turn to double over, but as she did so, she grabbed a handful of Kim's hair in both hands and yanked her head down so that the bridge of her nose hit the top of Davina's head.

They both slid to the floor, Davina retching and gasping, Kim momentarily concussed. As she came round, Kim was aware that the other woman had pulled off her shoes and was crawling up the steps leading to the hatch. The water was rougher now. Kim grabbed her, the barge rolled and they both fell backwards.

Davina groaned as her arm twisted under her, but she hauled herself back onto the steps.

Kim was struggling for breath. The fall had sent an explosion of pain up her back from her damaged ribs. She made a grab at her opponent's leg but only succeeded in getting hold of the hem of her trousers. Davina kicked out but Kim hung on, then something gave way and she was left with a pair of trousers in her hands and the sight of Pauline's naked legs disappearing through the hatch. A second later she heard the sound of a body hitting the water.

Kim's first instinct was to follow. Then she remembered the ticking clock attached to the engine behind her. It was clear where her first duty lay. She crouched by the bomb, aware that her nose was bleeding and her head was still muzzy. She rubbed her hand over her eyes and forced herself to concentrate. It was a simple device, only three wires from the detonator to the explosive. In the dim light of the cockpit it was hard to see the colours, but she was pretty sure the last one was white. She needed wire cutters. Now.

The timer was ticking. It read one minute thirty seconds. She cast around her in desperation then she saw a panel in the bulkhead with the word 'toolbox' stencilled on it. She scrabbled at the catch. It clicked open and there was the box and inside it, a pair of pliers. Kim grabbed them, took a deep breath to steady her hand and cut the wire. The clock ticked on to zero. Nothing happened.

Kim sank down on the steps and put her head in her hands. When she took them away there was blood on them. She looked around for something to use to wipe it away. There was a rag in the toolbox. It had been well used and was smeared with grease but she reckoned that would be easier to explain away than blood, so she wiped her hands and face as best she could, and ran her hands through her hair. Standing up, she straightened her uniform then climbed the steps out to the cockpit. For a few minutes she scanned the waters behind them. They were well out into the Solent now and she could see nothing except the heave and swell of the waves.

Even the strongest swimmer would fight a losing battle against these waves, Kim decided. She thought regretfully that she might never see Mouse's killer brought to justice. Unless, of course, she had had accomplices waiting to pick her up in a boat. She pondered that thought for a few minutes until a shout from somewhere ahead brought her back to her station on top of the cabin.

Ahead of the barge, a fleet of battleships was riding at anchor. The barge came alongside one called the Bullalo and the King went aboard. After spending a few moments talking to the captain and inspecting the crew, he returned and they moved on to the next in line. After that he visited several other ships, welcomed onboard each one with pipes and ceremonial salutes.

At one point the crew of the barge were invited onboard one of them to have lunch. Aware that her appearance must cause comment, Kim opted to stay on the barge, saying that she felt seasick and could not face anything to eat.

Later, the King boarded a fast motor launch and disappeared in the direction of the Hamble River to inspect some more landing craft. Kim was very glad to see him returning, knowing that they must be heading for home soon. The motor launch approached at high speed, creating a considerable bow wave which had the barge pitching and tossing. Jacky, standing in the prow to catch the mooring line, had great difficulty keeping her feet. As the launch came alongside, Kim heard the officers laughing.

Men, she thought bitterly.

The voyage back passed calmly and when they docked below Exbury House, Kim felt it would be better to hide in the engine room until the King had left. She heard him thanking the crew and complimenting them on their seamanship, and then voices moving away. At that point she felt it was safe to come out and join the others on land.

If the other girls were surprised by her appearance, they made no comment, assuming, she supposed, that it was due to the seasickness she had feigned earlier, which they tactfully refrained from commenting on. But when they reached the house, they found Captain Swinley waiting for them.

'Good God, woman!' he exclaimed. 'What have you been doing to yourself? You look a wreck.'

Kim met his eyes. 'It was a bit rough out there,' she said.

He gave a bark of laughter. 'A bit rough! She gets a few hundred yards offshore and she finds it "a bit rough". God protect me from delicate females!'

Kim controlled her temper with difficulty. 'Excuse me, sir. I must speak to you privately about a matter of national security.'

'National security!' He was ready to continue his mocking tone, but something in her face, or perhaps the memory of whatever briefing he had been given before her arrival, quelled the impulse. He took a breath. 'Very well. My office.'

After that, things moved quickly. A phone call to M.'s emergency number triggered a sequence of events that began with the arrival of a bomb-disposal squad from the nearest RAF station. Kim barely had time to return to her room and wash her face before a car arrived to take her back to London. She regretted not having a chance to say goodbye to Jacky and the rest of the crew. They would never know how close they had come to being blown out of the water.

In M.'s office he regarded her appraisingly. 'You look as though you should be back in hospital. Tell me exactly what happened.'

Fortified by a dram of his single malt whisky, she told him the story.

'The nation owes you a medal,' he said when she finished. 'Maybe after the war we can do something about that. But for now, what about Davina?'

'Pauline?' Kim said. 'I don't know. I'd damaged her. I don't think she will have made it to shore, unless she was picked up.'

'Unless,' M. echoed. 'But we can't wait to find out. We have all the evidence we need now. It's time to reel them all in.'

'You're going to arrest Westerham and the rest?'

'Yes. Before the news gets back to him that the plot failed.'

'Can I come?'

'You should be in bed, not traipsing around the country.'

'But I want to be in at the kill. And Foxy's there. Please?'

He looked at her for a moment. 'Oh, very well. It'll take me an hour or two to get organized. Take a taxi back to the flat and give yourself a bath and something to eat. I'll pick you up when we're ready.'

'You promise?'

He gave her a smile. 'After all you've been through, how could I let you down?'

CHAPTER 30

At the flat, Kim bathed and put on clean clothes. Then she made herself a pot of tea and rang the number pinned to the board beside the phone and ordered fish and chips. She had just finished eating when the internal house phone rang and M.'s voice said, 'I'm downstairs.' She joined him in the back of a police car and they set off, followed by a second car full of policemen and a Black Maria.

'What about the others, the ones Foxy identified?' she asked.

'They are being picked up as we speak,' M. told her.

On the journey she dozed intermittently and it was getting light by the time they drew up outside the Falcon's Nest.

The house was in complete darkness, but that was normal with the blackout regulations in force. M. rang the doorbell and they waited. After a few moments, he rang again and pounded on the door. 'Open up! Police!'

There was no response.

M. swore softly. 'Damn me, the birds have flown! We're too late.'

At his command one of the policemen broke down a side door and they all made their way through a kitchen and into the main hall. There was still no sign of life. A thorough search revealed clothes pulled out of closets but not packed, food left in the kitchen and a safe door left open to reveal the empty interior.

'But where's Foxy?' Kim demanded.

'Gone with them? Or following them?' M. suggested.

The search was extended to the wine cellar and the coal store beneath the building. In one place they found a heap of old blankets and a bucket half full of stale urine.

'They've sussed him. They've been keeping him prisoner.' Kim's throat was so dry she could hardly get the words out.

'That's only speculation at the moment,' M. said.

'It's the only explanation,' she insisted. 'Otherwise he would have been in touch.'

'So why have they taken him with them?' M. pondered. 'A hostage?'

Kim swallowed. 'Could be.'

M. turned to leave. 'I'll get an all-ports warning out. They are almost certainly trying to leave the country.'

Kim had been scouring the cellar. 'Look! Over here!'

In a corner, one flagstone had been swept of debris and on it, drawn it what might have been blood, was a circle marked with the points of the compass — E, W, S, N. An arrow pointed straight up.

'North!' Kim exclaimed. 'They've gone north.'

'Up to his place in Scotland?' M. speculated.

'They can't expect to hide out there for long,' she said.

'No. But it might just serve as a bolthole until they can arrange some form of exfiltration.'

'You think they are expecting Hitler to send a plane for them?'

'I can imagine they might have set up some kind of escape plan in case their schemes didn't work out,' M. said. 'Come on. We still need to have a watch on all the ports but I think it's worth checking out the house on Speyside.'

He used the phone in the house to make several calls, including one to a contact in the RAF. Then Kim called the house in Balham. A sleepy Prof answered.

'Get your gear packed, all three of you, and get yourselves to Northolt aerodrome,' Kim ordered. 'I'll meet you there.'

* * *

Lord Westerham descended from the overnight sleeper train at Edinburgh's Waverley station. He was followed by the man who called himself Dr Winkler and two muscular attendants. A large trunk was manoeuvred out of the guard's van and loaded onto a porter's trolley, then the porter followed Westerham and his party to the platform from which trains left for Aviemore. At Aviemore, a similar procedure was followed to load the trunk onto the train bound for Grantown-on-Spey. At the little station of Broomhill the party found two vehicles waiting for them — a green Riley saloon and a station wagon. The trunk was loaded onto the station wagon and the party drove to Glenfarr House. There the trunk was manhandled down to the cellar.

'Open it,' Westerham commanded, handing a key to one of his men.

The lid of the trunk was opened, emitting a strong odour of stale urine and other bodily fluids. Winkler bent over it.

'Is he alive?' Westerham asked.

Winkler put his hand on the throat of the man who lay bound and gagged in a foetal position in the trunk. 'Yes, just.'

'Get him out,' Westerham ordered.

The two men lifted the man bodily and sat him with his back leaning against the trunk. Foxy opened his eye and surveyed his surroundings.

'Untie him,' Winkler said. 'And give him some water.'

When his bonds were cut, Foxy at first made no attempt to move his cramped limbs. It felt to him as if he would never be able to unlock them again. A mug of water was held to his lips and he allowed a little to trickle into his throat. When it was offered again, he took a mouthful and swallowed with difficulty.

'Find some blankets,' Winkler said. 'And bring him food — soup or broth.'

'Do it,' Westerham instructed. 'We need him alive.'

CHAPTER 31

It was evening by the time three Scottish police cars drew up outside the locked gates of Glenfarr House. M. pressed the button on the intercom and a moment later Westerham's voice crackled over the line.

'You're quicker off the mark than I expected, but it won't do you any good. I have your man and if you make any attempt to enter the house, or the grounds, he will be shot.'

'How do I know you have him, and he is still alive?' M. demanded. 'I need proof.'

'Look at the window above the main door,' Westerham said.

A light came on in the room behind the window and the blackout curtains were drawn back. Kim gave a whimper of distress at the sight of Foxy, held up from collapsing by two men.

'Seen enough?' Westerham asked, and the light went out.

'What good do you think this will do you?' M. asked. 'The house is surrounded. We may not be able to get in, but you can't get out. Have you provisions for a long siege?'

'We shan't need them,' Westerham replied. 'If you follow my instructions, you might just get your man back unharmed. If not, I am afraid his prospects do not look good. He has already lost one eye. It would be a shame if he lost the other one.'

'*Bastard*! *Bastard*! Kim whispered.

'What instructions?' M. asked.

'We are expecting to be picked up by a submarine tomorrow night. We want safe conduct to the rendezvous. If we are allowed to board the sub unharmed, we will let your man go.'

'Where is the rendezvous?'

'I will tell you that when we have an agreement.'

'And what makes you think a German submarine will be allowed to get anywhere near our coast?'

'You'll just have to make sure it does. I am sure you have enough influence to have instructions passed to your naval commanders to make sure it arrives and leaves unharmed.'

'You flatter me,' M. said. 'I can't guarantee that your sub will ever make it to the appointed place.'

'Then I cannot guarantee the continued health of the hostage.'

M. was silent for a moment.

Then he said, 'I need time to make arrangements. I will come back tomorrow morning and let you know what I have been able to achieve. Meanwhile, make sure that our man is taken care of. If he dies on your hands, the deal's off. Understood?'

'He will not be any further harmed, as long as you abide by your side of the bargain,' Westerham said. 'Until tomorrow, then.'

The line went dead.

In a private dining room of the small hotel where Prof and the other two had stayed some weeks earlier, they gathered to confer.

'We cannot simply allow that man to board a German sub and get away scot-free,' M. said grimly.

'But we can't let him kill Foxy,' Kim pleaded. 'Or . . . or do something almost worse. God knows, he's suffered enough.'

'Haven't they agreed to let him go if they are allowed to board the sub?' Larry said. 'What's wrong with having a torpedo boat lying in wait to sink them as they head for home?'

'They're not fools,' Kim said. 'They won't let him go. They'll take him onboard with them as insurance. And then, when they get to Germany . . .' her voice thickened, 'they'll hand him over to the Gestapo, or worse still, they'll give him back to Klaus Barbie to get his revenge for making a fool of him by escaping.'

'We won't let that happen,' M. spoke soothingly. 'The problem is, how to get him out of their hands before the sub arrives tomorrow night. A frontal attack on the house would just result in his death.'

'Could we arrange an ambush?' Prof suggested. 'Maybe let them get as far as the beach, ready to be picked up, and then pounce?'

'I like the idea,' Kim agreed.

'It would need to be somewhere there is cover,' M. said. 'I have an idea that the beaches near here are pretty flat and open.'

'You know the area, Mac,' Prof said. 'Any ideas?'

Mac's eyebrows drew together in concentration. 'Aye, maybe I have. There's a wee cove about five miles north of the Spey estuary. It's surrounded by cliffs and there's only one way down, by a steep path with steps some of the way. But there are gullies running through the cliffs, where streams have carved out the rock, and they are filled with bushes and small trees. You could hide people in there, no problem.'

'Sounds ideal!' Kim said. 'But how do we ensure that that is where they expect the sub to pick them up. They must have agreed a position already.'

'Tell them the rest of the coast is mined,' Prof spoke eagerly. 'After all, most of the south coast is mined. They might believe the beaches here are, too.'

'OK,' M. said. 'So why isn't this one little cove?'

'It's used by the fisher-folk to haul out when the weather turns rough,' Mac suggested. 'There's a little fishing village a couple of miles further north.'

'Will they believe that, do you think?' Kim asked.

'It would help if we could convince them that the place they've already chosen really is mined,' Prof said. 'I suppose there isn't time to actually plant a few?'

'Westerham is refusing to tell me where it is at the moment,' M. said, 'but I think I can convince him that we need to know when we talk tomorrow. But I'm afraid getting hold of mines and planting them in the time available is not on.'

'We could put up warning signs,' Larry suggested. 'You know: DANGER MINES and a skull and crossbones.'

'We could knock up a few of them very quickly, given some board and some red paint,' Prof said.

M. was silent for a moment, while they all waited for his verdict. 'All right, it's worth a try. Mac, can you show me where this place is on a map?'

'Aye, no problem,' the Scot agreed.

The proprietor of the hotel was able to produce a map of the local area and Mac pinpointed the cove. M. made a note of the coordinates. Then he said, 'Tomorrow morning, you, Kim, and Mac, can go there and check that it is really possible to set an ambush. I shall go and try to convince Westerham to change the location of the pick-up. I assume he must have radio communication with the sub. Prof and Larry, your job is to create those signs. Now, let's get to bed. We all need a good night's sleep. I'll brief the police inspector in the morning.'

Kim did not expect to sleep at all. Her mind would not let go of the image of Foxy hanging between his guards. What had they done to him? How had they got him to Glenfarr? What had made them suspect him? How had he given himself away? The questions went round and round in her head. She had had very little sleep the night before and her body was still aching from her fight with Pauline, so she downed a measure of whisky and crawled into bed. She slept almost at once.

Next morning, Kim and Mac were picked up by one of the police cars and driven to the cove, while M. went in the other one to the gates of Glenfarr. Westerham answered the intercom immediately.

'Well, you've had time to think. Do we have an agreement?'

'In principle, yes,' M. told him. 'But if I am to ensure that your submarine is not intercepted and the pick-up goes smoothly, I need to know the exact location.'

'North side of the Spey estuary.'

'The Spey estuary?' M. feigned surprise. 'You do know those beaches are mined? If you were to attempt to get down there you and your . . . friends, or whatever you call them . . . would be blown to pieces.'

'First I've heard of it.' Westerham sounded slightly shaken.

'Well, unless you've been in the habit of bathing there, or walking the dog or whatever, there's no reason why you should know. The point is, as the commander of your proposed submarine presumably knows, that is an area where it would be easy to land troops. If your friend Herr Hitler wanted to create a diversion, what better place to land an expeditionary force? It was recognized as a security risk, hence the mines.'

'I thought you said we had an agreement.'

'I assumed you had done your homework. As it happens, there is just one place on this stretch of coast that hasn't been mined. It's a small cove north of here, used by local fishermen. It's too small for a mass landing, but it would work perfectly for your purposes.'

'Why are you telling me this?'

'I should have thought that was obvious. I want my man back, and I don't want to see him blown up. I do have your word that once you are picked up by the boat from the sub you will let him go?'

'Yes, yes. I told you that.'

'And you are a man of your word?'

'You have to trust me on that. Where is this cove?'

'Do you have a pencil and paper? I'll give you the map coordinates.'

A pause and a rustle. 'Go ahead.'

M. dictated the coordinates. 'And the time?' he asked.

'Moonrise. 3 a.m.'

'Very well. We shall be waiting to collect our man.'

'You, no others. If I see soldiers or police, I'll shoot him.'

'No, you won't,' M. said, 'because he's your passport out. Once he's dead, there will be no reason for us to hold back.'

'Just keep out of my way,' Westerham growled. 'That way we both get what we want.'

'Very well,' M. responded. 'Till tomorrow night — or rather the next morning.'

He ended the call and got back into the police car. 'Back to the hotel, quick as you can.'

In the yard outside the back of the hotel he found Larry and Prof busy with a can of red paint. Four boards painted with the danger warning were already finished.

'Get those over to the north shore of the estuary and put them up,' M. ordered. 'I have a feeling Westerham will be sending one of his goons to check up.'

Kim and Mac returned soon afterwards.

'It's perfect,' Kim declared. 'There's a gully about fifty yards south of the main path. We can lie up there and be completely hidden but have a full view of the whole beach.'

When Prof and Larry got back, Prof said, 'Good job we had those notices ready. We'd just put them up when along comes that green Riley, with one of Westerham's henchmen at the wheel.'

'Did he seem convinced?' M. asked.

'He stopped a woman walking her dogs, and she confirmed it.'

'Confirmed it?'

Larry grinned. 'She came along just as we were finishing, so I told her it was top secret, national security, et cetera. I said we'd just finished planting the mines and she'd better make sure her dogs didn't go down there. That's the thing about a uniform — people believe anything you tell them.'

'Well done!' Kim said with a laugh.

Shortly before midnight they got back into the two police cars and drove to the cove. M. had drawn weapons before they left London, and Kim and her three men were now all armed with Welrod pistols. They all carried flashlights, with instructions not to turn them on unless given the order. In addition, Larry carried a walkie-talkie which would allow them to communicate directly with M.

A road ran parallel to the shore, above the cove, and there were a few houses which, in peacetime, would have been rented out to holidaymakers. Now they were empty, and it had not taken Kim long on her previous visit to pick the lock on the door of one of them. It was agreed that M. would wait there, with the police inspector and four constables.

Prof, with some forethought, had brought Kim's grab bag, which he had picked up from the railway bridge at North Hykeham and taken back to the Balham house. As well as her climbing equipment, it held, among other things, a pair of dark trousers and a black sweater, which she was now wearing. The other three had also changed out of their uniforms into dark clothes. The cars dropped them outside the house and M. put his hand on Kim's arm.

'No heroics, now. We don't want to lose Foxy, but we don't want to lose you, either.'

She looked up at him. 'Don't worry, sir. I've been well-trained.'

'I know.' He gave her a tight smile. 'Good luck.'

Kim shook her head. 'What do we say, lads? *Merde alors*!'

She led the three men to a point where a stream ran in a culvert under the road and then spilled down the side of the cliff. The sides of the little gully it had made were clothed with gorse bushes and she was glad that her sweater was thick as she pushed her way through the prickly branches. The way was steep and it would have been easy to lose her footing, but from time to time small saplings which had taken root there gave something to hold on to. At the bottom, the gully widened out slightly and there was space for them to sit down on the sandy ground behind a screen of bushes. Kim looked at her watch.

'We've got a couple of hours to wait, so try to relax.'

The summer night was warm and the air was full of the coconut scent of gorse. A few yards below them, the waves sighed softly against the shingle. Kim closed her eyes and tried to empty her mind. She was well used to long waits but it was never easy and tonight it was harder than ever. The minutes ticked by and the eastern sky grew lighter. Soon the moon would rise.

A noise above brought all of them to full alert.

People were coming down the steep path to the beach and someone was swearing under his breath.

After a long pause, four men came into view. The tall man must be Westerham, she reckoned, and beside him the unmistakable, hated form of Leopold Kline. The other two were struggling to carry a heavy trunk across the yielding sand. But where was Foxy? She stared into the darkness. Surely they wouldn't have left him behind? Then she understood.

'The trunk!' Her voice was barely above a whisper. 'He's in the trunk!'

At that moment the moon rose and cast a path of silver across the waves. Westerham produced a signal lantern and flashed a message, and from somewhere out at sea an answering light flashed. Moments later they heard the sound of oars and a dinghy appeared, gliding down the moonlit pathway.

'When do we take them?' Prof whispered in her ear.

'Wait,' she whispered back. 'I want to see what they do with the trunk.'

At a command, the two henchmen lifted the trunk and began to carry it down to the water's edge.

'Now!' Kim said.

She drew her pistol and stepped out into the moonlight.

'Stop there! Put your hands up! You are covered from all sides.'

The two men dropped the trunk and put their hands in the air. Westerham swore and swung round to look for her.

Out at sea a German voice gave an order and there was a sound of oars splashing frantically as the dinghy went about and headed back for the submarine.

'Hands up, I said,' she repeated.

He raised his hands and a little behind him Kline did the same.

'Open the trunk,' Kim ordered.

One of the men said tremulously, 'I can't. He's got the keys.'

'Give him the keys,' Kim said.

Westerham put one hand down and reached into his pocket, but when he withdrew it, he was holding not keys but a revolver.

He fired and Larry, standing just to Kim's right, made a noise like a pig struck by a sack of wet cement and went down. Westerham fired again, but the shot went wide. Kim's hand was steadier, and as she fired, he went down screaming and clutching his shattered knee.

Kim took a few steps towards him and levelled the gun at his head.

'The key!' she repeated.

This time he pulled the key from his pocket and threw it awkwardly towards one of the men, who scrabbled in the sand for it.

'Open the trunk,' Kim said.

The man fumbled with the lock and, at last, lifted the lid. Kim glanced over her shoulder. Prof was on his knees tending to Larry, but Mac was right behind her, his gun steady in his hand.

'Keep them covered,' Kim instructed and walked to where the trunk lay on the sand. A sick feeling of anticipation rose up from her stomach as she looked down.

Foxy gazed back at her. 'Are we going to make a habit of this? Because I'm fed up with being kept in a box.'

She quelled the hysterical giggle that almost overwhelmed her and turned to the two men.

'Get him out of there and untie him.' She looked back at the place where Prof was still kneeling by Larry. 'How is he?'

'I've managed to stop the bleeding. I don't think it's fatal.'

'Get on the radio. Tell M. we need an ambulance — two ambulances — and the coastguard with those special stretchers. Say we have four prisoners — no, wait a minute, where's Kline?'

She scanned the beach. There was no sign of Kline.

'Where is he?' she demanded of Mac.

'I don't know,' he responded. 'I took my eyes off him for a couple of seconds . . .'

Kim strained her eyes. On the far side of the beach something was moving. 'He's making a run for it! Stay here and watch this lot. Tell M. I've gone after him.'

Without waiting to see her instructions followed, she took off at a run. Kline was heading for the cliffs on the far side of the cove. 'You won't get far,' Kim muttered to herself. 'Not up those cliffs.'

As she approached the base of the cliff, she saw that there was another gully, like the one where they had hidden. She stopped at the base of it, panting. Above her she heard pebbles falling under scrabbling boots. She took a breath and began to climb. This gully was more overgrown and she had to force her way through the gorse. The stream that had created it ran in a narrow, rocky bed to her right and there was a steep drop of seven or eight feet into it. Ahead she could hear laboured breathing, then suddenly, a noise of rocks falling, a cry and the crackle of broken branches as a body crashed down into the stream.

'Got you!' Kim exulted.

She climbed a little further, to where a small sapling had been ripped from its roots and a gap had been opened above the drop down to the stream. She reached for her flashlight and leaned down. Kline was lying in a crumpled heap six feet or so below her.

'Help me!' he begged weakly. 'I think my leg is broken.'

Kim redirected the light onto her own face. 'Remember me, Leopold Kline?'

She heard him gasp. 'But you are . . . it can't be, because you are . . .'

'Dead? Yes, that's right. You bricked me up in a cellar and left me to die. But now I've returned. I'm your avenging angel, Leopold Kline.'

He struggled to pull himself up and collapsed with a groan. 'No! No! Please!' he gasped. 'You must help me!'

'Help you? Why should I? Nobody else knows you are here. I shall tell them I lost track of you and you must have made it up to the road. They will search that area, but no one will look for you here.'

'No, no!' He was weeping now. 'You can't leave me here to die.'

'Why not?' she asked. 'It's what you did to me. Goodbye, Leopold.'

She turned round and slipped and slid back down to the beach.

There was a little cluster of people there now. Men were strapping Larry and Westerham into stretchers, and Foxy was on his feet, refusing to be carried. Mac and Prof were guarding the two henchmen and M. was directing operations. Kim ran to Foxy and wrapped her arms round him.

'Have they hurt you? Are you all right?'

He hugged her tightly. 'I may never stand straight again, but I'll live — thanks to you, my darling.'

M. came over to them. 'Well, you did it. Congratulations.'

'No, I took my eye off the ball. Is Larry all right?'

'He will be. It seems the bullet went straight through between his ribs and his hip, without touching any vital organs.'

'Oh, thank God for that!' She looked round at Prof and Mac. 'Well done, lads.'

'All down to you, Skip,' Mac mumbled gruffly.

'Come. It's time we went home,' M. said. 'Large whiskies all round, on me.'

'I'll drink to that,' Kim said. She slipped her arm through Foxy's. 'Can you walk?'

'With you? To the ends of the earth,' he replied.

As they turned away, Kim looked over her shoulder.

'Oh, by the way, Kline is halfway up a gully over the other side. I think his leg is broken.'

CHAPTER 32

Two days later the five of them, plus M., congregated around Larry's bed in a private room in the Queen Alexandra Hospital. Larry was still attached to a drip, but he was sitting up. Foxy was wearing a hospital dressing gown but sitting in an armchair. Much to his annoyance, M. had insisted that he spend a few days in hospital, 'if only to be sure that you're not getting up to mischief elsewhere'. Kim and Prof and Mac were clustered together on an assortment of chairs purloined from other wards.

'So,' M. began, 'to bring you up to date. The four men Foxy identified staying with Westerham have all been arrested: two in their own beds, one in a car en route to Liverpool, the fourth as he tried to board the Dublin ferry. Westerham himself is still in hospital under guard.'

'Will they be tried?' Prof asked.

'Perhaps, after the war. For now, they will be held under defence regulation 18b.'

'What about Pauline. I mean, Davina?' Kim asked.

M. looked at her. 'A woman's body was washed up on the beach near the estuary of the Hamble yesterday. We don't have an official identification yet but I'm pretty sure it's her.'

Kim nodded resignedly. 'I'd like to have seen her convicted of Mouse's murder, but I suppose this will have to do. Will there be repercussions?'

'For you? No. The coroner will register the death as accidental. She must have fallen overboard from a boat while trying to get a look at the fleet moored offshore.' M. turned his attention to Foxy. 'There's one bit of the story only you can fill in. What happened to cause you to end up in that trunk?'

'It was Kline's doing,' Foxy said. 'I think it had been nagging at him, the feeling that he'd seen me somewhere before. I didn't think he would make the connection, but he literally caught me napping. He engaged me in what seemed like an innocent discussion about an article in the newspaper and somehow managed to hypnotize me. It didn't work the first time he tried because I was ready for it, but this time I didn't see it coming. Apparently, he started speaking French to me and, of course, I responded in the same language, and I suppose that triggered a memory for him. I'm not sure what I said, but by the time he brought me round, I'd told him I used to cook at the Bistrot Le Renard Rouge, and that was enough. Before I knew what was happening, I was locked in the cellar.'

'You drew that compass, to put us on the right track, didn't you?' Kim asked.

'As they were bundling me down there, I heard Westerham giving orders to his staff to close the house down because he'd decided to spend the summer in Scotland.'

'But how did they get you there, without raising suspicions?' Prof asked.

'How do you think? In that trunk.'

'You travelled all that way, in a trunk?'

'Don't remind me!'

Kim had already heard most of this story. He had been drugged initially and had come round to find himself bound hand and foot, in darkness, his limbs cramped into the confined space. He had spoken of his terror that this was to be his coffin, that he was to be abandoned there, or buried or thrown into a deep lake. In a way, the realization that he was on a train had been a comfort. The agonies he had suffered, he left to her imagination.

Mac was saying, 'Do you mind if I ask you something personal?'

'Go ahead.'

'When they opened the trunk on the beach, I couldn't help overhearing what you said. What did you mean about being kept in a box? It sounded as if it had happened before.'

Foxy and Kim exchanged looks and burst into laughter. Briefly, Kim explained how they had smuggled Foxy into the Vercors in a coffin.

The three young would-be agents listened, wide-eyed.

'So what was the bistro you mentioned?' Prof asked.

'Le Renard Rouge? That was my place in Lyon. It was a cover for my other activities, of course, but I was the chef-patron.'

'So you're a cook, as well as everything else?'

'Best damn chef in France,' Kim attested.

The three were silent, shaking their heads in wonder.

'Which brings me to the subject of your immediate future,' M. said. 'You've had a small taste of clandestine work. Are you three still game?'

There was no equivocation about their response.

'But if the invasion is successful, will there still be a need for us?' Prof asked.

'Your role may be slightly different, but you will certainly be needed. We plan to drop small teams in uniform to work with resistance groups all over France, to demonstrate our commitment. Your job will be to organize actions to disrupt enemy troop movements or supply chains. In that way you could make a vital contribution to ultimate victory. But don't kid yourselves that if you were captured, you would be treated any better because you're in uniform. The Nazis have very little respect for the Geneva Convention. So, you've had a small taste of clandestine work. This will be far more dangerous. Do you want to go ahead?'

'Count me in,' Prof said.

'Me, too,' Mac added.

'And me, as soon as I can get out of this damn bed,' Larry said.

'Very well. You two can have seventy-two hours leave. You can go home to your families. I don't need to caution you again about the need to keep your real activities secret. Then it's back to Beaulieu to complete your training. Larry, you'll get home-leave as soon as you are well enough, but it will be a while before you're fit for active service. The most important thing for you all to remember is that, though you may never be able to talk about it, you have already rendered your country a great service. I congratulate you.'

Kim looked at her three protegees and saw each of them flush with pride. 'Yes,' she added. 'I'm proud of you all. Well done.'

'As for you two,' M. said, looking from her to Foxy, 'what am I going to do with you?'

'A spot of leave, then back to France?' Foxy suggested.

'Leave, certainly. Back to France? Really?'

Kim looked at M. 'What else are we going to do?'

'I think a spell as conducting officers back at Beaulieu, passing on your experience and expertise to the new intake might be a good idea.'

They looked at each other. 'Both of us?' Foxy said.

'Both of you,' M. confirmed.

For Kim, the prospect opened up of days spent in the peaceful countryside, working with more young men like Prof and Mac and Larry, more young women like Mouse, passing on the skills that might keep them alive in enemy country — and uninterrupted nights in Foxy's arms.

'I think,' she said, 'that sounds like a good idea . . . for a while, anyway.'

'For a while,' Foxy confirmed. 'Until we are needed elsewhere.'

M. stood up. 'There's one more thing before I leave you in peace. I think it's time you shed your sergeant's stripes, Foxy.'

'Shed them?' Foxy looked alarmed.

'It has occurred to me that you have been due for a promotion for some time. It is remiss of me not to have dealt with this before, so to compensate, I've jumped a couple of ranks.' He held out his hand. 'Congratulations, Captain Leroux.'

Kim had rarely seen Foxy at a loss for words. Now he swallowed hard and managed to get out, 'That's extremely kind of you, sir.'

They shook hands. 'Not at all. Well deserved.'

Kim saw the other three men exchanging looks. Prof got to his feet. 'Congratulations, sir.'

'Yes,' Mac said. 'The brigadier is right. Well deserved.' And Larry concurred from his pillow.

There were handshakes all round and Kim saw that Foxy, usually so suavely in control, was genuinely moved.

'Where will you go for your leave?' M. asked.

'Will your friend in the Wye valley have us back, do you think?' Kim asked.

'I'm sure she will be delighted,' M. said.

* * *

Two weeks of unadulterated joy, in the depths of rural Monmouthshire, were almost over when Kim turned on the wireless and heard the voice of the newsreader report, *'D-Day has come. Early this morning the Allies began the assault on the north-western face of Hitler's European fortress . . . Under the command of General Eisenhower, Allied Naval Forces with the support of strong Air Forces, began landing Allied armies this morning on the northern coast of France.'*

Operation Fortitude had done what was required of it. Until the dawn broke on 6 June to reveal the massed forces off the coast of Normandy, Hitler had had no idea where the invasion would take place, and so had no opportunity to concentrate his defences.

Kim and Foxy looked at each other.

'The beginning of the end?' she suggested.

'Perhaps,' he replied. 'But there's a long way to go yet.' He was silent for a moment. Then he said, 'You remember that little pantomime we enacted to get me out of Barbie's clutches?'

Kim felt a catch in her heart. 'How could I forget?'

'I've been thinking, perhaps we should do it again, for real.'

She looked into his eyes. 'Are you saying what I think you are saying?'

'It seems like a good idea, don't you think?'

'Marriage?'

'Yes.'

Her first impulse was to throw her arms round him and say 'Yes!' but something held her back.

He looked at her, wounded. 'You don't want to?'

'I want to, more than anything in the world but . . .'

'But what?'

'I feel like we're giving hostages to fortune. Getting married means looking forward to living together, having kids maybe. One day they will send us back to France. What are the chances of us living long enough to have a proper married life?'

'You mustn't think like that. We have to believe we have a future.'

'Didn't we say, a while back, that we don't need words in church to keep us together?'

'Yes, we did. And it's true. But I want to claim you as my own in front of the whole world, now and for as long as we both live.' He reached out and caressed her cheek. Then he added, with a grin, 'And there are practical considerations. If we are both going to be at Beaulieu, won't it make life easier if we are seen as a married couple? They might even give us married quarters, in one of the houses on the estate.'

Kim was silent for a moment. The prospect was almost too good to imagine. She looked at Foxy and saw the hope and the longing in his eyes. She put her arms round his neck.

'You're right. You always are.'

'Then the answer is yes?'

'Oh yes! Yes, please, darling Foxy.'

THE END

THE JOFFE BOOKS STORY

We began in 2014 when Jasper agreed to publish his mum's much-rejected romance novel and it became a bestseller.

Since then we've grown into the largest independent publisher in the UK. We're extremely proud to publish some of the very best writers in the world, including Joy Ellis, Faith Martin, Caro Ramsay, Helen Forrester, Simon Brett and Robert Goddard. Everyone at Joffe Books loves reading and we never forget that it all begins with the magic of an author telling a story.

We are proud to publish talented first-time authors, as well as established writers whose books we love introducing to a new generation of readers.

We have been shortlisted for Independent Publisher of the Year at the British Book Awards three times, in 2020, 2021 and 2022, and for the Diversity and Inclusivity Award at the Independent Publishing Awards in 2022.

We built this company with your help, and we love to hear from you, so please email us about absolutely anything bookish at feedback@joffebooks.com

If you want to receive free books every Friday and hear about all our new releases, join our mailing list: www.joffebooks.com/contact

And when you tell your friends about us, just remember: it's pronounced Joffe as in coffee or toffee!

www.ingramcontent.com/pod-product-compliance
Lightning Source LLC
Chambersburg PA
CBHW020302200626
46814CB00006BA/2037